Welcome to Menham. Perhaps you should start your tour by dropping by Lem Witherbee's saloon where all the customers have their own private drinking mugs which they talk to for advice. Tonight they're talking about Miss Hummer's new baby. Miss Hummer being the prim, man-hating virgin that she is, everyone assumes that the father is probably Arthur Moore. But Arthur doesn't have any use for Miss Hummer. He doesn't really have use for women at all except as lust receptacles. Arthur prefers the company of his rattlesnakes.

If you spend some time in Menham, you'll get to know Miss Hummer and her baby, Henrietta; and Arthur Moore, of course. Not to mention May Cline, who walks in her sleep and into the barn every night. And Minnie Muller, who is blessed with the kind of body that is the perfect match to all the men in town. And Peter Brush, the travelling salesman, who tries so hard to keep his customers happy that he ends up fathering a whole new generation of Peters. And don't forget Deacon Ormsby, who preaches against the sins of alcohol with a Bible in one hand and a bottle in the other.

Welcome to Menham . . . there's room for one more . . .

Men, Women and Rattlesnakes

"An astounding, perverted, brilliant and sardonically humorous novel . . . It is outrageously unmoral, degenerate and sadistic, so that we are not sure we should even mention it. If you are the kind to say that nothing shocks you any more, try this pornographic novel."

—Los Angeles Times

"Author and publisher ought to be taken by the scruff of their nasty necks and dipped into a vat of chloride of lime."

—Pittsburgh Sun-Telegraph

"A shocker."

—The Indianapolis News

"banned for import into Canada"

—The Vancouver Sun

"There is no moral."

—The Cincinnati Enquirer

"It leaves you crawling."

—The Cincinnati Post

Sin Is Man's Twin

"This is a sequel to '*Men, Women, and Rattlesnakes*'—a statement something in the nature of a warning. The shocking Mr. Collier . . . apparently has no respect for anything. . . . it's the kind of book nobody else should be allowed to read."
—The Cincinnati Enquirer

"by any thermometer the hottest thing of the week"
—The Birmingham News

"This is an hilariously nonsensical nightmare."
—The Buffalo News

Franklin P. Collier, Jr.

MEN, WOMEN, AND RATTLESNAKES

•

SIN IS MAN'S TWIN

by

Franklin P. Collier, Jr.

Introduction by
David Rachels

AN IMPRINT OF STARK HOUSE PRESS

Other Titles from Staccato Crime

Dust jacket of the first edition of
Men, Women, and Rattlesnakes

INTRODUCTION

"Nobody can say that I beat my wife."

—Arthur Moore

"Whoopee! I'm an angel!"

—Rev. Nehemiah Dick

The dust jacket for the first edition of *Men, Women, and Rattlesnakes**, published in 1933, proclaims the novel to be *THE MOST EVIL BOOK EVER WRITTEN*. Readers today, in possession of this fact, may find themselves amused and perplexed—amused because the book is very much a noir comedy and perplexed because the book is entirely too lighthearted to feel evil. Or perhaps I should say, the book is entirely too lighthearted to feel evil to me and you in 2023. Back in the day, *Men, Women, and Rattlesnakes* was evil enough to be banned from import into Canada.

Men, Women, and Rattlesnakes takes place in Menham, a farming community where little farming appears to take place. Barns are for trysting, and the general store serves as the town's saloon (only men allowed—women must improvise). While Menham's amoral landscape of drunkenness and fornication plays primarily for laughs in 2023—and perhaps played for shocked, head-shaking chuckles in 1933—a thread of evil nevertheless runs through the book. Androphobic Miss Hummer and misogynistic Arthur Moore embody the darkest elements of the novel. In a review titled "Cretins at Home," the book critic for *The Cincinnati Inquirer* found Hummer and Moore to be "impressively horrible." After Miss Hummer accidentally adopts a baby boy (not the girl that she had demanded), her fear of men fuels increasingly sadistic parenting. And Arthur Moore, who would like to lock a woman in a closet to be released only when he wants sex, considers rattlesnakes "the most affectionate of all animals" and appreciates their usefulness for killing people he dislikes.

---

* The title of the novel, properly written, contains two commas. The Oxford comma was omitted by the designer of the first edition's dust jacket (on the spine of the jacket, the title has no commas at all!), but on the title page of the book and in the running header, the title appears with two commas: *Men, Women, and Rattlesnakes*.

The dust jacket for *Men, Women, and Rattlesnakes*, after proclaiming the novel's evil, goes on to compare the book to Sherwood Anderson and William Faulkner: "Nineteen-nineteen had its WINESBURG, OHIO; nineteen-thirty-one, its SANCTUARY; nineteen-thirty-three has *MEN, WOMEN, AND RATTLESNAKES*." In reality, however, 1933 had *God's Little Acre*. Erskine Caldwell's novel would sell 6.5 million copies and so scandalize my Southern Baptist preacher grandfather that he would warn me, circa 1977, that I should never read it. (Thank you, Grandfather, for encouraging me to read it!) Thelma Browne Ziemer, book critic for the *Santa Cruz Evening News*, noted that *God's Little Acre* would "please those who want to read off-color stories under the guise of literature." The Georgia Literary Committee (read: Georgia Censorship Committee), which banned books from the state in secret to avoid feeding interest in the objectionable material, nevertheless declared publicly that readers of *God's Little Acre* should face jail time. Caldwell's book was so popular that the committee must have realized that their public condemnation could hardly make it more so.

God's Little Acre appeared more than ten months prior to *Men, Women, and Rattlesnakes*, so author Franklin P. Collier Jr. was positioned to ride Erskine Caldwell's million-selling coattails. Unfortunately, whereas *God's Little Acre* had the backing of major publisher, Viking, *Men, Women, and Rattlesnakes* appeared from Godwin, a publisher that specialized in selling to lending libraries. (Godwin also published the excellent noir *Room Service* by Alan Williams, which has previously appeared from Staccato Crime.) As a result, today *God's Little Acre* is a cultural touchstone while *Men, Women, and Rattlesnakes* is coveted by book collectors, but largely forgotten. In the January/February 2017 issue of *Firsts: The Book Collector's Magazine*, collector Boyd White wrote that he never expected to find a copy:

> [I knew only that] *Men, Women, and Rattlesnakes* was published by William Godwin in 1933. A cursory search on the Internet and the various websites of major rare book dealers turned up nothing more, nor could I find an entry for the novel or its author in any standard bibliographies or reference books on American writers of genre fiction or literature from the first half of the [1900s]. No contemporary reviews showed up on the

Internet, no copies of the book were for sale anywhere, and OCLC located only 3 copies in library holdings worldwide. I suspected I would never find a copy of such an obscure book.

Such has been the fate of *Men, Women, and Rattlesnakes* and also its sequel, *Sin Is Man's Twin*, which has a total of six copies in libraries worldwide.

Men, Women, and Rattlesnakes and *Sin Is Man's Twin* are connected by six half-brothers named Peter, boys in the original, young men in the sequel. The setting shifts from smalltown to city, and the marketing shifts from "The Most Evil Book Ever Written" to "A Hilarious Burlesque of Sex and Sin." In *Sin Is Man's Twin*, there are no characters with hearts as black as those of Miss Hummer and Arthur Moore, and the sexual content is even more scandalous. (To wit: Rival prostitutes Dorothy Dolly and Teresa Beetle compete for the professional distinction of hosting the biggest gangbang.)

The original packaging for *Sin Is Man's Twin*, while noting that readers "may be quite considerably shocked," also credits Franklin P. Collier Jr. with creating "an amusing and most attractive picture of many of the so-called minor vices." In other words, there are no snake-wielding serial killers in this book, and wouldn't life be a lot more fun if we all had lots of casual sex? Absent Hummer and Moore, *Sin Is Man's Twin* is certainly less noir than *Men, Women, and Rattlesnakes*, but darkness remains in the novel's ability to make its contents seem so "amusing and most attractive." (To wit: The "gangster activities" of the six Peters include serial mugging at gunpoint—is this a "minor vice"?)

Sadly, Franklin P. Collier Jr. is remembered today (if he is remembered at all) for being an incompetent communist. Years after his career as a novelist had come to nothing, Collier served as head of the Communist Party's chapter in Melrose, Massachusetts, and he ran the party's bookstore in Boston. Collier's communism came to public attention after he issued a party membership card to an undercover FBI agent, Herbert A. Philbrick, in 1946. As a result, he was investigated by the Massachusetts Legislature for his un-American activities, and in 1954, he was indicted. He escaped prosecution, however, because the federal government ruled that states cannot prosecute citizens for subversive activities.

In 1952, Philbrick wrote about Collier in his book *I Led 3 Lives: Citizen—"Communist"—Counterspy*:

> Collier was bookish, thin, sullen, and unhealthy. He rarely drank, but chain-smoked cigarettes, and his gaunt face had the pallor of ash. Frank had a deep appreciation of literature and a large library including the most complete private Marxist collection I ever encountered. Had Frank devoted to writing but a small portion of the energy he squandered on communism, I am sure he could have been at least a moderately successful author. Instead, he was only a mediocre newspaper hack. His eyes were bright and suspicious, and frequently flashed with his ingrown hatred of capitalism. I never heard him laugh. When he enjoyed a joke, as he frequently did, he chuckled inwardly with a wrinkled visage and a tightly closed mouth, and a "hm, hm" sound was swallowed up in his spare, hollow chest.

Philbrick appears to have had no idea that Collier wrote two novels, and Collier's books were not mentioned in his obituaries.

Collier hanged himself in the cellar of his Melrose home. He lived alone, and three weeks passed before a concerned brother-in-law found him. On November 24 and 25, 1958, Collier's death was widely reported via the United Press International, whose story appeared under an amusing variety of headlines. Here are ten examples in ascending order, concluding with the headline that the inwardly chuckling Collier might have appreciated most:

Petoskey News-Review: "Communist Takes Own Life"

The Memphis Press-Scimitar: "Red Commits Suicide"

The Tampa Times: "Top U.S. Red Found Dead in Own Cellar"

The Boston Globe/The Indianapolis News: "Red Who Gave Card to Philbrick Kills Self"

The Orlando Sentinel: "U.S. Red Who 'Goofed' Found Dead"

Shenandoah Evening Herald: "Red Spy 'Goat' Takes Own Life"

Lexington Herald-Leader: "Red Who Issued Card to FBI Counterspy Is Found Hanging"

The Cincinnati Post: "Commie Who Made Prize Boner Takes Own Life"
The Modesto Bee: "Boner Puller Of Reds Ends Life"
Port Huron Times Herald: "American Red Who Pulled Big Boner Is Suicide"

David Rachels
Newberry, South Carolina

13

MEN, WOMEN, AND RATTLESNAKES

CHAPTER I

*A MEETING OF THE WOMEN-SEEKERS' CHRISTIAN
TEMPERANCE UNION*

"There are millions! of drunkards in the gutters of Menham tonight!"

Deacon Ira Ormsby, the speaker, waved his right arm above his head and clutched the table before him with his left hand. He had been shrieking against the evils of alcohol for over half an hour. The small audience of farmers still listened with sober faces. Most of them were still wondering when Deacon Ormsby was going to take off his hat. His loud voice held their attention, too. Its echoes about the walls of the miniature town hall brought a noisy relief from the monotonous quiet of their country life.

This delay in their Saturday night drinking activities did not disturb them. They could soon catch up to their customary pace for any hour in question at Lem Witherbee's saloon by making the opening drinks longer and with shorter intermissions. And being forced to catch up to schedule in this manner was generally preferable to the customary slower start, as past experience had shown that such a beginning frequently resulted in a night of more intensified drinking.

"Millions!"

Deacon Ormsby repeated his charge that the gutters of Menham stretched far into the sky with piles of drunkards whose affairs of the evening had come to a sudden end. He hesitated for a moment to let the effect of his words attain its full significance.

The comment was somewhat inaccurate. To begin with, there were no gutters in the town of Menham. Sidewalks and roads there were one and the same. When it rained there was more water and mud in the centers of these lanes than on the edges. Another fact the deacon had overlooked was that the population was well below three hundred, and that the total number of former residents and visitors for all time did not approach even one million.

The deacon probably would have disputed the fact that there was not enough liquor in the surrounding county to enable millions of men to enjoy the beds offered by gutters. He might have replied: One drop, yes, even one smell of this foul poison is enough to send an upright man to the gutter a drunkard and disciple of the Devil! One bottle of the demon rum can send millions to the gutter!

There were no remarks. The thundering tones of Deacon Ormsby were of more than sufficient noise to make their truth remain undisputed. The farmers were under the spell of the noise. The words spoken did not make their impression as things of comprehensible meanings. There was a tense moment when Deacon Ormsby wiped his forehead during the pause. The audience thought the expected climax of the removing of his hat was about to occur.

Bulges in Deacon Ormsby's coat that draped awkwardly over his hip pockets suggested the presence of two pint bottles. His continued clutching of the table in a manner that made a third leg of his arm suggested that perhaps the bottles were not full. These details were taken for granted rather than observed by the spectators. None of them ever gave speeches when sober. They supposed it was the same with other people.

Deacon Ormsby being a visitor, they hoped he would set up drinks for the crowd over at Lem Witherbee's after the lecture. Lem Witherbee, who had closed his shop to attend the meeting, anticipated increased business. He expected a new customer in Deacon Ormsby and was certain the enthusiasm inspired by his words would lead to additional sales for the evening.

Deacon Ormsby belched with a loud report that was in keeping with his vocal tones and continued his address.

"Alcohol means death! corruption! insanity! wickedness! immorality! lewdness! rapery! murder! depravity! sodomy! lust! *pederasty!* cannibalism! crime! failure! Hell! disease! debauchery! the gutter! and the sink of iniquity!" he observed.

"He who acquires a taste for rum must have a taste for sewage. There is sewage in the gutters as well as drunkards. If the temptation to drink of liquor is ever upon you, remember! your next drink will be of sewage!

"Which of you gentlemen is the owner of this white horse coming down the aisle? Please remove him at once. At once, I say! He is walking on his hind legs and carrying a pitchfork! Take him away! He is chasing me! Help!"

Deacon Ormsby released his grip on the table and tried to run, shrieking in screams that were even louder than his speech. He staggered back and forth across the platform with one arm curled around his head.

The farmers watched curiously. They could not see the white horse that was chasing Deacon Ormsby with a pitchfork but were not concerned with this detail. The words "white horse" had brought that brand of whisky to their minds and the hope that the deacon would order it in buying the first round of drinks. They preferred an allegorical rather than a literal interpretation of the speaker's words and actions. Previously they had represented fireworks and excitement. Now they stood for White Horse Whisky and good times.

Deacon Ormsby dashed for the rear of the stage, stumbled, tripped, and fell headlong through a window that reached to the floor. But this was an anticlimax. He had snatched his hat from his head and thrown it at the wall just before the crash.

CHAPTER II

A MAN'S BEST FRIEND IS HIS WHISKY GLASS

Lem Witherbee's saloon was part of his general store. One counter was cleared of other merchandise on Saturday nights and covered with an assortment of glasses, tumblers, and cups. Each man kept his own drinking utensil there, identified by its individual size, shape, and cracks. A few of the containers had initials painted on their sides similar to those on the shaving mugs in the barber shop at the adjoining town of Westham.

John Lyman used a shaving mug decorated with ugly flowers and the large gold initials J. L. for his drinking. This had been a present from his wife, Anna, one Christmas. She thought it had been assigned a private niche at the Westham Barber Shop and had no suspicions that it was the most admired drinking cup in the Witherbee collection.

While Lem Witherbee kept a reserve supply of glasses of his own for use by visitors and in case any of the regular customers broke theirs, there was seldom any call for them. Each farmer held a sentimental affection for his chalice and took every precaution that its life should be prolonged indefinitely. These containers held memories and knew many secrets. They spoke with an intimacy that brought words and thoughts to mind in ways no human being could do. Their breaking brought more sadness to the owner than a death in his family. A broken glass would still be used and cherished if enough of it remained to hold a drink of whisky.

Making acquaintance with a new glass after the loss of one that had been a friend through the years was like picking up conversation with a sullen stranger and forcing him to fill the role of confessor.

None of Lem Witherbee's customers ever had any lack of a drinking companion when he found himself alone at the counter. Each man's glass furnished the best drinking companion he knew, and if the stay was extended the conversation became oral as well as psychic.

Sometimes, after a long tarriance, a solitary drinker requested that cups of his best human friends be placed on the counter and gave messages to them which it was understood would be delivered to the owners on their next visit. Often at such times conversations were held with dead friends after their glasses had been returned to the counter with proper tenderness and care. The ritual of downing a drink of whisky from the glass of the departed was usually observed during these latter conversations.

As custodian of the private drinking receptacles Lem Witherbee exercised all possible concern and caution in their handling. He kept them in carefully arranged order on covered shelves beneath the drinking counter, hidden from all eyes when not in use. He only moved them when placing them either on the counter or back in their allotted places on the shelves. The containers were never washed. The unnecessary risk of breakage involved in this procedure made it unanimously forbidden.

Whisky of the cheapest brand was the regulation drink at Lem Witherbee's. Occasionally rum was substituted, such as at times when Lem ran out of whisky. The liquor was taken straight without recourse to chasers.

The anticipated round of White Horse Whisky to be purchased by Deacon Ira Ormsby had not been provided. His disappearance from the platform of the town hall had caused concern for this reason only. The men had accompanied Lem Witherbee to his store without thinking to look for the deacon beneath the window through which he had fallen. If he had been waiting for them at the store they would have been reconciled. Since he was not there, it was concluded that he had taken this means of escape from his social duties, and there was a feeling of resentment.

At nine-thirty the farmers were abreast of the usual drinking schedule for that hour. Andrew Cline was talking about cows.

David Hume spoke of babies. Arthur Moore discussed women. A figure came through the door unnoticed and stopped on the outskirts of the group.

"I hear Miss Hummer is goin' to have a baby," said Alfred Dole casually. This was a stock joke that somebody always gave in some version every Saturday night. Miss Hummer was an elderly, prim virgin of pointed joints who always turned out the light before undressing for bed. In the morning she dressed in a closet. It was generally believed that she had never undressed to the point of nakedness but always wore some of her underclothes beneath her nightdress. In keeping with this theory, it was understood that she had never taken a bath.

"I wonder if it will be twins," Dole continued.

His trend of thought was interrupted by Lem Witherbee who suddenly said in a loud voice, "Evenin', Miss Hummer."

Dole had heard no-one enter and would have taken this remark to be a joke if the reply, "Evenin'!" had not resounded in a high-pitched voice almost in his ear. Miss Hummer was standing directly behind his chair.

Silence immediately interrupted all conversations that had been in progress with a hush like that preceding an explosion. Dole did not move. He wished he could vanish through a window in the same way Deacon Ormsby had done, but he was hemmed in by chairs, walls of shelves, and Miss Hummer.

The impossible had happened. The austere Miss Hummer had penetrated this drinking temple of men. By unwritten law Lem Witherbee's store was for men only on Saturday nights. Women always made their purchases at other times. Miss Hummer usually would not even walk past the store at any time of the day or night on a Saturday. Nobody would have been any more surprised if she had stood before them now naked.

The group resented Miss Hummer's presence, and her untimely arrival at the moment of Alfred Dole's comment about her expected baby was resented even more. Dole was the only man who could be the object of her wrath, but the sympathy of the others was deep, for any one of them might just as easily have been the victim.

Miss Hummer spoke again. Her words provided more than the anticipated explosion.

"How did you know I was goin' to have a baby?" she asked.

Nobody could have spoken even if they had been able to think of anything to say.

"I was tryin' to keep it a secret," continued Miss Hummer. "I knew rum made men see double, but I didn't know they thought double, too. The baby will not be twins, and I expect the child tomorrow. Now is there anything else I can set you right on?"

David Hume frowned. This announcement meant an end of the jokes that had been built around the tradition of Miss Hummer's exaggerated virginity.

"Why aren't you in bed?" asked Andrew Cline.

Miss Hummer shrieked.

"I knew rum was a demon, but I didn't realize it could be as bad as this," she shouted. "How can you accuse me of being an abandoned woman? This child will be delivered to me from the Scofield Orphanage. I am adopting it!"

Miss Hummer burst into tears and ran out of the store, having forgotten all about the vital purchases she had braved this den of iniquity to make. The thought that anyone could believe she was to give birth to a child without a ring on her left hand to prove the magic word of a clergyman had been spoken was too terrible for her comprehension.

"I didn't mean nawthin' 'ceptin' that it was way past her bedtime," said Cline, smiling for the first time that evening.

"She got almost as jumpy as the deacon when he mentioned White Horse Whisky," said Alfred Dole. "Maybe she thought we expected her to give us all a baby."

Witherbee poured drinks for all.

"We should have gutters here in Menham," commented Andrew Cline.

"Yes, the deacon said we ought to sleep in gutters when we drink," said David Hume. "Here in Menham we have to go home to bed."

"Ormsby prob'ly got disgusted and went to Westham to find a gutter," remarked Arthur Moore.

CHAPTER III

THE MALE CONSPIRACY FOR WICKEDNESS

Miss Hummer took a dislike to her adopted baby as soon as it was delivered.

After all, someone had given birth to it, and a stranger might assume it was she. Her visit to Lem Witherbee's saloon—vile sty of filth—had shown her that even the local residents were capable of believing she had committed a sin so foul, so contemptible, so low, so vicious, so criminal as to bring forth a smiling cherub.

Until then Miss Hummer had never thought it possible that any one could ever doubt her chastity. Her virginity had become a thing so precious, sacred, and holy that she had even been able to convince herself that she still possessed an unruptured hymen.

Andrew Cline's suggestion that she ought to stay in bed the night before giving birth to a baby had brought back a forbidden memory and an agony of shame. She recalled the day when she was a little girl that she had broken her virginal membrane with a candle. The men had known about the baby. Perhaps they knew about this incident, and perhaps their version of her broken maidenhead was as distorted as their conception of the origin of the adopted child.

Men!—they had never been able to drag her from the path of virtue (none had ever tried very hard), but in their filthy minds they could rape her over and over again. Miss Hummer thought she felt herself shudder at the thought. Her body might be chaste, but her name and effigy could be corrupted constantly in men's societies of iniquity.

Miss Hummer had been further outraged by receiving a boy baby from the orphanage. She had insisted on a girl and had told the superintendent she would not adopt a boy. The infant was given to her without a name, and she had assumed it was a girl until, with all innocence and modesty, she removed its clothes. What was the shock, horror, and infamy of her discovery that the sex was male!

As soon as she could collect her thoughts after wrapping the exposed nudity in a towel, she had decided to send the child back to the orphanage directly. Then she changed her mind and smiled. No. She would not send the child back. Instead of being in the dreaded power of a wicked man, as she had always feared, she now had a wicked man in her power. Anything of the male sex was wicked. She could dictate to this wicked man all his life and let him suffer for the wickedness the fellow members of his sex would like to have done to her. Perhaps she could keep him ignorant of the male conspiracy for wickedness. At any rate, she could prevent his giving his life to that cause while she was alive.

This plan pleased Miss Hummer so much that she decided the sacrifice of being forced to undergo suspicion of motherhood was not too high a price. She had intended to name the baby Henrietta. This very name would be a good means of starting her kidnaping of a man child away from the male coalition.

"Henrietta Hummer, how's that?" she asked the the baby. "Or let's make it still better: Henrietta Harriet Helen Hummer."

Miss Hummer could not accustom herself to the distasteful duties that had to be performed while the boy was indecently exposed. She looked forward to the time when he could take his bath alone and attend to other toilet necessities without assistance. She gave him as few baths as possible and made a bed for him on the kitchen floor. No man could share her bed or bedroom.

One night she awoke horrified by the thought that Henrietta was crawling towards her bed. She bolted the door at once. After that she locked the door before undressing.

CHAPTER IV

DEFLORATION

Miss Hummer's adopted baby gave rise to many theories.

In the new line of jokes it inspired for Saturday nights at Lem Witherbee's saloon the child was never considered as of any other mother but the spinster. Many interesting stories were built around various imaginary fathers and their methods of seduction, or of Miss Hummer's seduction—some said rape—of them.

John Lyman stuck to the story that the man had been kidnaped and blindfolded by Miss Hummer. Others had more variable accounts. No attention was paid to the obvious facts supporting Miss Hummer's explanation of the child's delivery from the Scofield Orphanage, which she took care to emphasize on all possible occasions. These facts were inconsistent with the overbalancing and more pleasing facts of their imaginations.

The women of Menham accepted the facts with reluctance but still had their theories. Some said the baby was an illegitimate child of an illegitimate daughter Miss Hummer had had many years before. Others said it was a child an old lover of Miss Hummer had found on his doorstep after refusing to be its legal father. Another version was that the baby was from a brothel Miss Hummer had been secretly conducting in Scofield.

One by one the women of Menham all called on Miss Hummer to see the child. Henrietta was, of course, fully clothed on these visits, and all agreed that she was a very cute and pretty baby girl. The name Henrietta Harriet Helen Hummer was heartily approved, and Miss Hummer was praised for her kindness and benevolence in adopting this poor helpless orphan.

Miss Hummer brushed the child off very carefully and placed it on a parlor chair when she saw the callers approach on these visits. At other times she went out of her way to pay it as little attention as possible. It crawled about the kitchen floor at random and sometimes became lost on journeys into other rooms. She especially liked to ignore Henrietta when he cried.

There were other times, generally at night, when Miss Hummer was especially attentive to the child. She held it in her arms, hugging it tightly and rubbing her face against its head. She had a man in her power. She was the master. He could not seduce her, but she had it in her power to seduce him. His whole life was in her hands. She could kill him, cripple him, torture him, do anything she liked to him.

She had outwitted the male conspiracy for wickedness. She could play the part of the demon now with one of its own members. Her long suppressed sexual urges and maternal love had found an outlet in a disguise of hatred and possession. Miss Hummer's subconscious resentment of the male sex's ignoring of her had found revenge.

Miss Hummer became happier, more congenial, and better natured. She sometimes smiled when she saw a man, taking care to turn her head away first.

Coming home across David Hume's meadow one evening after a trip to the store Miss Hummer saw a shocking sight. Alice Goode, a young and pretty girl, was walking through the twilight hand in hand with Felix Dole, whose father had spread the news about the baby. They were heading for a pine grove that bordered the field.

Such a sight aroused all of Miss Hummer's indignation, scorn, and bitterness. Such flagrant immorality! Their bodies were already fused in an uncouth handclasp, and Felix was taking her to a dark pine grove where their actions would be unobserved!

Miss Hummer felt faint. Should she run and try to separate them or go to the home of Alice's parents with the sad news? She was afraid to follow the couple into the woods. Felix was a large youth and would be quite capable of overpowering her with his immoralities, too. She hastened toward the Goode farm.

Silas Goode was lighting his pipe at the well by the back door when Miss Hummer arrived. Forgetting for the moment that he was a man, she dashed up to him with the words, "Felix Dole just dragged Alice into the woods there at Hume's meadow. Quick! There isn't a moment to lose."

"Glad to hear it," said the farmer, lowering a bucket into the well. "She's been wantin' Felix to go walkin' with her for a long time. She's prob'ly tickled to death that he finally asked her." Goode chuckled. "You say he dragged her into the woods? More likely 'twas she draggin' him in. How's your baby?"

Without waiting for an answer Goode started for the back door with a bucket of water, shouting for his wife, Emma, to tell her the good news of their daughter's conquest.

Miss Hummer was flabbergasted. Here was a father rejoicing at the defloration of his daughter, a man promoting the infamy of other men even when it ruined his own child. She waited to see Mrs. Goode's sorrow at the news. Her only comment was, "That's fine, but now I guess you'll have to help me churn the butter."

Miss Hummer went home in disgust, stopping to break off two birch sprigs alongside the road. Henrietta had crawled from his bed on the floor and was crying in a dark corner that imprisoned him. She picked him up roughly. Here was one person—and a man, too—who would not rejoice at this disgraceful moral turpitude.

She placed him face down in her lap and proceeded to whip him with one of the pieces of birch. The thuds of the branch as it struck and the child's loud screams aroused a pleasant sensation that she had never felt before. She made her blows harder and harder and found herself removing Henrietta's clothes to make the pain more intense. Miss Hummer had been smiling when she started the whipping. Soon she laughed out loud in the manner of one who is under the influence of liquor—or lust.

Once inside the confines of the pine grove Felix released Alice's hand. He talked about chores and a recent visit to Westham. Alice wished he would kiss her. Felix wished he could get up enough courage to take her hand again.

CHAPTER V

SOMNAMBULATING WITH AN UMBRELLA

May Cline walked in her sleep. These peregrinations did not interest her father, Andrew, but were of much concern to her mother. Mrs. Susan Cline was always awakened when her daughter climbed out of bed at night. She could never tell whether May was awake or not and did not dare speak for fear of awaking her if she were asleep. She firmly believed that waking a sleepwalker in action would result in insanity. She was not quite sure whether the crazed one would be the somnambulist or the one who woke him. The only way Mrs. Cline could tell whether or not May was noctambulating was to follow her.

May was seventeen years old and had black hair. When she walked during her slumbers she generally went outdoors. Her mother would precede her so as to open the doors in her path. In the winter Susan kept two overcoats at the foot of her bed, one for herself and one to throw over May's shoulders.

May had walked in her sleep since she was a small child. Only from the day of her sixteenth birthday had she taken to going outdoors on these wanderings. Since then she had left the house at night with regularity, usually on Sundays, Tuesdays, and Fridays, and generally at the same hour: eleven o'clock. This schedule had become almost a ritual with May and Mrs. Cline. Susan used to look forward to her daughter's menses. During these periods she slept soundly and did not leave her bed.

May walked slowly as long as she was in the house. As soon as she was outside she would break into a run. Mrs. Cline did not dare to follow her at this pace in the darkness and so sat down—on the doorstep when it was warm, in the kitchen when it was cold—to await her return. When she came back May was always walking slowly.

After becoming addicted to outdoor sleepwalking and running, May had adopted a habit of putting on her shoes during cold weather before starting. This pleased Mrs. Cline, who had been afraid her daughter would catch pneumonia by going outdoors barefoot in the winter.

"The body knows how to take care of itself," she had said to her husband. "May is sound asleep when she walks at night, but now that there's frost in the ground she puts on her shoes."

"Maybe if you'd hide her shoes she'd stay in bed at night," Andrew had replied.

May was usually gone for about half an hour. At first this prolonged wandering had alarmed Mrs. Cline. She was afraid May would collide with something in the darkness and be awakened, or walk into the wrong house to find her bed— Arthur Moore lived alone in the nearest house to them—and be awakened in a somewhat different way.

But after May had returned in safety a few times Susan decided that the extended scope of her nocturnal pilgrimages did not entail much additional danger. May seemed able to recognize her own house as well as her own bed when asleep. Perhaps she could detect obstacles in her path, too.

Sometimes Mrs. Cline saw pieces of hay in her daughter's hair after she got back. When snow was on the ground there were no footprints off the shoveled paths to the barn and road on mornings after. If it snowed after supper on the Sunday, Tuesday, or Friday walking nights, so that the paths were filled in, May generally stayed in bed, much to her mother's delight.

Susan had gone to the barn early one wintry Monday morning and noticed small cakes of snow clinging to rungs of the ladder leading to the hayloft. The snow had evidently been scraped from someone's shoes, quite likely those of May on her sleepwalking of the night before. Susan could imagine why May had climbed into the hayloft. Her body had become tired of walking and, since it was not yet time to return to bed, had gone into the soft hay to rest.

May Cline had a dislike for sewing during early childhood. When she was sixteen she took a liking to one form of sewing. Making pretty nightgowns and elaborating them with lace and designs of colored thread became a hobby. She always wore one of the prettiest nightgowns on Sundays, Tuesdays, and Fridays.

On rainy nights Mrs. Cline left an umbrella at the door. May opened it in the shelter of the small porch and held it overhead as she ran across the farmyard.

"Just imagine May usin' an umbrella when she's asleep," Susan said to her husband the morning after this had happened for the first time.

"Why does she bother goin' to bed at all?" Andrew replied.

CHAPTER VI

A WORKING DAY FOR THE LYMAN WHISKY MUG

John Lyman was talking with the ugly flowers on his whisky mug. It was not Saturday night, but he had gone to Lem Witherbee's store after his wife, Anna, began to tell him at breakfast that he would have to stop drinking. His brother had died from overdoses of whisky, and the same thing would happen to him, she insisted, while John looked quietly into space and hoped one of the other farmers would have a similar excuse to make this day a holiday.

After John had gone, Anna became more cheerful and sang as she did her kitchen tasks. When these were finished she changed her dress and took a seat in the parlor. Anna enjoyed having a holiday during the week now and then. Besides, this was the day Peter Brush, the peddler, was due to visit Menham. She liked to be alone when he came. He was always very polite and businesslike, but some day it might be different.

She rocked in her chair and looked at the narrow black couch stuffed with horsehair. She would ask Peter Brush to come in and show his wares. Why couldn't he forget to bring his pack so that this formality could be dispensed with? Or he might leave his load on the doorstep and come in alone. If he didn't have this pack he could pay more attention to her. Anna felt an envy for the peddler's pack. She could be very happy if Peter Brush carried her about the country instead of this load of goods.

John Lyman was the only drinker at Lem Witherbee's store. He had pulled up a chair to the counter at which liquor was sold and cleared a space there for his mug and a bottle of whisky among piles of boxes of all sizes, bolts of cloth, and trays of penny candy. Lem had made the clearing a little larger after placing Lyman's mug on the counter with a gesture that would have been motherly if he wore dresses.

An hour later John said to one of the distorted roses on his mug, "Yeah, I know, but don't you think Minnie ought to at least have gone into the barn with me to see what I wanted?"

There was silence while the flower replied in a voice discernible only to Lyman.

"Well, mebbee," he answered, "but seems like she might at least have said, 'No,' in a quiet voice. I ain't deaf. I didn't squeeze her arm very tight, and I showed her I didn't mean no harm by lettin' her go when she started to holler."

The flower seemed to agree with Lyman's point, for he smiled and nodded his head during the pause that followed.

"I'll try that next time," he said. "And I won't let go if she starts to make a noise. I proved my intentions are good. There's no need to do any more provin'."

Lem was waiting to make change when Lyman poured out another drink. Now that the spoken conversation with the whisky cup had started, he knew that John would be a customer for the rest of the day.

"Still thinkin' about that Muller girl?" Witherbee asked by way of polite discourse. He had taken her mother, Nancy Muller, on many walks when she was a girl.

"Yeah, I was thinkin' I might drop around and see her next time her mother's away," John replied.

John Lyman never noticed Minnie Muller when he was sober, but when he was drinking alone she always came into his thoughts as the first subject of the inspired conversation. Once he had gone to her house from the store when drunk. Minnie had been frightened by his greetings and ran away. She was a girl of many soft curves. Her mother had adopted the title Mrs. when Minnie was born.

Having shown a friendly interest in the subject at hand, Lem remained silent to leave John and his cup to their own thoughts. He sat down near John where he would be available if his opinions were wanted on any subject, and where he could watch the whisky bottle.

"Anna can always pick a good day for a holiday—'course any day makes a good day for a holiday, but she has a way of makin' 'em right now without any waitin'."

Lyman had shifted his conversation to the gold letter J on his cup. Before he could reply to the initial's comment on this introductory remark, he was interrupted by the entrance of Peter Brush, who immediately attracted all his attention by inviting him to have a drink. John drained his cup and placed it on the counter for the new drink with many thanks.

"I just been up your way," said Peter. "Your wife said I'd find you here."

"She buy anything?" asked John.

"No, she said she wished I wouldn't bring so much stuff around when I came."

"P'r'aps she'd rather you'd just come to call on her." John Lyman laughed heartily.

Peter Brush gulped his drink.

CHAPTER VII

FIRE BELLS FOR RAIN

When David Hume began his haying it was a sure sign of rain. Other farmers always waited until his crop had been spoiled before starting to cut their own. This year Hume had delayed the cutting of his hay. One morning he awoke to find that a corner of his meadow had been mowed during the night. It was raining heavily.

Arthur Moore was pleased by the drone of the rain that awakened him. A real service had been done to the countryside in starting Hume's haying for him. The annual three-day Hume storm had begun. After that it would be safe for others to do their haying. If Hume had continued to neglect his hay, the drought would have spoiled all the crops.

"Whoever cut that hay for Hume did him a favor," said Moore, winking at himself in his small mirror. "He'll get some hay of his own this year, and, with this rain, his other crops won't go bad."

The Hume storm called for a whisky conference at Lem Witherbee's store. Arthur Moore was the first to arrive. The news had spread slowly that the Hume haying had started during the night. Lem saw to it that the good news became known at once. He hurried to the town hall and pulled the bell rope. This bell had been installed as a fire signal but was seldom used for this purpose. Nobody thought of fire when its peals were heard. The farmers hurried to the conference.

The conclusion of Andrew Cline satisfied the others as to the cause of the conference, "Since David wouldn't cut his own hay I s'pose the weather man had to come down and cut it for him so's he could give us this storm."

David Hume suspected one of the other farmers might have helped the weather man but only confided this to his whisky glass later in the day after the storm had been forgotten by the others.

Alice Goode did not approve of the storm. She had hoped to take a walk with Felix Dole that night. He never asked her to go walking, but they had a way of meeting at certain times and places and continuing along together.

Felix had discovered a knack of taking Alice's hand. He often found her hand in his at times when he thought he was still trying to get courage to take it. He always held her hand very gently, so gently that Alice sometimes had difficulty keeping it in his. He had not yet dared to kiss her.

Minnie Muller did not appreciate the rain either. This was her night to go walking with Paul Turner. Paul did not treat her hands so gently. In fact, he paid little attention to them. He worked for Andrew Cline and was very strong. Minnie enjoyed her walks with Paul. They did not walk far but were never home very early.

Paul would not even call on her tonight. Her mother would not approve of her going to see his aunt in Westham in the rain. This was the best excuse they had found for getting away alone. If Paul should sit down with them for an evening of talk he would soon fall asleep.

Miss Hummer was also displeased with the storm. At first she had found it quite to her liking. Henrietta had to have a bath, and the rain could give her much assistance.

She had undressed the baby and put it in a large pan she used for making soap. This she had placed in her back yard. Then she had run to the shelter of the kitchen, where she could watch the effects of the rain beating down on the child. Red stripes that crossed each other in no particular pattern stood out on Henrietta's body.

Miss Hummer smiled as she watched the baby in the rain. If she left him there long enough he would surely be clean. The smile did not last long. Henrietta had been crying when he was indoors. Soon after Miss Hummer left him out in the rain alone his cries stopped. He seemed to be enjoying the splashes of the raindrops. Henrietta began to smile and gurgle and Miss Hummer to frown. She waited several minutes. The rain continued to delight the baby.

Miss Hummer brought the child indoors to finish the bath herself. Henrietta was soon crying again.

CHAPTER VIII

HAYCOCKS AND HAYLOFTS

After the Hume storm, haying began with justified optimism. There would be no more rain until the hay was safely in the barns. Even after David Hume cut the rest of his crop the sky would remain clear. Mrs. Cline put the umbrella that had been kept at the door for May to use at night back in the closet.

The whisky conference had been held for a very practical purpose of deciding upon a system of cooperation among the farmers. This subject had not been mentioned at Lem Witherbee's, but the morning after the storm the farmers met in a group at Andrew Cline's barn as though by appointment to start on the first field. The same haying schedule was followed each year, and its details called for no reiteration to the exclusion of more important topics at the conference.

Mrs. Emma Goode liked the haying season. It brought an atmosphere of excitement and a feeling that something was going to happen. This expected something never did happen, but each year Mrs. Goode had new nameless hopes that brought a pleasing anticipation and suspense. She was sure that if she was ever given a present of a million dollars or found a fine carriage in the barn it would happen during haying days. Whatever happened of a pleasant nature during the haying season would be quite in keeping with her frame of mind.

Haying days were hard-working holidays. Irritating things did not happen at this time. They would not be tolerated and so went unnoticed. Even when Mayhew Currier had been killed one year by falling from a hayrack onto Arthur Moore's pitchfork the event called for no serious concern until the holiday spirit of the haying season was over. Mrs. Goode felt happy, for pain as well as rain was dismissed until the hay was in the barns.

She had liked to play among the haycocks when a child. It was on a pile of hay that Arthur Moore had shown her many things she never knew before. Silas Goode had taken her to a pile of hay a few years later, and a few months after that Silas had married her.

Mrs. Goode looked at Alice, her daughter. Perhaps she would sit down to rest on a haycock this year. She wished she could change places with Alice for a few days. Silas was all right, but there was something nice about being taken to a haycock at night that he did not appreciate now. He had all he wanted of fresh air and haystacks during the day. At night he led the way to bed but not into the fields.

"You been seein' quite a bit of Felix Dole lately, ain't you?" Mrs. Goode asked Alice.

"We been walkin' a few times, that's all," her daughter answered. "I ain't seen him since it rained."

"Well, you better not go walkin' with him so much. It don't look good to be seein' one boy all the time, and Felix ain't a very good boy for you to be goin' with anyway."

Mrs. Goode smiled to herself. Things were supposed to be nicer when forbidden, and she certainly was not going to neglect her part in making Alice's meetings with Felix more enjoyable.

"Well, I won't be able to see him now it's hayin' time," said Alice. "He'll be busy days and tired nights."

Mrs. Goode had said, "That's too bad," before remembering she was reprimanding her daughter. "Your father didn't used to be tired nights," she added by way of encouragement.

Alice did not appreciate the holiday atmosphere with the same enthusiasm as her mother. She changed the subject and offered to go to the store for some needed groceries. Mrs. Goode gave her several coins from her pocketbook and, when her daughter had left, sat down in a reverie of haycocks with faces that smiled and winked at passing couples.

There was a knock on the door. Mrs. Goode opened it excitedly and found Arthur Moore standing outside. "And me wearing this old dress and spotted apron," she thought, her excitement increasing.

She had not been alone with Arthur Moore for many years. This sudden reunion without onlookers was a surprise indeed. It seemed as though he had just arrived back from a long journey. It was strange he should come to see her after she had been married all these years, but then, these were the haying holidays.

"What are you doin' way over here?" she asked.

"I sprained my wrist and thought I'd come to call," said Moore. "Silas won't be home to dinner."

"No, but Alice will."

"Well, let's talk it over in the barn. We can go out and see if the lofts are ready for the hay."

Being led into a hayloft by day was not quite the same as visiting a haycock at night, but for the moment Mrs. Goode thought it was even nicer. She walked into the barn with Arthur. The expected something that never happened in the haying season had happened.

Alice returned from the store running and without the purchases she had gone to make. Mrs. Goode was just coming out of the barn.

"Ma!" Alice shouted. "Pa's been killed. He was killed just like Mayhew Currier was! He fell off Cline's hayrack and landed on Arthur Moore's pitchfork. And there's Arthur Moore now!"

Arthur Moore had followed Mrs. Goode out of the barn.

"Oh, yes, I was goin' to tell you," he said. "Silas was fixin' the hayrack, gettin' it ready, and my fork was restin' agin a wheel. The railin' broke, and the tines went through him."

Mrs. Goode forgot the holiday spirit of the haying season for a moment. She looked into space.

"Well, you tried to break the news gently," she said to Arthur.

Arthur Moore was walking toward the road.

CHAPTER IX

A NOISY FUNERAL ENDS MERRILY

After the haying was over, the populace of Menham turned out in a group for Silas Goode's burial. The body had been kept in Mrs. Goode's cellar, as cool a place as could be found, but the weather had been hot, and there was an unpleasant odor for those who stood too close to the casket.

The coffin had been made by Andrew Cline to whom the duty fell since the death had taken place on his farm. He had nailed up the body while Mrs. Goode waited at the top of the stairs. The smell in the cellar had been strong. The coffin, with open spaces between the boards, resembled a crate more than a casket. There was a lining of newspapers.

The burying had been delayed by the haying ceremonies, which could not be interrupted by anything but rain. Despite the assurance of fair weather after the Hume storm, haying was still done with all possible haste. A burial at night would have been inconvenient.

Lem Witherbee was the officiating sexton. He designated a spot that he thought was well to one side of Mortimer Goode, Silas' father, the last one to be buried in the Goode plot. Witherbee and Alfred Dole dug there until Lem's pickax went through the end of a rotted wooden box.

Forgetting where he was, Lem thought that perhaps he had discovered buried treasure. He pulled off the broken board and saw a skull, which reminded him that he should have counted off nine paces from the gravestone instead of seven. But the hole was deep enough, so, after enlarging the bottom, the grave was declared ready.

After the group had assembled, the coffin was lowered into the hole by Andrew Cline, who brought it from Mrs. Goode's cellar, and Lem Witherbee. Miss Hummer had been one of the first to arrive and was enjoying herself immensely, although her dejected countenance was the most mournful in the gathering.

A man was dead. There was one less man to inflict himself on women. The male society for the promotion of wickedness could not coöperate with him any more. He was simmering in the flames of Hell now and adding his groans to the chorus of men there.

Miss Hummer stood as close to the grave as she dared. She smelled the stench from the coffin and almost smiled. A man could not conceal his true nature when dead. This awful odor which permeated his being was concealed during life, but in death it became the perfume of his soul. Neither the smell nor the soul could hide within the body then.

John Lyman, being a cousin of Silas Goode, was to say a few words over the grave. He had written something on a small piece of paper and began to read, "Silas Goode was a fine farmer and was always good to his wife and child. He was free from sin and—" Lyman could not read his own writing. "He was born in 1872 and—" Lyman held the paper at a different angle to the light in an attempt to decipher the next word.

At this point there was a general surprise by the appearance of Deacon Ira Ormsby. On his last visit to Menham the deacon had been found asleep behind the town hall by Little Mary Dole while playing the morning after his temperance speech. He had stood up and walked away hatless without saying a word and had not been heard from since. The window that had been broken on his fall was still broken.

Deacon Ormsby was wearing a hat when he joined the funeral company. He walked through the group, stumbled, and turned back to face it from a spot directly in front of John Lyman. He began to talk in a very loud voice as though he had been an announced speaker whom Lyman had just introduced.

Lyman was pleased by this conclusion to his part in the program. Perhaps the deacon would buy the White Horse Whisky this time, and perhaps he, as Silas' cousin, could have the drink that was due Silas. Being so close to Deacon Ormsby he could not help noticing large bulges in his hip pockets.

"It makes me very sad to come upon you in this hour of suffering and sorrow," roared the deacon, "but I am only too pleased to be able to do my part in sending your lost"—he hesitated between the words "brother" and "sister" then said— "friend into the eternal happiness."

"I knew and loved the deceased well,"—he hoped the corpse was not a woman—"so well that I can be one of you in your sorrow. I am sure our dead beloved is now enjoying the happiness of Eden, drinking the cup of bliss—"

Deacon Ormsby became entangled in the threads of his thoughts. "Drinking" and "cup" were cues for a different sort of discourse. He paused, belched, staggered slightly, pushed his hat back on his head, clenched his fist, and yelled, "Ladies and gentlemen, let us take this example of the evils of whisky—the terrors of alcohol. Death and the horrors of Hell await those who drink liquor. All the torments of Hell have been exceeded in the saloon. Far more men come out of saloons dead than escape alive. Dead, ladies and gentlemen. Death and whisky are synonymous. Whisky is poison, the worst poison the Devil has conceived. Death comes to those who drink whisky. Death, shame, degeneration, and Hell. Death."

Deacon Ormsby paused abruptly. His threads of thought had untangled themselves and left him in an embarrassing position. He pushed his hat forward hastily and added in bellowing tones, "But this dead comrade is an example of an unsullied body, free from the poisons of whisky, plucked into Heaven by God's own hand to be His bosom companion. Our dead friend is now conversing with God, telling him perhaps how he escaped the ruin of whisky and how—"

In his enthusiasm Deacon Ormsby swayed too far to one side, lost his balance, and took a quick step in an attempt to right himself. His foot came down in thin air. He found himself falling. He disappeared into the open grave.

CHAPTER X

DEACON ORMSBY BUYS THE DRINKS

Except on occasions of extreme necessity Deacon Ira Ormsby never bought whisky in the towns where he spoke. He made his tours of the countryside on foot, speaking at one town and drinking at the next. Unscheduled speeches were frequently given in the saloons of the latter towns, but these were inspired talks that God called upon him to make in these foul dens of iniquity where they could do the most good. His hip pocket supply made it possible for him to drink in towns where he gave formal lectures, even though he did not purchase liquor there.

To seem to violate his own precepts by drinking the very poison he assailed was an inconsistency that Deacon Ormsby could readily explain, and in such a loud voice that the skeptic could offer no further arguments that would be heard.

Whenever this question was brought up, whether facetiously by fellow drinkers or in earnest by indignant temperance fanatics, Deacon Ormsby would strain his exaggerated dignity to a new maximum reserved for such times—if he still had sufficient control of his bodily faculties. This increased dignity alone would often frighten the questioners and provide all the explanation needed, but Deacon Ormsby would not let the doubters off so easily. He would assume an expression of pity, righteous indignation, and violated virtue all in one. Then would come the blast of noise that usually did not stop until the questioners had withdrawn for shelter.

"Such a question shows a mind unable to comprehend the sufferings of true martyrdom, the pains of Jesus Christ on the cross and of His companions on either side," the deacon would say.

"I am a *martyr* to my cause. I have devoted my life to fighting whisky and saving the souls that it would otherwise lead to graves in the gutter. I drink this poison myself for this one purpose: so that others cannot have it. Poison that goes into my body cannot contaminate another's. I drink to save others. I suffer the torments of whisky so that they shall escape. The more I drink the less there is left.

"God has granted me a special immunity from death by this poison but protects me from none of its pain. He has made me a martyr to show others what will happen to them if they succumb to whisky. By my example, when I sleep in the gutter all those who see me there are frightened into a life of temperance. Your question overwhelms me. It is unbelievable that my work could be unappreciated by even such a handful of skeptics."

Deacon Ormsby could go on in this vein as long as he had a listener. Then he would sit down—if he had been able to stand beforehand. At any rate, he would have a drink.

There were those who said Deacon Ormsby conducted his temperance campaign to prevent others from drinking liquor that might otherwise be his. The motto, "The less others drink the more there will be for me," had been ascribed to him.

This defamation was equally easy for the deacon to answer. "There were those who ridiculed and persecuted Jesus Christ, too," he would say. "As His messenger, I have been cast into jail and slandered by the unrighteous. This additional invective is only another burden for me to carry as a martyr to the cause of temperance."

For various reasons, Deacon Ira Ormsby usually did not follow the same route twice or stay in any town more than one night. His return to Menham had been as unexpected to him as to the residents. He had thought he was on the road to Lakeville when he found himself at Silas Goode's funeral in Menham. This was his day for drinking rather than speaking, but he could not resist the opportunity afforded by the already assembled funeral group.

Having spoken there, he could continue on to Lakeville without visiting the Menham saloon and make tomorrow his drinking day. This plan would have been feasible had it not been for the open grave. When Deacon Ormsby landed on the coffin he heard a cracking of breaking glass and felt wet. The lower part of his body was dripping, and a smell of whisky replaced the stench of the corpse when Lem Witherbee and John Lyman helped him out of the hole.

His reserve supply of whisky was gone. He could not continue on to Lakeville in this condition. It would be necessary to visit Menham's saloon and at once. Deacon Ormsby picked pieces of broken glass out of his hip pockets. He felt partly undressed without the padding of these two pint bottles.

"I could not leave without proving my nearness to our beloved dead friend," he said, making no attempt to account for his wet trousers.

"What d'you do, strike a whisky well down there?" Andrew Cline whispered to Lem Witherbee, wishing the drops that were coming from Deacon Ormsby's trousers could be dripping into a glass.

"No, but the deacon prob'ly wishes there was a whisky well handy," Lem replied. "He didn't get away this trip. He'll have to come to the store now. And he sure gave Silas the drink that was comin' to him."

Deacon Ormsby walked out around the group to the road and continued on his way, while all the women except Miss Hummer applauded the uproar of his remarks. Even his fall into the grave had been taken as a symbolic expression of something very sacred and appropriate. Only a few had laughed. The men had been watching for some such irregularity and were glad the grave had a bottom.

"Silas was lucky to have the deacon come along when he did," said Mrs. Dole to Mrs. Goode.

"Yes, but Silas prob'ly won't appreciate it," she answered. "He never cared much for show."

The men had no doubt but what Deacon Ormsby was heading for Lem Witherbee's saloon. It had been closed for the funeral, and he would have to wait there to have the broken bottles replaced. Lem would be neglecting his self-imposed duties if he went back before the grave was filled in. He and Alfred Dole proceeded to shovel dirt onto the whisky-stained coffin with much haste, while the others urged them on to greater efforts.

Deacon Ormsby was sitting on the doorstep of the store asleep when the farmers came running up in a body. He was having a bad dream in which the storekeeper told him no liquor was sold there. When Lem Witherbee opened the door the deacon fell through it backwards and awoke. The farmers politely waited for him to get to his feet before entering, forming a wall around the door that prevented an escape in their direction.

"Is this Menham's foul den of iniquity where whisky can be purchased?" asked the deacon, shaking himself into a position of dignity.

"Yes, indeed," said Lem proudly.

"As a martyr to my cause, I am called upon to demonstrate what no man should ever do. Give me a glass of that horrible poison known as whisky."

"I ain't got no poison whisky, but I've got a nice bottle of White Horse," Lem replied.

"Any kind at all will do. Poison is poison under any label."

Lem Witherbee arranged the glasses of all those present in a row and opened a quart bottle of White Horse whisky that had long been secluded in a dusty corner of his liquor shelf.

"Last time you were here, you know, you promised us a round of White Horse," said Andrew Cline meekly.

Deacon Ormsby was concentrating his attention too closely on the bottle in Lem's hand to pay any attention to the remark. He placed a bill on the counter with the words, "I must suffer the tortures of whisky to save the souls of others."

Lem seized the bill, and, starting at the opposite end of the counter from the deacon, poured a drink into all the glasses. The deacon drank his with the manner of a man dying of thirst who is given a thimbleful of water and called for another.

"Did I pay you for the first one?" he asked, fumbling in his pocket.

"Yes, just right," replied Lem. "Is this next one goin' to be for every one or just for you?"

"Just me, of course," the deacon bellowed. "I would die before I would buy whisky for another."

Lem poured the deacon's drink and reached for a different bottle from which to serve the farmers. He was used to inconsistencies in his customers' remarks, and, after all, the deacon had only promised one round of drinks.

CHAPTER XI

HENRIETTA HARRIET HELEN HUMMER'S FIRST TOY

Silas Goode's whisky cup, a thick white mug with overlaying networks of cracks, was placed with proper dignity in the niche reserved for customers who could drink no more of Lem Witherbee's beverages.

This was an internment attended by sympathy and sentiment on the part of the farmers. Burial of the body was a routine duty—Silas had left that, and the corpse hardly resembled him. But putting his whisky cup on the shelf of the dead was a sad rite—Silas was still a part of the cup and could use it no more. The part of Silas that had been buried had escaped from further work. The part that still remained had been deprived of further pleasure.

This would happen to all of their cups some day. Perhaps they would have to watch the world from this niche to the end of time, owning a cup and unable to drink from it. Even when a friend used a glass on the reserved shelf in communicating a drunken message to the owner, only the living friend could drink the liquor.

Deacon Ira Ormsby's example was considered quite fitting for the occasion: drink all you can now because you can't use your whisky cup when you're dead. The deacon had even interrupted the silence that came when Lem Witherbee placed Silas Goode's cup into its new sanctuary by calling for another drink.

"Do you s'pose Silas could taste whisky if we put some in his cup?" reflected David Hume.

"He could if he was here," said Arthur Moore, whereupon the subject shifted to horses.

Miss Hummer returned home from the funeral happy that another man was gone and unhappy that still another man had arrived to take his place and to be applauded. She plucked small birch branches from trees as she passed. She had quite a supply of these in her kitchen now, but it would never do to run short. She kept the switches in a pile beside the stove, where they would be mistaken for kindling by a visitor. She had a bouquet of long twigs as she entered her yard.

Henrietta was sleeping in his bed on the floor. He usually slept when Miss Hummer went out. She had left him crying and crawling on the floor. He had crawled to the bed somewhat like a tired kitten that has a box of rags in a corner. Miss Hummer wakened Henrietta at once. The baby remained on the bed as though waiting for another opportunity to take a nap.

Miss Hummer had found a large crib in her attic which she now kept in the parlor. She placed Henrietta there when she had a visitor. The baby had only slept in this crib once: when Mrs. Whiter had made a long call during which the conversation turned from babies.

"I've got some nice new birch switches for you, Henrietta," said Miss Hummer pleasantly.

The baby began to cry.

"You'll cry louder than that when I use them." Miss Hummer struck the child across the chest. "How do you like that?" she asked.

The baby stopped crying but began again as soon as Miss Hummer left its side. She paid no more attention to the cries than though she had just wound a clock and left it ticking behind her.

It was a hot day. Miss Hummer wanted to take a nap, but if she did it would mean this man in her power could sleep, too. She didn't want Henrietta to escape the heat, but she supposed it was necessary to let him sleep a lot if she wanted to continue to keep him in her power. Well, she could make sleeping a little harder.

Henrietta was wearing a long dress and a variety of underclothes. Miss Hummer placed him in a chair and put another dress on over these garments. Now he could go out in the hot sun and sleep or cry, whichever he preferred. She left the baby on a stone step outside the kitchen door and went to her room to lie down.

She awoke during her nap resenting the fact that it is necessary to take such care with babies in order to keep them alive. Henrietta might have had sunstroke outdoors while she was asleep. It would be no great loss if he died, but if she wanted to have a man in her power she would have to keep him alive. If he were dead now there was nothing she could do about it. Miss Hummer went to sleep again.

When Miss Hummer finally came back to the kitchen door the baby was not on the step nor in the yard beyond. She went around the corner of the house and saw Henrietta sitting in the shade of the woodshed. She saw something else, too, and was terrified. There was a large black snake in the baby's lap. Henrietta was playing with the snake and laughing, fingering its body and lifting its tail into the air. He shook the tail, and there was a noise like a rattle. The snake's head was on the baby's chest and moving nearer to his face, its tongue flickering in and out between two fangs like flashes of fire.

Miss Hummer had a horror of snakes. The sight of a snake came like an electric shock and left her nervous for a week or more. How did this awful monster get into her yard? How could she get rid of it? How could she prevent seeing it again? She ran back into the kitchen trembling and locked the door.

Then she thought of Henrietta. She shuddered, not out of concern for the baby but for herself. The male conspiracy for the promotion of wickedness was asserting itself. The man she had dominated was now dominating her. He held her at bay. She could not even approach him. He was torturing her worse than she had tortured him. The thought of the snake brought back the electric shock.

Henrietta had been laughing like a fiend as he fondled the snake. Where had he learned to laugh? This writhing horror must be a messenger of the male conspiracy for wickedness. It had led him into the shade and taught him how to laugh. What other secrets had it brought? Perhaps it had told Henrietta his real sex and brought some poison with which he could kill her. The male depravity was even worse than she had imagined. And its secret powers were incredible.

Miss Hummer regretted that she had kept the child. She had asked for a girl. The delivery of a boy had been a mistake. The whole thing was probably part of a male conspiracy against her.

The snake might be outside the door now, waiting for her to open it. It would crawl all over her, rape her, while Henrietta beat her with the switches she had gathered to use on him, or perhaps with bigger sticks.

She sat still in terror. The male conspiracy must have inspired her to put Henrietta outdoors. This horrible suspense. What was going to happen to her? With an extreme effort of courage Miss Hummer forced herself to a window where she could see the woodshed. She saw Henrietta and the snake still in conference. The snake's head was now curled around the baby's neck. She ran back to her chair.

At intervals of several minutes Miss Hummer bravely brought herself to the window again. Each time the snake and the baby were in new positions, and Miss Hummer felt new agonies.

On the fifth trip to the window the snake was starting to crawl away. Miss Hummer giddily seized the curtain to hold herself there and saw the snake disappear through a small hole beneath the woodshed. She continued to stand there for several minutes until the baby began to crawl after the snake.

This roused her to action. She would not let the male coalition kidnap her baby while she stood idly by. She unlocked the door, ran to the child, picked him up, and dashed back into the house.

Henrietta seemed to be just the same as before. His strength had not increased, and he no longer laughed. Miss Hummer searched about his clothing for a vial of poison. There was none. This man was in her power again. She had thwarted the male society for the promotion of wickedness. She wished she had dared to kill the snake.

Miss Hummer hastily removed Henrietta's clothes and proceeded to select the largest switch in the pile.

CHAPTER XII

DARKNESS FOR CLOTHING

It was Tuesday and May Cline's night for sleepwalking. Mrs. Susan Cline, who had been keeping a record for twenty-eight days, decided that, although it was Tuesday, it was not May's night for sleepwalking. For this reason, she did not leave the umbrella at the door, even though it had looked like rain at bedtime.

Mrs. Cline slept soundly, expecting her daughter to do the same. She was not awakened when May sat up at eleven o'clock and put her feet on the floor. May remained in this position for many seconds, but her mother continued to snore. Without her mother to guide her in leading the way down the dark hall and stairs to the door May anticipated some difficulty.

She considered waking up her mother but was afraid that to do so would waken her father, too, and he had always been in favor of forcing his daughter to remain in bed when she started to walk at night. May started down the hall alone, helped by the side of the wall.

At the head of the stairs she groped for the railing and then started the descent timidly. Her mother had been of even more assistance than May had realized. She collided with a chair in the kitchen and found herself barricaded by the kitchen table. Considerable fumbling freed her from this prison, then her thigh struck the door knob. She drew the bolt, turned the key and the knob, and was outdoors.

It was raining. May felt for the umbrella in its usual place, but it was not there. Why had her mother been so careless tonight? The pretty blue nightgown she was wearing for the first time would get all wet. She thought of leaving it in the kitchen and going on her way without this only garment, but perhaps her mother would be waiting there to lead the way back to bed when she returned. She took off the nightgown and placed it on a dry part of the porch. Her mother probably wouldn't come out in the rain, and a nightgown could be put on quickly and quietly.

Well, she knew her way now. May began to run, both from force of habit and because of the rain which struck her naked body with cold splashes. She entered the barn through a small door that was open and was greeted by the pressure of a man's body with his arms around her. She tried to kiss him, but in the darkness she could not find his lips, which she soon learned had been seeking her breasts.

There were no spoken words. The man took May's hand and led her to the rear of the barn, where the floor was piled high with the hay that had been left over after the Cline lofts were filled with the new crop. In the darkness, all movements had to be felt and not seen.

The horse stamped, and the two cows could be heard swinging their tails. In a sty underneath the stalls two pigs grunted occasionally. May did not notice these sounds, nor did her companion. The sense of hearing had fallen into disuse for the time being.

When May returned to the house she did not mind the rain. Its drops were cooling and felt nice. She walked slowly to enjoy them. Puddles and mud splashed about her bare feet and ankles, but even this seemed nice.

She was about to open the kitchen door when she remembered the discarded nightgown. She felt around for it indifferently, but was roused to a more careful search when her fingers touched nothing but wood. May fumbled about the porch again but only made her fingers dirtier. The nightgown had disappeared.

"I'll bet Ma's been out here," May concluded.

"Well, t'ain't my fault if the wind blows off my nightdress when I'm asleep."

She opened the door and entered the kitchen. Her mother was sitting at the table in the dark. Mrs. Cline started up the stairs followed by her daughter.

When she awoke the next morning May saw her blue nightgown at the foot of her bed and was somewhat worried. She did not get up until her parents were downstairs.

At the breakfast table Mrs. Cline said to May, "I like to broke my neck trippin' on a nightgown of yours on the back porch last night. I guess it blew off the clothesline."

"Yeah," said May, "I meant to take it in 'fore I went to bed."

"Musta been hangin' in mid-air," said Andrew Cline. "I took in the clothesline just 'fore supper."

This clinched the point for May. Mrs. Cline would not let the facts interfere when her husband disputed her. Once she had established a proposition it remained dogmatic regardless of what he might prove to the contrary.

"And I put it up ag'in just after supper," she answered.

CHAPTER XIII

A SNAKE AND HIS WIFE BECOME PROPERTY OWNERS

The power Miss Hummer exercised over a man was reciprocal after Henrietta's interview with the snake.

She held him a prisoner in her fortress, but he had communicated with the enemy and taken possession of her lands. Miss Hummer no longer dared go into her back yard or even to leave her house by the kitchen door for fear of meeting the black snake.

She kept the kitchen door locked and bolted. When she had to go out of the house she used the front door, which formerly had always been more of a decoration than a practical part of the dwelling. Going outdoors at all was a risk that was taken as seldom as possible. The snake could crawl around to the front yard and lie in wait for her.

Henrietta had become more than a potential member of the male coalition for the promotion of wickedness; he was now a full-fledged and active member. Miss Hummer saw to it that he was kept indoors and away from further contacts with things outside.

To have her property taken over by a snake was a horror that would have caused her uneasiness even in imagination. Miss Hummer was in continual fear that the snake would find its way into the house. There was always the dread that it would be lurking under something she was about to touch, or curled up behind some object either directly ahead or behind her. When Miss Hummer undressed with the light out at night and went into her closet to dress in the morning, she could almost see the snake hiding in the darkness.

Several times Miss Hummer had looked out a window and seen the snake crawling about near the spot where it had been with Henrietta. Once she had seen it lying there motionless, evidently waiting for either her or the baby. On these occasions she had whipped Henrietta immediately to let the snake hear his screams.

Being barricaded like this caused many inconveniences. It kept Miss Hummer from going into her barn or woodshed. She had no animals to feed, but she did want to cook food for herself. Without wood for the fire she could not do any cooking.

While Miss Hummer was imprisoned by the snake Mrs. Nancy Muller came to call for the first time since the baby had been adopted. Mrs. Muller was very deaf and, in common with the men of Menham, did not accept the story of Henrietta's adoption. It is doubtful if she had actually heard this story, but if she did she rejected it as due to some new defect in her ear drums. She knew babies could be obtained in only one way, and she knew Miss Hummer had a baby.

Miss Hummer had been doing sentry duty at a window overlooking the woodshed and did not hear Mrs. Muller until she began to pound on the back door. Was this the snake demanding entrance? Miss Hummer felt electric shocks running over her body.

She went to another window and saw Mrs. Muller's rounded shoulders. Only a visitor, and a woman, too! The relief was so great that she started to open the kitchen door. Then she reconsidered. She could not take any such chance as this. Mrs. Muller would have to come in by the front door. Miss Hummer went out the front door to call her there.

When Miss Hummer got her first full-length view of Mrs. Muller she thought she was going to faint. Mrs. Muller was holding one arm out in front of her on a level with her shoulders, and in her hand was the long black snake, which hung down to the ground. A woman was cooperating with the male conspiracy! Mrs. Muller had been ready to pounce upon her with the snake as soon as she opened the kitchen door. Miss Hummer was about to run back into the house and lock the front door when Mrs. Muller saw her.

"I just killed this rattler in your driveway," she said. "Thought you'd like to see it. Biggest one I've seen in a long time."

Killed? The snake was dead? It must be a trick of some kind.

"Put it down!" yelled Miss Hummer. "Don't bring it near me!"

Mrs. Muller was walking toward her to let her get a better look at the snake.

"Ain't he a big one?" she said proudly, while Miss Hummer ran for the door.

"You must be a'scared of snakes." Mrs. Muller threw the rattler to the ground and followed Miss Hummer to the door. "How's the baby?" she asked.

"Be sure and take that snake away when you go!"

"I know how it is," replied Mrs. Muller. "Havin' a baby and no husband. I've been through it all." She sat down in a parlor chair.

"Don't leave that snake out there when you go," said Miss Hummer, so distracted she did not realize this enemy was dead.

"Yes, and knowin' who the father is, seein' him every day, and him actin' like he'd never seen you before. I've been through it all."

Miss Hummer opened a drawer where she kept pencils and paper. She wrote in large letters, "Take the snake away when you go," and handed this message to Mrs. Muller.

"What would I want with it?" she replied. "I killed it, ain't that enough?"

Miss Hummer wrote another note, "I'm afraid of snakes. Please put that one where I can't see it."

"Oh, all right," replied Mrs. Muller. "But as I was sayin', it's irritatin' when a man says he'll marry you while you're enjoyin' yourself with him, and then when you have a baby he says it's someone else's. But p'raps it's better not havin' a husband around to bother you. Did you have a boy or a girl?"

"I adopted my baby, and it's a girl," said Miss Hummer, recovering most of her dignity.

"You're lucky. I wish I'd had a boy. At least he can't have a baby, and maybe he can be a little help when he grows up. All Minnie can do is wait for night to come so's she can go walkin' with Paul Turner. First thing I know *she'll* be havin' a baby. She'll prob'ly want me to take care of it."

Miss Hummer felt much better now. She was shocked rather than horrified. But she would have to set Mrs. Muller right on two important points. She wrote, "I adopted my baby and it's a girl."

"So you got a girl, too," replied Mrs. Muller. "Too bad. We both got girls, and we both didn't get husbands." She laughed. "I know how it is. I've been through it all. Now you better change your name to Mrs. like I did. You're the same as married if folks call you Mrs."

Miss Hummer summoned her loudest voice, "It's not my baby, I adopted it! Adopted it!"

"Yeah, mine hurt a lot, too," Mrs. Muller answered.

Miss Hummer could not let Mrs. Muller continue to have this horrible opinion that she, a virgin and a benevolent foster mother, had given birth to a child. She wrote, "It's not my baby. I got it from Scofield Orphanage."

Mrs. Muller laughed when she read this. "I found mine growin' on a tree," she replied. "You better just change your name to Mrs."

Miss Hummer was indignant. How could this woman say such things? She wrote again, "But it's true."

"There, there, of course it's true," said Mrs. Muller. "Every baby has to have a mother. There's no use tryin' to deny where you got it when you find a baby in your belly. Only Christ's mother could think up a story anyone would believe. And if she'd a been a virgin the baby would'a had a hard time gettin' out."

Miss Hummer's exasperation and scorn became as intense as her horror had been previously. This callous infamy with which her character was being stained was more of the suffering she must go through to have a man in her power. This sacrifice was too great. She was becoming a martyr. She would see that Henrietta was made to feel each of these cruel words as keenly as she had.

The argument came to an abrupt end when Mrs. Muller stood up with the remarks, "Babies are a nuisance. Well, you've learned your lesson now. Don't have any more. I've got to be goin'. I'll try to remember to call you Mrs. after this."

She went out the front door, while Miss Hummer remained in her chair. Mrs. Muller picked up the snake and dragged it behind her out to the road.

The snake was dead now. Miss Hummer could get some wood for a fire and cook a meal. The enemy had been killed, the male coalition defeated again. Mrs. Muller had done her a great favor after all. She locked the front door and unlocked the kitchen door, pushing Henrietta out of her path with her foot.

Miss Hummer walked toward the woodshed. She owned her yard again. Henrietta had no more power over her. Then she looked down. Directly in front of her was a live black rattlesnake, larger and longer than the other. Electric shocks that should have brought sparks surged through her.

Miss Hummer ran for the kitchen door. Mrs. Muller's visit had been a ruse. She was part of the male conspiracy, one of its whores. She had taken the other snake home to have supper with her, to sleep with her.

CHAPTER XIV

ARTHUR MOORE'S SNAKE STY

Arthur Moore lived alone. His parents became ghosts, as he expressed it, when he was a boy, and his wife had died two days after he married her. He had a theory that neighbors at a distance were bad enough and numerous enough without having more and having them live in his house. He regarded matrimony as a gigantic swindle conducted by women. He would never be caught again.

He only had to see neighbors occasionally and usually on a friendly basis. He would have to see a family more often than his cows, whether on a friendly basis or not. It would probably be unfriendly. Besides, he didn't like to see people as often as he did his cows. There were plenty of women without bringing one home to support, and having her breed children that he couldn't be sure were his.

Arthur Moore gave very little thought to the breeding of children. They were the result of carelessness. There was a bounty on rattlesnakes. He preferred to breed them.

He had a pen of these snakes that he fed and tried to fatten. When they became too numerous for comfort in the quarters provided, he killed some of them and collected the bounty. He had enlarged the pen several times.

The snakes were kept behind the barn, where they could bask in the sun. A wooden cover was let down over the wire netting top when there was a visitor. Callers saw only a large wooden box. Nobody but Arthur had ever seen the inside of this pen of snakes.

Arthur Moore liked snakes, especially rattlesnakes. He liked them for pets as well as for the bounty they brought. He found them the most affectionate of all animals. He often took two or three rattlers out of the pen and let them crawl over his shoulders and arms. They did not try to get away and never bit him. When one fell to the ground it often curled about his leg.

Sometimes he put the snakes to practical uses. He would take some of the largest and let them drag themselves about among his crops with their tails tied to long pieces of twine fastened to stakes. They would eat harmful insects without damaging the plants.

He usually waited until the crops were high enough to hide the snakes before employing them in this way. If any one did notice one of his fields of tethered snakes, Arthur would explain that he had set some snake traps and was waiting to get some ammunition to shoot them. He didn't dare try to kill them any other way because they were poison.

Rattlesnakes were useful in another way, too. They would bite other people, and their bites often meant death. Nobody could accuse him of having anything to do with somebody's being bitten.

When he took a strong dislike to a person Arthur Moore enjoyed leaving one or two big rattlers near that person's house while walking by at night. If they happened to bite anyone, he would agree that it was too bad. If they didn't, or if the wrong person was bitten, he could take another walk by the house at night. If the dislike he felt was strong enough he could bring more than one or two snakes.

Arthur Moore regretted the loss of two favorite black snakes that had escaped from their tethers in his potato field. They had been fine snakes, and, no doubt, would like to be back in the pen. They were the only black ones he had. Perhaps they had been stolen. He had been saving them to use when he had a real enemy, someone whose funeral he really wanted to attend. If two other snakes had come loose from their leashes it would not have been so bad, but these were special favorites. They would have won first prizes if there were snake shows.

Arthur had looked all over the potato patch and adjoining field without success. He gave the other snakes a meal of live toads and frogs and went to call on Mrs. Goode. Perhaps the lost snakes had crawled onto her property.

He had visited Emma many times since Silas Goode's death. He usually took her walking, as he had when she was a little girl. He had to keep her out of sight of her parents in those childhood days. Now he felt that he had to keep her out of sight of Alice.

CHAPTER XV

A SECRET SEXUAL PLEASURE

One day when Arthur Moore was a young man he had decided to marry. Marriage was a mystery that many people indulged in, and his curiosity as to why they did so got the better of him. There must be something more to marrying a girl than having sexual intercourse, he thought. It was not necessary to get married to enjoy this pleasure. There must be other pleasures, other bodily contacts that could be revealed or performed by a girl only after she had married a man.

Having made this decision, Arthur began to consider the possibilities in the way of girls. There was Nancy Muller—she was Miss then—but he had had too much trouble convincing her to stop and lie down when they took walks together. There had been one night when she would not do anything but walk.

If she was as contrary as this in accepting such pleasant sensations, she was probably just as stubborn in other ways. She might refuse to eat—but that would not worry him—or she might refuse to reveal the new pleasures that marriage permitted.

There was Jenny Taylor. She had not been contrary when they had gone on walks. She would be a nice girl to enjoy any sort of pleasure with. Arthur felt that he was making improper advances in asking her to marry him. He was suggesting a new form of intercourse whose nature he did not know but which she did know. She might consider it an insult.

He waited until they returned from their walk that evening before proposing. If she considered his proposition indecent and refused to have anything more to do with him, at least he had enjoyed a final evening with her. To his great surprise, Jenny kissed Arthur when he asked her to marry him.

They went to Scofield the next Sunday to have the ceremony performed. Arthur had harnessed his horse to the carriage at daybreak so to get an early start and be back that night. Jenny was happier than he had ever seen her before. The marriage-pleasure must be an intense sensation if its anticipation had this effect on his bride.

Arthur had never gone anywhere with Jenny by daylight before. She kept an arm around him and kissed him frequently, which annoyed him. Why was it necessary to get the permission of a minister to obtain this new pleasure? Such a formality seemed ridiculous. But so many others had done the same thing before him that there must be some good reason for it. Perhaps the minister sold some contraption which was necessary for the full enjoyment and which could only be used by one couple.

The Scofield minister did not sell Arthur anything but his marriage certificate. "Is this all we get?" Moore had asked with the feeling of a man who has paid for a house and been given a paperweight model of one. The wedding had been so meaningless and nonsensical that he thought the clergyman was lying when he said they were now man and wife.

"He must be too lazy to marry us right," Arthur thought when the minister assured him that was all.

Jenny seemed willing to believe it was all over and tugged at his sleeve to come away. If she was ready to show him the new pleasure, that was all he wanted, but it seemed a pity that they had needed to waste a whole day just to hear and say these few words and get this piece of paper. He felt that someone had played a joke on him. Why couldn't Jenny have come alone?

Arthur watched Jenny carefully as they got into the carriage. How soon would she show him the new pleasure? Should he stop as soon as they were out of sight of the houses of Scofield? He drove the horse at a gallop until there was nothing to see but trees.

"Shall we stop here?" Arthur asked.

"If you will, please," Jenny answered.

Arthur started to follow her into the woods, but she laughed and said, "You use the other side."

Arthur got back into the carriage. He had used the toilet at the minister's house. Evidently Jenny did not want to show him the new sensation yet. Driving on to Menham, whenever they passed through a particularly dense stretch of woods, he asked if she wanted to stop. She only laughed and said, "No."

Arthur became irritated and indignant. Why was she keeping him waiting? They were married now—or at least so the minister had said. He was entitled to know what marriage was. The minister should have let them use a room of his long enough for this initiation. There should be no more delay or suspense. Jenny only talked nonsense and seemed to have no intention of letting him know what she had in store for him until they got home.

Arthur's rage and desire increased as the ride continued. At last he pulled the horse to a stop alongside a field. There was one pleasure of which Jenny did not have exclusive knowledge. He could at least enjoy her in the ordinary way he always had when they went walking, and it was no longer necessary to hide. He stepped from the carriage.

"Come on," he said to Jenny, starting to walk toward the field.

"What for?"

"You know what for. Come on."

Jenny followed him. She was his wife now. They did not have to wait for darkness. As soon as they were off the narrow road, Arthur placed her on the ground and started to fumble with her petticoats.

"We're married; I can do that myself now," said Jenny.

CHAPTER XVI

ARTHUR MOORE IMPROVES ON BEATING ONE'S WIFE

When they drove on, Arthur Moore did not feel so much concerned with the new pleasure of marriage. He could wait until they got to Menham to know about that. He pulled up in his yard more interested in food than his wife's body. Jenny had brought a lunch which had been eaten—most of it by Arthur—before they reached Scofield.

The bride prepared supper, which the groom ate hastily. When Jenny started to clear off the table Arthur interfered by holding her wrist.

"You can do that in the morning," he said. "It's bedtime now, and you've got a lot of things to show me."

"But it's still light," Jenny protested.

Arthur led her to his bedroom without comment.

"I didn't bring a nightgown or any of my things," said Jenny. "I thought we could get some of them after we came back."

"You won't need a nightgown," Moore replied.

Jenny undressed and got into bed. Arthur had undressed faster and was waiting for her there.

"Now what do we do?" he asked.

"What do you mean?"

"We're married. What are we supposed to do?"

Jenny laughed. "Why just act like you always have when we've been together, like you did on the way home."

"Yes, but we didn't have to get married to do that. What else do we do? Don't keep me waiting any longer."

"There isn't anything else," laughed Jenny. "At least nothing I know about."

Arthur knew Jenny was joking, but he didn't like her sense of humor. She had made him wait all during the ride home, and now she was still refusing to provide the new pleasure. He wished he had married some other girl.

"I can't wait any longer," he said.

"You don't have to wait," she replied. "It's you that's keepin' me waitin'."

"But we're married. What are the things to do after gettin' married? What do people get married for? Hurry, I've waited too long now."

Jenny laughed again, or, rather, continued to laugh. She had not stopped laughing since this conversation started.

"There's nothin' to marryin', 'cept that I live in your house, and people call me Mrs. Moore," she said. "We can sleep together now instead of goin' walkin'. And if I have babies people won't look at me funny and act like they was better'n me."

This was carrying the joke too far. "What d'you s'pose I married you for?" Arthur demanded. "Come on now, show me what marriage is all about."

"I can't give you a baby yet," Jenny replied. "You'll have to wait a while. All we can do now is try to get one started."

Arthur began to have a horrible suspicion that Jenny was telling the truth, that marriage was all a hoax. If there were any other physical pleasure it seemed as though he would have heard some inkling of what it was. He had heard plenty of stories about other bodily affairs of men and women.

Arthur said no more. He satisfied himself with Jenny in the usual way, then dressed and went out to feed his rattlers. Watching the snakes tangle and untangle themselves silently in the twilight brought meditations.

It might be that Jenny was still joking and trying to see how long she could keep him from knowing the new pleasure, but it seemed more likely that there was nothing new to marriage, only what he had been doing all along.

Marriage was nothing but a trick women had for forcing men to support them and their children the rest of their lives. No wonder Jenny had laughed when he asked her what marriage was. She had swindled him into buying her. It was as though he had bought a cow with the understanding that it would give whisky only to find that it was even dry of milk. He was worse off than though he had bought a dry cow. He had only seen Jenny when he wanted to before. Now he would have to see her every time he went into the house. Perhaps she would even come out to the barn and fields to see him.

The secret of marriage was only that women had nothing new to show their husbands. Women were all fakers and robbers, each with this one aim in mind: to live with a man and make him feed and clothe her until she died. And he had let one of these bandits into his house! Why couldn't he have seen through this trickery of women? Jenny must have hypnotized him.

Arthur Moore spoke very little to Jenny the next day. When no new pleasure was revealed that night, Arthur was sure his conclusions were right: he had been defrauded. He came in from the barn for breakfast the next morning in a very happy mood. He joked with his wife and told her he was going to build a closet for her clothes.

After he had gone, Jenny was bitten by a large brownish rattlesnake as she went out the back door.

When Arthur came home from the fields for dinner the snake was sunning itself on the doorstep. Jenny was on the kitchen floor, dead.

"Nobody can say that I beat my wife," he said to the snake, laughing for the first time in two days.

Arthur put the rattler back in the pen and then measured Jenny for a coffin.

CHAPTER XVII

A WITCH'S BROOM THAT DID NOT FLY

It was the belief of David Hume that his mother, Sarah, was a witch.

She had one companion: a broom, which he thought she used nights for trips through the sky. The broom was seldom out of her hands. She carried it everywhere she went on the farm. When she had to use both hands for something else, the broom was placed nearby and picked up again as soon as possible. When she went to bed, the broom was left leaning against a chair within easy reach from her pillow.

Mrs. Sarah Hume smoked a pipe and often talked to herself—not very often to other people. She seldom used the broom for its customary purpose but carried it more as a man carries a cane. When she did sweep, it was with energy that raised a mist of dust which settled onto the walls, ceiling, and furniture.

She never discussed the nocturnal broom-flights David suspected. David did not dare mention them, so she had no knowledge of this power. Had he told her of these air trips, the idea would have been an inspiration to Mrs. Hume. The thought of flying through the air on her broom at night would have appealed to her, and she might have tried it by jumping from her second-story bedroom window astride of the broom.

David Hume was afraid of his mother and her broom. She had a way of staring through her wrinkles at him without speaking that made him feel cold. He avoided her presence as much as possible, only coming into the house from the barn or fields when he felt hungry. He frequently took his lunch when he left in the morning.

In the winter he spent the daylight hours in the barn, talking to the horse and cow. He could not afford to talk to his whisky glass more than once a week.

Mrs. Hume usually forgot to get the meals. When she did do any cooking she usually forgot her son and prepared only enough food for herself. David preferred to get his own meals. Witches had access to strange potions which might be put in the food and cause any desired change in him. He felt that his mother could turn him into anything from a cow to a blade of grass.

On the rare occasions when Sarah Hume did make a meal for two David lost his appetite but ate his share for fear of angering her if he didn't.

He never disputed his mother's whims. Whatever he thought she wanted he did or provided at once insofar as possible. If she broke her silence, David listened intently. This might be his death knell. Every word she spoke was either a reflection of dogmatic truth or a command that must be carried out instantly. If she had asked him to set fire to the house he would have done so immediately and without removing any of his belongings. An angry witch would cause worse happenings than anything a pacified one could order him to do.

David Hume bought tobacco for his mother's pipe and left it on the kitchen table where she would see it. Once he had left a bottle of whisky there while he went to get a cup. He returned with the cup, but the bottle had disappeared. He went out to the barn, where he was awakened from a nap by his mother's singing a dirge that frightened him. He spent the night in the barn, afraid to return to the house. The next morning he found the whisky bottle on the kitchen table with only a little of its original contents remaining.

Hume used to have very poor success with his crops. It was said that only he could tell which were his gardens and which his hay fields. Another account was that he forgot which fields he had planted.

The fact was that he had relied to a large extent on his mother's powers of witchcraft to tend the crops. He thought she should be willing to make the few magic motions necessary to eliminate weeds and bugs. When the weeds became higher than the plants he went to work with a hoe, disappointed at his mother's indifference to their mutual welfare.

His crops had improved after David came to the conclusion that his mother's powers were only for evil doings. She could not exercise influence in a way that would be beneficial. After that he tended his gardens without waiting for the assistance of witchcraft and was pleased with the harvest.

But the stock jokes about his hay gardens continued as accepted conventionalities. David Hume was not annoyed by these jokes. He enjoyed having his name used as a topic for conversation and listened to all versions of his gardens with a happy smile.

He was especially proud of the fact that an important annual event had been named after him: the Hume hay storm. The fact that his hay crop was spoiled by this rain was incidental. It was this storm bearing his name that all the farmers waited for before starting their haying. This storm made him an important figure in Menham.

One night Mrs. Hume was talking to her broom and fondling the handle affectionately as David came into the kitchen for supper.

"No, George," she said. "I don't want to go way up in the loft. Why ain't it all right right here? No-one will see us. Oh, come on. What are you scared of? Well, if I do have a baby I've got a father for it, ain't I? David will think it's his, and I'll name it after him. Well, all right then, let's go up in the loft." Mrs. Hume paused and sighed. "Poor George," she continued. "It's too bad David found us. But anyhow we named it David after him."

David always stayed away when his mother was entertaining invisible callers. He had run into the barn for shelter.

CHAPTER XVIII

ALICE'S SECRET FOR FONDLING

Alice Goode was having very poor success with Felix Dole. He still went walking with her and took her by the hand, but walking hand in hand is a poor way of answering the biologic urge in question. Alice was becoming discouraged. Her summary of the case was, "He acts as though I had some disease."

Felix could never think of anything to talk about when he was with Alice. The hand that held hers, or in which she kept hers, became lifeless during these contacts. The heat went from it, and its fingers became paralyzed. Alice felt as though she were holding a piece of damp wood. And Felix seemed to be trying to walk at arm's length.

The death of Silas Goode had given Felix a topic of conversation that he seemed to enjoy. Over and over again he told Alice how sorry he was that her father had been killed and how much he had liked the funeral oration of Deacon Ira Ormsby. (Felix had not yet joined the farmers' drinking fraternity.) He said he had wanted to help fill in the grave and had regretted ever since that he forgot to bring a shovel.

He spoke these sentiments as though he were reciting something he had memorized. His words did not vary from night to night, and, after the first few recitals, were monotonous for Alice, who began to interrupt and change the subject. Except for Felix Dole's reiteration of the matter her father's death would have left her mind much sooner.

Felix had offered to help Alice and her mother tend the crops Silas had left behind. This was welcome assistance and pleased Mrs. Emma Goode very much. Arthur Moore had not even mentioned the crops. It pleased Alice, too, but she would have been more pleased if Felix had offered to kiss and fondle her.

Alice arranged to work in the fields whenever Felix was there. Felix worked harder and faster when Alice was near. His one interest in life seemed to be the weeding or hoeing he was doing. He would not look up from his labors and took no rest periods, having the manner of a worker being watched by a factory foreman. If Alice had left the field he would have taken a long rest and with much relief.

Felix had had dreams about Alice. He knew many of the so-called secrets of sex and had enjoyed the versions of them he had had while asleep. He did not know the secret combinations of his body's inhibitions, which insisted that he make no allusions to such matters in the presence of Alice's material body.

He felt that even if they were married he would be afraid to go to bed with Alice, and that if he should go to bed with her he would be afraid even to touch her hand. He had a feeling of relief when he was alone after a walk with Alice, yet he was soon looking forward to another walk.

He wondered if the magic words of a marriage ceremony could show him how to make himself deliberately and calmly go about trying to give a girl a child. If he were sure this secret would be revealed he would have asked Alice to marry him. Perhaps this was why people got married: to get the secret for obtaining the courage to embrace one another. Perhaps if he and Alice attended a wedding they could get this secret without being married themselves. But he would not dare invite her to go to a wedding even if there were one to take her to. It would be like asking her to take off her clothes and lie down.

Felix did not dare ask Alice to marry him. If the necessary secret were not revealed, he might have to spend the rest of his nights sitting in a chair in their bedroom or sleeping on the floor. Then, too, it would take just as much courage to ask her to marry him as to go about making the advances that marriage called for. More, in fact, for in starting to make the advances he would not have to get up the extra courage needed for a vocal request. He was stronger than Alice and could overpower her physically. But first he would have to overpower himself mentally and find out how to act toward her as he did in his dreams. Perhaps if he could go to sleep while he was with Alice.

While they were working together in a field one evening Alice had an idea. Why was a girl supposed to wait for a boy to take the aggressive? If she should kiss Felix it ought to help matters. Then he might kiss her and start to squeeze her breast and force her to lie down with him.

When darkness came Alice suggested that they take a walk. This was a routine suggestion. At an isolated spot Alice made use of her plan. She gave Felix a hasty kiss and waited to see what he would do.

Felix stopped walking. His whole body took on the characteristics of the hand that held Alice's. His hand dropped from hers. He had a feeling of resentment. She was telling him she knew how to make him get up courage and at the same time saying she wouldn't let him know the secret. Alice knew the secret and was taunting him for not knowing it. If he could only fall asleep—or if she would tell him the secret.

Alice could not get Felix to take her hand again during the rest of the walk.

CHAPTER XIX

PETER BRUSH REMAINS FAITHFUL TO AN AGREEMENT

It was a happy day for Mrs. Anna Lyman. This was the day Peter Brush, the peddler, would come to Menham and to her house with his wares. He had promised to arrive early on this visit. She had sent her husband, John, to his whisky cup at Lem Witherbee's before breakfast by giving him an inspiring lecture on the evils of liquor while he dressed.

Walking along the road from Westham to Menham, Peter Brush suddenly recalled this engagement, but he could not remember who the hostess was to be. There was only one woman in Menham who had done anything but buy or refuse to buy his goods, but who was she?

This lapse of memory annoyed him. What should he do: kiss each woman in Menham as she came to the door or merely try to sell his wares as usual and wait until one of the women kissed him?

The second process of elimination would be safer, yet would the woman in question take the aggressive after he had greeted her in such a cold manner? She might be insulted and think he was insisting that she buy something before he would change from his role of a polite peddler. She had led him on before, but this time she would expect him to show a similar interest in her.

Perhaps he would recognize the woman when she came to the door. This did not seem likely. He knew all of the Menham housewives by sight. As he brought their faces to mind in an effort to force his memory to respond, the only thought that accompanied most of them was, "I hope it's not her."

Instead of kissing each woman, he might change his manner of greeting and say, "Good morning, dear," or, "The days have been years since my last visit, my love," or, "Seeing you again is the biggest event in my life, darling."

If the woman did not react with the proper spirit he could change the subject at once and start to discuss his goods. If she seemed pleased at the greeting he would know he had found the right party. Peter Brush rehearsed numerous possible greetings involving affection.

The first house he came to in Menham was that of Mrs. Sadie Sadler. He waved to her husband, Jonathan, working in a cornfield some distance from the house. The woman he sought had a husband, he remembered. This might be she. He knocked at the farmhouse door with his lines of love running through his mind one after another. Mrs. Sadler, with red cheeks and a body that was plump but by no means obese, opened the door.

"Er, darling, I have looked forward to seeing you again since, er, good morning, dearest," Peter mumbled.

Mrs. Sadler looked about the farmyard hastily. No-one was in sight.

"Won't you come in," she said.

He had found the right woman on the first guess. Peter Brush removed his pack and entered the kitchen. He pulled Sadie into his arms and squeezed and kissed her. She stepped back in surprise at first but offered no resistance. She said nothing when he led her to a sofa he saw in the parlor.

There came a pause in their love-making, which had soon become mutual. Peter rose to his feet. Mrs. Sadler sighed and lay motionless.

"Why haven't you been like this before?" she asked.

Peter Brush sat down. Was this true? Had he made a new conquest instead of finding the woman he had arranged to make love with today?

"You never used to do anything but try and sell me things," Sadie continued. "Next time you come to Menham I'll see to it that Jonathan is away, and we'll have the whole day to ourselves."

Yes, it must be a new conquest. He would have two women in the same town each expecting him to spend the day with them when he came again. He would have to arrange to get away from the first one at noon and apologize to the second for his late arrival. Whether or not he would be physically equal to the assignment was a still more important problem.

At any rate, he had to keep his other appointment for today. Peter assured Sadie he would come prepared to spend the day with her on his next trip to Menham and made her a present of a metal plate in the shape of a cow's head for a weather vane decoration. If his memory should fail again, this vane would tell him which was the right house. Sadie kissed Peter, and he went on his way to find today's correct mistress, who, his memory did not yet recall, should have been Anna Lyman.

The next house was that of Edward Jones. He was nowhere in sight, and Mrs. Edna Jones came to the door, smiling and slender.

"Darling, I have looked forward to this day ever since my last visit," said Peter.

Mrs. Jones asked him to come in. This must be the woman he had been looking for. He kissed her. She kissed him back. They were soon on the parlor sofa. Words were not necessary and were not used until Edna sat up and said, "Why haven't you done this before? Why have you always been so businesslike until today?"

Peter felt something jump inside him. This must be still another conquest.

Mrs. Jones said he would have to leave soon because her husband would be home, but proceeded to make plans for Peter's next visit. She would have Edward spend the day at Lem Witherbee's. Peter could do nothing but agree with her arrangements. He gave her a weather vane in the shape of a cow's head and left with the understanding that they would spend the day together when he came again.

Peter Brush was perplexed. Now he had three women to deal with in something besides his wares, and the stock required was limited. He had only thought of these farmer's wives as customers before. Now they were all suddenly becoming his mistresses in the same day and in a most inconvenient manner. He felt that he must remain faithful to his original agreement for today, yet this seemed an unpleasant duty and an effort now rather than a pleasure.

There were four more houses before reaching the Lyman farm. But, faithful to his promised role for the day, Peter continued to greet the women there with rehearsed tenderness. One of them might be the one he was to visit, and he must act accordingly.

He was only repulsed at one of these dwellings. At this house the woman spoke first and said she wanted to buy some needles. This was a relief for Peter, who was certain that the one he sought would have a more personal greeting.

Each of the other three women had parlor sofas, and their husbands were in the fields. Not until the sofas had been used did their remarks inform Peter that they were new conquests. Each agreed that her husband would not be on the farm when he came again and that Peter would spend the day with her.

Peter gave each a weather vane in the shape of a cow's head. He was certain that each new effort on a sofa was his last, but more energy seemed to develop between houses for another final attempt.

With each finale came a feeling of consolation. He had found the right woman and been able to prove true to their agreement. He could soon go about his usual trade in peace. Then came a question from the woman as to why he had not offered this stock in trade on a previous visit, and his troubles and worries were multiplied.

Most of the women had had very little to offer him in the way of beauty. They seemed still uglier in Peter's overworked state. Peter's tradesman's attitude told him he was paying high prices for merchandise he did not want, but his sense of faithfulness assured him that women appeared to him as something entirely different than this ordinarily. Perhaps with this assurance he was too tolerant in overlooking physical distortions when making his greetings.

Peter had taken a nap in a field during the noon hour. When he finally neared the Lyman farm it was late in the afternoon. After his fifth new conquest Peter had decided he would have to change his tactics. He would revert back to his customary sales talk and wait for the woman in question to greet him. It seemed too bad to have to approach her so coldly, but there were limits even to faithfulness.

He walked to the Lyman kitchen door feeling tired and emaciated. He hoped the woman he had the appointment with had moved to some other country, or that her memory was as vague as his. Perhaps she had forgotten him, and any efforts to remain faithful were only advances to other women. He might have been faithful to his agreement already without either he or she realizing it.

Anna came to the door. She showed evidences of anger and impatience. "Where have you been?" she demanded. "You promised to be here early in the morning, and here it is almost night."

So this was she. He had found the woman at last. Peter took a cow's head weather vane from his pack and gave it to her at once.

"Darling, I have walked all night to be with you," said Peter, feeling that he could now elaborate on the greetings he had rehearsed that morning, and at the same time having an idea. "I have reached my goal at last, but I am so tired I can hardly stand."

"You poor man," said Mrs. Lyman tenderly. "You lay right down and rest. But it's funny you never seemed to have any trouble before gettin' here on the right day."

"No, never before," agreed Peter, lying down on the parlor sofa and hoping that a little sleep would enable him to be faithful. This would actually be the final attempt, the grand finale, and he must rouse all his reserve energies to make it a success.

"Five and one is six," he thought, closing his eyes. "At least there won't be a seventh."

"You're sure it wasn't some woman who made you late?" asked Mrs. Lyman with pretended suspicion.

"No other woman has been in my mind," replied Peter. "I've been faithful to you."

CHAPTER XX

GRADUATION EXERCISES

Henrietta Harriet Helen Hummer was learning to walk on his hind legs. He was proceeding in a manner that probably compared poorly with that of his first four-legged ancestors who had tried this.

He had an advantage over these evolutionary ancestors in having the example of Miss Hummer walking on two legs to imitate. But he also was at a disadvantage through being a baby. The ancestors probably had waited until they were adults before making the attempt.

Henrietta was further handicapped through having to carry on his experiments in secret for any degree of comfort. Miss Hummer gave him no assistance or encouragement. In fact, when she saw him standing erect clutching to a table leg or chair she released his grip and let him fall to the floor. Had she realized her manner of walking could be of any assistance as a pattern for his efforts she might have crawled on her hands and knees when in his sight.

Miss Hummer was resigned to the fact that Henrietta probably would learn to walk eventually, but she wanted to keep this man in her power groveling before her on the floor as long as possible. She became nervous at the evidences of growth he was showing. She had the feeling she was raising a monster that was developing strength to overpower her.

What would she do when Henrietta did walk on two legs and grew into a strong man? The strength would not be diminished even if she could make him believe he was a woman. He would still be in her power legally, but she would be at his mercy physically. But perhaps he would not grow to be a *strong* man. Miss Hummer consoled herself with this thought.

Her war with the male conspiracy for the promotion of wickedness was a very serious matter. The enemy had taken over most of her territory and was trying to turn her prisoner into a beast of its own kind that could perform all sorts of tortures on her.

She must not let Henrietta have access to any such powers. She would prove her superior strength daily and accustom him to the fact that he could never be her equal. She could not surrender in this war in which she had become engulfed. It was a fight to the finish, and she was the winner as long as she kept this man in her power, regardless of the disadvantages involved.

The kitchen door had remained bolted ever since Miss Hummer's second encounter with a snake near the woodshed. She was afraid to go anywhere on her land except out the path from the front door to the road. Even this was a risk. She felt as though she were running a gantlet of snakes whenever she attempted it.

She had had piles of wood placed against the front of the house. This provided a fuel supply on reasonably safe ground and acted as an extra barricade for her fortress.

Having lasted out most of the summer in her house, Miss Hummer had come to believe that this was a safe citadel. She had not seen the second snake since her one meeting with it, but was sure it was in hiding, waiting to attack her and to communicate with Henrietta. All windows were kept locked. Henrietta had drafts of fresh air only when the front door was slowly opened and hastily closed by Miss Hummer on the few occasions that she went out.

Having safely brought in an armful of wood one day and pushed Henrietta's hands from the wall, which was holding him upright, Miss Hummer had a very pleasing thought: as Henrietta grew in size she could use correspondingly larger switches in demonstrating her authority and power.

The small birch branches she had been using would not be so effective when Henrietta increased in size. She could use larger sticks at each evidence of increased strength on the part of the prisoner. Pieces of kindling would be very good when Henrietta became a little bigger. Then larger pieces of wood, and larger and larger until—Miss Hummer gasped: suppose he should get so big she could not wield a club large enough to hurt him?

But the former thought was too pleasing to be frightened away by a danger of no immediate concern. The larger Henrietta became the more of him there would be to hurt. The stronger he became the more she could hurt him without too serious results.

She could use more energy together with the larger sticks. The whippings could last longer and be given at more frequent intervals. An unpleasant thought came to mind again but was hastily driven out: suppose he became so strong she could tire herself out without chastising him properly?

Miss Hummer examined the wood she had brought in. She began to sort it out in rows according to size. She went out several times for more varieties until small piles of wood stretched all along one side of the kitchen. Kindling was at one end and small logs at the other with gradual increases in the size of the sticks in each pile.

Now she could look forward to Henrietta's growth. As he increased in size she could increase the size of her weapons accordingly by merely drawing from the next pile in the series. If he should suddenly obtain new powers, she was ready to meet the emergency. Miss Hummer wished Henrietta were a little larger now so she could graduate him from the birch twigs. She looked at him. He was larger than when he had been delivered from Scofield. She began to sort out the pile of switches behind the stove, breaking the smaller ones and saving the largest ones.

She looked at Henrietta again and then at the twigs she now had in store for him. They would not do. Henrietta had grown faster than she had realized. He might be laughing to himself at her whippings already. This unpleasant thought was of immediate concern and could not be dismissed.

Miss Hummer took a knife from a drawer and went out the front door to brave the gantlet of snakes and collect a new assortment of branches by the side of the road.

Henrietta continued his secret experiments in walking. He crawled to the piles of wood and pulled himself onto his feet by means of one of them.

CHAPTER XXI

JOHN LYMAN SEEKS JUSTICE FOR MINNIE MULLER

There were many theories as to which farmer in Menham Minnie Muller's features most resembled.

Every member of the Saturday night drinking fraternity who was old enough had been carefully diagnosed in loud sessions of mirth and shown to have been the pattern she had followed. David Hume wished he were older so that he could be included in these discussions, but he had been only a little boy in the days when Mrs. Nancy Muller was eligible.

At other times Minnie and her parentage were forgotten while the farmers compared stories of walks they had taken with Nancy. Often the younger men invented accounts of their own so they could participate in these memoirs, but such admissions never made them eligible for mention when the topic of parentage was before the meeting. The older men had to elaborate their versions still more in order to keep abreast of these less accurate stories.

David Hume would have given an account of his walks with Nancy Muller but for the fact that he could not think of anything that had not been said.

When the latter topic came up at a properly timed point in John Lyman's conversation with his whisky mug, his thoughts of the moment about Minnie were intensified.

Why all this talk about Nancy Muller? It was time Minnie received more acknowledgment in such dissertations. Her mother had been a celebrity long enough and had her full share of renown. Minnie was not yet considered as anything but somebody's child. She was a very pretty girl and deserved appreciation as such. Minnie could become just as celebrated a figure as her mother and deserved a proper share of distinction. She was obscured by her mother's fame. Steps should be taken to overshadow her mother by hers.

At these times John Lyman felt that he had received a call. He had more than a physical desire. It was his duty to bring Minnie into repute. It was unjust that Nancy should still have the prestige her daughter was now entitled to.

Stories about Nancy had become myths and fables. Stories about Minnie would be current and timely news. There would be a new topic for diversion at Lem Witherbee's. Some of the farmers who had a factual basis for their accounts of walks with Nancy would at least have to change the name of the heroine in order to contribute stories to the talks about Minnie.

There might come another new topic involving parentage and the farmer who most resembled the child. Then Minnie would be of equal fame with Nancy. The older farmers would be neglected in the new discussion as the younger ones had been before.

There would be two distinct schools of expression at Lem Witherbee's. Perhaps the newer school would prove its own superiority as well as Minnie's by producing a second child. Then Minnie would rank far above Nancy, and the older school would suffer ridicule instead of the prominence it now enjoyed.

Usually a distraction—such as the discovery he was talking to one of the initials instead of a favorite rose on his whisky cup—interrupted John Lyman's meditations about Minnie.

This night he looked down at his cup and saw the rose listening patiently. The rose told him there might be some who could claim membership in both schools but that this was incidental. He should heed the call and help Minnie attain the distinction that was her due.

John drank what was in his cup, bought another drink, and swallowed that. He placed the mug on the counter with unspoken good-bys that only it could hear and left to find Minnie Muller.

It was Minnie's night to walk with Paul Turner, her only male companion. He might have started the new school had he been an attendant at Lem Witherbee's. Andrew Cline had told him when he hired him that he would have to remain sober, so Paul had looked for other diversions.

Walking toward Minnie's house, John Lyman passed the town hall and saw two figures coming out from behind it. He felt the desire to talk to someone and stopped. One of the figures was walking away from the other. In a disinterested tone it made the parting remark, "All right then, I'll see you Wednesday."

John recognized Paul Turner and saw that the other figure was a girl. This latter observation recalled his mission, and he asked with sudden enthusiasm, "Is that Minnie Muller with you?"

"Yeah," Paul replied without stopping. He did not like the smell of liquor when he could not drink. "I'm all through with her; go to it."

CHAPTER XXII

TWO GLASSES AND A ROW OF KEGS

Alfred Dole had two whisky glasses, one at Lem Witherbee's store and one in his barn. The latter receptacle had received its apprenticeship at the store and then been transferred to new duties at the barn. There it was seldom used for whisky but proved itself equally capable of embracing hard cider.

At first Dole had thought he would be unfaithful to the original glass in adopting a second one to share his confidences and act as his most intimate friend. He had tried taking the glass with him when he went from one drinking resort to the other, but this involved the danger of breakage. He had fallen down more than once on this trip between his barn and Lem Witherbee's.

Before employing a second glass for permanent use, Alfred had apologized profusely and, drunkenly to the first, which replied in favor of the idea and advised him that if it were kept in the seclusion of his barn they could have more privacy and see each other more often.

Most of Alfred Dole's work around the farm was done in the morning and early afternoon. He made frequent visits to his glass during this time, but usually it was not until late afternoon that the conversation became of sufficient importance to justify suspending all other operations to continue it.

Alfred Dole worked hardest when his apples were ripe. He picked and sorted them carefully, saving out the poorer ones for eating and cooking purposes. All the others were run through his cider press. The juice was kept in large kegs that formed a symmetrical double row along the rear of the barn.

A drinking corner had been prepared at one end of the row. There the keg being used was propped up in front of a chair. When not in Dole's hand, the glass was hidden in a niche above a beam overhead.

Other farmers had called on Dole when he was settled in this corner, but very little hospitality was extended. Sometimes Dole would speak to the visitor. Usually he continued to speak to his glass. Despite the number of kegs, there was only one chair and only one glass. It did not take long for a visitor to realize that Alfred could get along very nicely without them.

When little Mary Dole was still younger she had once come running to her mother with the startling discovery, "Ma, Pa's talkin' to himself."

"No, he's not," Mrs. Jessie Dole had replied. "He's talkin' to his whisky glass."

While Felix Dole was attending to the nightly chores around the barn his father would sometimes look up from his glass and talk to him. A father should give his son good advice and show some interest in his welfare.

"How is it you never come over to Lem Witherbee's on Saturday nights?" he would ask. He had heard Felix's answer to this question many times and so continued without waiting to hear it again, "You ain't got no money? Well, that's too bad.

Hmmm. Well, maybe Lem would trust you for a few Saturdays. Get your whisky cup into trainin' there and maybe it'll tell you how to keep it goin'. A whisky cup will give you a lot of good advice. And Lem always likes to get a new customer. I guess he'd trust you all right for a while."

Felix was never very interested in this advice, principally for the reason that it came from his father. If Alfred had advised him to keep away from Lem Witherbee's on Saturday nights Felix probably would have run up as large a bill there as Lem would allow.

Alfred Dole would lapse back into his reveries and direct his conversation to the cup again. If it was getting dark by this time, he would make some comment about the excellence of the cider crop and ask Felix to bring a lantern—he had never asked him to bring a cup.

The Dole cider glass had one secret it had not revealed to Alfred: it had two users. Since the glass was kept in a secret hiding place, Alfred Dole had no suspicion that any one else could use it. Nor did he believe his glass capable of such infidelity as to become another person's companion even once without telling him.

But Mrs. Jessie Dole had located the container and acquired a taste for hard cider both at the same time one morning. Since then she had watched from the kitchen window for her husband to enter and leave the barn during his working hours. When he left she entered. She would time her return to the kitchen window so as not to conflict with his next arrival. After he had come and gone again, she would go back to the barn.

This program interfered with her housework but was much more pleasant. Mary Dole had learned to do many household tasks and was given an opportunity to learn more.

Felix Dole noticed his mother had become somewhat hilarious and sometimes did strange things, but gave the matter little thought. If she wanted to sing and stagger about the kitchen, that was her affair. Alfred Dole noticed no change. Any increase in verbosity or gayety was quite in keeping with his mood when he came in for dinner.

After her husband began his extended conversation with his glass late in the afternoon Mrs. Dole had to suspend her visits to the keg for the day. She regretted this, but there seemed nothing she could do about it.

One day she got up courage. When Alfred Dole came to the barn from the fields for the last time he saw an unexpected sight. At the opposite end of the row of kegs from his drinking corner was another chair. His wife was sitting there engaged in conversation with a glass of cider in her hand. There was a spigot in the keg in front of her.

This tapping of his cider supply was bad enough, but the glass in her hand was his. Alfred seized the glass. Jessie seized it back again. She raised it in the air as though about to throw it to the floor.

"Don't!" cried Alfred. "Don't break it! Give me the glass, and I'll let you stay here. You can have that corner, and I'll stay in this one."

Mrs. Dole returned the glass to her husband. "Remember, now, this corner is mine," she said. She stumbled back into her chair and reached beneath it. Her hand encircled a cup she had brought from the kitchen, and she lifted it to the spigot.

After that there were two drinking corners, two chairs, and two hidden glasses in the Dole barn, and Jessie no longer kept a lookout from the kitchen window.

CHAPTER XXIII

THE WOMEN'S CHRISTIAN INTEMPERANCE UNION

Another drinker, with equal rights and privileges, to help drain the Dole cider kegs was not in keeping with Alfred Dole's conception of a sanctum. He was being robbed of his solitude as well as his cider.

The situation was still worse because the other party was a woman, and even more objectionable because the woman was his wife.

When he and Jessie Dole occupied their respective drinking corners, filling their glasses from their respective kegs, Alfred did not converse with her, but neither did he talk with his glass as freely as before. Alfred took no steps to eject Jessie. Having established herself, she became an accepted part of the barn routine, somewhat the same as though the roof had disappeared and rain was discomforting him. Only in this case Alfred had no recourse to an umbrella.

Jessie's drinking schedule was patterned after Alfred's. During the day she alternately visited the barn and helped Mary with the housework. Usually at precisely the same time that Alfred established himself in his corner for a prolonged stay Jessie did the same in hers. She also became intimate with her glass, and a close friendship was formed which involved daily conversations.

Alfred continually thought of planting more apple trees and filling more kegs. Perhaps the present supply would be exhausted before this year's cider was ready. Another year the kegs would surely go dry too soon. Such worries increased his discomfort. He had watched over the contents of these kegs like a miser. Now his resources were being squandered by an invader. Jessie was quite happy as long as the spigot before her brought forth a brownish-white flow.

Jessie sometimes had trouble getting back to the house at night. She was given no assistance by Alfred, who enjoyed her difficulties unless he were having too much trouble keeping himself upright to notice them. Once Jessie had woke in the morning on the barn floor, another time on the steps of the back stoop.

But Alfred Dole's worries and discomforts were to be increased. When Felix Dole, pleased at having a topic for conversation, told Alice Goode that his mother had established a drinking corner in his father's barn, she became interested for the first time in what he had to say.

Mrs. Emma Goode came to call on Mrs. Dole the next day in the barn. Other women promptly made similar visits one after another, some panting as they arrived. Mrs. Dole greeted them all cordially. She got another glass from the kitchen when Mrs. Goode came, and each new caller filled it.

The women of Menham saw hopes of emancipation. It was possible for them to usurp the drinking pleasures heretofore reserved for men. Why should they continue to be denied them? They were men's equals. They should enjoy men's privileges. These thoughts possessed each woman in turn as she saw the enlightenment that had come to Mrs. Dole. The opinion was intensified after sampling the cider.

Alfred Dole was almost frightened away several times when he entered the barn and saw two women drinking his cider. He said nothing but wished they had been taking poison. His row of sacred kegs was being prostituted. His shrine was being defiled.

"Women are a lot of robbers," he told his glass in a psychic manner that could not be overheard by Mrs. Sadler and his wife.

"Stealin's their line. If I didn't know these damn women I could shoot 'em, but since I know 'em I s'pose I got to stand for their stealin'."

The following Saturday night a new institution was established. The women of Menham—with the exception of Miss Hummer—gathered in the Dole barn in a body. Each brought a glass or cup, and a women's drinking fraternity got under way.

The men in their bachelor quarters at Lem Witherbee's knew nothing of the women's meeting until they started home. The women had just adjourned and were seeking their domiciles with uncertain steps. Groups of men and women bound in the same directions became mingled. Many men were surprised to find themselves talking to their wife or to somebody else's.

John Lyman was still talking to Mrs. Sadler when he arrived at his bedroom. But since Anna Lyman had stopped to talk with Edward Jones, there were no disagreements until she arrived home and could not find room in the bed.

Mrs. Whiter started to accompany Arthur Moore to his farm, but gave up the attempt after she fell down without his noticing her disappearance. There were other confusions, but in due time all couples were sorted out in the usual manner, and all members of both fraternities were in their own beds, except for Mrs. Muller who slept in front of the town hall.

Having asserted their rights and become emancipated, the women of Menham continued their Saturday night gatherings as religiously as the men. Although there was no set time for abandoning the cups, both groups always seemed to disband at times that brought their members together. Alfred Dole could not believe the stories that these meetings were being held in his barn until an alarming depletion in the cider supply showed him that this, or something equally serious, was the case.

It was a sad situation. One robber had discovered his treasure and led a horde of companions there to help carry it away. His privacy was not so important now. Soon he would have to talk to an empty glass.

The women realized that the Dole kegs could not always be full and made plans accordingly. Apples would soon be ripe. They would hold a fair to help raise money for kegs of their own and would press a crop of apples themselves.

They would move to new quarters, too. The town hall had no use as such. It had been the gift of a wealthy man who once lived in Menham and had the desire to be a selectman. He had adopted the title, and Menham had found itself the possessor of a town hall to prove his right to it. They would store the kegs in the town hall and hold their meetings there as soon as the new cider crop was ready.

The women contributed money for new kegs, and the fair held in the town hall brought nearly three dollars more. Mrs. Dole was made treasurer. It was agreed that she had given her share of apples already and that the present crop would all be furnished by the others.

A cider press loaned by Mrs. Goode was brought to the town hall when the apples were ready. Kegs had been delivered there, and apples were provided in wagon-loads by the women. For two days the women worked. Mrs. Dole even neglected her daytime visits to her barn, although she brought a bottle that required her attention quite often in the entry leading to the stage.

When all the kegs were filled and placed in proper arrangement, a padlock was applied to the door. The women had taken over the town hall, and men were barred.

"We're all selectwomen now," said Mrs. Dole.

"Yup, p'raps if we think of it some Saturday we can pass a few laws," laughed Mrs. Cline.

CHAPTER XXIV

PETER BRUSH IS FAITHFUL TO SIX WOMEN

Although it was not Saturday night, there were six farmers drinking at Lem Witherbee's store. They had arrived early in the morning and showed no intentions of leaving until bedtime or later. It was the day Peter Brush was due to peddle his wares again in Menham.

The farmers were pleased to be able to form such an unexpected gathering, each having come with the thought that he would have only his whisky glass to talk to. All realized that unpleasant words of their wives had sent them there, and no questions were asked as to the subject matter involved.

Lem Witherbee was heartily in favor of this group of customers he suddenly found established before the drinking counter. He hoped this was an indication that local farmers were becoming more sensitive to the words of their wives.

The conversation started along the new conventional lines. Edward Jones gave the cue. "Who'd you go home with last Saturday night?" he asked, looking at the ceiling.

"Mrs. Sadler," replied John Lyman, smiling at Jonathan Sadler. "We got to my place and she said she'd have to rest, so I took her in the parlor and let her lay down."

"And while you and her was in the parlor," said Jonathan, "your wife and I was upstairs in your bed. We was helpin' each other along the road and decided your house was nearer than mine."

Both men laughed.

These pleasantries about the mix-up of wives on Saturday nights were intended only as an exchange of wit. Each man seemed to laugh a little more heartily when his own wife was involved. Every farmer relied wholly on his imagination for facts and realized the others did the same.

There were often no recollections of any actual details of happenings after leaving Lem Witherbee's. Any basis of truth that found its way into the accounts was accepted as the same sort of fiction as the rest. The confusion that now came on Saturday nights gave too free a rein to the imagination to let memory interfere. The actual mix-ups involved were not even considered.

The discussion of the previous Saturday night's post-drinking events continued until all members of the women's fraternity were properly mated with new mates.

John Lyman was soon thinking of other things. Should he start Minnie Muller on her path to fame now? On previous Saturday nights he had been tempted several times to broach this new subject which would soon be the most important topic of all, but he always decided to wait.

He had a chance to collect a number of anecdotes that would give him a long head start on the others. And this topic would call for accounts of fact not theory—at least at first.

It would be better to make his important announcement regarding Nancy Muller's daughter on a Saturday night, at any rate, when all were present, John decided. In introducing his protégée he would want a full house to hear the facts. Lyman relaxed after this decision. The longer he kept Minnie's name out of the forum the longer he could have her practically to himself.

Six farmers' wives, each of whose husbands had installed a new weather vane in the shape of a cow's head on the barn, had put on their best dresses and taken seats at windows that gave a view of the road from Westham. Each was alone in her house and had very pleasant thoughts of a happy day ahead.

Peter Brush had not forgotten any of these ladies this time. They had been in his mind almost constantly since his last visit to Menham. And so had the problem of how to spend the same day alone with six different women in six different farmhouses.

He had to be faithful to six women this time. He could not keep his promise to all of them, and he did not dare brave this gantlet of women again in the manner that he had before. He considered omitting Menham from his route. But, no, he could remain faithful to one of the promises. This would have to be at the first house. He could not pass by any of these farms without being seen.

Spending the day with Mrs. Sadler seemed quite agreeable to Peter Brush, and he continued toward Menham. It was better to keep one promise and break five than to break all six.

An idea came to Peter as he walked. If he had a messenger and knew the names of all the women involved, he might send a note to the other five and apologize for a tardy arrival. He might arrange to visit them on successive days and sleep at night in fields or woods between houses.

So long as nobody but the woman of the day saw him, the next one would assume he had just arrived in Menham, and the others would think he had gone on to the next town. He liked the idea but did not know how to obtain the essentials necessary for its execution. He had no messenger and was not sure of most of the names.

Just as he had decided that the scheme was impractical, Peter was overtaken by the mailman's buggy and given a ride. The mailman knew the names of the women and would leave letters for them. He also had envelopes. Peter had a pad of paper and a pencil.

He began to write, "Dearest Edna, I am sorry but I will be a day late getting to Menham and your house on this visit. I can hardly wait to see you again. Much love, Peter Brush."

The envelope was addressed to Mrs. Edna Jones. Peter began the next note, "Dearest Doris, I am sorry, but I will be two days late…" He wrote three others of similar nature. The last note informed Mrs. Anna Lyman that he would be five days late.

The mailman took the letters and stopped to let Peter Brush out at Sadie Sadler's house.

CHAPTER XXV

ARTHUR MOORE ENVIES HIS SNAKES

Arthur Moore had a banquet for his rattlesnakes. In addition to the usual frogs and toads, he had several lizards, a rabbit, a rat that was still half alive, a large cage of mice he had allowed to breed and fatten after their captivity, and a brood of garter snakes he had picked up one by one as they began their solution of the mysteries of life.

Next to his whisky glass, Moore liked the companionship of his snakes better than any other. He liked to feed them the delicacies they enjoyed. He liked the way they ate, holding their struggling dainty in their mouths as though enjoying its suffering more than its flavor, and slowly forcing the morsel further inside them until most of the struggling was being done within the snakes' bodies.

Sometimes a snake took too big a mouthful and appeared to be suffering itself as the live food became stuck, still partly in the fresh air, but most of it too far within to be ejected. Such a state of affairs never acted as an emetic on the snake and would sometimes be prolonged for hours.

"That's only the first course," Arthur Moore would say to a snake in this predicament. He liked the way the snakes slept after a hearty meal, often for days. He envied their hedonistic existence.

"They're either hungry and enjoyin' food or sleepy and enjoyin' sleep," he once told his whisky glass. "Never any work. And there's plenty of womensnakes for 'em to curl up with. They get tangled up with a lot of women all at the same time—or else it's the women that get tangled up with them. That's prob'ly it. But anyhow they don't try to get the men to marry 'em. It's me that's supportin' 'em all. I'd like to try bein' a snake and have a lot of women get curled up with me like that. I can only have one woman at a time now."

There was no particular occasion for today's sumptuous banquet. Arthur Moore was generally kind to his snakes and, having the food on hand, decided he would surprise them with this hearty repast.

"Everything but the knives and forks," he said, as he threw the small animals into the snake sty, much to their objection.

As he watched the snakes turn connoisseurs and select their courses, Arthur Moore began to think of women. He decided he wanted the use of a woman. At times such as this he wished it were possible to keep a wife hidden in some closet of his house, where he could take her out and lock her up again at will. As it was, he would have to walk way over to Emma Goode's farm, which was more than half a mile even by the path through the woods.

Moore spit into the mass of snakes, with their staring eyes that never closed. He felt inferior to these creatures that he raised. "They don't have to walk no half mile to get a woman," he thought. "It must be nice to live in a snake sty." He left the snakes to their pleasures and walked toward the Goode farm.

Alice Goode was working in the kitchen when Arthur Moore arrived. He resented her presence. He would have to take her mother into the barn or somewhere out of her daughter's sight. "Snakes don't have to worry about no-one seein' them," he thought.

"Where's your ma?" he asked Alice.

"She's gone over to see Mrs. Lyman," Alice replied.

What! Emma was not home! Arthur felt as though she had broken a promise to meet him at this exact time and place.

"How long 'fore she'll be back?"

"Oh, not for an hour or more. Want to come in and wait?"

Arthur Moore thought of his snakes. They didn't have to wait upon a woman's convenience. Their women couldn't go calling. He became impatient and thought of other women. Then he looked at Alice. She was a woman, and she was here at hand. Perhaps her mother had left her behind to attend to him.

His eyes stared at Alice in a way that brought the two thoughts, "This man's pitchfork killed your father. But Arthur was a long ways off when it happened."

"There's something I was goin' to show your ma out in the barn," said Moore. "Come on out, and I'll show you."

Alice followed Arthur into the barn.

"It's up in that hayloft," he said.

Alice went up the ladder first. Arthur Moore smiled. He was glad Mrs. Goode was away. If he couldn't hide Emma from her daughter, he could hide her daughter from Emma. He should have thought of this before.

"If only I was a snake I could have 'em both at once," he mused as he followed Alice up the ladder.

CHAPTER XXVI

A BAWDY BABY

With the coming of winter to Menham, Miss Hummer regained her captured territory from the enemy. After the first snowstorm she unlocked her kitchen door and stepped into a drift with a feeling of conquest. She wished she had a flag of some sort she could unfurl in her back yard.

She looked for marks left by a snake's body among the soft white crystals. She knew snakes did not thrive in snow, but the one that had surrounded her house was more than a snake: it was a representative of the male conspiracy for the promotion of wickedness. There were no tracks of any kind, and Miss Hummer walked into her woodshed with confidence and without being attacked. To prove her victory she brought as much wood as she could carry back into the kitchen.

She considered letting Henrietta go out and play in the snow. She could outfit him in a nice light summer dress. There were no mittens or hats for him, and the shoes he had worn upon being delivered from Scofield would no longer go on his feet. He could play in the snow barefooted and bareheaded.

Then she reconsidered. The enemy had communicated with him when she left him outdoors in the summer. They might do the same now in some diabolical manner. She could not take this chance. Her prisoner must be kept in confinement. Henrietta had once enjoyed it when she left him out in the rain. He might like the snow, too.

Henrietta now walked on two feet with considerable agility, although when Miss Hummer was near he generally dropped to his hands and knees. He did not cry as much as he had at first, even though he had been graduated to the first pile of sticks in the long series for his whippings. He almost never cried except when one of these sticks was in use. He seemed to realize that the sooner he cried on these occasions the sooner Miss Hummer's pleasures would be ended, also that the louder he cried the sooner this climax would come.

At other times Henrietta made strange noises with his mouth. Miss Hummer did not think he was talking, for she could not understand what he said. Yet he might be talking in some other language. He might be calling to the enemy.

He uttered these sounds in a monotonous way that annoyed her. She had often tried to silence him, but the cadence would soon start again. Once she had stuffed a handkerchief in his mouth, but Henrietta finally removed it.

Sometimes Miss Hummer was certain Henrietta was talking in a mysterious tongue. He would address his remarks to a chair or table, the very things that had helped him learn to walk, or to the floor or one of the piles of wood. These listeners did not answer him, but they might understand what he said. This made Miss Hummer uneasy. At other times Henrietta only mumbled or shouted to himself. Miss Hummer seldom talked to him.

On the day of the first snowstorm a small package was left in Miss Hummer's mailbox. Miss Hummer seldom received any mail. She was elated by the recovery of her property and became jubilant when she saw the flag on her mailbox go down. She had been waiting for this parcel.

"We'll have some fun now," she said to Henrietta.

Miss Hummer put on her overshoes and watched for the mailman's sleigh to disappear. She never went to the box until the mailman was far out of sight. The package contained a can of powder, a bottle of perfume, several sticks of rouge, and one black stick for the eyebrows.

Miss Hummer had a bitter contempt for anyone who used such things. A painted woman was a depraved woman. Powder and perfume were only added so that others could smell as well as see the flagrancy they flaunted. Painted faces were those who, in their shame, wished to cover up and disguise their own features.

Miss Hummer would as soon have asked Lem Witherbee to sleep with her as to have inquired if he carried rouge or eyebrow blacking. She had answered an advertisement in a magazine and in the same mail canceled her subscription to this immoral journal in which the needs of whores were displayed in such a disgraceful way.

But Miss Hummer had no intention of contaminating any part of her body with such lewd coverings or odors. She had a man in her power and was bringing him up to be a woman. She could not only make him a woman but a depraved woman of the lowest sort. She could cover him with these foul signs of iniquity and teach him to use them himself. Miss Hummer put on an old pair of gloves before opening the box. She handled its contents with the extreme tips of her fingers.

Even if Henrietta ever did find out his real sex, she could always gloat over the stigma of his early depravity. This would be a permanent stain. He had begun life with the garb of a prostitute. The contact with paint and powder would be a permanent blemish. These obscenities probably contained some germ that would infect him with the bawdy qualities they represented. He would be a demoralized woman and at the same time a man.

Miss Hummer placed Henrietta on her lap. She sprinkled powder and perfume on his head. She painted his lips red and his eyebrows black. She put large red spots on his cheeks. She would have to wear these gloves whenever she touched him now.

Henrietta had been surprised to find that it would not be necessary to cry after Miss Hummer had taken him into her lap. Miss Hummer placed him back on the floor and handed him a stick of rouge. He began to mark on a chair but was rudely interrupted.

He put one end of the rouge into his mouth. Miss Hummer brought it out to his lips and moved his hand back and forth until Henrietta looked as though he had been drinking from a jar of jam.

"You'll learn," she said.

Miss Hummer smiled at Henrietta's appearance. Immorality, scandal, and shame were emphasized in his face more than in any other she had ever seen.

"You're a slut," she told Henrietta.

Henrietta said something that sounded like, "Slut."

"Yes, 'slut,'" replied Miss Hummer slowly, trying to teach him the right pronunciation. "You're a man, and you're a 'slut.'"

"Slut," said Henrietta, laughing. Such friendly attention when no visitor was in the house was something new.

Miss Hummer did not like to have Henrietta laugh. What was he laughing at now? at her? at the pollution with which she had covered him? He probably didn't know the seriousness of this stain. Wait until he grew up and found other girls and women shunning him for his profligacy, crossing to the other side of the road when they saw him.

And other men—Miss Hummer paused in her reflection. Suppose men should be attracted by Henrietta's show of indecency? This would lead to a discovery of his true sex, to his escape from her. She could not let this happen. She would make him so depraved that even men would be repulsed.

Miss Hummer picked up Henrietta again. She removed his dress and proceeded to scribble over his body at random with her red and black cosmetics.

CHAPTER XXVII

THE PATH OF VIRTUE BRINGS REGRETS

All the women of Menham who were eligible now had keys to the padlock on the town hall. Saturday night festivities had been transferred there from the Dole barn with due ceremony, which included a parade, cups and glasses in hand, from the barn to the hall.

Mrs. Whiter was a full-fledged member of the sorority, but some thought she enjoyed more than her proper privileges. Her home was only a short distance from the hall, and she used her key and cup at times during the week unspecified by the other members.

Her informal visits were not always more than once a day, but frequently they were prolonged until dark. Sometimes she brought matches and a lamp. Other lamps had been contributed by other members, but Mrs. Whiter always preferred to bring her own. She had a fear that other people's lamps might explode. This made her restless during the first few drinks on Saturday nights with lamps on all sides of her flickering at the point of explosion.

Mrs. Whiter's explanation of her visits to the town hall at times other than Saturday nights was that she was acting as sentinel. The kegs of cider were too valuable to be protected only by a padlock. A watchman should be on duty there at all times.

"So I have appointed myself guardian," she would say. "Whenever I can spare a minute, I go to the hall to make sure there are no burglars. If I can stay longer, of course I do."

Mrs. Whiter lived alone. Mrs. Muller did not understand why she should bear the title Mrs., having neither children nor husband, so she called her Miss Whiter. Mrs. Whiter sometimes retaliated by calling her Miss, but Mrs. Muller knew nothing of this.

Mrs. Muller had not heard of her neighbor's professed sentry duty, but she had seen her returning by night many times with a lighted lamp that followed a course somewhat like a leisurely firefly.

"Want any help?" Mrs. Muller had once hollered from her bedroom window.

"Yeah," came the reply, "there's more cider there than I can drink."

Mrs. Whiter had followed a path of virtue as prescribed by a maiden aunt and, barring an omission by Nature, had better proof of virginity than even Miss Hummer.

She had been brought up to consider her body as something obscene and indecent, a stigma of vice and dishonor that must always be covered with as many clothes as means permitted. A new petticoat was another covering in which to hide her awful body, and had always been a welcome addition to the mattress of clothes she wore already.

As a girl she had been ashamed that most of her wicked face had to be exposed through a network of veils. She considered it immodest to wear less than two veils. Her hands, of course, were always hidden in long gloves. She had been a pretty girl, but nobody had known it.

There had come a man who had an interest in hidden things and wondered how long a time it required for this girl to take off all these clothes. He also wondered what she looked like. The young lady always put on her hat and at least one extra veil when he called. His name was Whiter.

His curiosity became so great that one afternoon, in the presence of the aunt, he had asked if the girl would marry him. She, in response to nods by the aunt, finally said, "Yes."

After he had left, the girl was horrified by a partial revelation by the aunt of the wicked practices of married people. Not only her face but all of her indecent body would have to be exposed. There were many tears, and both the girl and her aunt went to bed without any supper. The girl had promised to become a bawdy martyr in order that the human race might be continued.

The marriage ceremony was performed, and the girl, dressed in black, became Mrs. Whiter. But, when the man had opened the door of his home to allow her to enter first, the girl had revolted. She could not suffer an exhibition of her obscenities. She ran from the porch. Financed by her aunt, she eventually found her way to Menham. She was still Mrs. Whiter, but she had escaped an exposure of the wickedness of her body.

Mrs. Whiter talked with other women and heard other accounts of bodily relations. Her ideas slowly changed, but so slowly that the day she had first gone outdoors with her face exposed Andrew Cline, the only one to recognize her, said merely, "Won't you get cold without them veils?"

The only remark of men after she had discarded six of her petticoats was, "You're gettin' thinner, Mrs. Whiter."

These immodesties, which she had thought would surely make every man want to rape her and would probably bring a few of them into action, had been in vain. After that Mrs. Whiter tried harder to make herself attractive to men. She dispersed with her gloves and the rest of her petticoats. She went out without a hat and without stockings.

She wanted a man. But she no longer had any physical attraction. Her beauty had remained hidden until it wilted. The path of virtue was the only path available.

"If we could only start life as old women and then get to be girls again we'd be a lot better off," she thought. "We'd look forward to not bein' a virgin instead of livin' in fear that some day we might not be a virgin."

She did not give up her efforts to make some man interested in her body. Lem Witherbee had accepted invitations to eat supper at her house, but he simply thanked her kindly after the meal was over and went back to his store.

Even when she had exposed most of her bare legs upon lifting her dress to protect her hand in taking a hot pan off the stove, Lem Witherbee had watched without interest in anything but the contents of the pan.

Drinking was a pleasure Mrs. Whiter had always abhorred as a wicked vice, but, having learned that she enjoyed it, she proceeded to make up for lost time. She was also sincere in her insistence that she was watching for burglars when she visited the kegs alone. Burglars never came to her house. Perhaps one would come to the town hall and could be persuaded, under the influence of cider, that her body had not wilted too much.

CHAPTER XXVIII

PAUL TURNER PRESCRIBES AN ABORTIFACIENT

May Cline was very much irritated by the fact that she was going to have a baby. She had been complimented on her increase in size by her mother, who was pleased to have her daughter gain weight and assured May that the extra poundage would soon be circulated about her body in a more proportionate manner.

"What we eat goes into the stomach, you know, and stays there until the body takes it to other places," she said.

Andrew Cline's comment, "Is it goin' to be a boy or a girl?" had been squelched by his wife's reply, "Your evil mind will be askin' next whether Miss Hummer's baby's goin' to have a baby."

May's somnambulations had not been made on the usual regular schedule of late and had recently been discontinued altogether. When nobody else was in sight, she often spoke to Paul Turner, who worked for her father and lived in a room in the rear of the kitchen. He tried to avoid these private interviews.

"You can't say it was me," he would insist before May had a chance to speak. "It's so dark out there in the barn you couldn't tell who it was."

"But it was you, and you've got to do something about it," she would reply. "You said everything was goin' to be all right."

"And so 'tis," he would answer, "I can prove I been goin' with Minnie Muller all this time."

"But you said you was just goin' with her so they wouldn't suspect us."

"And so I was. I been goin' with her. You don't know who you been goin' with."

May Cline did not want a baby. What would she do with it? It would be like playing with a doll again except that this doll could move and cry whenever it wanted to. She couldn't throw it into a corner and forget about it when she wanted to play something else.

A baby would play with her, rather than she with it. Whenever it screamed she would have to go and see what it wanted, or try to find out what it wanted. A baby could only make noise. It couldn't talk so that she could understand it. She would have to bring silence by experimental offerings of things she thought might be desired. It would be like trying to silence a live and drunken idol that insisted on having a certain sacrifice placed before it but could not remember what it was.

This live doll would be her dictator. Whenever it decided to call her, day or night, she would have to respond. Babies probably cried several times a day just to amuse themselves by having their mothers run to them.

If she could have had a baby when she was a little girl and liked to play with dolls it would have not been so bad. She would have enjoyed the live doll part of the time at least. And, being nearer to babyhood herself, she could have understood its whims better. She might have been able to understand what it was talking about. If she had had this baby then, the discomfort she was experiencing now would be over, too.

A baby would have to be fed, and washed and housebroken. It would be a long time before it could do anything for itself. May wished her baby could be a kitten or puppy. A baby of this sort would not require much attention and could soon do everything for itself. By the time a human baby learned to walk the kitten or puppy would be a sophisticated adult.

Perhaps her mother would help her take care of the child. She had had experience and could tell her what to do. Her mother would also suspect her motive for sleepwalking in the past. She could claim her being asleep must have been responsible for the baby, but then, another time, her mother might follow her right into the barn.

One day Paul Turner went out of his way to speak to May alone. He handed her a package from which the label had been removed.

"You take some of this and go to bed," he said. "That'll fix you up."

May went to bed, but she postponed taking the medicine when she heard her mother coming up the stairs. Mrs. Cline saw the package under the bed. She tore off the cover, and her mouth fell open.

"Your father must have gone crazy!" she cried. "What's he doin' leavin' his blastin' powder under your bed? Is he tryin' to blow you into pieces, and me, and the house? Wait'll I get my hands on him."

Mrs. Cline dashed from the room to find Andrew.

CHAPTER XXIX

HENRIETTA, MAN OF ONE WORD

The first word Henrietta Hummer learned to say soon became known in Menham. Mrs. Jones hurried from Miss Hummer's house to tell Mrs. Sadler the news.

"I went to see Miss Hummer, and her baby called me a slut!" she said.

"Did it say anything else?" asked Mrs. Sadler.

"Prob'ly," replied Mrs. Jones, "but when anyone calls me a slut I don't wait to hear any more. The baby's prob'ly swearin' a blue streak by now."

"Prob'ly," agreed Mrs. Sadler.

"She had the baby all painted up like an Indian, too," continued Mrs. Jones. "She said she'd given it some crayons to play with and it wrote on its face."

"Prob'ly she paints its face instead of washin' it," Mrs. Sadler suggested.

"I guess that's what she does," agreed Mrs. Jones. "And when the baby called me a slut Miss Hummer acted surprised and tried to tell me the baby has an evil mind and says words she's never heard before."

"Well, come in. Tell me some more."

Other women called on Miss Hummer. Henrietta paused in his vocal jumblings to say proudly and clearly to each, "Slut." Whereupon the visitor left with a gaudy display of indignation.

"She must call Miss Hummer that all the time," the women agreed.

"And think of all the other things she must call her," Mrs. Sadler always added.

The baby's painted face called for considerable theorizing:

"Maybe it ain't paint. Maybe it's her real color."

"Maybe Miss Hummer's too lazy to wash it off."

"Maybe the baby turned out to be a nigger, and she's tryin' to disguise it."

"Maybe she thinks babies are *s'posed* to be painted, same as furniture."

Each visitor felt obliged to give a slightly different version of her encounter with Henrietta, and, as a result, he became accredited with a larger vocabulary.

It had previously been commonly supposed that Miss Hummer did not know even such an evil expression as, "God." How she, the baby's only teacher, had come into this knowledge of profane and obscene remarks was a mystery.

"Perhaps Miss Hummer's always been so aloof and proper because Menham people didn't know enough profanity to suit her," suggested Mrs. Lyman.

"Maybe she thinks she's teachin' the baby to pray," said Mrs. Jones. "And, not knowin' which are the right words, she's usin' all the words of that kind she's ever heard."

"Is she teachin' the baby, or is the baby teachin' her?" asked Mrs. Whiter.

"If I had a baby I wouldn't bother teachin' it to swear," said Mrs. Sadler. "It'll swear enough when it's older anyway."

"Miss Hummer p'raps wants her baby to be different than others," said Mrs. Dean. "She keeps it painted and doesn't teach it nothin' to say but swear words. P'raps she learned the swear words just so she could teach 'em to the baby."

Miss Hummer and her eccentric baby became as important a topic for discussion at the women's sessions in the town hall as were Mrs. Nancy Muller and her daughter at the men's forum. It became an accepted fact that no-one could pass the Hummer house without having obscene insults shouted at them by the baby. It was becoming an accepted fact that Miss Hummer joined in this shouting and was almost as indecent in her defamations as Henrietta.

John Lyman stopped at Miss Hummer's house one afternoon to try to sell her some wood. He walked into Lem Witherbee's store a few minutes later.

"You know, that Hummer baby can't tell a man from a woman," he said. "It called me a slut just the same as though it was my wife 'stead of me it was talkin' to."

CHAPTER XXX

NATURE PLAYS A TRICK ON MINNIE MULLER

The appreciation of Minnie Muller's right to fame and distinction equaling that of her mother was still confined to a very limited circle: John Lyman and Paul Turner.

John Lyman's realization of the full justice due her was the greater, as he knew more of the tradition attached to Mrs. Nancy Muller than Paul. John still intended that Minnie should make a sudden rise from comparative obscurity to become the subject for a new topic and tradition at Lem Witherbee's, but, as yet, he felt that more than one competitor for her hand and body would not be fair to him who was to be her sponsor and deserved a head start on the others.

John and Paul shared Minnie in a gentlemanly manner. There were no offers of duels or fights. Instead, there was a standing appointment that Minnie should be on the town hall steps directly after supper each night. During the winter this place of meeting became the Goodwin farm, a long-deserted abode. The man who arrived first had precedence over the other. The second left politely and returned at a reasonable time, when Minnie was surrendered to him.

Paul had no objection to this arrangement. Andrew Cline might discharge him some day, and John Lyman would be a potential employer. If he opposed the sharing of Minnie, Lyman might connive with Cline to find work for him to do at night. And the gentleman's agreement now practiced provided a means for his leaving Minnie with less delay and needless conversation than in the past.

Usually at least one of the men came to the meeting place. Occasionally neither would put in an appearance, and Minnie would waste much time in waiting that could have been put to more profitable use in her mother's kitchen.

Until her encounter behind the town hall with John Lyman, Minnie had considered intersexual love as a physical compatibility peculiar to individual couples: a mutual conformity in the bodies of the man and the woman involved that made them suited to each other with no alternate choices available to either.

Each man was physically able to love only the one woman whom his body matched, and each woman only the one man for whom her body was built. She had found the man who matched her in Paul Turner, and so considered herself in love with him. All other men were physically unadapted to her.

She thought herself fortunate in locating the proper key to her body so close at hand. She had been afraid the man she was built for might be looking for her in some other country.

Then came John Lyman, who proved himself capable of creating the same bodily responses as Paul Turner. Minnie discovered she was doubly fortunate in having two lovers who were built to match her body, and both of whom lived in Menham. As a result, she was in love with two men.

One Saturday night John Lyman's desire for prominence became greater than his desire for Minnie Muller. He had kept her from acclaim long enough. It was time to perform his humanitarian duty and present her to the audience that would substitute her name for her mother's. It was too bad she could not make a personal appearance and verify the things he had to say.

He waited for the proper dramatic moment, the pause that preceded a change in the topic then under discussion. Miss Hummer and her baby would have been introduced as the next subjects for consideration if Lyman had not interrupted the usual program with a startling new text, of which only he could speak authoritatively.

He became the center of the gathering, despite his seat in a corner. All eyes and ears were attentive to him. There were no interruptions. John Lyman was making the most important announcement since the birth of Nancy Muller's baby. He was the pivotal public figure of the moment. He had made history and was relinquishing his rights of conquest in order that others might benefit. He was founding a new school of expression which would have many members by the next Saturday night.

"Minnie Muller's the girl to go walkin' with; she's a lot better than her ma ever was," he began, arousing unspoken controversy and determined investigators at one and the same time.

He continued with descriptive details that left no grounds for skepticism of his facts, but obviously withholding much of the material available for use at another session when he would meet with rival accounts.

He closed with the words, "Yup, you fellows who went out with her ma are welcome to her. Even if her ma was standin' here just like she was at her best you could still have her. I'm sure glad I had to wait and get Minnie."

Candidates for the new school expressed themselves at once. John Lyman was besieged with questions. Other topics of discussion were forgotten. Minnie Muller had made good.

The old school asserted itself in the voice of Andrew Cline, who insisted, "Nobody could measure up to Nancy Muller. Minnie's prob'ly better'n most, but that's only 'cause she's Nancy's daughter."

Whereupon the older men began a discussion of their own upon the merits of Mrs. Muller. The question period over which John Lyman presided was not disturbed or distracted by this. Lyman, the spokesman and authority of the hour, felt that he should have made Minnie known sooner and come into this prominence with her before.

Minnie was not roused from her bed that night, but she was not kept in ignorance of her popularity much longer. Men put themselves out to speak to her and pinch her breasts. They asked her to go to the Goodwin farm or to their own barns.

Minnie Muller became aware of a surprising fact. There were more than two men whose bodies were built to match hers. Most of the men in Menham had been constructed in the manner that was compatible with her body. They had been formed in the pattern necessary to be her lover.

She found herself in love with many men. Through some whim of Nature, the mold for her mate had been filled many times. Since they were built to be her lovers, she must treat them with equal affection. There was only one Minnie Muller. She was the only girl they could love, so she must love them all.

John Lyman regretted the fulfilling of his duty toward Minnie. He now had more of Paul Turner's companionship than Minnie's, and on the following Saturday night he found difficulty making his presence heard, despite the fact that he was the original authority on the subject at hand.

CHAPTER XXXI

BE KIND TO MICE

On every possible occasion Mrs. Sadie Sadler expressed a theory that people are reincarnated as mice.

She constantly warned Menham residents not to kill a mouse, as it might be some deceased relative or friend. Mice, she said, must not only be tolerated as household companions but treated generously and kindly. Having become mice, our forebears return to the homes of their descendants expecting a fitting greeting. Only a monster could welcome those responsible for his existence with fiendish mousetraps and poison.

Mrs. Sadler's house was a home for mice. She walked with cautious steps, looking from side to side and taking all precautions not to step on one of them. She fed the mice large meals on the kitchen floor. She would rather have served them on a table, but it seemed much easier for them to eat on the floor. She laid down a cloth to make the eating place seem more attractive, and put the food in china dishes.

Hundreds of mice attended these dinners, which were given every noon and night. They paid no attention to Mrs. Sadler, who watched over them devotedly. At each meal she identified the mice she thought were her mother and father, but each time she selected different ones. She had discovered all of her dead relatives she had known at these mouse picnics and was always pleased to point them out when requested.

Mice ran about the floors in large numbers. Mrs. Sadler could only sweep when her husband was in the house. The mice noticed his presence and hurried to sheltered places. Jonathan Sadler often amused himself by killing mice. There were many that could not find room in the hiding places. But he never indulged in this pastime in his wife's presence.

Mrs. Sadler had a horror of cats. Cats killed mice. A stray cat might kill some of her ancestors. Any cat that found its way into her yard was soon put to death. She liked to entice neighbors' cats to follow her home and then kill them.

Mrs. Sadler wished she knew more of her genealogy so she could identify more of the mice that lived with her. She was convinced she was being hostess to all of her forefathers, even as far back as Adam and Eve. She could always single out this latter couple to her own satisfaction.

Mrs. Sadler did not speak to Mrs. Muller. Mrs. Muller had suspected as much from the way in which Mrs. Sadler walked away when she started to talk. So Mrs. Muller stopped speaking to Mrs. Sadler.

The breach had been caused by a visit of Mrs. Muller's to the Sadler farm. Unaware of the relationship between Mrs. Sadler and the mice, Mrs. Muller had seized a broom and started killing these creatures that were everywhere beneath her feet. Mrs. Sadler's screams had done no good, and over fifty mice were dead or dying by the time she was able to wrest the broom from Mrs. Muller. Mrs. Sadler had burst into tears after the tragedy, and Mrs. Muller had offered to lend her a mousetrap.

Whenever she was awakened at night by mice running over her bed Mrs. Sadler got up to prepare them a lunch. This was their way of letting her know they were hungry.

Mrs. Sadler bought mousetraps at Lem Witherbee's store whenever there were any for sale. She destroyed them as soon as she arrived home. One of her ancestors might call on a neighbor and be caught if someone else bought these insidious devices for execution.

One Saturday night Mrs. Sadler nearly disrupted the women's meeting. A mouse jumped out of the folds of her dress and ran across the floor. Other women jumped and screamed.

Mrs. Sadler spent the rest of the evening hunting for the mouse—it looked like her grandfather.

CHAPTER XXXII

ARTHUR MOORE, DEALER IN WOMEN

The unannounced visits of Arthur Moore to the Goode farm were awaited with equal enthusiasm by both Mrs. Emma Goode and her daughter Alice. They were rivals for his choice and never knew who the lucky one would be the next time he came.

Whenever Moore was seen approaching, each hoped his motive was something other than benevolence. For Arthur had shown himself to have this characteristic, too. He had convinced Mrs. Goode that he was only showing a fatherly interest in her daughter, and had assured Alice that he only discussed business affairs with her mother.

When coming to perform such impersonal kindness in a private conference with one, he could not, on the same visit, show his customary affection for the other. His moods were fixed in either benevolence or passion. Each visit was either to give moral guidance and kindly advice to the one or to enjoy a pleasurable indulgence with the other. On only one occasion had Moore taken both mother and daughter from the kitchen in turn.

Arthur Moore's schedule of appearance and choice was most irregular. Sometimes he would come two days in succession and select either Emma or Alice both times. He might not come again for a week or a month, or he might be back two days later. His choice might be the same as before, or it might not. He might come during the day, or he might rouse them from bed at night.

Both Emma and Alice had taken to wearing their best clothes seven days a week. Each liked to look her best when before Arthur for inspection, hoping that his mood might change if it was paternal and revert to her. Their housework had to be done in a fastidious manner, and much of it was neglected to protect their dresses.

Arthur Moore would escort, or at least accompany, the lady of his choice—usually to the barn—but he never saw her back to her home. Following his charitable advice, he left without words or ceremony, only walking away faster if asked for some hint as to when he would come again. He had a head start coming down from the hayloft, as his clothes did not require much adjusting, while those of his companion were somewhat ruffled by the hay.

Arthur Moore's manner of greeting was brief. "I've got something to tell you," he would say, adding the name of the one he wanted. She would follow him happily, while the other would go and change her dress.

Alice Goode's interest in Felix Dole had both increased and decreased. It seemed a waste of time to bother with him, but there must be some way of making him more like Arthur Moore. If Felix could change his tactics she could be more sure of him than she was of Arthur. She could make definite appointments with Felix and know when she would see him again. And she would not have to wonder whether he would invite her or her mother to accompany him when he came to their house.

Arthur Moore had qualified as one of Minnie Muller's lovers, but had done so principally for social reasons. This made him a full-fledged member of the Minnie as well as the Nancy Muller school of thought at Lem Witherbee's. His taking of Minnie to the Goodwin farm had been an initiation he felt obliged to make to attain this distinction. Otherwise his imagination might be found in error in some intimate detail involved.

He did not consider any woman worthy of the popularity Minnie Muller was enjoying and felt humiliated in having to let her know that he, too, was obliged to make use of her. He thought it degrading to the superiority of man over woman for more than one man to show continued affection for any one girl. He had tried to show as little affection as possible during his encounter with Minnie and had left a scar on her wrist.

Every man should have a number of women at his disposal, Arthur Moore had told his whisky cup. A woman should share one man in common with other women. A woman with a number of admirers had too high an opinion of herself: she was something necessary to as many men. If her male companions returned only a few times it was not quite so bad. She could conclude she was not good enough to belong to any one man and was only doing her duty to men whose other women were not available at the moment.

Women, as you know, were not held in very high esteem by Arthur Moore. "They're all the same," he said in announcing his membership in the Minnie Muller clan. "Anyone that went out with Nancy knows what Minnie's like. I forgot whether it was

Nancy or Minnie until I pushed her hair off her face so I could see."

Arthur Moore pondered these opinions as he walked toward the Goode farm for the first time in two weeks. Perhaps he was showing these ladies too much attention. Each thought she was the one woman in his life at present and that he not only was faithful to her but had so much interest that he was acting as a friendly eunuch to the other.

Each probably thought she had him in her power. One of them would be asking him to marry her or trying to rob him in some other way if he was not careful.

He should correct their opinion of him. He had better let them know that, as an upright man maintaining the dignity of his sex, he had more women at hand than he could ever use. He was doing them a special favor in calling so often when he had so many better women to choose from. He must not let their debasing ideas about him persist.

Arthur Moore knocked at the Goode kitchen door. Emma and Alice stood before him side by side in expectant readiness. He looked at them without comment. Then he stepped closer and began to pinch and slap in various places each of their bodies in turn, as though examining a pair of horses.

He seemed to be comparing their physical attributes and trying to determine which was the better for his purposes. He felt of corresponding parts of both at the same time and shook his head silently.

In their anxiety to hear who his choice was for today, Emma and Alice remained motionless and indifferent to this unexpected greeting. Which one did he have something to tell?

Arthur Moore stepped back and studied them, with one hand holding his chin and another his elbow. "Well," he said, as though to himself, "I guess I'll go over and see Minnie Muller."

CHAPTER XXXIII

YOU CAN LEAD A HORSE TO BRANDY, TOO

Arthur Moore was not welcomed at the Goode farm for a week, the interval that elapsed until his next visit. Instead of having to use the reconciliatory methods he had planned, he found Emma and Alice waiting with similar tactics to regain his favor. He immediately changed his intended submissive rôle to one of tyranny and interrupted Mrs. Goode's invitation to have tea by telling Alice to come out to the barn.

He went home a short time later thinking about Teresa Brown, a girl in Westham. He also thought of his snakes. He had not seen them since they got tangled up for their winter's slumber. Moore covered their pen with hay when cold weather came. It would soon be time to uncover them. He visited the Goodes several times before the weather permitted the awakening. He shortened his manner of greeting to, "Come, Alice," or, "Come, Emma."

Arthur Moore's spring reunion with his snakes was a happy occasion. He looked forward to the event and saved up choice morsels of food to bring to them. This year he had a newly hatched brood of chickens to give them. He missed the snakes during the winter. After they had been awakened by the warmer temperature he picked many of them up to receive the intricate embraces of their crawling bodies.

The rattlers enjoyed the chickens and other fresh foods Arthur gave them this spring. In return they provided all the coiling embraces he desired. He did not see the Goodes for over a month after that but visited the snakes daily.

After the revival of the snakes Arthur Moore went to the store to have a few words with his whisky cup. There was a strange horse and buggy outside Lem Witherbee's. He did not approve of this. Somebody he didn't know would be inside. He took an immediate dislike to the man drinking brandy at the bar. He did not like strangers, and he did not approve of brandy as a substitute for whisky.

Moore tried to avoid the visitor. He sat down at a distance from the drinking counter and pushed away nearby empty chairs. Without comment, Lem Witherbee brought his whisky glass filled so that it resembled a cup of tea. The stranger pulled a chair to Moore's side and started to talk.

"Glad to see yuh," he began. "As I was just sayin', it's a nice day for drinkin' and a nice place to drink. Nice brandy, nice store, nice town, nice weather."

Arthur Moore moved restlessly in his chair and looked at Lem Witherbee.

"Have some brandy," said the stranger. "It's a lot better'n that stuff you got there."

Arthur Moore went to another chair. The other man followed him. Moore emptied his glass and walked to the counter. The man was still beside him and emitting a flow of noisy words. Moore drank another cup of whisky.

"S'pose my horse ud like a drink of brandy?" asked the man.

Moore spoke for the first time, "Yes, he told me when I came in that he was thirsty." This mission would take the man away from his side.

"I'll bring Brandy right in for his brandy—that's my horse's name, Brandy," said the man, starting for the door.

Lem Witherbee objected to this proposal. "You better take the drink out to him," he suggested. "There ain't room for him to get through the door."

"I'll unharness him, and he'll squeeze through all right," replied the man.

"No," Lem remonstrated, "you can't bring him in here."

Arthur Moore sat down to enjoy the argument. The stranger might not be such a bad sort. He was all right as long as he was talking to somebody else. And his idea of bringing the horse to the bar was a good one.

Lem's arguments had no effect. The man insisted that his horse was going to come in for a drink. "He won't hurt anything, and he's good company," the stranger maintained. "I shouldn't of left him out there all alone in the first place." Lem followed the man outdoors, and Arthur Moore poured himself an unrecorded glass of whisky.

Lem buckled the harness in place again as the stranger unbuckled it, but the stranger worked faster and was able to lead the horse out of the shafts when the contest ended. Lem went ahead intending to bolt the door, but Arthur Moore was holding it open.

The horse arrived at the bar despite further interference by Lem Witherbee. He announced that he charged double rates for liquor served to horses in the store, but the visitor could not be discouraged. Lem poured a drink of brandy, and the man poured it into the horse's mouth. The horse did not live up to its name. It threw its head down, shook its body, and backed away.

Arthur Moore was standing beside the horse. A harness buckle struck his whisky glass. He looked at the glass and saw a crack in its side. The stranger and his horse had seriously damaged this priceless receptacle and almost broken it, a felonious offense.

The glass would always bear this terrible scar. It was weakened, disfigured, and more liable to break than before. He would have to protect the honor of his whisky glass. Moore handed the glass to Lem Witherbee and seized the stranger by the arm.

"You and me is goin' for a walk," he stated. In a lower tone he explained to Lem Witherbee, "I'll take him out and let him sober up."

Lem expected more serious consequences. A cracked whisky glass called for more than a walk for the party responsible. He led the horse out the door after them and reharnessed it to the buggy. The stranger's utterances grew less audible as Moore forced him down the road in the direction of his farm.

An hour later Arthur Moore returned alone. He had a drink from his damaged glass and examined the crack mournfully.

"I came back to get that fellow's buggy," he said.

"Too bad about your glass," condoled Lem. "I tried to keep the horse out. I knew something like that would happen."

"Yeah, damn shame," replied Moore. "I knew the bastard didn't mean to do it, and I just took him outside so he couldn't do any more damage."

Lem eagerly awaited the account that this alibi was introducing.

"We got down the road and a rattlesnake bit him. I tried to pull him away, but he didn't know what he was doin' and tried to pick the snake up. I guess he's dead by now, but if we get him in his buggy the horse'll know where to take him."

"His folks'll know it was a rattler bit him, will they?" asked Lem skeptically.

"Oh, sure. I didn't do nothin' to him. There's only the snake bite."

Lem Witherbee put Arthur Moore's glass back in its place with even more care than usual.

CHAPTER XXXIV

MRS. JONES DISPLAYS HER WINGS

Once a year on a warm spring day Mrs. Edna Jones went to the Menham graveyard to eat lunch. She used the Blake family stone as a back rest. Her father's name, the last of the list, had been placed on the stone the day he was christened, "Nathan Manuel Blake 1839—," but the year of his death was not filled in after he died. There had not been room on the stone for her mother's name.

Mrs. Jones did not hold to the theory of Mrs. Sadler that our predecessors become mice. She believed that people remain in the ground where they are buried.

Mrs. Jones liked the quiet atmosphere of the graveyard. There were a number of people there, but none of them could talk aloud. She had a feeling of superiority. Whatever she might say could not be disputed. People whom she had not liked she could call names, or say anything about them that she wished.

Those who were buried had to stay there. She could come or go at will. No matter how much better or more well-to-do than she they may have been once, there was nothing they could do to prove it now. Her house was a palace compared with theirs, and she was far better than their remains.

Then, too, a periodic visit to the grave of her parents was a duty that should not be neglected. She did not call her father and mother names, but carried on a pleasant monologue summarizing the gossip of the past year. They were probably pleased by her visits. Her presence gave them a certain dignity and superiority. Two of the other graves had small stained statues. During her stay she provided a live and talking statue, one that brought news and could call any of the other graveyard inhabitants any name desired.

Surely this was better than a stone statue. These statues had to stay there, and in silence, while she could go wherever she wanted to and could talk about the merits of her parents if she so desired. She could even break the other statues if she went to the trouble of bringing a sledge-hammer.

Mrs. Jones had considered making a pair of large wings to wear while at the graveyard. The statues had wings, and that might be one point in their favor in comparison with her. But she had always put off making the wings until the day she decided to go to the graveyard, and then it was too late.

Spring had brought warm weather to Menham again, and Mrs. Jones was preparing a lunch to take to her parents' grave. She was interrupted by the tappings of a spring shower on the windows. She decided to postpone her visit and in the meantime to try her hand at making wings.

The next day Mrs. Jones walked out of her yard with a lunch basket in one hand and two redesigned sacks decorated with hens' feathers tied to her back. The sacks had been cut and sewed into triangular shapes and given rounded corners by a stuffing of rags. These wings probably would not take her into the air, but neither would those of the stone statues permit them to fly.

Mrs. Jones had difficulty keeping her wings in place as she walked to the graveyard. She had to stop and readjust them several times. The stuffing of rags settled until the wings were drooping at the top and bulging at the bottom, and many of the feathers blew off.

"Y' got quite a load there, Mrs. Jones," said Howard Dean as she passed his farm. "Want any help?"

"Isn't it a nice day," she replied, ignoring his question.

At the graveyard Mrs. Jones was free from further impertinences. Other people only came there for a funeral. She laid her basket on the Blake lot and circled the statues. She displayed her wings to them in a haughty manner with her head raised.

"They can't say your statue hasn't got wings now," she told her parents. "I could teach these other statues to fly if they were alive."

One of the wings slipped down her back. She pulled at the rope attached to it and prevented it from falling to the ground. Then the other wing began to descend.

"My wings want to take me into the air now, but I'm going to stay here and talk to you, Ma and Pa," she said.

The first wing came loose from the rope that held it.

"I can take my wings off when I want to, too," said Mrs. Jones, picking up the wing and tying it back in place. "I don't have to wear 'em all the time."

The Blake stone, like the others, was thin, flat and oblong, rising into the air for a little over two feet at an angle that deviated noticeably from the vertical. Mrs. Jones sat down in her customary position there after squeezing the wings together so that they acted as a cushion for her back. She began to talk. When she became hungry she reached into the lunch basket.

Her meal was interrupted before she had proceeded far with the year's gossip, and before she had begun to address any one besides Mr. and Mrs. Blake. Another spring shower started pouring from the sky. Mrs. Jones was doubly annoyed. It was not right that she should be humiliated in the presence of her inferiors. They were protected from this rain that was drenching her. They were exhibiting an argument in their own favor.

She would have to bring her visit to an abrupt end, or else sit there and suffer in the rain. This was humiliating. She could come again, but those below would always remember this time when she was driven away.

Mrs. Jones felt like a dignified queen at a formal function who has tripped on her train and fallen into an awkward sprawl. But she could cause humiliation, too. She untied her wings and walked to the statues. She placed the open end of each sack over the head of one of the images. The rags fell about on the ground, and both statues were left covered.

Mrs. Jones hurried home. She had asserted herself under trying circumstances. In covering the statues with burlap bags she had shown the ready means for retaliation at her disposal and her superior powers.

But the glow of pleasure that this consolation brought became a second dose of humiliation. The bags would protect the images from the rain, and in providing this protection she had shown that her wings were not real.

CHAPTER XXXV

THE VIRGIN MAY

Mrs. Susan cline still insisted that her daughter, May, was gaining weight in a healthful manner, which was true. Andrew Cline made no inference to his wife that May might also be acquiring a child, but he had told his whisky glass several times that he hoped the baby would not be twins. May's hatred for men, babies, and pregnancy had increased with the size of her body.

One afternoon May felt as though the baby were turning somersaults inside her and lay down. Mrs. Cline hurried to her with an indigestion remedy. May wondered whether her mother would be as pleased by the baby as she had by the enlargement of her body. Her mother ought to be even more pleased, May thought. The baby had been the cause of the large stomach and would grow to be much larger after it was born.

For a long time Mrs. Cline had wondered what the proper occasion would be to inform her daughter of the secrets of life and sex. May was a big girl now and ought not be kept in ignorance much longer. As Mrs. Cline sat at May's bedside, she decided that this might be a good time for the revelation. It would divert May's thoughts from her indigestion.

"There is something I've got to tell you," she began. "I s'pose you've wondered how we get babies."

"Yes," replied May. Evidently her mother was going to give her some assistance. Perhaps there was some way of luring a baby out of the body like catching a fish. May did not like this conception of childbirth. Her baby might refuse the bait and keep right on growing inside her.

"Well, before a woman can have a baby she has to sleep with a man," her mother continued.

May did not approve of this. She did not want to sleep with a man. In her present condition this would be quite painful. "Why?" she asked.

"Well, er, you see men and women are made different," Mrs. Cline explained. "A man can't have a child, but he can give a girl a child. She can't have a baby without his help."

"What does he have to do?" May asked, dreading the answer. She didn't want any help from a man. Having a baby must be more complicated than she had realized. She had heard of midwives but not of midhusbands. And suppose Paul Turner wouldn't help her?

"A man, er, well, the man sleeps with the woman, and after that she can have a child," Mrs. Cline answered, somewhat bewildered.

May felt frightened. There was something her mother was holding back, something terrible, some awful ordeal in store for her. "Doesn't he do anything but sleep?" she asked, trying to obtain some hint of her fate.

"Why, yes, but, well, that's what I'm trying to explain. The man does something that isn't nice, er, oh, you know what they tell about in dirty stories."

"But I never heard one about how a man helps a girl to have a baby," May replied.

Mrs. Cline was bewildered. Why had she started telling May these things? She wasn't old enough yet. May hadn't heard of dirty stories, and now she would have to tell her about them.

"Well, either at the beginning or the end of a dirty story the man and the girl lay down together," she began. "Perhaps you'll see what I mean better if I tell you one. A girl was undressing, and a burglar opened the window—"

"Yes, I've heard that one," said May when Mrs. Cline had finished. Her mother must just be trying to cheer her up and avoid telling what a man would have to do to her before she could get this baby out of her stomach. May's pains grew worse. She had been awakened by pains in the same region the night before, but then the baby had only been kicking her. Now it was biting, kicking, and scratching all at once.

"Now, when a man sleeps with a girl he does the same thing," Mrs. Cline continued. "And the girl has a baby just the same way."

"But the burglar didn't come back to help her," said May dubiously. She could not bear the thought of sleeping with a man now. She had heard of women dying in childbirth and was certain this final requisite her mother spoke of would kill her.

"Men are like that," said Mrs. Cline. "They like to run away from their babies and let the mothers bring 'em up. They don't come back and help once they get away. Your father was too lazy to run away, so—"

Mrs. Cline was interrupted. May needed assistance.

• • •

It was a girl. When Mrs. Cline held the baby in her hands she realized the limited scope of her knowledge. She had thought there was only one way to get a baby. Surely no man had ever done this to May. Until just now May had not known how men gave women babies. Her big stomach had been caused by food. Evidently a woman had to be careful of her diet as well as of men.

CHAPTER XXXVI

MISS HUMMER FINDS A ROPE

After the snow had gone Miss Hummer again abandoned her yard to the male coalition and its snake. The warm spring days were lovely weather for snakes, and she was not going to take any unnecessary chances of meeting Henrietta's emissary or any of its progeny.

She did, however, contrive an experiment to determine how active a watch the enemy was keeping in its encampment. It was a great risk and involved a maximum of bravery and courage. This might be just the opportunity the snake had been waiting for to slip through her defenses and twine itself around her. She did not even consider the poison fangs of the black rattler in her thoughts about it. The twisting body of the most harmless snake inspired her capacities for fear and horror to a maximum of effort.

Miss Hummer had to unbolt and open the kitchen door to try her scheme. She first tied a heavy rope securely and tightly about the waist and shoulders of Henrietta. She tied the other end to a leg of the stove, so that if she should lose her grip on it the rope would still be held fast within her fortification. Then she hastily opened the door, pushed Henrietta and a slack of rope through the opening, and slammed the door behind him.

This dangerous procedure having been accomplished, Miss Hummer clutched the rope and sat down at a window to watch Henrietta. He had been given a long enough leash to permit him to reach the woodshed. If the snake appeared she would yank him back into the kitchen before there was any chance for communication.

If the snake did not appear it might mean either that the enemy had given up the siege or was lying in ambush waiting for her to become a victim of the ruse. Miss Hummer did not think an ambush was likely, for the delay in seeing Henrietta had been so long that the snake would doubtless try to make use of this chance to deliver new messages.

Being outdoors was like visiting a new country for Henrietta. For nearly a year he had been confined in the Hummer fortress. He rose to his feet, made loud noises, gave his version of laughter, and tried to run. He was succeeding well in this latter attempt when he reached the end of the rope and was pulled to the ground. His laughter stopped, and Miss Hummer smiled.

For twenty minutes Henrietta played in the area granted by the rope. He looked at the sky and picked up many objects from the ground, but none of them was a snake. Miss Hummer was sure he was looking for the snake, yet his search might be a sham. The serpent could be hiding somewhere and whispering secret messages.

Or perhaps the snake did not recognize Henrietta with his rouged face. Miss Hummer had painted him every day and had had to obtain new supplies of cosmetics from the mail order house. Perhaps the male coalition had come to believe that Henrietta was a girl, or perhaps she had already succeeded in making him loathsome even to men.

Henrietta picked a toadstool and held it in his hand as though wondering whether or not to taste it. Miss Hummer smiled at the thought of what a complete and overwhelming victory for her it would be if her disguised prisoner ate this poison while the snake watched from its hiding place unaware that this depraved girl was the man it sought. But the snake might not be watching. And she could not let Henrietta escape. She wanted him in her power.

She unfastened the door and pulled the rope. Henrietta found himself being dragged along the ground on his back. His head struck the step outside the door. He coöperated with Miss Hummer in her efforts to drag him over this obstacle and was pulled into the kitchen on his stomach.

Henrietta got onto his hands and knees but did not stand up. If he had been allowed to walk through the door he would have dropped to this position before coming within range of Miss Hummer. She had him trained in this respect. He still crawled when in her presence.

Miss Hummer untied the rope from the stove but did not untie Henrietta. She liked having him on a leash like this. She could interrupt any move he started to make merely by tugging on the rope. She struck him light lashes with the loose end. She did not feel like whipping him just then. The rope would make a nice whip, though. She struck Henrietta a little harder. It might be better than the wood she had been using. Henrietta had been graduated to the second pile in the row of sticks. She swung the rope still harder, hard enough so that Henrietta cried. She stood up and struck him.

Miss Hummer became flushed. Her eyes became bright. She felt like whipping Henrietta now, and she had a whip to use that might prove the best thing yet. She sat down and lifted the child into her lap.

Miss Hummer forgot the heavy nature of the rope in her furor. She let it fall with hard slashes. She had not removed Henrietta's dress. A red splotch appeared through the fabric. It might be rouge, or it might be blood. A rope was best to use on this man in her power, much better than a stick. She would use the sticks for the stove. She swung the rope madly with an expression of wanton delight on her face.

The last lash came with a sigh from Miss Hummer. Then it was quiet. Henrietta had stopped crying. She noticed this when she started to put him back on the floor. She placed him on the table instead. She had a terrible thought of a long snake climbing a tree with its tail coiled in a noose around her neck. She untied the rope from Henrietta and wished she had let him eat the toadstool.

If this rope had caused his escape, the male coalition could obtain revenge by tying her to a similar leash in a slightly different manner.

Henrietta soon began to cry again. Miss Hummer was so pleased she unconsciously leaned forward with the intention of kissing him. But she checked herself abruptly. She had been on the verge of kissing a man! The horror of this realization replaced her previous fears.

She washed Henrietta's back and looked for bandage. For several days, at least, she would only be able to paint him. She would throw the rope away. The sticks were better after all.

CHAPTER XXXVII

MRS. WHITER MAKES SANDWICHES

What little spare time Minnie Muller now had she spent in front of the town hall waiting for her next lover. When she was available, the legitimate members of the new school at Lem Witherbee's knew she could be found there. During the evening—except on Saturday—this became a congregating spot for men of Menham. Minnie then waited behind the town hall, and in turn the men withdrew from and reentered the discussions at hand.

Lem Witherbee did not approve of this temperance group Minnie had organized. He feared that such teetotalism was having a bad effect on his whisky sales. If the men were not interested in Minnie they might form these gatherings in front of his drinking counter. This abstinence might even be extended to Saturday night.

Some of the men came in for a few drinks on the way home, but what were a few drinks in comparison to those of a whole evening? Lem had suggested that the men do their waiting at his store, but they seemed more interested in trying to be one of the first to reach the town hall.

Lem Witherbee was a member of the old school. Even if eligible, he would not have become an official member of the new school because of the temperance meetings it sponsored.

During the day Minnie did not have to pass much of the time alone either. She frequently brought her lunch. Farmers had discovered that a period of rest from their labors long enough to make a brief visit to the town hall was often beneficial. These rest periods were scattered throughout the day, so that there was seldom a gathering in front of the hall until after supper.

Minnie Muller was sure other women must be jealous of her body for which so many men had been built. The disparaging looks and vulgar remarks they provided for her benefit indicated a feeling of envy underneath. Most of their husbands did not match them properly. Minnie felt sorry for the women who walked past with their noses pointed toward the sky during her moments of leisure on the town hall steps. Perhaps no male counterpart had been made for them. At any rate, they hadn't been able to find him.

Mrs. Whiter did not try to disguise her envy of Minnie. She always left the door ajar while on sentry duty at the town hall, but none of Minnie's callers could be enticed. When she was able to be alone with Minnie, Mrs. Whiter was very friendly and usually sat down on the step beside her, cider glass in hand. Minnie had so many admirers that perhaps she could spare just one for her.

Often Mrs. Whiter was sitting on the step alone when a man came. But smiling, fawning, or flattering did no good. She could gain no more recognition from him than, "Howdy, Mrs. Whiter. Minnie been gone long?"

In the evening Mrs. Whiter became more aggressive. She would bring the men drinks of cider and invite them one at a time to come inside and have more. Those who went in indulged in nothing but the cider. She would pass out sandwiches she had made in the morning and tell jokes she had heard at the women's meetings. The men would eat and laugh and continue their discussion of the moment. If she lost her balance and fell the man nearest would help her to her feet, but his hands were removed as soon as this duty was performed.

Mrs. Whiter had tried taking a man's arm and suggesting, "Let's go for a walk." The man would only politely help her home and say, "Good night." Lem Witherbee was enraged by her giving glasses of cider to the men. He regarded such hospitality as deliberate robberies from his cash box.

Mrs. Muller did not hear much that was said about her daughter, but she had an active imagination that kept her abreast of all new accounts. She did not approve of Minnie's activities. Mrs. Muller did not like to have to do all the housework.

Whenever Mrs. Muller asked Minnie to do something that would call for much delay she was given a slip of paper bearing the words, "I'll do it Saturday night." Minnie kept many such messages written in advance. She only had to see Paul Turner on Saturday nights. He called on her after Mrs. Muller had gone to the town hall for the meeting.

Mrs. Muller had an intuitive resentment of Minnie's usurping her place at Lem Witherbee's. She felt that her daughter was depriving her of something else besides her companionship. Nothing in the house was missing. There was very little that would have been worth the bother of stealing. But Mrs. Muller sensed that something was gone.

She could only express her displeasure by repeating the warning, "If you go havin' a baby you'll have to take care of it yourself. I won't help. I brought up one baby, and that's enough."

Minnie would make no reply. Her mother would not have heard it anyway.

Sometimes Mrs. Muller would add, "And havin' a baby ain't no fun. The laborin' pains are fun compared with the work that comes after that. And we can't have two Mrs. Mullers in the family. You'll have to get a new name if you get a baby. You better stay home more."

Minnie did not take anything Mrs. Muller said very seriously. Her mother couldn't hear her own voice. Perhaps she thought she was saying something altogether different, or perhaps she didn't know she was talking.

CHAPTER XXXVIII

PROHIBITION: BIG BUSINESS FOR LOCKSMITHS

Prohibition came to Menham, as it did to other parts of the United States, with the passing of the eighteenth amendment. Lem Witherbee learned of the new law when a bulky policeman from Scofield calmly started to rob his store.

He helped himself to a bottle of whisky and a glass and sat down in front of the bar. He poured out drink after drink, ignoring Lem's indignant demands for remuneration. When Lem tried to wrest the bottle from him the officer pushed him away roughly with the reprimand, "What's a matter with you? *I*'m a cop! *I* got a gun!"

The policeman's desires were not confined to whisky.

"Open a can of them sardines, and gimme some crackers!" he demanded. "Hurry up! And put some more of them bottles here on the counter where I can reach 'em!"

Lem Witherbee would have run from the store to get someone to help overpower this burglar, but the officer placed a blackjack on the counter in an authoritative and threatening manner.

"Make it snappy!" he ordered. "And get me some cigars!" Lem did as he was told.

In a short time a billy and a revolver had been placed beside the black jack. All the bottles on the liquor shelf had been opened and put on the counter within reach of the policeman, also the only two boxes of cigars in the store. Every variety of prepared food available had been brought to the officer to be sampled. Cans, boxes, bottles and their contents were scattered about the counter and floor. Lem Witherbee stood at the policeman's side, can opener in hand, acting as waiter and hoping the bandit's eyes or thoughts would not light on the cash box. A command by the policeman accompanied by a glance at one of his three weapons would have obtained even this.

The thirst, appetite, and stomach capacity of the officer seemed unlimited. He kept several glasses lined up before him filled with beverages from different bottles. He munched food from cans and boxes with increasing ravenousness and gulped it down with several swallows from one of the glasses. Lem had been ordered to keep these filled. This guttling was only interrupted when the policeman paused to light a new cigar. The edge of the counter had a fringe of cigars that had been lit and left to smolder out.

Lem Witherbee could not help admiring this magician's ability to make such quantities of food and drink disappear inside him. The bandit had a stomach like a barrel, but he seemed to have eaten enough to fill it many times. Lem sadly reflected the amount the burglar's indulgences would have brought if he were paying for them. He had lost count in his mental arithmetic shortly after the man had demanded food.

The policeman got up once to stretch and yawn. He walked behind the counter and, by another feat of magic, casually produced the cash box from its hiding place.

"This all you got?" he growled, scowling as he put the money in his pocket.

The officer returned to his seat. The few steps he had taken had had the effect of a constitutional on his appetite. Later he started a brief conversation.

"How about some money?" he began. "I didn't come way out here for nothin'!"

"You've took all my money," answered Lem, starting to tremble.

"You got plenty more tucked away somewhere! What a you say, you gonna make me a proposition, or do I close this joint up?"

Lem had a surge of courage. "You should be payin' me. You're stealin' everything in the store."

The officer laughed. "Wise guy, huh! What kind of a racket do you think you're runnin', havin' a cop pay you? You'd oughta be on the stage!"

The dialogue ended there. The policeman's pride had been hurt. The inference that he should pay for things in the same manner as an ordinary person was a burning insult that he tried to quench with the contents of the glasses. He might have hesitated before accepting a bribe now had it been offered.

The officer had a large nose as well as a large stomach. The nose was red when he arrived. It grew redder as time passed. Having displayed this organ at a maximum of brilliance, he concealed his weapons about his person and spoke again.

"Get me an ax!" he demanded.

Lem Witherbee provided the ax, and the policeman went to work. He stood up with apparent difficulty and staggered about the store wielding the tool. He slashed the shelves and walls, producing avalanches of cans, bags, bottles, and hardware. He hacked the counters into a pile of broken wood and ruined merchandise. He chopped the floor; he chopped everything on the floor. Lem Witherbee kept out of his way.

He hewed flour and sugar barrels, bags of grain and mash into one thoroughly mixed heap. He broke the chairs and benches into small pieces. Cans were opened with carefully aimed blows of the ax, bottles broken, boxes strewn about the floor, or sent through the holes he had made in the floor. The stove pipe was dissected amid a shower of soot. The show case provided a shower of glass. The windows were broken, the door smashed through.

Nothing was left in its original position. The policeman swayed about through the ruins, swinging the ax at any articles of merchandise still intact. He came to what had been the drinking counter and put two bottles that had not been broken into his pockets. He chopped aimlessly at the rest of the pile there. Only a keg of nails had escaped destruction. The officer picked this up and dumped the nails onto the debris.

Lem Witherbee had been struck on the cheek by a piece of flying glass and was swabbing the wound with his handkerchief. The policeman interfered with this by putting one brace of a pair of handcuffs around his wrist and twisting it in a way that brought new wounds. Then the officer made use of his billy. He hit Lem across the forehead.

They walked out of the store, the policeman prodding Lem with the club and supporting himself with his other arm thrown around Lem's shoulders.

There were three counts against Lem Witherbee at the Scofield court: drunkenness, resisting an officer, and carrying concealed weapons. The policeman produced an ax in court which Lem, he said, had had concealed about his person.

"He was so drunk he was tryin' to find the trigger," the officer attested. Before reaching Scofield, he had finished the contents of the bottles brought from the store, so, for lack of evidence, he omitted the charge of keeping and exposing liquor for sale.

The judge interrupted Lem Witherbee's account of the wrecking of his store by advising, "Next time don't carry an ax." He complimented the policeman on his bravery in overcoming such a desperate drunkard. He ordered Lem to pay a heavy fine and placed him on probation.

Lem arrived back at Menham with a lock, a keg, and the announcement that whisky prices had gone up.

CHAPTER XXXIX

TIN CUPS AND A KNOT HOLE

It might have been easier to build a new store than to rebuild the old one, but Lem Witherbee set to work to restore the original. The memories, sentiments, and traditions based around this shrine and its drinking counter made moving, even to an adjoining site, something of a sacrilege.

The destruction of the drinking counter had been a serious tragedy. Only two whisky glasses were salvaged: Jonathan Sadler's tin cup, which was restored after much bending, and John Lyman's decorative shaving mug, which had a miraculous escape. Parts of most of the others were found. These were given to the owners, who kept them for pocket pieces.

The ruins were carefully examined by the farmers for all fragments. Each broken piece that was found had the effect on the man who claimed it of discovering some part of the body of one's most intimate friend who has been killed in an explosion.

Parts of the cups of dead members of the drinking fraternity were preserved by Lem Witherbee. They might still be able to carry messages to their owners. At any rate, they were all that remained of their most cherished possession. Pieces that could not be identified were also saved by Lem. Perhaps they could make themselves known on a Saturday night.

Alfred Dole still had the companionship of the cider cup in his barn, but the others were left with only a few bits of glassware for solace. The first Saturday night after the raid was a sad evening. The men all brought tin cups. These receptacles were strangers. There was nothing in common to discuss, no unsettled problems to reconsider, no mutual secret intimacies over which to ponder. The new cups might not prove to be friends. They had each selected an outsider at random in the hope that he could fill the role of a cherished friend.

The men drank and stared in silence. The keg of whisky Lem had brought back from Scofield was not the same as before, or perhaps it was being contaminated by the new cups. The store was different. A new drinking counter had been built and new chairs and benches provided. These things were strangers, too.

They had a cold indifference to what was going on. The men shifted in their seats. They could not get into their favorite Saturday night positions. Customary objects on which they fixed their gaze were gone.

The front part of the store was still a mass of debris. The men tried not to look at this, but even the broken stove pipe in the rear told of the horrible manner in which the whisky glasses and their surroundings had been demolished. The usual topics of conversation were ignored. The tin cups knew nothing of these subjects and could furnish no inspirations for reviving them.

John Lyman and Jonathan Sadler were affected by the melancholy atmosphere. Their cups had had a narrow escape and had not yet recovered from the shock. Later in the evening other men produced pieces of their broken whisky glasses and brief monologues ensued. Most of the bits could still communicate with their owners. The men dipped the pieces in their whisky. Some of them placed a piece of the glass in their tin cups.

Lem Witherbee had barricaded the door and windows of the store with heavy boards. No more policemen or other strangers would be admitted. The door was kept locked from the inside. Customers all had to be identified through a knot hole before they could have entrance.

"There's a law now that we have to drink with the door locked," Lem explained.

The women's drinking quarters in the town hall were similarly secured. The padlock on the outside of the door was snapped into fittings inside when members were there. Mr. and Mrs. Dole placed locks on all doors of their barn. All strangers were shunned. Every one in Menham would have fastened every lock and bolt on his property if a policeman were reported in the vicinity.

The attitude of the farmers toward their new cups became less reserved as subsequent Saturday nights and intermediate visits developed their acquaintance. The cups showed themselves to be friendly and talkative and quick to catch on to the ways of their predecessors. They possessed an intuitive knowledge of the subject matter of topics discussed by the group and of secrets revealed only to the lost glasses. Probably the pieces of glass that had been introduced to them had passed on much of this information.

It became a common practice to drink with one of these pieces in the cup. In this way a man had two drinking companions when alone.

The friendship of the old glasses when they were intact was not forgotten. The new containers did their best, but whisky did not taste the same from them and became worse as time went on. It was contended that having a piece from the old glass in the cup improved the flavor, but no-one argued that it brought the taste back entirely. But the effect was the same. They should probably be thankful that only the taste had been lost.

John Lyman and Jonathan Sadler could not understand why their cups did not produce the old flavor. They must have sustained some permanent injury when the store was wrecked.

One Saturday night Lem Witherbee brought out the box of unclaimed bits of glass. These were passed among the men and exchanged for trial conversations until all were positively identified. The next day some of the farmers noticed that the new pieces did not match the texture of the others in their pockets. This was attributed to the abstinence from whisky while kept in the box. This discovery provided an excellent reason for coming to the store at once, and an informal group gathered to soak new pieces of glass in tin cups of whisky.

New supplies of groceries and other products were delivered to the store. Those who came to purchase these things were admitted in the same way as those who came for whisky. Lem looked at them through the knot hole and then unlocked the door.

One day Miss Hummer came to buy some sugar. When Lem Witherbee looked through the knot hole he drew away in pain. She had stuck her finger in his eye. Lem feared another fat policeman was outside. He made no sound. Miss Hummer identified herself by shouting, and Lem unlocked the door with great relief. After she had gone he fitted a piece of window glass into the hole.

CHAPTER XL

PETER AND HIS BAND

Peter Brush had not come to Menham for eleven years. The six women in the six houses on the Westham road that used to be his first stops remembered him best. They all had young sons, and all were named Peter. The boys were of the same age and were often confused by their parents.

This addition to the population of Menham had come in a manner that made parturition seem like a contagious disease. Mrs. Jones gave birth to the first Peter. Before this baby had been properly discussed, Mrs. Sadler was taken ill and produced another one. Then, with intervals of but a few days, came Peter Lyman, Peter Dean, Peter Pike, and Peter Hatch.

Other women became worried. Babies were not usually born in such rapid succession. One a year was a high average for Menham. Was this some plague that brought sudden pregnancy? Some new germ perhaps had settled in Menham, capable of giving babies in a few hours. Women went to bed with the fear that they might be awakened by the pains of childbirth. Miss Hummer slept with all her clothes on.

Men were frightened, too. Perhaps the germ could impregnate them. It would be hard for a man to live down the reputation he would obtain upon giving birth to a child. But, after the sixth Peter, the mysterious germ became inactive, and the baby scare died out.

After the babies became boys they were usually together. They ran about the town and its environs, quite often with somebody chasing them. They preferred running to walking. Their energy was inexhaustible. They liked to break fences and windows.

They flew about Menham like so many birds, running, hiding, reappearing, disappearing. Fields, roads, and woods all offered them equally suitable routes. They were always going somewhere, trying to be many places at the same time. A call of, "Peter," anywhere in the town would bring forth from one to six of them as though by magic.

"One of the Peters done it," was the explanation for all damaged property. No-one of the six could ever be singled out as the guilty party.

Anything unusual that happened outdoors in Menham was attended by them. Private scenes in hidden places were their especial delight. With intuitive knowledge of the exact time to be there, they would be hidden in waiting at such spots, and running would be postponed.

When two events worthy of their audience were scheduled for the same time at different places, the Peters divided into two groups and compared notes after the performances. They could have added interesting facts and details to Menham gossip, but they did not divulge their secret knowledge to others. In this way they were able to get pieces of cake and pennies for candy by making subtle hints to certain housewives.

The boys had no secret knowledge about Mrs. Whiter, but they paid her flying visits both at the town hall and her home. She kept pies and candy ready for them. Others did not welcome their calls or even the sight of their approach. They felt more at ease when the sextet was running past their property than when it was approaching.

"So long as they keep on runnin' it's all right, but when they stop, you can never tell what they'll be up to," said David Hume. "They'll all be highway robbers as soon as they get a little bigger."

"Or else detectives," replied Alfred Dole. "I expect to find 'em all hidin' under my bed some night."

Mary Cline was about the same age as the boys. They stopped at her house sometimes, but only to get the cake her mother, May, provided. They would say, "Yes," and, "No," to Mary's remarks but refrained from more intimate comments. They ran away again before she could say much.

The Peters talked about Mary when alone. Each insisted she was to be his mistress and that he would desert the band as soon as this had been arranged. Before stopping at the Cline farm each maintained that he would stay there this time and court Mary. But there were always six runners when they left.

Mary wished the boys would come to see her instead of her mother, or that they would call some time when her mother was not home. They always stayed away when May was not there.

Running past the Cline farm on an occasion when they did not stop, the six boys saw Mary waving to them. Each insisted it was he she was waving to, and each contemplated stopping to further his suit with her. But none waved back, and they all kept on running.

"That was a signal for me to meet her tonight," said Peter Pike.

"It was a signal for me to see her right now," claimed Peter Hatch, "but I'd rather go where we're goin' and see her ma."

CHAPTER XLI

MISS HUMMER WINS THE WAR

Henrietta H. H. Hummer had become tall and very thin, with a scowling countenance, a distorted mouth, and a pronounced limp. He was still a girl to Menham residents, a harmless eccentric girl whom everybody looked at but whose companionship everyone avoided.

John Lyman expressed the attitude of the men toward Henrietta, "Seems good to have a girl idiot for a change. Now the women can't tell us only men can be that way."

Arthur Moore had an additional comment, "Women are all idiots anyway."

Henrietta wore long dresses. His hair was long, too, and covered his shoulders in a mass of snarls. He carried a pocket mirror in his hand and every few minutes made use of this in rubbing more rouge or eyebrow pencil on his face.

He applied these colors abundantly and in peculiar patterns. Sometimes the black would predominate: black circles around his eyes, a black forehead, black nose, black lips and chin, and black cheeks with trimmings of red. Other times the red would be substituted with black trimmings. And sometimes the two colors would be used in more equal amounts, one black cheek, one red, a black nose, red forehead, black chin, red eyebrows, one red lip and a black one.

Henrietta carried a powder puff and perfume atomizer which he used both on himself and others. He liked to come up quietly behind a woman and spray her neck with perfume. He daubed the powder puff on men when they were within reach. Bystanders would coöperate with Henrietta in holding a victim's attention while he stole up from the rear. All of which caused amusement for Menham.

Miss Hummer delighted in letting Henrietta walk about Menham, using his vile cosmetics wherever he happened to be and with no more concern than though he were alone. No evidence of bodily corruption could be more vulgar and convincing than this. Although too young to be a whore, he was already a street walker unable to find customers.

Henrietta was exhibiting Miss Hummer's victory in the war with the male conspiracy. She had not only eluded the snares of men to seduce and corrupt her, but she had turned one of their sex into a depraved woman. Men still thought Henrietta was a girl, and every one shunned him except for purposes of ridicule.

Henrietta played his part well, contaminating other men with powder. Such immoral advances alone were full proof of his female sex. And the filthy powder he put on men was a stigma that added to their repulsiveness. Miss Hummer was not so heartily in favor of Henrietta's perfuming of women. This might arouse suspicion. Still, she did not like these women, and his attacks with foul perfume offered satisfying revenge for her to chuckle over.

As soon as he entered Miss Hummer's house Henrietta dropped to his hands and knees. If he met her when out walking he did likewise. He crawled with the aptitude of an animal that uses all four legs as such. Miss Hummer kept him fastened to a leg of the stove on a leash when he was indoors. She had a fear of this man in dresses despite his trained submission to her. She was the victor in the war with men, but there might be a revolution. Henrietta might discover his real sex and turn on her with the lust that this information would bring.

In her victory over the male coalition Miss Hummer had retaken her yard from the enemy. There had been no further evidence of a snake. The hostile forces had been completely outwitted. Her piles of sticks had been reduced to three: large clubs for use in emergency, a smaller size to correspond with Henrietta's next indication of growth, and the size now employed.

Henrietta responded to his whippings with loud wails. He made no opposition, accepting the blows as part of the scheme of life. Miss Hummer could no longer take him in her lap. She stood above him, while he remained motionless on his hands and knees. His moans could be heard at other farms but were accepted as another of Henrietta's peculiarities. Probably he was calling for food.

Henrietta's interest in the English language had stopped with the learning of the word "slut". He knew a few other words, but he said, "Slut," with a pride of accomplishment. People still acknowledged him when he said this. It was a word that attracted attention to him and brought responses from others. It was evidently a universal greeting of some sort.

Men laughed in reply when he greeted them with this conception of, "How do you do." Women spoke back or lifted their heads. These were their ways of saying, "Howdy," in answer.

There was one woman citizen of Menham who did not pretend to resent Henrietta's favorite word. Mrs. Whiter laughed in an embarrassed way and acted as though he had paid her an undeserved compliment when he greeted her with it.

Miss Hummer did not enjoy the reputation Henrietta's greeting had given her. She had to take the blame for his vocabulary. Tradition maintained that Henrietta knew other words of this sort. Miss Hummer thought that perhaps he did have this knowledge and was afraid to use the other words in her presence. She was blamed for something she had nothing to do with. It was not her fault if men were born with minds full of obscenity and profanity. But she could not escape the disgrace Henrietta caused her without making his male sex known. At any rate, in his garb of a woman he was bringing still more disgrace upon himself by using these words people accused him of.

Henrietta mumbled to himself and others in a language of his own that was translated to suit the theory of the listener.

His monologues to inanimate objects no longer worried Miss Hummer. If his utterings were understood, they were also ineffective. If he was trying to enlist other powers for assistance in an uprising against her, he was having poor success.

A tree out of sight of Miss Hummer's house was Henrietta's most intimate companion. He liked to stop there when he went for a walk. He talked to the tree and made red and black marks on its bark. The tree rustled its branches in friendly response. On a windy day when the tree was especially talkative Henrietta would sit down there and go no further.

Sitting there silently one day listening to the tree, he was greeted by a black snake that crawled from behind the trunk. It was a harmless milk adder, and not a rattler, but it recalled a pleasant sensation to Henrietta's mind. Here was another friend.

The snake had not noticed Henrietta, who put a hand around its body when it came within reach. He drew the snake into his lap, accepting its wigglings and writhings as a form of friendly embrace. He stroked the serpent gently and mumbled to it. The adder seemed to understand Henrietta's words of affection mingled with the swishing introduction made by the tree. It ceased its resistance and crawled over his lap and body. Henrietta laughed happily.

Arthur Moore happened to walk by just then. He saw the adder and seized it from Henrietta's grasp. This would be a tasty bit for his rattlers. He forced the snake into a small bag he used to carry such foods that he happened upon and went his way.

Henrietta looked at the tree, but it could do nothing to rescue the snake. Its branches only produced a dreary dirge that told Henrietta, "We were lucky that he didn't take one of us instead."

CHAPTER XLII

BABIES

From all outward appearances, the initiation of members into the cider-drinking sorority consisted of giving birth to a child. This organization had enrolled three new members since its inception: May Cline, Alice Goode, and Minnie Muller. Each had had a baby daughter before attending her first meeting.

Mrs. Cline's explanation of the dietetic cause of her daughter's child was amusing but not convincing to others. May Cline offered no further explanation and insisted her mother's theorem was right. The theories that had resulted as to possible fathers amused Mrs. Cline, for she was sure May could never have been a party to the usual practice for begetting children. They amused May because Paul Turner was not even mentioned.

Mrs. Emma Goode had no unusual theories about her daughter Alice's baby. Arthur Moore had been guilty of an atrocious pun in convincing her he was only showing a fatherly interest in Alice. To have a pregnant daughter as evidence of the unfaithfulness of the man she thought was her private lover had been a displeasing revelation for Mrs. Goode. She had hoped Felix Dole was the party responsible, but Alice confided in her that Arthur Moore was the only man involved.

With intuitive foresight, Moore remained away from the Goode farm after this confession, and the two women were left without a lover. Alice named the child Blanche, and gossip took its course.

Minnie Muller's baby had been a long-prophesied event. When it finally showed evidence Menham women breathed sighs of relief. This girl who had captivated their husbands was not to escape the discomforts of childbearing. Only two did not approve of this: Mrs. Nancy Muller and her daughter Minnie.

Mrs. Muller had insisted that Minnie change her name, but Minnie did not see how this would help matters. The outcome was that Mrs. Muller called her daughter Mrs. Black, while everyone else in Menham called her Minnie Muller. The baby was named Elsie.

Minnie did not return to her standing appointment at the town hall for several months following the birth of the child. The baby required too constant attention to permit her to spend much time away from home, even though so many lovers had been built to match her body. These men called at her house on occasion and took her for short walks despite interference by Mrs. Muller, who always insisted, "Mrs. Black is busy."

Minnie Muller's maternity had been a crowning achievement for the new school of expression at Lem Witherbee's store. Until then the old school had had the strong point in its favor of having created this girl who refused to be made fertile by the attentions of the new school. The baby brought out the fallacy in the charges of impotency that until then had been directed against the new school members.

The long-awaited discussions as to whom the child would most resemble began on the Saturday night following the birth. All new school members came in for a full share of alleged paternity, this despite the fact that none of the men had seen the baby. The old school provided a counterdiscourse, using the conventional topic of whom their child Minnie looked most like.

The elated new school outnumbered the others and was not distracted by their conflicting theme. This new subject was to be a definite part of Saturday night discussions from now on. Arthur Moore found himself in glory when both groups in turn discussed his resemblance to the children in question.

Felix Dole had become a member of the drinking fraternity but not of the new school. He had never been able to get up sufficient courage to more than say, "Howdy," to Minnie Muller, much as he would like to have done more. This fact was overlooked by his drinking companions, who read his features into those of the baby with the same careful analysis given the legitimate members.

This both irritated and pleased Felix. He did not like to accept credit he did not deserve, but the charge of parentage showed that the other men at least thought he was capable of fatherhood. Felix had never waited in line for Minnie's attentions, but the other men insisted she had been seeing him at other times.

Minnie Muller's baby had not been of particular concern to Felix, but he had been annoyed by Alice Goode's offspring. Until its delivery he had thought Alice was his girl, despite their lack of intimacy. Then one night he called for her and was greeted by the roar of a howling baby.

"Yes, it's mine," Alice told him. "It almost drove me crazy while it was inside, and now that it's out it's starting right in where it left off."

Felix continued to visit Alice Goode, but his courage was not increased by her proof of lost virginity. He took no steps toward instigating another baby, for which she was both glad and sorry. She did not want another baby. Arthur Moore turned his attentions to May Cline, and Paul Turner continued to call on Minnie Muller. The babies grew into childhood with Blanche Goode and Elsie Muller a little younger and Mary Cline a little older than the six Peters.

CHAPTER XLIII

ARTHUR MOORE DIAGNOSES HIS DAUGHTER

The affair that developed between Arthur Moore and May Cline was merely another expression of a biological necessity as far as he was concerned.

He enjoyed his walks with her but would have preferred to be able to forego these pleasures. Women were the only laxative for a third form of bodily poison of which his system had to be cleaned. Affection was as far removed from the relation as from relations with his privy. Being forced to depend on women for this former function was a degradation to the male sex in Arthur Moore's opinion. The female sex could not be degraded any further, he thought.

Women held men in their power through providing living latrines whose friendship men must cultivate as a necessity to health and comfort. Moore's contempt for women increased as he approached sterility. He looked forward to this state. When his body became capable of living happily without recourse to women he could act differently toward them. He could let them know that his memories of their sex were not among his pleasantest.

Babies, even his own, as offsprings of women were also held in low esteem by Moore. True, he had been born himself, but the event was something over which he had no control. It was not a state he had accepted voluntarily, and he was within his rights in being contemptuous of it. Whenever he saw a baby he thought of his snakes. Some day he would like to include a newly born baby with the toads, frogs, and other reptiles he fed them.

May Cline attributed Arthur Moore's silence in her presence to bashfulness. A man can be bashful with words, she thought, while at the same time very aggressive in conduct. She was pleased by his bashfulness and equally glad that it did not extend beyond the use of words. Paul Turner had lacked this fear of words and ridiculed the fact that he was the father of her child. She thought Arthur Moore would marry her in case of another baby.

Moore called on May at unannounced times, just as he had on the Goodes. During the child's babyhood he was often irritated by having to wait until she finished tending to it. Then he would lead the way to a stretch of woods near her house. May would talk about Mary's latest feats, and Moore would wish women were born without tongues.

Mrs. Susan Cline was not in favor of these walks, but she tolerated them as daytime substitutes for May's former somnambulations. Mrs. Cline no longer had to lead the way downstairs for the sleepwalker and was pleased at this change in events.

Her daughter assured her that she and Arthur only picked flowers on their walks together, and May always brought back a bouquet as proof. In the winter, she explained, she helped Moore with his housework. Her mother could not understand this, for the household tasks at the Cline farm were numerous enough without deliberately going out to find more.

Mrs. Goode, on the contrary, assumed that her daughter Alice was enjoying herself with Felix Dole. She felt a distinct resentment toward Alice for having frightened Arthur Moore away with her baby. If Alice had stuck to Felix, Mrs. Goode probably still would have had Arthur Moore. She felt that the just thing for Alice to do would be to share Felix with her as Moore had been shared, but Alice evidently did not think so.

Arthur Moore avoided Blanche Goode as well as her mother and grandmother. One day Blanche surprised him by appearing at May Cline's when he called. She was playing with Mary.

"H'lo," she said. "My ma tells me you're my father."

"Your ma's a liar," Moore replied angrily. The depths to which a woman could go to slander a man were bottomless. Why had Alice told this child who her father was? Arthur restrained himself from slapping Blanche's face.

"My ma ain't no liar," Blanche responded, "but she said you'd be a liar if you tried to say you weren't my father." Moore slapped her face. "Call me a liar, will you?" he challenged.

"Well, she ought to know who my father is," Blanche sobbed.

"She don't seem to. You tell your ma she's crazy."

May Cline appeared on the scene at this point, and Moore led the way toward the woods. He broke his usual silence after they had gone a short distance.

"I think that girl of Alice Goode's is loony," he said.

CHAPTER XLIV

MRS. WHITER POURS

After Prohibition had brought its poorer grade of liquor for the men, Menham women conceived a new type of fair, much to the chagrin of Lem Witherbee. It was decided to raise money for more kegs and locks by selling cider one evening. The men arrived at the town hall in a body on the night set—all except the storekeeper. He could not be a sponsor of such rapacious rivalry.

This was the first drinking the two groups had done together. Mrs. Whiter was much pleased by the response of the men to the occasion. She made a valiant effort to do all the serving and was so concerned with the well-being of the men that she usually forgot to collect any money.

Arthur Moore did not enjoy the presence of the Goodes, but he did enjoy the cider. May Cline kept one glass filled for him and Mrs. Whiter another. He soon became acquainted with both receptacles, as did the other men with their strange drinking glasses.

Infused with community spirit, Mr. and Mrs. Dole had deserted the cider kegs in their barn for the evening to join the others in patronizing this worthy cause of the ladies' drinking sorority. Alfred Dole was ready for conversation when he arrived. The other men could only furnish an audience until Mrs. Whiter had accomplished the miracle of turning their glasses into informers.

Alfred Dole had brought his own glass, having been in the midst of a very interesting conversation when he left his barn. He continued the discussion and sipped a last drink of his own stock on the way to the town hall, arriving in time to have the glass refilled before it was empty.

"There's nothin' will annoy my glass so much as to get empty when we're talkin'," he told Mrs. Whiter. "It's likely to shut up like a cup of tea if I don't keep it filled."

"You needn't worry about its gettin' empty while I'm around," she replied. "I'll keep it talkin' so much you won't be able to get a word in."

David Hume had accompanied his mother to the drinking place, and, in gentlemanly manner, carried her broom for her. Mrs. Sarah Hume had adopted this household comrade as her drinking companion and always took it with her to the town hall. David's belief that she used this device for flying about the countryside in her capacity of a witch had been communicated to others during alcoholic intimacies and come to be an accepted fact.

As long as he carried the broom, Hume believed his mother would be unable to use it to get into the sky and frighten him. He realized that the broom might take him into the air instead as he walked along with it, but this did not terrify him so much as the thought of seeing his mother dash into the air and swoop down on him from overhead. When exercising herself in this manner of witches she would probably forget that he was her son.

Mrs. Hume smoked her pipe and talked to the broom when she drank, just as she did at home. She often listened to others but had very little to say to them in reply. The broom served as a support as well as a companion for the homeward trek. She would have preferred to have the broom carry her through the air to her bed, but she had not yet learned of this power with which she was credited.

Most of the conventional drinking topics of the men had to be considerably abridged because of the presence of the women. Women found the presence of the men a similar handicap. Miss Hummer and Lem Witherbee, the only absentees, furnished the only subjects that could be discussed safely. Conversations started around such abstract questions as the weather.

Jonathan Sadler introduced the equally familiar theme of Miss Hummer and daughter. He started in a customary manner, "I saw Henrietta Hummer this afternoon, and she called me a—" He stopped in confusion, recalling the presence of the ladies.

Both drinking sects had enlarged their own vocabularies of profane adjectives and exclamations in thinking up new expressions with which to quote Henrietta, but to compare notes was embarrassing.

"I know," said Mrs. Cline, "she's called me that, too. Isn't it awful the things that child says?"

Sadler wondered which quotation he would have made if he had continued his remark.

"All she can say is swear words," said Mrs. Jones. "I've never heard her say anything else. We'll have to admit Miss Hummer is original, only teachin' her child words like that."

"Miss Hummer knows a lot more than we used to give her credit for," commented Andrew Cline. "She must of been quite a girl in her day."

This censorship of the subject was not satisfying. The Hummer discourse was ordinarily a battle of wits to see who could think up the most impressive invectives.

Arthur Moore was about to take May Cline for a short walk, but he reconsidered. This would be even less advisable than making use of her right here in the hall before all the gathering. His absence would give the others a chance to name him definitely as the father of Miss Hummer's child and Mary Cline, and to think of him as the father of the six Peters, Blanche Goode, and even Elsie Muller. There were other things, too, they might talk about regarding him. Moore crossed his legs and shifted in his chair.

A mouse ran across the floor. Mrs. Sadler and Arthur Moore both rushed after it from force of habit. With practiced agility, Moore pinned the animal into a corner with his foot and reached down to pick it up.

"Give it to me!" cried Mrs. Sadler. "That's my great-great-grandmother. Don't hurt her!"

Mrs. Sadler's theory of reincarnation was well known, and the laughter was not as loud as might be supposed.

"You mean great-great-grandfather, don't you?" asked Moore, examining the mouse.

"Perhaps," admitted Mrs. Sadler. "They tell me he used to like cider. Anyway, let me have it."

Moore could think of no reason to give why he should want a mouse, so he handed it to Mrs. Sadler regretfully. This would have been a nice appetizer for one of his snakes.

"That reminds me, I've got half a dozen mice home that I've been saving for you," said Mrs. Pike.

"That's fine. I'll take this one home now and stop for the others when I go by your house." Mrs. Sadler left with her ancestor.

Conversation became less reserved as the evening continued, but did not reach its customary standard. Nobody acknowledged Mrs. Whiter's repeated suggestions that the two groups meet in this manner each week, nor did any of the men mean it when they agreed to accept her invitation to call.

CHAPTER XLV

PROLIFIC PETER

The six Peters started their day's running. Peter Sadler ran from his empty breakfast dishes to the house of Peter Jones, who raced him to Peter Dean's residence. There the band was augmented by the arrival in a sprint of Peters Lyman, Hatch, and Pike. The six boys disappeared in a clump of trees bordering the road.

They appeared at the Goode farm suddenly and silently as though out of thin air. They dashed into the barn and disappeared to watch for Blanche Goode's appearance. Blanche was a second favorite of each Peter for his mistress in the event that he did not succeed with Mary Cline. Individual courtships were always put off until the next day, but the band as a group kept in close touch with these girls as well as Elsie Muller, each boy's third choice.

Blanche came out to the barn with swill for the pig, timing her arrival to correspond accurately with the hiding of the Peters. She had never tested the boys to see how long they would wait for her entrance in the morning. She emptied the orts and looked about her. The guests remained quiet and hidden, but Blanche was fully aware that she was being carefully studied by them.

She sat down on the grain box, smiled, and made faces. She liked to have the Peters call on her but would have preferred having them come out and play. She swung her legs so that her heels struck the grain box with loud bangs. There were bangs of greeting from various parts of the barn in response, and six running boys raced past her out of the door.

"Hello, Peter," shouted Blanche, as though surprised by their presence.

There was no reply. The runners soon disappeared again behind trees, and Blanche returned to the house with her swill bucket. Some day she hoped one or more of the Peters would stay behind with her after this morning visit.

Henrietta Hummer was the next host. Each boy hoped he would not have to select her for his mistress, but each believed that she would be the only choice for one of them, and that two of them would be left without girls when mistresses were finally apportioned. They had not yet discovered any flaws in the theory of monogamy.

The Peters watched Henrietta go from the house to the woodshed to bring in an armful of sticks. When he had loaded his arms to their capacity, Henrietta suddenly found six monsters surrounding him and uttering appropriate yells. They liked the way Henrietta dropped the wood and ran in fright each morning. He did not run toward the house, and they chased him for a short distance to hear his weird cries of alarm.

Miss Hummer enjoyed this part of the Peters' daily program. She saw to it that Henrietta went to the woodshed at the proper time each morning and watched from the window as he ran screaming in terror across the Hume meadow. Henrietta's scare was especially pleasing to her since it was caused by men. These six Peters thought they were tormenting a girl, not one of their own sex.

The boys raced back to the Dole farm. Locks on the barn prevented their running inside as had been their habit before prohibition. But they stopped long enough to look through knot holes and cracks to make sure Mr. and Mrs. Dole were starting their day's cider menu. Felix and Mary Dole now carried on all the work at the farm, but their activities did not often interest the Peters.

They galloped to Mrs. Whiter's abode, where she was waiting to give them their first cake of the day. They hurried away, cake in hand, for two figures were walking toward the deserted Goodwin farm. The boys were in their hiding places when David Hume and Minnie Muller arrived.

They ate their cake and took mental notes on the proper way to handle a mistress. The Peters were calling on Elsie Muller when Minnie arrived home. Elsie was playing with a doll in her yard, and the boys were watching her from the barn. They ran from their hiding places and were given an apple pie by Minnie. Elsie would have liked a piece of the pie, too, but she realized any suggestion she made that they cut it in seven pieces would be ignored. The boys hastened away as though they had been unaware of her existence.

They stopped next to listen to Mrs. Sarah Hume talk to her broom. They had long intended to spend a whole day there to see her take to the air on this vehicle, but there had always been too much else to do for this to be accomplished. Mrs. Hume was calling the broom Jack and insisting she did not like it and that it might just as well stop making advances to her. Then she called it by a different name in a different tone and asked why it had stayed away so long.

The Peters raced on past the town hall and store to Arthur Moore's farm. He appeared from behind the barn and chased them, rehearsing expressions with which he would quote Henrietta Hummer on the next Saturday night. They laughed and tipped over a wheelbarrow full of apples as they shot past.

Mary Cline was waiting at the next farm and sighted them before they could go into hiding.

"Hello," she said, "want to play tag?" Mary hoped that some day one of them would answer, "Yes." Each Peter was sure that the next time they came there he would say, "Yes." There was no reply today. The boys ran to the back door, took the cookies May Cline had for them, and disappeared.

This cursory review of Menham and the four girls it was providing to be their mistresses having been accomplished, the six Peters sprinted back to their own end of the town. The intuitive mechanisms that told them when to be at certain places were informing them that something was worthy of their attention. They dashed past their six houses and continued along the Westham road.

They saw a strange man walking toward them with a pack on his back and went into hiding. The man stopped opposite the hiding places. He hesitated a moment and then removed his pack and sat down on it. He appeared nervous rather than tired. Letters on the bag spelled "Peter Brush."

Strangers always interested the Peters. They watched this one intently. Since he did nothing except stand up and sit down again several times, they came out of their hiding places to see him closer to. Peter Brush shuddered at the sight of these six boys. They were in the pattern of a mental picture that had been troubling him.

"Hello," he said. "What are your names?"

"Peter," answered one of them.

Peter Brush shuddered again. "And the rest of you?" he asked.

"We're all Peter," he was told.

The peddler felt weak and white. "Have your mothers all got cow's head weather vanes on their barns?" he asked.

"Yes," they answered in unison. "How did you know?"

"I guess I'm on the wrong road," said Peter Brush. He picked up his pack and walked with a rapid stride back toward Westham. The six other Peters followed him for nearly a mile, much to his embarrassment.

CHAPTER XLVI

OMNIPOTENCE

Henrietta Hummer did not know what suicide was. Otherwise he might have investigated its merits. Or he might not have. Life is a peculiar property with qualities of an expert salesman. It thrusts itself upon us and convinces us to keep it even when we might be far better off without it. Perhaps our ego is horrified by the thought of nonentity.

Henrietta had few thoughts of the future. He had few thoughts of any kind except those based around a fear of a woman who struck him with a piece of kindling wood and smiled. She was the goddess of Henrietta's universe. Resistance would be dangerous heresy. The pains of life cannot be eliminated. His fear of Miss Hummer was a terror of life, this state in which he was a captive of a body that was a captive of this goddess.

To walk about Menham alone was considered a great privilege and pleasure by Henrietta. He might have tried to escape from Miss Hummer during one of these periods of freedom, but he regarded her powers as omnipotent. He believed she could see him wherever he was and that he was just as much in her power whether or not he could see her. He stayed away as long as he dared but always ended his walks at her residence.

Henrietta began his walks by running until out of sight of Miss Hummer's house. Even though she had just as much control over him then, he felt more secure if he could not see her. The invisible powers of his goddess had been proven in Miss Hummer's absence by body pains such as stomach, ear, and teeth aches. Henrietta accepted these as the blows of a club she wielded that he could not see. All pain was caused by Miss Hummer.

Henrietta did not stop after leaving Miss Hummer's house behind until he came to his friend the tree. His back and buttocks were sore on this occasion and his limp more pronounced than usual. He mumbled to the tree and put more paint on his face. Cosmetics had been his principal toys. They furnished a diversion for which he was grateful to Miss Hummer.

"Put some black on your forehead and chin," the swishing of the tree's branches told him.

"All right," Henrietta's jargon told the tree.

"You're lucky to have nice paint like that," said the tree, "and to be able to use it. Even if I had any paint I couldn't put it on me."

"You can have some of mine," offered Henrietta, "and I'll put it on you." He rubbed rouge and lipstick on the bark.

"Thank you," said the tree. "I wish I could go for a walk with you now, but I can't move from here."

"That's too bad," replied Henrietta. "But, then, you don't have to be whipped every day like I do. I'd like to change places with you."

"Too bad that woman who rules us couldn't change places with me," suggested the tree.

Henrietta powdered the tree and squirted perfume on it from his atomizer. He continued on his way, promising to visit the tree again when he returned. A short distance down the road he met Mrs. Anna Lyman, who was coming home from the store.

"Slut," said Henrietta, using his most friendly tone.

"Bastard!" replied Mrs. Lyman, turning her head away.

Henrietta laughed happily. This woman had spoken to him. He ran toward her, squeezing the bulb of his atomizer. Mrs. Lyman pushed him away roughly.

Further on he met Elsie Muller playing in the road.

"Hello," she said.

"Slut," responded Henrietta. He squeezed perfume on her, and Elsie laughed. He would have put paint on her face, too, but Minnie Muller sighted him and called her daughter.

"Get away from here," she told Henrietta.

"Slut," said Henrietta cheerfully.

At Lem Witherbee's store Henrietta sat down on the steps. He could spend the afternoon here among friendly people. They would speak and shout to him. He would speak to them and show his friendliness by letting them share his perfume and powder.

He heard sounds of chopping in the distance. Miss Hummer was probably beating someone else.

Mary Cline came to the store on an errand. Henrietta asked her to sit down with him, but she thought he was trying to frighten her by making funny noises.

"You can't scare me," she said, but she hurried to the door without stopping to let Henrietta make further attempts. Lem Witherbee opened the door after examining her through the glazed knot hole.

Mary left by the back door. Henrietta watched her walk down the road. He would like to have played with her. He felt a very pleasant sensation and wondered if she would hit him if he should follow her. He wished he could paint her face, paint her bare legs, paint her whole body from head to foot. He would like to have had her paint him. He wished they could both be alone and naked, painting red and black designs on each other.

"Slut," he muttered, meaning the term as one of endearment. Henrietta remained seated. Mary had too long a head start now for him to overtake her conveniently.

Other people came and went. They listened to what Henrietta had to say to them. The men laughed. The women walked away with pretended indignation. They believed their translations of his mumblings, which they would quote with additions on Saturday night, were correct.

Late in the afternoon Henrietta applied more rouge to his cheeks and started back toward Miss Hummer's house. He would stop and see the tree again on the way. He looked for its branches in the distance. They did not appear at the usual place.

When he neared the home of the tree he saw a dazzling white stump where his friend had stood. The tree lay on the ground. David Hume had cut it down to widen the road and was chopping off its branches with a shiny ax.

Henrietta sobbed loudly. He wished the last words of the tree to him could have been realized and Miss Hummer could have changed places with it. Perhaps this punishment had come to the tree for having had such a thought about the tyrant.

He did not think of the loss of the tree in terms of death, but rather in terms of extended torture. Its body had been cut off. Next it would be sawed into logs, then split and chopped into small pieces. Every part of it would be dissected. Later the many parts would be burned and turned into flames and ashes. The tree, Henrietta assumed, would feel all this.

Miss Hummer bought wood from David Hume. Some of the pieces of this friend would probably be used for Henrietta's whippings. Henrietta wondered how much longer he could be so fortunate as to escape with only the pains of an intact body.

CHAPTER XLVII

HENRIETTA CONGRATULATES HIMSELF

Miss Hummer was glad Henrietta's intellect had been retarded. Otherwise he might have been able to discover his male sex for himself. As it was, he would not understand even if someone were to explain to him the difference between men and women.

Miss Hummer had a feeling of pride in the realization that she had probably been responsible for this reformative alteration in a being who had been born a member of the male society for the promotion of wickedness. Instead of devoting his life to raping women in the manner of his sex, he had become a harmless simpleton who everyone thought was a girl.

She had a dread that Henrietta might expose himself on some occasion and reveal his real sex to others. To have it known that she had been living with a man would be a scandal that would detract considerably from her victory over the male coalition, even though Henrietta would remain her prisoner. Menham citizens could never be convinced that she had always kept him locked out of her bedroom.

If Henrietta's sex was ever discovered Miss Hummer hoped it would come as a result of some man's trying to rape him. For a normal man to find that he had been attempting to practice his trade on one of his own sex would be such a good joke and such an overwhelming victory for her side that the satisfaction would overbalance the resulting scandal built around her.

While gloating in her accomplishment, Miss Hummer wished the reformation of Henrietta had not been quite so complete. He could do many things for her if he understood just a little more about his environment. She would have taken great delight in having him do the housework and obey whatever orders she might issue.

To be waited on by a man-prisoner would be mastery indeed. After he had learned to cook, sew, and keep house, she could teach him to raise crops, chop wood, and wash clothes. The only useful thing she had been able to teach him so far was to go out to the woodshed for sticks.

Miss Hummer resented having to wait on Henrietta as much as she did. She had to prepare his food and wash his clothes. She never made his bed, for he did not have one. He still slept on the kitchen floor with a few blankets either underneath or on top of him.

The births of the six Peters and three girl babies had been nine shocking events for Miss Hummer. The fact that the mothers of the six boys had husbands did not lessen their sins in her estimation. She had reached the conclusion that the begetting of children was a wicked practice that only furnished proof of bawdy body relations. Life made up of such walking and talking proofs of sin was necessarily foul, vile, and wicked.

Others should follow her example, she maintained, and put an end to childbearing and the life that it perpetuated. In adopting a child she had not begot one. Henrietta was proof of someone else's sin. And in bringing him up in her reformed way she was preventing his engendering children.

Everyone, she told herself, is unfortunate in having had to be born as a result of someone else's misdemeanor. We should see to it that this transgression is not duplicated and this stigma of life passed on to someone else. Miss Hummer would not have approved of contraceptives. What she advocated was castration. She would have campaigned in favor of a twentieth amendment for the prohibition of testicles.

Miss Hummer had never heard of Sadism as such. She would have justified the practice of this sexual perversion by maintaining that people, being live proofs of sin, should be punished. And that men, being members of the male coalition, deserved far more punishment than women, their victims. Pleasure attending the chastising of a man was only the just reward of the one who gave this criminal his due.

Miss Hummer did not understand how other people could be so wicked. Their carnal propagation and immoral consumption of alcoholic drinks were fiendish atrocities. Their foul minds were filthier than offal. And if an inhabitant of some other world should make a visit he would assume her to be of the same habits as the rest.

Henrietta's birthday was celebrated by his foster mother each year. This was the day that marked the horrible sin of his nativity and called for appropriate observance. He was whipped as soon as Miss Hummer awoke and then locked in a small closet for the rest of the day without food. Miss Hummer arose early on the morning that Henrietta reached his thirteenth birthday. This was an occasion for special ceremony. Henrietta was to be graduated to the next to last pile of sticks in the series. She awoke him with a thrust of her foot and examined the new pile of scourges with sparkling eyes.

She had replaced the original sticks of the size in this pile with green wood of a new supply purchased from David Hume. These would make Henrietta moan with new tones of pain. This wicked man in her power would not have such an easy life from now on. There was an extra satisfaction in knowing that Henrietta had brought this wood into the kitchen himself. Miss Hummer had tossed and turned most of the night in happy anticipation of this birthday revel.

She selected a piece of wood with careful deliberation. Drunk with lust and grinning with glee, she staggered toward Henrietta. Miss Hummer started to raise her arm. This movement was checked abruptly. A rheumatic cramp sent the arm back to her side. She put the stick in her other hand and felt another pang of pain when she tried to raise it.

Neither arm could be lifted high enough to give Henrietta more than a gentle pat. She hit him a few light strokes with the stick, but the pain was too great for her to continue. What incredible injustice that her rheumatism should interfere with an event such as this.

Disappointed and chagrined, she kicked Henrietta with her foot until he cried. She dropped the stick onto his back and went to find her rheumatism salve. This criminal was having his punishment postponed, while she, his jailer, was being made to suffer. But she would make up for this probation as soon as one of her arms was well.

Henrietta picked up the stick. He saw red and black marks on a piece of bark that still clung to it. This must be part of his friend the tree. Henrietta mumbled to it.

"It was too bad you had to be a tree," he tried to say. "I was certainly lucky to be a child."

CHAPTER XLVIII

FELIX DOLE'S DREAM

Alice Goode had long since given up hope that Felix Dole would ever provide anything but spiritual companionship. She had hoped that the birth of her baby would inspire him to more physical and satisfying methods of approach, but no. Felix had never been able to acquire the courage in Alice's presence that he had in his dreams. The proof that she had the same courage whether asleep or awake only made him more nervous.

He still called on her. They took walks together. Arthur Moore had started a story most people believed that Felix was the father of her child. But their only bodily contacts came when Alice held her hand in his, while he kept it at arm's length. Felix seldom talked to her. Alice wondered why she bothered going to walk with him. Felix wondered why he could not have his bashfulness in his dreams and his gallantry when with Alice.

Alice and her mother had lived very chaste lives since Arthur Moore noticed the first signs of gestation in the family. Mrs. Goode's opinion—that since Alice had made a mutual lover of Arthur, and been responsible for frightening him away, she should now be entitled to share Felix with Alice—was expressed to her daughter while stumbling home together from the town hall one Saturday night. Her daughter was willing to make this sacrifice and even offered to ask Felix to call for Emma and her on alternate nights.

This proposal pleased Mrs. Goode. Felix did not dare refuse to ask her to walk with him after Alice suggested that he do so. Emma and Felix went out together one night. They did not get home until late, and Mrs. Goode did not rise until noon the next day. Alice suspected that her mother had had more success than she, and felt a little jealous.

Mrs. Goode seemed to awake with difficulty. "I'm lame all over," she groaned. "All he did was walk. We must have gone fifty miles."

On many Saturday nights Alice and Felix had found themselves together on the way home from their respective drinking gatherings. Alice always stopped to rest in front of the deserted Goodwin farm. Felix always waited for her to recover her energy. Once when she stopped there Alice found that she was with Alfred Dole instead of his son.

"Sorry," he said, "but I think that's my wife comin' right behind us."

But on one Saturday night Felix Dole found himself walking in his sleep. Inspired by the advice of his drinking glass in reaction to a new brand of bootleg liquor at Lem Witherbee's, he deliberately sought Alice among the wabbling women who came from the town hall. He took her by the arm with a firm grasp and led her away from the group in a surprising manner. Alice squinted and blinked.

"Is that you, Felix?" she asked in astonishment.

"Yup. Less get away from this crowd where we can be alone."

"But why?" asked Alice, stumbling as he caused her to quicken her pace. She could think of no good reason for being alone with Felix.

"You'll see," he said. "Wonderful liquor at Lem's tonight. Less hurry. I hope you feel as good as I do, sweetheart."

Alice looked at her companion. No-one had ever called her "sweetheart" before. And, of all people, Felix had shown the least inclination to do so.

Felix tripped in his haste and would have fallen down but for his grip on Alice's arm. When they reached the Goodwin farm they were almost running. Alice did not have a chance to stop outside. Felix led her on up the path and through the front door.

They could not see anything in the darkness, but Felix soon knew where all the principal parts of Alice's anatomy were. He kissed her a few times, too. Alice expected to wake up any minute, but she kissed him and hugged him tightly on the chance that this might not be a dream.

Felix pulled her onto the floor beside him. The boards of the old house creaked. Alice realized that hay was much softer, but, having Felix in this transformed state, she could not complain about the spot chosen. Being in more of a dream than a state of consciousness, Felix acted accordingly. At last he had realized his ambition to be able to go to sleep in Alice's presence. Alice decided she must be awake but could not believe this was Felix. For the time being, she did not care who it was.

Felix did not awake as usual when his dream came to a climax. Having discovered that he was not afraid to make love to Alice, he summoned still more courage and asked her a question.

"Will you marry me?" he inquired. Convinced now that he would dare go to bed with her in the event of a wedding ceremony, it was safe to propose.

Alice had not thought of marriage. She was not thinking of anything very definite at the moment. The proposal brought her back to reality with an unpleasant jolt. Marriage would mean a lot more housework than she had to do now, but it would also be a means to a permanent lover.

"Whya, I guess so," she replied skeptically.

"That's fine," said Felix. "Y' didn't bring a drink with you, did y'?"

"No." Alice kissed Felix and led him by the hand to the door. He was staggering more than before he had come in and seemed in no mood for further attempts at running.

"I'll take you home instead of you takin' me home," Alice offered.

Felix did not reply. She held him by the arm and accompanied him to his back door. She kissed him and headed toward her house. Felix fumbled for the knob on the wrong side of the door and then slumped into a heap on the porch.

The next morning Felix awoke when his sister, Mary Dole, opened the kitchen door and tripped over him. His head throbbed painfully, and his stomach felt like a slowly rising elevator. He had no memory of events after dark on the night before. There was some trace in his mind of a dream about Alice Goode, but he dismissed this with the usual jealous indignation that his waking self felt for his courage when dreaming. The only thought he formed clearly was, "How soon will I die?"

That afternoon Alice Goode came to the Dole farm. Felix was sitting in a chair leaning against the barn. He felt very little like having a visitor and hoped she would not see him.

But Alice walked up to him. She greeted him with a kiss and casually asked, "What day shall we get married?"

Felix wiped his mouth with the back of his hand and spat. It was very poor humor for Alice to torment him like this because he did not dare make love to her. In suggesting that they get married, she was thinking how funny he would look sleeping on the floor. He felt a hatred for Alice and wished he had never seen her.

"Go to hell!" he said, and walked toward the road for Lem Witherbee's store.

Nine months later Alice Goode had another baby. She told Felix Dole that he was its father, but he did not even laugh. Alice's humor when directed against him was very depressing. He was not mentioned among the possible fathers in the discussions based around the new infant at Lem Witherbee's, despite the fact that it was named Felix.

CHAPTER XLIX

MINNIE BECOMES ADEPT AT HIDE AND GO SEEK

When her child was a baby Minnie Muller sometimes sat holding it in her arms at her old post on the town hall steps. This site held many pleasant memories. These were not duplicated with regularity until she was able to leave Elsie to play by herself, but when two men came by together they arranged to take turns holding the baby. Minnie abandoned this station after Elsie learned to walk efficiently. The child established annoying practices of following its mother when she tried to seek privacy, and of finding Minnie after she had eluded it.

Mrs. Whiter, who continued her duties as watch-woman over the town hall cider kegs, would have taken the child in charge if requested. Minnie had a secret fear that, knowing little of the habits of children, she would entertain it with cider. Minnie did not like the thought of being greeted on her return by Elsie staggering and stuttering in a drunken condition.

Children generally acted as though in a somewhat drunken condition, even though they did not drink intoxicating liquor as a rule. She thought that their bodies, being in a stage of development, might not have acquired the faculties necessary to become sober again after drinking. A child, already drunk by nature, would be a difficult problem if it became drunk with alcohol as well and was unable to do anything to check its effects. Then, too, when it finally sobered up in later years it would probably find life rather dull.

Minnie Muller retained her popularity with Menham men even though she deserted the original meeting place. Only the few of her followers who had legitimate claims to membership in the old school objected to calling for her at her home. But all men received the same reception if Mrs. Nancy Muller saw them first.

"Mrs. Black is not home," she would shout. "Go on away. Get out of here."

These cries would be heard by Minnie if she was there. She would make her presence known by calling from a window, "I'll be out in just a minute. Wait for me down the road."

She made this announcement once when a man whom she did not see called to sell bear oil that would cure all ailments and prolong life. When Minnie caught up with him, she was embarrassed by finding him to be a stranger. But she soon learned that she had not acted with impropriety. This was another lover whose body was built to match hers.

The Goodwin farm became the established year-round meeting place where Minnie saw her callers after they were driven away by her mother. A bolt was applied to the inside of the door there and the windows boarded so that Elsie could not gain admittance while trying to find her mother.

Minnie did not start from her house until the man who called was out of sight. Then she left in haste to join him, and both her mother and Elsie thought she was playing hide and go seek. Elsie began the hunt after merrily counting to one hundred. This head start enabled the couple to reach their retreat before being overtaken. Minnie would jump out in front of Elsie from behind a tree or other hiding spot on the way home.

The fame and distinction acquired by Minnie Muller had gone far beyond the imagination of John Lyman when he selected her as a prodigy, in every respect but two: her child had not been twins, and she had only been a mother once. These facts were the only arguments of the old school members in attempting to maintain their equality with the new school in being the exploiters of Mrs. Nancy Muller.

Both girls, they pointed out, had only had one child, and so Minnie had no claims to superiority over her mother. But even if Minnie should be conceded to be superior, this was because she was the product of the old school.

These arguments held little weight, for the new school members outnumbered those of the old and could win any point at issue through their greater volume. They insisted that Minnie had had but one child only because she was the daughter of the old school. She had not been endowed by these impotent fathers with sufficient fertility to produce another offspring.

Minnie, they asserted, had been active over a much longer period than her mother. Her methods were far superior and her obligingness and cooperation much better. She had won many more lovers than her mother. And the stories built around Minnie not only included all those told by the old school about Nancy, but new ones that far exceeded these both in number and excellence and that were constantly being added to.

The two schools of expression at Lem Witherbee's had become separate units. The old school assembled in one end of the store for its discussions of Nancy, while the new school exchanged anecdotes about Minnie. Lem Witherbee, an old school member, had to desert the ranks in order to keep the glasses of the new school members filled. An interchange of thought at the close of discourses on these topics on Saturday nights came in boisterous debates in which the old school had to admit defeat by suggesting the next subject for consideration.

Minnie Muller was glad she had never married. Having so many natural husbands, it would have been unfair for her to wed any one of them to the exclusion of the others. If Paul Turner had proposed in the days before she had learned of her additional lovers, she would probably have agreed to the ceremony, and these other men, with equal claims to her, would have been neglected.

Wedlock she considered as having been conceived on the theory that each woman has but one man patterned after the mold of her body, and each man is built according to only one woman. When a properly mated pair find each other it is fitting that they should celebrate with a wedding or other appropriate observance. She had invited Paul Turner to her house for dinner.

Her case was an unusual one that did not fit into the scheme of marriage. Having a unique body that was adapted to several men, she was not restricted to only one. Polyandry was not recognized in the marriage regulations, so she could not get married without being unfaithful to all but one of her mates. She hoped her daughter would prove to be equally fortunate.

Minnie Muller often laughed at the thought of how envious other women would be if having more than one husband were permitted, and she wore the wedding rings of all her lovers.

"I wouldn't need to wear gloves," she grinned, looking at her bare hands.

CHAPTER L

A WHITE MARE NIGHTMARE

A man with black glasses, hat, suit, and tie drove slowly into Menham, in a small truck. He stopped in front of the store and walked to the door. When his pushes failed to open this entrance, he sat down on the steps and brought a large bottle of hair tonic from a pocket. Other pockets showed bulges similar to the one that this action had leveled. He lifted the bottle to his mouth and took several swallows. He continued to sit there, quietly staring in front of him except when of necessity looking at the sky in order to drink again from the bottle.

Lem Witherbee did not recognize the visitor at first and became frightened. This might be another policeman with a truckload of axes and improved means of destruction. He watched the man through the knot hole. The brand of liquor he had with him was not known to the storekeeper. It was probably some high-priced cordial he had saved out for himself in destroying the last saloon visited.

Then the man started to talk.

"I've told you I don't need a horse, especially a white horse, now that I've got this truck," he said. "Run along. Stop following me around. If I ever did get a horse it wouldn't be a white one anyway. Get away! I know you can dance, but I don't want you. There's some nice grass in that field. Go have some breakfast and do your dancing over there."

Lem Witherbee recognized this voice. He had heard it say, "White Horse," before. This was Deacon Ira Ormsby. Lem opened the door to let the customer in before he could drink any more of his own stock. The deacon hurried to shelter and slammed the door.

"I'm glad you've got some locks inside," he said, sliding a bolt and snapping a padlock into place. "I guess they'll keep that white mare away from me for a while. I got an automobile just to show the horse I didn't want her, but she still keeps followin' me around."

Deacon Ormsby sat down in the end of the room opposite from the door and took a drink from his bottle of hair tonic with considerable relief.

"Hey, I still keep whisky here," shouted Lem, indignant that he should lose still another sale.

"Glad to hear it," said the deacon. "That's what I came to see you about. I've got a few cases of the real stuff I can let you have real cheap."

Deacon Ira Ormsby had a new schedule now. Instead of alternately buying his liquor in one town and preaching against whisky in the next, he sold bootleg liquor, spoke for prohibition enforcement, and drank hair tonic in all towns.

While his merchandise was genuine bootleg whisky, the deacon preferred hair tonic for his personal consumption. He could not put a bottle of moonshine to his lips with the same confidence as one containing a mixture of kerosene and alcohol for the hair. His favorite brand was always of the same flavor with a uniform base of reliable grain alcohol. It was not as good as the whisky he used to denounce, but he knew how each drink would taste and react on his system. He also knew it was not poisonous.

But Deacon Ormsby did not admit these facts even to himself. He still had explanations to cover any situation in which he was found that seemed to be inconsistent with the views of his lectures.

His humanitarian mission of drinking the venomous pre-prohibition whisky so that it could not contaminate and corrupt others had given way to a still more worthy cause. Hair tonic had become a beverage, bringing massacre and havoc with even worse devastation than moonshine. He was consuming this deadly hair tonic so that others could not have it. The kind and benevolent Lord was keeping him alive to drink this awful poison that would be fatal to another.

Those who escaped as a result of his sacrifice and still insisted on violating the laws of temperance would have to choose the lesser of two evils. They would have to drink bootleg liquor, which, foul and bad as it was, would not kill or corrupt them so quickly. He was keeping these depraved sinners out of the fires of Hell just so much longer.

In keeping with this work, he was selling bootleg liquor—and at a loss, he insisted—so that the poor unfortunates who drank might have access to this rather than hair tonic. Moonshine was poison, liquid corruption, and a quick road to Hell, but it could not quite equal the agonizing death torments of hair tonic, death torments which he suffered constantly, kept alive by our munificent and gracious Saviour.

Lem Witherbee was in no mood for buying liquor from a man to whom he had expected to sell a day's supply. His moonshine was delivered regularly by a Scofield bootlegger, whose labels read, "Fresh And Pure Rye Whisky. Wash And Return All Bottles."

"I'm sellin' whisky, not buyin' it," Lem told the deacon emphatically. "And if you want to drink here you'll have to drink mine."

Deacon Ormsby did not want to leave this retreat and face the white horse that he knew was smiling and waiting for him outside. In an outraged manner, he told Lem that he did not drink whisky, and offered him a dollar to let him stay in the corner where he was and take his medicine.

"Medicine to save living souls from Hell," he would have added if Lem had asked for details.

The deacon did not leave the store until evening. He had announced to all of Lem Witherbee's customers during the day that he would conduct an open air temperance rally in front of the town hall that night. Lem approved of the gathering. It would be a means of getting the men congregated for a mid-week meeting at his store. The deacon drove his truck to the hall, following a course that would have won the affection of a giant serpent.

Mrs. Whiter had been waiting for him. The rest had not arrived. Deacon Ormsby began his lecture at once, despite the small audience.

"We must keep our nation alive by enforcing prohibition by ridding our land of the plague of liquor that is singeing its innocent souls with Hell fire," he declaimed. "We must free poor, unfortunate addicts from the tenacles of moonshine. We must—"

The deacon paused. He saw a white horse standing in the doorway. Then he recalled that this was the place he had first met this mare that had either followed or led the way over his routes ever since. The horse was home again now. Perhaps he could elude it while it was renewing old acquaintances.

"Deacon Ormsby, won't you come in for a glass of cider?" Mrs. Whiter asked.

The deacon did not answer. He started his machine and rolled away as quickly as possible. This was a wonderful opportunity to escape his unwelcome companion who tried to entertain him with its antics. The horse would be obliged to accept the hospitality of its former friends, and he could be far away by the time it was able to start the pursuit.

Deacon Ormsby's smile suddenly went awry. He saw the white mare trotting alongside the truck and displaying a gold band on its left front ankle. He looked to the other side and saw a black horse running in step with the white one. It was sprinkled with confetti and wore a large silk hat. The black horse was a stallion. The road had become unusually bumpy. The deacon discovered that he was driving across an open field.

CHAPTER LI

A CLAMOROUS HEADLINE

For a long time Arthur Moore had been tired of May Cline. He had gone with her longer than any other girl, and had been tired of her longer than any other. He attributed this satiety to the inadequacy of May, in common with all women, in her ability to interest a man for long.

Moore felt ashamed of his relations with May. He had given her grounds for the thought that she had dominated him and been an essential figure in his life over this long period. Such degeneracy on his part had not only been degradation for him but disloyalty to the male sex.

A woman, he contended, is made to be but one of several mates for some man. Each man, with his superior abilities and powers, is intended to have a number of women at his disposal, and it should be considered a supreme achievement for a woman, at some time in her life, to be one of those on call for some man.

While he had told May of other women with whom he shared his attentions, she must have realized that they were largely fictitious. In allowing her to be the only woman, he had provided her with contentions for vanity and a feeling of superiority. She could assume that she was the equal of him and of all men. As his only girl, she could maintain that she dominated him in being the only one to provide an essential bodily function. She could consider herself capable of dominating any other man in the same way.

Women had had a declining interest for Arthur Moore during the past few years. He had seen May Cline less and less frequently. After each visit he insisted vehemently that he had taken his last walk with a girl, and so no plans were laid for obtaining a different woman for future usage.

Later, like a recurring illness, he would feel the need of a woman again. Surely this would be the last time. It would be easier and quicker to call on May just once more than to go to the bother of soliciting the attentions of another woman. And so the affair continued.

Moore tried to convince May that she was not a dominant or even an important individual in his life. He generally twisted her arm, slapped her face, or squeezed her breasts in a painful manner before departing. Once she had had a dark blue border under one eye when she arrived home. On other occasions there had been similar marks on other parts of her body. Moore considered these past proofs of his superiority feeble and unconvincing, for he had always gone back to May at some future time, which gave the impression he could not get along without her.

The recurring biological urge had returned to Arthur Moore and become greater than his contempt for this woman whom he had allowed to elevate herself in imagination into the ascendancy of the male. He would have to call on May Cline this one last time and take another step downward in his dishonor. After this final visit he would show her that she could not even affect the mechanism of his memory, to say nothing of his life.

He decided to go to Lem Witherbee's store first. A few drinks from and words with his whisky glass would enable him to invoke this defilement with a less reproachful feeling of shame.

"At any rate, May Cline is only *your* girl," his glass told him. "She doesn't think all the men in town have to have her, like Minnie Muller."

When Arthur Moore left the store he had a better opinion of May. He hoped that this might not be his last walk with her. He was not too old to go with women regularly. He would get another girl, too, and let May see him with her. He could tell her he had been going with this new girl and others all along.

This would drop May, out of the heights into which her imagination had lifted her, back to ranks of women. The higher she had risen, further she would fall, and the harder she would land. These thoughts made the approaching meeting with May seem very desirable. It would boost her to a point just so much higher for her fall.

Henrietta Hummer had been sitting on the store steps. He interrupted Moore's reverie with a deluge of powder that descended on his shoulders and back. Arthur was enraged by the affront to his masculine dignity and jerked an arm into the air to hit the offender. The arm returned slowly to his side. He felt as though he had just discovered something: Henrietta was a girl, young, but still a girl.

There was something lawless and freakish about the way Henrietta's face was painted, something attractive. Unsymmetric red and black patterns on his cheeks and forehead, together with a black nose and red chin, gave the impression of a courtesan savage out of the past come in modern dress to test her wiles on modern man.

This girl was at his disposal as well as May Cline. When he was a boy he had played house with girls as young as this and provided imaginary bedrooms for actual indulgences in the manner of a father and mother. It was strange he had never thought of Henrietta before.

Without comment, Arthur Moore took Henrietta roughly by the hand and started down the road toward his house. It was a new and pleasant experience for Henrietta to have someone walk hand in hand with him. He ran every few steps to keep up with Moore's longer strides. He was delighted by this novelty and joyfully uttered, "Slut."

"Yup, you're big enough to be a slut now," replied Moore.

Moore walked slowly past the Cline farm. He wanted May to observe that she was of no more importance to him and could do nothing more for him than this little idiot girl. Such a realization should topple her from her usurped pinnacle.

Arriving at his farm, Moore led the way into the barn. A rustling sound gave the effect of a large rat running for hiding in the hay.

"There's a lot of other girls that would like to be in your place right now," said Moore, boosting Henrietta up the ladder into the hayloft. He was not going to take any risk of letting this brainless girl think he was obliged to choose her. Being a fool, she might assume he had devoted his life to chastity while waiting for her to be born and grow up.

"I'm doin' you a big favor," he added.

The six Peters arrived at top speed at Lem Witherbee's. When Lem opened the door he was greeted with an astounding announcement that was too sensational and important to be suppressed.

"Henrietta Hummer is a *boy!*" they shrieked.

The six Peters ran on to spread the information, while Lem shouted after them excitedly for details.

CHAPTER LII

MOORE'S SECOND INSPIRATION COMES TOO LATE

Arthur Moore took Henrietta gently by the by hand and started down the road toward the store. He walked much slower than before, making far more allowance than necessary for the boy's limp. He watched Henrietta's face with an expression of pain and wondered again why he had not thought to bring the child to his farm before. Henrietta would have preferred adjusting his steps to Moore's longer ones as he had on the way out to the farm. This new pace was too monotonous.

Feelings of bitter hatred and of maddening sympathy whirled about in Moore's mind and overflowed into his body. He felt both stimulated and stunned. Miss Hummer, a woman, had actually made a man inferior to her own sex. She had not only brought him down to the level of women but had pushed him still lower.

She had succeeded in disguising him as a human privy, an offal receptacle of her own kind. The disgrace and humiliation had been so great for this boy, being overpowered by a woman and forced to appear as a girl, that he had been driven out of his senses. A woman had made a man into what had appeared to be an idiot-woman.

These thoughts and others like them almost brought tears from Arthur Moore. The male sex had been ridiculed by a woman. It had been degraded and defamed much more than by his own activities in letting one woman think she dominated him or in those of other men in letting Minnie Muller assume she was so important to all of them.

Miss Hummer had made a man into a woman, an idiot, and had even crippled his body with this limp. Moore's imagination could go no further. It could not have gone as far as this without actual, tangible proof. Moore felt as though he had awaked in a horrible dream and that reality had disappeared instead of the fantasy.

During all these years Miss Hummer, no doubt, had gloried in the thought that she was the equal, perhaps even the superior, of men. She was able to take a boy baby and distort and deform him into a limping girl, not only that but a fool. With her head in the air, and her prim and haughty manner, Miss Hummer had been laughing at men all the while, expressing contempt for their authority. Perhaps she had let other women know her secret, that Henrietta was a man. Perhaps all the women in Menham were laughing. Shooting or hanging was too good for Miss Hummer. She had committed a new crime that called for a new extreme of punishment.

Other passions were crowded out of Arthur Moore's mind and body. He did not notice May Cline wave from her yard as he passed. If he had seen her he would have sworn and probably thrown a rock instead of waving.

Moore's pity for Henrietta was an intense sensation arousing delicate brain parts that had almost atrophied during his lifetime. This boy, the superior of every woman, had found himself the imprisoned slave of one of them. He had been tortured into idiocy by the degeneracy into which she had sent him. She had given him a girl's name, made him wear dresses and petticoats, and let his hair grow long.

Being able to change his garb and name now that his sex had been discovered, Henrietta could assert himself as the superior of women, but he would still be inferior to other men. He would still have to go through life bearing a stigma inflicted upon him by a woman.

Arthur Moore stopped at the store to obtain the advice of his whisky glass. Not even on the night of his marriage to Jenny Taylor had he felt the need of such counsel so greatly. Lem Witherbee stared at Henrietta as though he were a new kind of animal.

"Is she really a boy?" he asked.

"Yes!" shouted Moore. "That damned Miss Hummer thought she could fool us forever! Give him some candy, and get me some whisky."

Moore led Henrietta to a chair. Such attention was unprecedented. The boy expected some new kind of pain to follow and felt frightened. After Witherbee opened a small box of candy for him Henrietta experienced a new sensation of pleasure. He had never had candy before. He ate piece after piece until the box was empty. Moore had been watching every move.

"Give him a bigger box," he said.

Half of the sky was a blinding red when Arthur Moore left the store. It had taken his whisky glass a long time to reach any conclusion, but its recommendation had finally come like a divine inspiration. He was glad he had not left sooner.

"Keep Henrietta here till I get back," he said to the storekeeper. Lem unfastened the bolt, which seemed to elude Arthur's fingers.

Moore walked toward Miss Hummer's house. He walked slowly, but not because this was his wish. His feet seemed uncertain where the next step would take them. Actually he was in a hurry. He was fulfilling his duty to avenge the tremendous insult to his sex inflicted by a woman. To kill her in an ordinary way would not be enough. His whisky glass had furnished the solution for this problem of an appropriate death.

Miss Hummer saw him staggering toward her door and was afraid. She was not frightened because he was drunk. All men were always drunk. A member of the male coalition was on her property. He must be intent on some wicked purpose: rape, arson, murder. This was the snake returned in its real form. The snakes she had seen before were probably Arthur Moore in disguise. The male conspiracy was declaring war again. She had been the victor in the past war, but the enemy must have new and more deadly tactics to be attacking her so openly.

At first Miss Hummer determined not to answer the knock on the door. Then she realized that Moore could break his way through. She could lock out the snake but not a man. She opened the door. Moore was leaning against the side of the house for support. Miss Hummer saw that he had already been in position to smash down the wall.

"Henrietta's hurt herself over to my place," he said politely. "You better come over and get her."

Miss Hummer started to say, "You tend to your affairs, and I'll tend to mine," but checked herself. She would have to profess a more kindly interest in her child. And she would have to get him away from Moore before his real sex was discovered. Evidently Moore had not found out that Henrietta was a boy. He had referred to him as "her".

The six Peters had not visited Miss Hummer in making their rounds.

"That's too bad," said Miss Hummer. "I'll come right over."

This mission of the male society seemed peaceful. Perhaps she was not in unusual danger. Of course, going with a man to his farm was a precarious undertaking that no respectable woman would be a party to, but she would have to show herself willing to make this sacrifice to decency in the interests of Henrietta. She would have to allow herself to be contaminated by the companionship of a man during this walk.

Miss Hummer's worries were dismissed entirely for the moment when an amusing thought came to her: probably Moore had injured Henrietta, assuming him to be a girl. Her smile soon vanished. Perhaps Moore would injure her in the same way.

He suggested that they take a short cut across the Hume meadow. Miss Hummer reluctantly agreed. She supposed it was necessary to show her desire to get to Henrietta as soon as possible. Thoughts of possible hideous crimes this man might perpetrate on her person while out of sight of habitation made her shudder. But then, if she refused to go by this lonely route he might force her to accompany him, perhaps drag her by the hair.

There was one consolation: she probably would not be seen in the company of a man. This would be a protection for her honor unless Moore told others she had walked with him.

The pair walked slowly and silently, Miss Hummer keeping as far behind Moore as she dared. She hoped Henrietta was not hurt badly enough to delay for long the revenge she anticipated in return for this risk she was being forced to take with her chastity on his account. Moore staggered considerably and tripped over many rocks and humps of earth. The path led to the rear of Moore's barn. He walked to a large, oblong box that provided an annex to this building.

"Henrietta fell through the floor of the barn," said Moore. "We can get to her this way best. Give me a hand with this door, will you please."

Arthur Moore and Miss Hummer raised the hinged cover from the rattlesnake sty. Moore leaned it against the side of the barn. Miss Hummer found herself staring at a tangle of snakes. The whole male army was assembled to meet her. Electric shocks shot through her. She felt numbed to all feelings but terror and pain. She was helpless. She knew she could not run or even move. She heard sounds that she thought were her death rattle.

Moore stepped behind her. He placed his hands on her shoulders and pushed with all his strength. Miss Hummer fell through wire netting and struck headfirst amidst the snakes. Several pairs of fangs were buried in her body. What was even worse for her comfort, several snakes crawled over her and squirmed out from beneath her. She prayed for death, but her body refused to lose consciousness.

"Poor women; God is a man," she muttered incoherently.

Arthur Moore was elated. He reached into the pen to exchange embraces with one of the snakes. He leaned too far and lost his balance. He fell, landing on top of Miss Hummer.

Either the snakes did not recognize him in this horizontal position, or they failed to distinguish his features in the twilight. Three of them sprang at him with open mouths. A fourth joined them but missed its aim and sunk its teeth in Miss Hummer.

"You dirty, stinking bitch," groaned Moore, as though Miss Hummer, and not the snakes, had bitten him with venomous fangs. "I should have thrown you down the backhouse seat and nailed the cover on."

CHAPTER LIII

A COFFIN FOR TWO

News of the deaths of Arthur Moore and Miss Hummer was announced before their hearts stopped beating by the six Peters. They galloped triumphantly from house to house with the new bulletin and broke their speed record established that day in proclaiming Henrietta Hummer's masculinity. Mrs. Nancy Muller had not heard either account but was one of the first to arrive at Arthur Moore's farm the next morning.

Because of the rattlers and the darkness that had fallen and blended with the murk that came to Moore and Miss Hummer, no-one went to the scene that night. Nobody went very close to the snake sty in the morning.

Only a few of the snakes had escaped from their pen. The rest were happily catching flies and sunning themselves in interwoven groups occupying perches on top of the two bodies. Mrs. Muller looked at this scene from a distance.

"Humm!" she muttered to nobody in particular. "So Moore was the father of her baby. Well, they picked a poor place for their last get-together."

Others made mental notes of these conclusions for future reference but were concerned for the time being with a matter that did not seem so obvious. How were they going to get the corpses away from the rattlers without being bitten themselves?

"There's no reason why we should take any chances just to get them out of there," said John Lyman. "What good will it do to risk our lives? You can't save the life of a dead person."

"And they're certainly dead by now," commented David Hume.

"We don't want to let them snakes get out and come visitin' us neither," said Andrew Cline.

"No," said his daughter, May. The visits of rattlesnakes could not compensate for the visits of Arthur Moore.

One of the snakes seized a mouse from somewhere and held it in its mouth.

"That must be either Moore or Miss Hummer he's eatin'," said Mrs. Sadie Sadler.

"Looks more like Arthur sprawled there across Miss Hummer to me," replied Alfred Dole.

The six Peters were not in hiding at this gathering. They were officially present and a center of attraction second only to the contents of the snake sty. Everybody wanted to know everything about the catastrophe. The boys continued to provide details after they ran out of facts. They enjoyed being public figures and wanted to continue in this capacity as long as possible. They remained together so that their accounts would coincide in essential points.

"Moore took off her dress and said he was goin' to take her under the barn," narrated Peter Dean.

"And her petticoats—he took them off," added Peter Jones.

"How many did she have on?" asked Mrs. Goode.

"Er, six," said Peter Sadler.

"No, ten," corrected Peter Pike.

"How did she get her clothes back on?" asked Mrs. Cline.

"Well, when she saw the snakes, she grabbed her clothes and dressed," replied Peter Pike. "She didn't dare run without havin' them on."

"And the snakes jumped out and pulled her in with them," added Peter Lyman.

"And they didn't like the taste of her, so they grabbed Moore," said Peter Jones.

"I thought you said Moore pushed her in," said Mrs. Jones.

"No, he jumped in to save her," said Peter Hatch.

"You just said the snakes pulled him in," insisted Paul Turner.

"Well, they helped him in," explained Peter Dean.

These conflicting versions were furnishing material for many long discussions at both the town hall and Lem Witherbee's store. A concordant account that left no inconsistencies to justify personal opinions and arguments would not have been as satisfactory.

At length, becoming a little too involved, Peter Pike picked up a long pole and knocked down the cover of the snake sty with it. This changed the topic.

"There, we should of thought of that before," said John Lyman. "Now we can bury 'em, snakes and all, right here."

"Yeah, and they've got a good big coffin in case they should want to turn over sometime," added David Hume.

Arthur Moore's horse and cart brought several loads of dirt to the rear of the barn. This was dumped and stamped down on the closed snake sty. The men cooperated in the burial. This was the best means of getting rid of the rattlesnakes.

There was still another problem to be settled. What was to become of Henrietta Hummer?

"He's too old to go back to the Scofield Orphanage and not crazy enough to go to a lunatic asylum," said Andrew Cline.

"He's been in my store all night," said Lem Witherbee. "I've had all I want of him."

Mrs. Whiter blushed and entered the conversation. "I thought p'raps I might adopt him," she volunteered timidly. "I'll change his name to Henry and change his clothes."

A troubled look on Lem Witherbee's face became one of pleasant surprise. He had not expected to get rid of Henrietta so easily.

"Let's go get him now," he said, anxious to permit as little time as possible to elapse in which Mrs. Whiter could change her mind.

They walked side by side toward the road, each intent on getting to the store as soon as possible.

"I'll cut his hair and wash the rouge off his face," said Mrs. Whiter happily.

She had a man.

THE END

SIN IS MAN'S TWIN

CHAPTER I

NATURE'S FINEST

". . . With the cross of Je-sus Go-ing on be-fore!"

Beating civilized tom-toms in poor harmony, a band of Salvation Army workers was sadly indulging in a street-corner concert.

Dorothy Dolly, lady of joy, smiled as she passed. But it was not her trade-smile. She knew these men were broke.

"Poor fellows," she commented to herself. "Even if they were drunk, that would be a poor drinking song—and they're cold sober."

"Christ, the royal Master, Leads against the foe . . ."

"They look as though too much temperance had left them with a bad hang-over. Except that fellow with the blood-shot eyes. I wish he had a two dollar bill."

"For-ward in-to bat-tle . . ." The savage basso of elevated cars to the soprano accompaniment of their wheels on a curve replaced the next few words of the song.

Dorothy Dolly placed a coin in the receptacle held by the man with blood-shot eyes.

"Here, go buy yourself a drink," she said. Mentally she remarked, "I'd like to put a bottle of whisky on one of their tambourines and see what would happen."

"March-ing as to war. . . ."

Dorothy Dolly stopped smiling. This phrase, detached from the word sequence of the song, came to her as a personal insult. She was very easily offended by any inference that might be construed as charging her with inefficiency in her profession.

"Marching as to war, huh," her mind repeated. "Just because I've walked three blocks without a customer—just to get a little exercise—they come out and say I'm in for an all day hike. Trying to make out I'll have to use a gun to get any money out of a man. I'm marching as to war, am I? Wise guys. Just because they haven't got the price to come along with me, they're trying to make me look cheap. And after I gave that fellow a quarter, too. Well, they ain't going to get away with singing about me like that."

In a loud tone Dorothy remarked, "Chorus boys, hey. Sore 'cause I ain't a big handsome man, huh." Using the highest pitch to which she could raise her voice, she added in intended mockery, "You mean old violets!"

The singers started another stanza. Dorothy continued with her walk, unaware of any of the song's verse except the phrase, "Marching as to war." Her new attitude toward these men in wrinkled uniforms gave her an excellent opportunity for further mental comments which soon brought a smile of satisfaction, her third type of smile. Her reasoning allowed no such details to interfere as deep bass voices or the fact that the man with blood-shot eyes had winked at her.

"An honest girl can't walk the streets these days without being insulted by some of the lavender boys," her cerebral reflexes informed her. "It's getting so a girl has to compete with the bleached hair boys to land a man. They're ruining our business. But no they ain't neither. There's plenty of real men left who sock the lilies in the teeth and go for the sex that's got a right to use a lipstick. They're ruining Nature, those pansies who curl their hair and use rouge—damn fluffs with their powder puffs. They're jealous 'cause they ain't girls. Well, thank God all the men ain't jealous—I ain't starving yet."

Dorothy Dolly regarded her profession as a worthy and honorable calling bestowed upon certain favored members of the female sex as a gift from Nature. No other occupation had such divine sanction, for others were all dependent upon discoveries and inventions of men. They were vocations which had been wrested from Nature only after long struggles and experiments. The minority which practiced prostitution comprised Nature's chosen girls, inspired to their calling by one of the rival immortal powers. Most people said Satan became the victor at this point, but Dorothy had her doubts. God, not the Devil, had created the tree with its forbidden fruit.

Dorothy remained neutral in her attitude toward the two immortals. Each opposed the other, and each had been credited with occasional victories. When the final winner had been definitely proven, she would side with him.

The one point of certainty Dorothy drew from primeval evidence was that she and her chosen sisters of to-day and of past ages were Nature's hand-picked nobility. This female aristocracy existed as a result of direct selection, not blood ties. Aristocracies which could only trace back their lineage a few centuries to King So-and-so were nothing but rabble in comparison. Dorothy and her chosen sisters had proof of the origin of their nobility with the fall of Eve.

Girls who were not inspired to Nature's profession were jealous, Dorothy's reasoning explained. It was necessary to keep the respectable—as they called themselves—in the majority in order to allow a reasonable income for the chosen. Being in the majority, they had been in a position to oppose Nature and to advocate such doctrines as the reversed code of morals that demanded monogamous marriage instead of promiscuity. Some men did not approve of prostitution either. They were members of the twilight sex.

Being one of the chosen girls of Nature, Dorothy Dolly was quite pleased with herself and with things in general as long as she earned a sufficient supply of money. She did not like to be confined to housework. Free lancing was her preference.

When "on the make" Dorothy Dolly always wore a white rose, as she called it—it was really a carnation—over one ear. This she believed to be a good luck symbol as well as an additional touch of something she believed to be beauty, and a sort of trade-mark.

Once she had explained to a man with a pale bald head, "I wear a white rose to show off my black hair, but my real trade-mark—"

"We won't go into that," he had replied, walking away.

Dorothy's trade-smile replaced her smile of satisfaction as she started the fifth block of her walk. She saw six young men approaching in a group. To get six customers ("six clients for her services in the profession endowed by Nature" would have described Dorothy's attitude more accurately) might establish a new record for her neighborhood. Four was the present record, held by Teresa Beetle, who lived across the street from Dorothy Dolly on Tinker Avenue.

If she could get all six of these men to come with her, it would be a big day for her and for Tinker Avenue. Dorothy could already picture Teresa Beetle's envious scowl when she saw the new record of six men trailing behind her. She would pause at the door of the apartment house and pretend to look for the key so that all girls of the section who were at leisure could witness her accomplishment.

Dorothy adjusted the white flower, then innocently lifted her dress as though to see if a run had started in the upper part of her stocking. Which reminded her that she had not worn stockings to-day, but this fact did not spoil the gesture.

As the six young men drew near, they spread out into a side by side position, forming a wall across the sidewalk. The wall moved forward, and the two ends closed around Dorothy. She found herself in the midst of a circle of men who could make her the most talked of girl on Tinker Avenue. The situation was working out even better than she had hoped.

"How are you, big boys?" she remarked.

"We're looking for a girl," replied one of them.

"Well, you've got one," said Dorothy with an engaging smile.

"Yes, but you may not be the right girl," another one answered. "Is your name Teresa Beetle?"

"Sure, that's me." Dorothy was delighted. Here was a chance to beat Teresa's record while posing as Teresa herself.

"Well, we were on our way to Tinker Avenue to see her. One time she let four friends of ours walk home with her—"

"For nothing," interrupted another one of the six insistently.

"For nothing? She—I mean, I did?" So this was how Teresa had come into neighborhood fame, the fourflusher. Just wait till Tinker Avenue heard about that! Teresa was undermining the reputation of Tinker Avenue's business girls. If this news became widespread, it would reflect on all of them. They would be bothered by all sorts of panhandlers looking for handouts. Regular customers might even start refusing to pay. Teresa was a skunk to have done such a thing.

Anyway, this was a chance for Dorothy both to denounce Teresa and her record and to establish a better record of her own. The notoriety of these achievements, together with the satisfaction of having prevented Teresa from setting this new mark, would be compensation enough. And not even Teresa would know that this was charity, too. Dorothy's smile of satisfaction replaced her trade-smile.

"Why, yes," she added. "I'm always glad to help a fellow out. Let's go."

CHAPTER II

JUST CALL US PETER

Six young men filed out of room 16 at 220 Tinker Avenue. Beneath the number 16 on the door was a card which said, "Dorothy Dolly, Chambermaid." Inside, a white carnation had been placed in a glass of water on the bureau.

"Don't bother about us—stay right there," the last man remarked. "We can find our way out all right."

As soon as the men reached the street they laughed in chorus.

"I wonder why she didn't charge us nothin'," one of them commented. "It cost those other four guys two bucks apiece."

"Maybe she was pullin' an advertisin' stunt," said another. "She told us to bring our two dollar bills next time."

"Yeah, they make you pay for everything in the city. Back in Menham we didn't need to do no tradin' with girls."

"Even if you picked the wrong one in the dark, it was all right."

These six youths had come to the city from a small country village called Menham eight years ago. They were each twenty-four years old now, and, by the strange coincidence of having had the same father (who had caused something of an epidemic of babies in the process of selling his peddler's wares), each had this swain's given name of Peter.

Most people thought they were sextuplets. Those who knew them were seldom sure which of the six Peters was which. Nobody really cared which was which, except the Peters themselves, and they could not have proved that there was not an interchange of bodies among them from day to day.

They were so much alike that, should a heavenly jester have exchanged the bodies of any two of them, the transfer would probably have gone unnoticed, unless one of them had happened to have a bruise of some sort. The new occupant of this body would have been at a loss to explain how the sore had suddenly appeared, as would the other Peter of the transaction to explain how his skin had miraculously healed.

No one would have dared confide information to one of the Peters that he did not want the others to know, for he could never be sure which Peter he was talking to when one was segregated from the other five.

The one word "Peter" was sufficient in greeting one or all of them. The Peters assisted in the confusion that attended the task of identifying them by their last names—which were, if you would like to try it: Jones, Sadler, Lyman, Dean, Pike and Hatch. If a new acquaintance, still trying to get their names straight, called one of them by the correct surname on a lucky guess, another Peter would interrupt to say that the name in question was his. This diversion would be indulged in by the six Peters until the other party either abandoned the attempt to remember their respective surnames or, by persistent perseverance, managed to get the wrong name attached to each of them.

The six Peters were more like one individual with six bodies than six different beings. They were invariably together and had been almost constantly from the time they had learned to walk. There was nothing of consequence—and very little of insignificance—about any one of them that the other five did not know. None of them could have kept the rest from knowing everything about him except his unspoken thoughts, for it was very seldom that any one of the six stayed away from all of the others for long. And their thoughts, being the reactions of identical bodies to twenty-four years of identical situations, were so similar that they permitted very few secrets.

It almost seemed as though their bodies exerted some kind of mutual magnetism that forced them to remain in a group. They lived together in two rooms, slept together in two beds, and worked together in various ways to obtain money. Not all of these ways were dishonest, but holding up pedestrians on lonely streets was.

Their technique of approaching a person who looked as though it would be worth the trouble to rob him was somewhat different than the manner in which they had surrounded Dorothy Dolly when they met. One of the Peters would appear from a hidden spot wearing a mask and a cap. The other five would be nowhere in sight.

The lone Peter would produce a gun and say, "Hands up, please." They all enjoyed seeing this remark quoted in the newspapers and reading accounts about the polite bandit. Having taken the man's money, the polite Peter would say, "Thank you, sir," and quickly disappear. Watches or other valuables were seldom taken unless they could be put to personal use. Such articles might be identified if they tried to sell them.

Almost immediately the frantic victim would then be confronted by all six Peters, who would suddenly come running up in a body from an opposite direction to that in which the robber had apparently fled. All would be wearing felt hats, the cap and mask having disappeared along with the bandit, for the thief was now in the rôle of a champion of law and order.

"We saw it, mister," one of the Peters would shout excitedly. "Come on, we'll help you catch him."

The six Peters and their victim would run in pursuit of the gunman as far as their companion was willing to go. If he lacked the courage to start out after this man with the gun, they would egg him on and assure him that the robber probably would be afraid to shoot.

Running after the thief, through alleys, up side streets, and across vacant lots, was always a source of amusement for the Peters. Generally the victim would soon become tired out and give up the chase. He would pant out thanks to the young men who had tried to recover his money for him and never suspect that one of these kind faces had worn the mask. Each of the victims would have been willing to appear as a witness for the defense if any of the Peters had been brought to court on a charge of robbing him.

The six Peters had started their gangster activities shortly after arriving from Menham when they were sixteen. Stealing bananas and coconuts from fruit store displays furnished a supply of food for a few days. Then they had started earning money by selling newspapers. After shouting about holdups for two weeks, they decided it would be more profitable to go into that business than just to shout about it. A cap pistol soon earned enough money for them to buy a real revolver.

Their honest tasks since then had not been as remunerative as the robberies. Three of them had worked in the city stables at one time, while the other three had driven city dump carts. These latter three were later transferred to the Sanitary Division and assigned to three swill wagons. All six had worked as city laborers and in a similar capacity for a contracting company. They had applied for jobs as bankers, chief engineers, policemen, and fashion designers but without success.

On one occasion when they had been entirely without funds, a few dollars were obtained from the Public Welfare Department. Their first purchase had been a box of cartridges for their revolver. Of their various experiments with money making, holdups, having proved the most effective, continued to be their favorite method.

Their departure from Menham had been quite unexpected. One morning six farmers had found their horses missing from their barns. That same morning the six Peters were all missing from their breakfast tables. Meanwhile, the horses had been found twenty miles away tied to six door knobs of stores in the town of Daisyville, where there was a railroad station.

"They've run away to be pirates," was the popular decision in Menham.

Mary Cline, a girl of the same age as the Peters, knew better. The night before she had told them, "You'll have to nurse it and everything," while insisting that, if she had a baby, she was going to make them bring it up.

CHAPTER III

HALF RATES FOR MONKEYS

Dorothy Dolly lost very little time in spreading the news on Tinker Avenue that Teresa Beetle's professional record had been made without compensation. The record now held by Dorothy was accepted as the new mark, and Teresa found herself subject to ridicule from her neighbors.

When such allegations were made, Miss Beetle, who had of course received remuneration, only laughed and replied with some such comment as, "Any time I sink to charity you can say, 'Well, she used to be sane.'" But inwardly she considered various schemes for revenge on Dorothy Dolly.

She started a counter report about Dorothy, but Tinker Avenue seemed skeptical of this information. The charge that Dorothy's accomplishment, too, was an amateur and not a professional feat lacked originality. Teresa was obviously stealing Dorothy's gossip-ideas. If she wanted to be given credence, she would have to use other tactics to humiliate her persecutor.

Teresa had a tattoo mark high on her right thigh. She considered hiring somebody to take Dorothy by force to a tattooer's to have her face decorated—preferably with obscene pictures. Good an idea as this was, Teresa hesitated to go through with it. For Dorothy would doubtless attempt and probably succeed with similar tactics in return.

She had never liked Dorothy Dolly. They often argued and had called each other many uncomplimentary names. On their last coming together, Teresa had greeted Dorothy with, "You're an eel's gut." Dorothy had replied with several words which are said to look very poorly in type—so let us not investigate that theory and run the risk of offending our esthetic senses.

Teresa had spent several years as a Vestal Vertical in a sacred but secret religious colony before coming to Tinker Avenue. There were two types of holy women in this group sponsored by a wealthy spinster who believed herself to be God's true interpreter on earth. Vestal Verticals spent their daily hours of devotion standing before the altar, their arms stretching toward the skies, in representation of rising souls en route to Heaven.

Vestal Horizontals passed their devotional hours lying face down, and forming a row behind the Vestal Verticals, with their arms stretched out on the floor toward the altar. The Vestal Horizontals symbolized the human race, their souls chained to wicked bodies—foul mechanisms of sin—to whose temptations God was subjecting them as a test to determine their eligibility as celestial citizens.

"I would have stuck it out," Teresa explained, "but one day another girl and I stole a bottle of Holy Wine." (Lucretia Longbeam, sponsor of the cult, would sometimes isolate herself for private ceremonies involving Holy Wine. This beverage was not allowed in the diet of her followers. During these mystery services, the prayers of Miss Longbeam—Vestal Longbeam was her adopted title—became rather noisy and could be heard at a considerable distance from her locked door.) "We got a little drunk and sneaked out to look for excitement. We met a couple of sailors who had some gin and told them we'd been to a masquerade. The next thing I remember I was watching a fish peddler cook some breakfast for himself on an oil stove. I was glad he didn't offer me any, because I didn't feel like eatin'. I couldn't go back to the colony, so I had to go to work."

Teresa had kept her religious robes and still tried them on occasionally. One of Vestal Longbeam's theories had been that the sins of the body could be prevented to a considerable extent by covering up the body, hiding it both from the eyes of its inhabitants and from the eyes of others. This had to be done, of course, in a much more thorough manner than by wearing ordinary clothing. Vestal Longbeam's followers, who obtained free board in this capacity, wore loose tunics which were tied at the neck and draped on the ground around their feet in a way that made walking difficult.

These women—no men were allowed—often tripped and fell down, but the purpose of the long robes was more important than these inconveniences. The feet were a part of the body, and Vestal Longbeam thought they should be concealed by something other than shoes.

Members of this flock also kept their heads covered by a hood which came down over their shoulders. Two small openings for the eyes were reluctantly tolerated by Vestal Longbeam. It was hard to keep these slits in front of the eyes. Since the cloth was opaque, the women often bumped into one another and into other objects.

The colony had been located on Vestal Longbeam's large country estate where there were no automobiles. It had been hard to teach the horses not to rear onto their hind legs at the sight of these cloaked figures.

There were difficulties at mealtime, for the hoods were not removed on these occasions of compulsory bodily sin. Food had to be located on the plate by means of the eye holes and a mouthful segregated upon a fork or spoon. (The hands, wearing long gloves that covered the whole arm, were allowed to protrude through slits in the sides of the robes at the table.) Conveying these morsels intact under the hood to the mouth required practice.

This cult was known as The Vegetarian Vestals. Eating meat was one of many sins of the flesh its members could escape, though there were quite a few others.

Robes of the Vestal Horizontals were striped with the pattern of convict costumes. This had seemed to Vestal Longbeam to be the best design for these women who represented the human race with its soul imprisoned in its unholy body. The Vestal Verticals, symbolizing the liberated soul, wore white. Spies from the surrounding countryside had reported that "Lucretia Longbeam's place is full of plain ghosts with zebra ghosts for pets."

Teresa Beetle's white robes had obtained several regular customers for her since coming to Tinker Avenue. Some men who had learned the story of the garments' religious origin liked to have her dressed as Vestal Beetle when they arrived.

Teresa—while thinking about Dorothy Dolly rather than Vestal Longbeam—saw an organ grinder with a monkey on one of her walks about the streets and had an idea. She could hire this man to take his monkey to 220 Tinker Avenue. A small sum would persuade him to come out of the building remarking, "Da monk he like Dorothy fine. Dorothy Dolly da monk's girl."

She could have him talk in a loud enough voice so that some of the other girls would hear, and the news of Dorothy's business dealings with a monkey would replace the accounts of Teresa's alleged philanthropy as a conversational topic.

She managed to explain to him what she wanted said and done. The man went to 220 Tinker Avenue and proceeded to carry out his instructions. He hid inside the doorway long enough to convince any who had watched him enter that this was no mere joke. Then he came back to the street telling of the monkey's fondness for Dorothy Dolly.

Dorothy was coming out of the door just at this time and found herself right behind a strange organ man who was making the announcement, "Da monk like Dorothy Dolly." She had been expecting some reprisal from Teresa. She overtook the man and made him another business proposition. In a few moments he was under way again, saying in a loud tone, "Teresa Beetle like-a da monk. . . ."

CHAPTER IV

AN UNCLE AND A GOD

Alfred Wopple was one of those who liked to have Teresa Beetle wear her religious robes when he called. He paid her an extra dollar to appear in this garb each Sunday morning at eleven o'clock.

Wopple would drive to Tinker Avenue from church and leave his wife and car parked outside Teresa's apartment while he went in "to visit a sick friend."

To have a daughter of joy in this dress of a daughter of God added greatly to Alfred Wopple's illicit enjoyment on these occasions—or, rather, was in itself the chief pleasure. He was an active church-member through necessity rather than choice. His uncle, a very rich and equally pious man, would have eliminated the name of a beneficiary from his will if there had been any suspicion of religious doubts. Murder or robbery he might possibly have pardoned with true Christian forgiveness, or even cruel or inhuman torture, but agnosticism—never!

The satisfaction of fooling his wife so openly while she waited at the curb was another inducement that led Mr. Wopple to Tinker Avenue on Sundays. He enjoyed letting her remind him to buy some fruit for the sick friend each week. This fruit served as Teresa's breakfast. One Sunday he had persuaded Teresa to walk out to the street with him when he returned to his wife and car. Teresa had refused to wear the hood over her head but had appeared in a white tunic several sizes too long.

"This is Vestal Beetle," he told his wife. "Bill was pretty sick to-day, and she came to call on him, too. He goes to her church, you know—The Vegetarian Vestals."

Mrs. Wopple had never heard of this order, but she did not let the religious lady know of her ignorance.

"What did she wear that funny dress for?" Mrs. Wopple. commented, after they had driven away and left the lady in robes to buy a paper for the sick man.

Her husband explained that white symbolized purity and that the more white cloth the members of Vestal Beetle's church could drape onto their bodies the purer they became, according to God's rules as prescribed in their creed.

Mrs. Wopple had also been surprised to see rouge and powder, and to smell a blend of perfume and cigarettes on this lady of God.

"She has to study the petty abuses of personal habits of the modern girl at first hand in order to be able to censure them intelligently," said Wopple.

Wopple liked to fool his wife just for the sake of fooling her. Sunday mornings it was quiet and orderly on Tinker Avenue, and she had no suspicions that this was part of the red-light district. On their first visit Mrs. Wopple had asked to go along with her husband to help cheer up his friend. He let her walk up the steps to the front door and then recalled that Bill would be taking an electrical sun-bath in the nude at this hour. She had hastened back to the car.

Any chance to ridicule religion in secret was a welcome one to Alfred Wopple. His religious pose had become so important a guise—being employed, as he was, by his uncle and due for an independent income when this relative died—that it seemed to be his real attitude, even to many who thought they were his intimates. And he could never speak blasphemy to a respectable stranger, for this stranger might know his uncle.

He looked forward to the Sunday following his uncle's death, when he could stagger into church and let his drunken whims take their course. A stained-glass window showing several sad angels heavily laden with wings had long been an intended target for a pint—or perhaps a quart bottle on this merry occasion.

He anticipated a few days in jail, or at least a heavy fine, as a result of this drunken outbreak but was willing to pay whatever it might cost in time or money—after he had his uncle's fortune safe in his own name.

Wopple gave the impression of being forty and pure. His nature was exactly like that of a small boy just learning to swear. At home and amongst all who knew his relatives he was a model Sunday School boy. When with trusted friends, he made a hobby of profanation. He did not dare include his wife among these trusted friends, for, if they should ever have a serious disagreement, a knowledge of his impiety would put a very effective weapon at her disposal.

God and Uncle Ben were somewhat synonymous to Alfred Wopple. Without his uncle there would be no God to bother him. In paying tribute to God, he was only paying tribute to his uncle. When blaspheming God, he was invariably blaspheming his uncle, too. One important difference between these two beings was that his uncle, for all practical purposes, had actually created the universe as far as Alfred was concerned. Everything he had ever owned had come from his uncle. God was only a part of this world his uncle had provided, and a very undesirable part because of the restrictions his uncle had introduced with Him.

Wopple had inaugurated noonday Bible talks for employees at his uncle's offices. He reprimanded those who did not attend regularly and secretly resolved, when he took over the business, to discharge those who did. His Sunday visits to poor sick Bill on Tinker Avenue were quite in keeping with his apparent belief in the love-thy-neighbor doctrine.

He brought his car to a stop in front of Teresa's apartment on this occasion and smiled. His uncle was sitting beside his wife in the back seat, having accepted an invitation to have dinner with them.

"Just wait a few minutes while I pass along the word of God to one of us whose health will not permit his attending church at present," he said.

"Shall I come, too?" asked the uncle.

"No, his health is so poor now that he can only see one visitor at a time," explained the nephew with great earnestness. He departed on his Christian errand.

Teresa had watched the arrival from her upstairs window.

"Why didn't you bring the other guy up?" she asked him.

This former Vestal Vertical could be Wopple's confidante in matters carefully guarded from his wife. There was no danger of Teresa's ever knowing his uncle.

He replied in words that gave him more pleasure than all of Vestal Longbeam's disciples could have provided: "That's that damn son of a . . ." (His vocabulary contained a choice selection of terms which might involve unesthetic combinations of type.) "uncle of mine."

CHAPTER V

WE MIGHT HAVE BEEN FIG TREES

The six young men named Peter were walking in two rows of three along one of many crowded city streets. They had just befriended the victim of a robber by chasing with him after the bandit for six blocks, and in one of Peter Pike's pockets were the missing eighteen dollars and sixty-two cents. Peter Hatch had a five dollar bill which the man had given his attempted benefactors from a hidden wallet the thief had not found.

"Damn it, we could have retired with the money in that pocket book," said Peter Dean. "How'd you ever miss that?"

"It was a dirty trick—him hidin' his money like that," replied Peter Pike.

"Talk about a polite bandit—Pike not only says, 'Please,' and, 'Thank you,' but he doesn't even take the guy's money," remarked Peter Lyman. "The papers will take us for a ride for this."

These six men had long arms and legs that were never properly fitted by their ready-made clothes. Thick wrists dangled out of the coat sleeves. High ankles kept the trouser cuffs far above the pavements. The Peters had been raised in a community of overalls. Their bodies had never been able to adapt themselves fully to the change into city clothes. But they would not have cared, even had they been aware of their unconformity.

They could have been nudists with as little concern as they accepted department store styles in clothes. Tattooed or painted wardrobes, with earrings, nose rings—and loin cloths for neck scarfs would have been just as satisfactory as sack suits and underwear, probably more so. They were not nudists because none of the civilized tribes of this city had adopted nudism—on the street.

Their manner of greeting people with whom they had dealings other than robbery needed but a slight change of costume to be mistaken for a band of head-hunters pouncing upon an intended trophy. They would spread out side by side into a moving wall, just as they had in approaching Dorothy Dolly, and then form a close circle around the individual that left no possible openings for escape.

They preferred to come up from the rear and take the party by surprise. A favorite amusement after forming the circle was to put the wall into motion again and provide a merry-go-round effect for the person in the center. This added to his confusion in telling one Peter from another, and, if he were very drunk, generally furnished additional confusion in his problems of equilibrium.

Surrounding people in this way was perhaps the result of atavistic instincts from ancestral savages, perhaps merely a natural means for getting seven beings into the smallest possible space on a city sidewalk. The revolving circle effect, too, may have been a savage expression of satisfaction in the capture. It may have been merely an expression of restlessness, or perhaps was only the joke that they intended.

"Well, anyhow, we've got twenty-three dollars," consoled Peter Pike. "We won't need any more for to-night."

"Yeah," said Peter Sadler, "and there's a dame coming now."

The girl, who was not a Tinker Avenue lady, was frightened when she found herself surrounded by these six men. She screamed.

"Shut up," said Peter Jones. "We'll pay you."

"Let me go!" shrieked the girl.

Passers-by were slowing down their paces to watch the fun. The girl was pretty, but these six men were exceedingly husky. No heroes came to her rescue.

"I guess she ain't the right kinda girl," decided Peter Hatch.

"She's one a them crazy ones that howl at the moon," remarked Peter Lyman.

Girls were of three kinds in the category of the Peters: those who charged, those who didn't, and those who screeched. Their selections were generally from the first group.

"Beat it," said Peter Dean, stepping out of the circle to let her through. She darted out the opening somewhat like a mouse that has been freed from a trap, except that she used only her lower limbs for running. The Peters watched her disappear into the crowd on the sidewalk. They were puzzled by this type of girl. They had found girls to be suitable for but one function, and those who refused to do even this were indeed useless members of society.

"She'd make a good siren for a fire engine," said Peter Sadler.

Another maiden, one who did not scream, was soon in the center of the Peter circle.

John Dew lived on the ground floor beneath the six Peters on One-Tenth Street. It was a crowded street full of small stores, continual noise, and many small children whose shouts were an unnoticed part of the general clamor. John Dew was a white-haired man who spent the warm seasons on the sidewalk seated in a chair that leaned against the front of a variety store now run by his two daughters. His hands shook, and he mumbled to passers-by.

Sometimes he mumbled about business. "I gotta nice-a tomatoes for you," he would mutter into space. "Da best. Da best! Twenty cent to you. Da best. Twenty cent."

If anybody became aware of this sales talk and asked to see the tomatoes, or whatever other kind of merchandise was being quoted, John would grunt and start to talk about something else. "Nice-a day," he might add, or, "Drinka two glass a wine every meal. That's a pretty good for you. Big glass. Bigger da glass, better da good."

John's daughters were large gobs of waddling fat. They puffed about the store, and the kitchen and other rooms behind the store, with apparent effort, moving slowly and with no attempt at gracefulness. Two masses that filled the upper half of their dresses swayed from side to side as they walked. Both women were over fifty and spinsters. They had the one point in common that they liked to eat a lot. And they joined their father in his customary two glasses of red wine at each meal. The father drank from a tumbler. The daughters used beer steins.

Ortensia Dew liked to paint pictures. The six Peters liked to encourage her in this hobby, not because they appreciated her work, but because they were pleased with her reactions to their praise. To say, "That's a fine picture," was an assured means of obtaining credit for cigarettes or other commodities—providing Tabitha, her sister, was not within hearing. Tabitha knew that it would be impossible to identify the debtor at any future time.

Since Ortensia's work conformed to no known school of art, it might be said to have constituted an entirely new school of its own. Unlike paintings by other artists whose results might be similarly classified, some of Ortensia's portrayals could be identified by the layman.

Human faces could be distinguished in many of her paintings that covered the walls of the rooms in which the Dews lived. Whether these depictions were men or women was generally a matter for conjecture. One large picture, however, was obviously a woman, or at least a female.

At the moment, Ortensia was engrossed in a painting of a nude man, at the bottom of which the name "Adam" stood out in large letters. It was after dark, but electric illumination had no effect on her choice of color tones. Ortensia did not approve of omitting any essential details. She believed in painting things as they really were and consequently was now confronted with a problem.

"Tabitha," she said, "what does a naked man look like?"

"What's the matter, you losin' your memory?" laughed her sister.

"No, I've never seen one—it was always dark."

"Well, offer one of them boys across the street a stick of candy, and he'll pose for you."

"No, I've seen young kids. I'm painting a picture of Adam. Wouldn't he look nice if I made a boy out of him! I want to know what a *man* looks like."

Six men entered the store just as these words were spoken, but this did not seem to solve the problem. The Peters were amused to hear Tabitha whisper to Ortensia, "No! No! Don't ask them!"

Tabitha did not like to admit that her ignorance was as great as her sister's. Aloud she said, with a tone of authority, "Give me a pencil. I'll show you."

"Don't look," Ortensia warned the Peters.

Tabitha proceeded to sketch her conception of a fig leaf, taking particular care in drawing the stem.

CHAPTER VI

A FALLEN WOMAN DEFINES A "FALLEN WOMAN"

Miss Mabel Shoe, wealthy social worker, had organized the Society for the Resurrection of the Fallen Woman. At the head of the society's stationery was printed the slogan, "Redeem the Souls of Lost Bodies." At the bottom was another motto, sometimes misconstrued by non-members, "Make the Prostitute a Respectable Woman."

Miss Shoe showed great indignation whenever the latter maxim was taken to mean Make Prostitution a Respectable Profession. She refused to change its wording and insisted that, "Only a filthy-minded guttersnipe could read any but the noblest of motives into this precept. I guess it's time I started a Society for the Cleansing of Nasty Minds."

Miss Shoe had founded many societies of her own for moral reform. Strictly speaking, these "groups" each comprised one active member: Mabel Shoe. She preferred to conduct social work according to her own ideas rather than to be but one of the many members of existing organizations. Other members for her societies were always welcome but, it is sad to relate, were not usually forthcoming.

She found it easier to obtain converts than workers. Once she had enlisted nearly five hundred followers in the Society to Put Silk Hats on Hobos, whose slogan had been, "Back to the Pullmans." She had made a public announcement through the newspapers that the conversion of all hobos who were willing to reform and sign a pledge never to ride the rods again would be celebrated at a banquet in their honor at the Ritz Spitz Hotel that night.

The overflow from the private dining room hired for the occasion had been accommodated in several shifts on banquet tables hastily assembled in the main ballroom. The guests had each signed the pledge, as requested, on departing.

"I been goin' in for hitch hiking lately anyway, lady," one of them had remarked.

Miss Shoe seemed to make a hobby of getting out stationery bearing her name in new official capacities. For she announced the starting of new societies by this means at very frequent intervals. "Miss Mabel Shoe, President," was always printed on the letterhead beneath the name of the group and the slogan. This sort of writing paper was used for all of her letters. Some suspected she kept a correspondence file, telling which society's paper was used each time, by means of which she was able to send every correspondent a different letterhead whenever she wrote.

None of these societies was ever officially disbanded, but Miss Shoe's chief interest always centered around the newest one. All others were, for practical purposes, merely letterheads.

The newest one of the moment was the Society for the Resurrection of the Fallen Woman, which Miss Shoe believed to be her most worthy enterprise to date—her usual attitude upon thinking up a new name for a society. There was something wicked-sounding about this latest group. Reforming erring sisters was not like reforming other types of recalcitrants. The evil associated with prostitutes was the most famous form of immorality. Some of the outstanding sinners of history had been women without morals. And she would come in contact with their wantonness in associating with daughters of—her thoughts started to form the word "joy" but quickly substituted "evil."

Miss Shoe felt a vague and strange stimulation, a slight sensation of excitement. There was something fascinating about the thought of this association with girls of sin her new duties would require. She felt as though she were doing something naughty and quickly assured herself that her efforts might put an end to the harlotry stigma which had persisted through the ages.

The new society had been announced two weeks ago, but active work had not yet started for lack of fallen women. Miss Shoe had been uncertain just where to go to find genuine prostitutes. She had a terror of approaching a girl she suspected might be a harlot and having the maid turn out to be an honest woman.

Being over forty and without experience in the ways of men with women, Miss Shoe was debarking for very unfamiliar lands in starting her newest society. The inevitable thrill of the traveler in distant countries had possessed her, and she was anxious to arrive at port. Where could she find a brothel?

She had heard of free lancers. Perhaps, if she took a walk about some of the undesirable sections of the city, she might see one of these girls plying her trade. She became aware of another stimulating flush. In walking the streets like this, she would be, literally, a streetwalker herself. Would any man accost her? She might carry a gun for protection. She decided not to. The glow continued. She knew she was working in the interests of society, but still she felt strangely wicked.

Mabel Shoe had often gone about the city streets on foot, but never before had she felt the way she did now. It seemed to her that every man was looking at her as though considering how much he should offer. This feeling alternately frightened and shocked her. Surely she did not look like a woman of easy virtue—then why did she suddenly feel like one?

Was she becoming evil-minded? Surely not, she told herself. Her benevolent interest in the harlot had become so great that, in her sympathy, she was beginning to see the world through her eyes. Her mental censor eliminated the thought that perhaps her body's appearance of being so many sticks stuffed in a dress would have prevented aphrodisiacal reactions on the part of men who chanced to notice her.

Miss Shoe was possessed by more qualms as she walked along One-Tenth Street. Would the eyes of the world still see her as a benevolent social worker if she were espied talking to a degenerate girl? Would passing men realize that she was trying to reform her companion and was not her partner in sin? Suppose the streetwalker, reluctant to become an honest woman, spoke to a man as they stood there together? The man would probably think both of them were seeking his patronage. Suppose he chose her?

"I must not wince in the face of danger while fighting for my cause," Miss Shoe assured herself.

But Miss Shoe did wince and at that very moment. A *man* was speaking to her! He was sitting in a chair on the sidewalk, evidently reviewing passing girls of lost reputations. She had been able to make out the mumbled words: "Twenty cent," but had overlooked the rest of his remark, which had been about oranges. Miss Shoe's wince had been the start of an immediate impulse to run, which she did. John Dew did not follow her.

Her reflex actions of fear, terror, and panic quickly changed into the more reasonable feeling of anger. This man had only offered her twenty cents. Miss Shoe became released from her emotions long enough to realize that she was running and that the white-haired man was not chasing her. He had actually said she was only worth *twenty cents,* and he was not sufficiently interested to bother running after her.

Of course, she would not have wanted to be chased by a man, but she had enough pride to realize that this man's reaction to her had been most indifferent. His twenty cent bid and evident lack of interest were even more of an insult than his having mistaken her for a loose woman.

Miss Shoe stopped running. She wanted to scream but didn't dare. Other men might think she was shouting to them. She wanted to go back and make a fitting retort to the white-haired rowdy. But she couldn't do that, for it would amount to accosting a strange man. Nor could she go up to a policeman and say, "That man only offered me twenty cents."

She was provided relief by a shocking sight which distracted her agonizing thoughts and recalled the cause for which she was fighting. Just ahead a young woman—unquestionably scarlet—wearing a white carnation over one ear, was speaking to a man. She could hear her say, "How are you, *deerie?*" The man answered, "Busy," and did not stop.

Miss Mabel Shoe hurried to the assistance of Miss Dorothy Dolly. The social worker had one last minute misgiving: was this really a prostitute? The man might have been a relative.

She found herself saying, "Are you a fallen woman?" and expecting the unfortunate female to burst into tears and sob forth, "Yes, is there *any* escape for me?"

The sensitive Miss Dolly was a more literal version of a scarlet woman for the moment. She saw scarlet. To be called a fallen woman was a "when-you-say-that-smile" expression in her vocabulary. No chosen girl in the profession endowed by Nature could tolerate any such insult as this from one of Nature's unfortunate outsiders.

"Fallen, huh, do I look as though I need any help getting back onto my feet?" she replied. "Here, I'll show you what a fallen woman looks like."

Miss Dolly gave Miss Shoe a vigorous push that threw her at full length upon the sidewalk.

Miss Shoe felt very embarrassed but not only because of her awkward sprawl. She had insulted an honest woman. The man this girl had spoken to must have been a relative.

CHAPTER VII

CURTAINS SHOULD BE PULLED DOWN

Business had been good, both for the six Peters and for a cut-rate clothing store that was featuring jaunty suits of black and purple checks. The six Peters had each purchased one of the garments and gave the appearance of a walking billboard conspicuously depicting these clothes of "Unusual Price and Pattern."

They usually all bought apparel of similar nature. It aided in the confusion of others in trying to tell one from another, and sometimes caused similar confusion among themselves. This uncertainty of identity was increased by such additional details as their customs of always having their hair cut at the same time, shaving at the same time, and getting drunk at the same time.

The Peters could usually tell each other's surnames by their slight variations of voice and individual mannerisms: Peter Pike wore his hat further back on his head than the others. Peter Jones said, "Oh boy!" whenever his enthusiasm was aroused by anything. Peter Sadler always took a chaser of water when he drank whisky—the others used beer. When at a bar, Peter Lyman always drank Peter Sadler's beer chaser as well as his own—since it was free and unclaimed. Peter Hatch always insisted on being first with a girl. Peter Dean did not like gin.

Having several dollars left despite their expenditures for clothes, the Peters began to consider a somewhat customary program of pavement nymphs and liquor—that is, five of them were thinking of procedures in this direction. Peter Hatch was having an unusual thought: how could he get away from the others without arousing suspicion?

A strange meditation had been bothering him to-day. (He had been the one who suggested buying the new suits.) A girl's face and figure had persisted in depicting themselves in his mind. She was not just a girl of unscanned face of the sort usually pictured with thoughts of women. This girl's face appealed to him as much as her body. For some inexplicable reason he wanted to have her just for himself. He did not want the others to know about her.

Peter Hatch was bothered by these thoughts because they were so abnormal. He felt rather guilty in wanting to keep this attractive female a secret from the rest. They had shared other women, and had all known about those who had not cared to have more than one of them. None of the Peters had had any girls on the sly without telling the rest the essential details. Why should *he* want to be so underhanded with this one?

Peter Hatch was frightened, too. Was he being hypnotized by the mysterious power that blinded men into marrying girls? There must be some such temporarily deranging force that caused sane men to agree to support wives and their children for life. He thought he was beginning to feel that living with this girl—even as her husband—would be tolerable.

"God! I better be careful," he told himself. "What a ride I'd take if I ever signed up with a dame for life. I s'pose I could have one of the others dress up like a minister—Hell! am I going crazy!?—thinking about getting married. I wouldn't even go through the motions for a joke. There might be some hitch to it. I'll tell them about this tramp now—no reason why I shouldn't. She's no different than the rest. What's a girl to get all excited about!"

Despite this decision, Peter Hatch's spoken words were, "I ain't feelin' so good. I think I'll go home and take a nap."

"See you later," said Peter Dean.

The night before, Peter Hatch had gone into a store alone to do an errand. The girl who had waited on him was the one who had been bothering him to-day. During a brief conversation, she had agreed to meet him at five o'clock to-night on the corner of Hathaway and Rood Streets. He arrived at this meeting place at four-fifteen.

"I hope she doesn't show up," he said to himself. "Damn it, what's the matter with me anyway? The other Peters are out having a good time, and here I am acting as though this thing in a dress had me covered with a gun. There's plenty of women. Look at them go by. Probably any of them would fall for this nifty suit."

Girls continued to pass without greetings from Peter Hatch. His mental processes insisted that he ignore them and wait for the saleslady, despite his reiterative arguments to himself pointing out the senselessness of this procedure. He stamped back and forth along the sidewalk but never got out of sight of the corner of Hathaway and Rood Streets.

He explained to himself that it would be only natural if he felt foolish, but there was no reason why he should continue to feel guilty. What difference did it make whether or not he told the other Peters about this girl? They were having their girl, or girls, too. He wasn't going to have anything that they weren't.

There were so many more girls that it would take a million times six Peters to handle them all. What difference did it make if he chose out just *one* for himself? Why should he feel obliged to account to them for this particular girl? That was as ridiculous as telling them about an extra cigarette he had smoked. Having convinced himself with this reasoning, he was immediately prodded by the question: "Why don't you want to tell them about her?"

At ten minutes past five Peter Hatch was still pacing about the corner. His former thoughts had been replaced by others which proved even more disturbing and repeated themselves over and over: Where is she? What's happened to her? Was she just kidding when she said she'd be here? Am I on the right corner? Why isn't she here? What's keeping her?

Then Bertha Render came into sight crossing Hathaway Street in a mass of traffic. Peter Hatch ran in front of a mammoth truck and a speeding taxicab to get to her.

"What's the matter, drunk?" she asked.

"No, I'd know better if I was," he replied. He was referring to his attitude toward her rather than his leap in front of the death-dealing vehicles. The traffic on her side of the street had stopped, so they were able to reach the sidewalk there in safety.

"Where shall we eat?" he asked, and then wondered why he had. He hadn't made this date so he could pay for the girl's supper. He wasn't saving much money by going out with her. But something seemed to inform him that he would enjoy watching her eat. It would be worth the price of the check to sit across from her and watch food enter her body. This thought seemed to stimulate him, and there was something about the girl's hair that seemed to have the effect of a shot of whisky.

Bertha Render agreed to let Peter Hatch come up to her room after they had eaten. He was pleased with himself for having retained enough of his former sanity to recall that four Ward Eights will present a very good argument as to why a girl should provide the hospitality of her own quarters.

Peter left early. It would not do for him to be out if the other Peters returned unexpectedly. He was already thinking up new ways to elude them for future dates with "Bicycle" Bertha—on the way home from the restaurant she had insisted that her head was going round and round like a wheel. Perhaps girls were good for more than one thing after all—or at least perhaps this one was. He was probably crazy, but at any rate his form of insanity was a happy one.

As Peter Hatch stepped out onto the sidewalk from the hallway, he suddenly found himself surrounded by five other men in black and purple checked suits. One of them was holding his foot in the door to prevent the snap lock from fastening.

"What did you think we'd been doin', buyin' aspirin for poor, sick Peter Hatch?" asked Peter Lyman.

"We watched you from the fire escape," said Peter Jones.

"You found one who was O. K. and thought you could put one over on us, huh?" said Peter Dean. "Well, we followed you."

"Yeah, and it's my turn now," announced Peter Sadler. "We been drawin' lots."

CHAPTER VIII

AN IDEAL COUPLE

Bertha Render wished Peter had not been in such a hurry to leave. She liked to have pleasant flame-sensations fanned and kept aglow as long as possible—not extinguished by a sudden departure. She wished Peter had stayed to hug and squeeze her more.

"But that's a man for you," she told herself. "As soon as they get well acquainted, they pull up stakes and beat it."

There was a knock on her door. A low voice announced, "It's Peter again."

Bertha jumped up from her couch excitedly and admitted Peter Sadler.

"I couldn't stay away," he told her. "I had to come back. You got me so excited, I had to go out and get a breath of cool air. And it felt like an iceberg after rubbing noses with you."

Bertha was very pleased. Her dampened flame-sensations burst into active fire again. This man in the black and purple checkered suit wasn't so bad after all.

Peter Sadler sat down on the couch and pulled her into his lap.

"It's great to get my arms back around my Bicycle Bertha," he told her. Five Peters had heard the sixth apply this delightful nickname to Miss Render.

"But you had a green necktie on when you went out a minute ago," she observed.

"Did I? Oh, yes. There was a guy outside selling ties, so I bought this gray one. You had me so hot under the collar it spoiled my necktie."

"Better take this one off so you won't spoil it."

Peter Hatch, on the sidewalk outside the door, remained surrounded by four other Peters. He had made no attempt to interfere with their program with Bicycle Bertha. Despite his confusion at having been caught so unawares, he retained enough logic to realize that one unarmed man could offer very little opposition to five—or even four—others of equal physical strength, especially when he was the center of a circle of which they were the circumference.

But only a very fleeting, hardly noticed, thought had suggested his making a physical effort to keep Bertha for himself by trying to fight off the others. Then, instead of being indignant at having been traded, he had a feeling of relaxation and relief. The appearance of his five half brothers had brought him out of his trance and back to reality.

They had provided the cure for this hypnosis which overcame so many men and left them helpless for a woman to drag up in front of a minister. Keeping this girl for himself might have been the first step toward asking her to marry him. That was what marriage amounted to: getting tied up with one woman.

Bicycle Bertha was a nice girl, and all that, but there was no reason why he should be victimized by her. He could enjoy her just as much by sharing her with the others. What would be the point of having her just for himself? His imagining that he had enjoyed watching her eat was a lot of nonsense.

He could still buy her more Ward Eights if he wanted to. There had been something attractive about her expression when she drank. And the red beverage had blended nicely with her rouged lips. "God! am I going batty again!?" he said to himself. "Next time I'll buy her Tom Collinses."

Peter Sadler meanwhile had accomplished his mission with Bicycle Bertha. "You've got me all steamed up again," he told her. "I'll have to go outside and cool off or you'll have to find a big dish to put a broiled Peter on. I'll be right back though."

"I'm next," said Peter Jones when the street door was opened.

"Better tell her you bought a new tie," Peter Sadler told him. "I forgot mine."

"Peter's back again," Bertha was informed, together with another rapping on her door.

"Didn't take you long to cool off," she said.

"No, it's like walking into an ice box when I get away from my little Bicycle."

"You sure can pick 'em," Peter Sadler told Peter Hatch, stepping into Peter Jones' place in the circle.

Peter Hatch again insisted to himself that these five men had done him a favor. They had brought things back to normal. These others had rescued him from the dangers of tempting that type of insanity which could lead to matrimony.

But, then, if the rest grew tired of Bicycle Bertha, he could have her to himself again. "Damn it!" his mind retorted. "Why in hell do I want her all to myself?"

Peter Jones returned to the group, also minus a necktie.

"Me next," said Peter Dean.

A short time later six men in checkered suits of black and purple, five of them without ties, walked away from the apartment house in which Miss Render resided.

"Some girl!" remarked Peter Pike.

Bicycle Bertha, lying on her couch, was trying to fan herself with five neckties.

"Some man!" she said aloud.

CHAPTER IX

HIGH HEELS AND A PINK BOW TIE

Mabel Shoe did not give up her hunt for a genuine maid of the gutter, despite her degradation in having become, in a literal sense, both a streetwalker and a fallen woman herself on her first quest. The Society for the Resurrection of the Fallen Woman must go on. In order to continue its good work, in fact, in order to start, it must have a strumpet.

Miss Shoe knew that prostitutes existed. Such creatures had even been mentioned in the Bible. So she was not looking for anything purely mythical. And, since these vulgarians were public women, flaunting their wares to all mankind, she was not looking for anything that should be hard to find.

She had a mental image of a large black pit—the underworld, the obvious den of all fallen women—where the unfortunate girls were screaming for help, praying (or, at least, wishing) for just such life-lines as she was anxious to throw them. If she could only find this pit. Where was the underworld? Of course, it wasn't actually underground, but it had to be hidden to a certain extent to keep out policemen—and the workers of any society which intended to rescue its ladies.

Miss Shoe had done social work in the slums and other undesirable portions of the city. She had heard some of these sections referred to as sites of the underworld. But never had she seen a girl there whom she could definitely classify as a prostitute. A few maidens had aroused her suspicion in times past, but she could not mentally apply the scarlet letter to any of them with certainty. After her unfortunate experience with that innocent girl who had been so "obviously" fallen, she would have to be doubly careful in accosting girls whose incontinence could not be established beyond all possible doubt.

Miss Shoe had suffered in sympathy for this poor girl, thinking how insulted and disgraced she herself would feel if any one should ask her if she were a fallen woman. The girl had disappeared before she could get back onto her feet and apologize. And what good would an apology have done? The insult had been made, and its words, implying that the lady resembled a woman of the streets, could never be erased from her mind.

This fact was indisputable, for Miss Shoe could speak from experience. She knew her own encounter with the insulting white-haired man could never be forgotten. He had done more than just speak to her, but there are limits to our emotional capacities. She would not have been much more upset—terror and anger can each be equally overpowering—if he had only spoken in a businesslike way and made no reference to a twenty-cent offer.

The lady she had spoken to had perhaps become hysterical. Miss Shoe was sure that she herself would have except for the shocking sight of this girl apparently accosting a strange man.

This had aroused her missionary ardor and enabled the inner tension to revise itself into the fighting spirit of a reformer. The other insulted girl, having no such inner change, might have collapsed under an accumulation of nervous indignation, and the shock might have led to serious derangement.

Then there was another point to be considered: If the girl ever did recover her normal senses, what would she think of this woman who had apparently been in search of a loose woman? There had been no chance to explain her real mission. If a man had approached the girl, at least he would have been acting according to a somewhat normal instinct. But what sort of a shady person would she think a woman was who sought consort with prostitutes? No wonder she had pushed her so rudely to the street—to be approached by such a depraved character had doubtless been taken as a two-fold insult.

Miss Shoe felt that she had disgraced herself even more than the girl. She had only implied that the girl was a party to a normal vice. This implied that she was seeking her services and thus had amounted to an apparent admission that she herself was a party to some abnormal and far more vulgar vice. Of course, the lady was a stranger, but suppose they should ever meet again?

Miss Shoe's frantic thoughts along this line led to conclusions that seemed to endanger the perpetuation of the Society for the Resurrection of the Fallen Woman: she could not run the risk of having her motive so misunderstood again. Even if she succeeded in identifying a real slut, to accost her might arouse her suspicion. The girl might throw this seeming invert, who apparently had fallen still lower than she, to the street before she had a chance to explain her benevolent purpose.

How could she seek harlots without running this danger? She must not abandon her cause! A true social worker must, like a soldier, be willing to make any sacrifices in fighting for the welfare of others. But it seemed impractical to continue the search for fallen women if she was to be knocked to the sidewalk on each encounter.

This problem seemed without solution until Miss Shoe had a very sudden and practical idea: she could disguise herself as a man. This inspiration aroused all the fighting strength of the society. Miss Shoe called her butler and explained that she was going to a masquerade. Could she borrow a set of his street clothes?

All of her original stimulation returned while putting on masculine attire. She felt strangely wicked again. The guilty feeling of having disgraced herself, and an innocent girl, departed. She could justify and tolerate this wicked feeling. It *was* rather unladylike and naughty to go out on the street dressed like a man. But it was a harmless vice, like a childish prank. She could enjoy this pleasant glow of excitement upon preparing to seek out the harlot now.

The pants gave her a strange sensation. They fit tightly around the stomach and hips and made her feel somewhat immodest. It seemed as though she were wearing only underdrawers. At any rate, in this costume, she could not be mistaken for a fallen woman of any type. She managed to push all of her hair under the butler's derby. It would not be necessary to tip her hat upon approaching a fallen woman. This scheme was working out fine!

The butler's shoes did not fit. Well, she could wear a pair of her own. The heels were high and the toes pointed, but there was no reason why a man could not wear shoes like this. Cowboys did. The butler's necktie was rather drab. She would use a bright pink ribbon of her own and make a nice bow tie for herself. Men wore bow ties.

Mabel Shoe stepped onto the sidewalk with confidence. Surely nobody would recognize her. Hardly had she told herself this when two men on the other side of the street, in voices strained to their highest pitch, shouted, "Oh, yoo hoo!"

She did not know them. Were they speaking to her? Perhaps she looked like some man they knew. She felt she must maintain her masculine pose and not appear offended because two males had spoken to her. She waved. The men laughed loudly.

A few steps further, two men approaching her laughed and remarked in chorus, forcing high-pitched voices, "Oh, swish!" This hardly seemed like a greeting, so Miss Shoe did not respond. But one of them added, "How's the la-de-da boy?" He was evidently speaking to her, so she replied, "Fine." The laughter grew louder.

There were many more such greetings and comments that she did not understand as Miss Shoe continued along the street. This man whom she resembled must be quite popular. But why did his friends all laugh so heartily? And why did they say such silly things? Comments about violets, lilies, pansies, fairies, and fluff did not seem like particularly manly topics. This initiation into masculinity was perplexing.

The constant salutations were interfering with Miss Shoe's mission. She would have to improve her disguise so that, besides not being a woman, she could escape being mistaken for this popular man. She had better take a taxi to another section of the city. Perhaps the man would not be known there. And, in taking a taxi, she could drive right to the underworld, perhaps right to the door of a brothel.

She was a man now. She could speak to the driver as man to man. Men doubtless knew where strumpets resided, especially a man so familiar with the city as a taxi driver. It would take courage to ask. But she must fight for her cause. And she must think of some vulgar word for "brothel," some "man's" term. She walked to a cab parked at the curb.

"Do you know where there's a whore-house?" she asked timidly.

"Sure, lady, jump in," said the driver.

Mabel Shoe ran toward her residence with more speed than her legs had produced since she was a girl.

CHAPTER X

HEAVEN'S BARTENDER

Uncle Ben Wopple, of nephew Alfred Wopple, prided himself on the fact that, in forty-nine years, he had not: 1. Had any gods before God; 2. Committed idolatry; 3. Taken the name of the Lord in vain; 4. Profaned the Sabbath Day; 5. Failed to honor his father and mother; 6. Committed homicide; 7. Committed adultery or fornication; 8. Stolen; 9. Borne false witness; 10. Coveted his neighbor's wife, maid-servant, nor anything that was his neighbor's.

Uncle Ben had always been very careful to address his prayers to God Himself, not to Jesus, the son. The appearance of this latter deity had been a trap, he believed, to lure the unwary into a violation of the first commandment. By worshiping the son of God, people were putting another god before God. God being the only God, it was evident that the son could not be a God, too. Jesus had warned his followers that he was only the son, but they had succumbed to temptation. Jesus should be highly respected, he thought, but not worshiped as a second God, for his Father was a jealous God.

Uncle Ben would not have been lured into the sin of idolatry even if he had a genuine statue of God Himself to bow down before. Graven images, even of God, would constitute idols, he thought, and would be traps to tempt violation of the second commandment. When kneeling for prayer, he specified that he was bowing to God alone, not to the son, and not to any invisible idol that the Devil might be holding in front of him in an attempt to make this a technical infraction.

Blasphemy was a sin which he hoped he understood correctly. He was not guilty of swearing, but he trusted that calling on the Lord in prayers for favors which had not been subsequently bestowed did not constitute taking the name of the Lord in vain. He was not sure whether the expression "Jesus Christ" (and its various derivatives), as an exclamation, amounted to profanity or not. God, being admittedly jealous, might be pleased to have his rival, even though it were His own son, spoken of in a light manner. On the other hand, He might resent having His son's name used as alleged profanity. It was an indirect reflection on Him to have His son insulted. Uncle Ben took no chances. He used no exclamations that referred to Jesus.

Working on the Sabbath was something that Uncle Ben Wopple would not be a party to, even to the extent of shaving.

He had always honored his parents, now dead, but had been careful not to let this adoration approach worship which might arouse God's jealousy.

The only possibility he could conceive of his killing another person would be while driving an automobile. He avoided this contingency by hiring a chauffeur.

The urge to commit carnal sin was an insidious trap for God's followers. Not having taken a wife, Uncle Ben had found glandular relief by mechanical means which sinful Satan makes no effort to condemn. Some say God's wicked rival of pitchfork and tail gives psychic broadcasts which go into additional details besides the mere fact of his lack of disapproval. But Ben Wopple had not accepted his discovery as a suggestion from Satan. He interpreted the commandments in a literal manner. The commandment in question was specific. An escape from the sins enumerated in its two well-known translations was a holy procedure.

Uncle Ben had never had any occasion to steal, having had practically all tangible objects that he wanted all his life.

Bearing false witness could not be attributed to him, he thought. He had appeared in two of his company's court cases and had spoken nothing but the truth. More of these truths might have resulted in verdicts for the other parties, but he had not run any unnecessary risk of unintentionally violating God's orders. It had been best to say as little as possible. The more he spoke, the greater became the danger of bearing false witness because of the chance that there had been some incorrect recording by his memory.

As for coveting his neighbor's wife, maidservant, or anything that was his neighbor's: a maid-servant, discharged by a neighbor had once applied to Uncle Ben for a job. He had slammed the door in her face. Whenever he invited any neighbors to call, he always specified that it was to be a stag affair. Neighbors' wives were not welcome at his home, and he did not speak to them on the street. To prove that he did not covet such females, he frequently told God in his prayers that they were all "daughters of bitches."

Uncle Ben Wopple might have been termed a religious roué. He had dissipated his life in religion to the neglect of other pursuits. Chastity and piety were to him what lechery and inebriation were to another. Uncle Ben had been on what amounted to a long religious drunk, with permanent effects that corresponded to those left upon the libertine. Liquor had become a habit and a necessity for the drunkard. Religion had become a habit and a necessity for Uncle Ben.

His temperance in worldly liquors had intensified his intemperance in the psychic intoxicants to be found in religion. Heavenly spirits had been a very effective substitute for alcoholic spirits. Alcoholic intoxication would have interfered with his spiritual intoxication. He had merely been rejecting an unnecessary and unwanted indulgence when he added the eleventh commandment, "Thou shalt not get drunk," later changed to, "Thou shalt not imbibe at all."

Sunday, the Lord's Day, was for Uncle Ben an occasion of highest ecstasy, comparable to other men's Saturday night excesses. He did not go to revival meetings. Nor did he shout and get into fights and police cells. Apparently he was quite docile and orderly. But inside him was stored the drunkenness of religion at its peak, the climax of each week's dissipation.

Beneath his serene appearance was the exhilarating agitation of religious hysteria. He was one of God's chosen! There was a reserved palace for him in Heaven, where every luxury awaited him! Not just luxuries such as he had known on earth but the luxuries of God! Luxuries that a mortal could not even conceive! Going into one of God's palaces from the earth would be like crawling from a coal mine into the throne of Louis XIV at the Palace of Versailles. His visions of Heaven and its joys obliterated all else from his mind and approximated the elaborate dreams of an opium eater. To all outward appearances, both the opium eater and Uncle Ben might have been concentrating on some Bible text.

The joys of Uncle Ben in religion were not those of self-sacrifice or humility but of self-indulgence. He indulged in religion as others did in alcoholics and narcotics. Religion was his vice. But the more he gave into it, the better man he became, he believed. The more he reveled in this debauchery, the nearer he came to being angelic.

He could and did indulge in religion every day, but weekday exaltations, delectable as they were, did not approach the climax that the Lord's Day brought.

The orgasmic peak of Sunday's delights came at the close of church services. He would remain seated in apparent meditation while the others all filed out of this kingdom of Heaven—exiled into Hell—leaving him and God alone amid their palaces, joint rulers of the universe.

CHAPTER XI

SEXIGAMY

Peter Hatch's reluctantly recognized reaction regarding Bertha Render remained resistant to renunciatory reasoning. For ten days he had continued to tell himself that he did not want Bicycle Bertha just for himself. And for ten days his thoughts had continued to tell him that he did want Bicycle Bertha just for himself.

He had conceived an apparently excellent compromise for these two conflicting opinions: On the next visit by the six Peters, he could return to see her a second time and take her to a theater or night club. Surely the others would not object to his having the rest of the evening alone with her after they had all concluded their visits. They would laugh and accuse him of insanity—and they would probably be right in this charge—but he would have to undergo their abuse if he wanted to escape another form of insanity. The restlessness caused by his persistent mental disputant, who did not need logic to refute contrary arguments, would doubtless lead to more violent acts than taking a girl to a show is allowed to continue.

So, when the sixth Peter had rejoined the group following their second visit to Miss Render's apartment, Peter Hatch had casually announced what seemed to be the extemporaneous idea of going back to invite her to the movies. Each of the five other Peters had instantly insisted that he had been planning to offer her a similar invitation. And, in a chorus immediately following, six embarrassed young men found themselves trying to account to each other for having expressed such a silly intention.

None of the excuses offered would have been convincing, even if distinguishable amid the sextet of voices. Each man was trying to clear himself of having spoken such a hasty and unmeant thought as the desire to take a girl to a theater merely for her companionship. The other five might have been ridiculing him as far as the impression made by their words was concerned.

But they soon realized that all had been a party to the same blunder, the same slip of the tongue. Instead of forgetting the incident, however, it was insisted that one of them should be made a laughingstock for his utterance. They would draw lots for the dishonor of wasting the rest of the evening in this inane manner. (Peter Hatch maintained that he did not want his usual precedence with women in this case.) The one who drew the shortest match would be the loser, as usual, and would have to return and offer himself as Bicycle Bertha's escort.

Peter Dean was the lucky loser, and there was much noise intended as laughter. The joke was so good that it was decided to draw lots again to make a second Peter undergo similar humility after their next visit. Miss Render had soon been assigned an escort for each of the next five alternate nights.

That had been a week ago. The six Peters had called on Bertha Render three times since then, and, after each visit, one of them had accepted his relegation to the senselessness of taking her out alone. Five others had ridiculed him and departed to finish the evening in a sensible manner with a series of drinks.

Despite the derision to which the sixth Peter was subjected, it seemed to be understood that Bertha would continue to be taken out in this manner even after they had each paid their forfeit by being her escort once. It was taken for granted that on the seventh night Peter Dean would explain how, since this ridiculous precedent had been established, it would be necessary to keep it up or lose Bertha's services as the hostess of the group.

Whereupon, Peter Dean would submit to taking her out again, while blaming the others for having taught a girl who formerly had been no hand at business to demand their time as well as their money. Meanwhile, the other five would accuse him of such contemptible offenses as having fallen in love and having bought an engagement ring for Bicycle Bertha. If he did not claim his turn on this occasion, Peter Dean knew that Peter Sadler, who had been the second loser on the night of the drawings, would.

Peter Hatch had been the last man to lose, and it would be three more days before he could go out with Bertha. The Peters had called on her every other night since their first meeting and planned to continue on this schedule. They would see her again to-morrow night, and Peter Jones would be the escort after all six had paid her their short visits in turn. Peters Pike and Lyman had each taken her to theaters following her dates with Dean and Sadler.

On the evenings they saw Bertha the Peters were more careful than usual in selecting identical wearing apparel. They dressed together and began by choosing underwear of the same color. Then socks, neckties, shirts, shoes, and hats all had to be the same, as well as their suits. Peter Sadler's gray necktie in contrast to the green ones worn by the others had almost interfered with their plans on the first night. Bicycle Bertha might not like it if she knew that she had six callers every other night instead of one.

After partaking of Bertha's hospitality, her five non-escorts for the evening did not attempt to trail her and the sixth Peter to their destination. Each Peter feared that, if one should be secretly followed, he himself would be similarly spied upon when it became his turn as escort. They decided it was best on these occasions not to run the risk of letting Miss Render see her five paramours that she was unaware of.

Peter Hatch could not remain pleased for long by the arrangement which forced him to share Bertha with the other five for social engagements as well as in other ways. As soon as he told himself that this circumstance was fine—fate was intervening to prevent his succumbing to the insane desire to have her to himself—he received the mental reply, "How in hell can I get her away from these other Peters? How long will it be before they get tired of her and let me have her alone?"

He could have her to himself for a few hours in three more days—and then again twelve days later. He looked forward to these longer periods with Bertha fully as much as to the shorter visits he would pay her meanwhile—with five others waiting outside.

He had carefully planned the first "outdoor" date many times. Instead of attending a theater, they would go to the same restaurant they had patronized before and drink Ward Eights in a private booth. His plans had consisted mostly of mental pictures of Bicycle Bertha sipping one of these drinks. He had forgotten his resolution to buy her Tom Collinses. Five other Peters had noticed that Ward Eights were now Peter Hatch's favorite drink.

And these same five had each noticed points about Bicycle Bertha that made escorting her very pleasant. Peter Dean enjoyed the way she moved her nose when she took up a glass of champagne. He also liked to look down her throat when she swallowed this sparkling liquid. (He had not suggested such a lowly beverage as Ward Eights.)

Peter Sadler liked the way she occasionally winked at him when she talked. Peter Pike liked the way she applauded in a theater and the irrelevant comments she made. Peter Lyman enjoyed rubbing his thigh against hers in a theater and looking at her profile in the dim light. Peter Jones liked her affectionate manner. He looked forward to bringing her back to her room tomorrow night.

Six sets of busy thoughts were also able to consider the problem of eluding the vigilance of five other Peters for possible secret dates with Bertha.

CHAPTER XII

DON'T DISCREDIT ALL MYTHS

Bertha Render did not try to conceal the fact from herself that she was in love. She had the *nicest* man! If she were *not* in love with him, she would have had suspicions about her sanity. Peter. This had become her favorite name. Hatch was a nice name, too. (Since Peter Hatch had told her his real name, the others had had to use the same one.)

At first she had regarded him as just another pick-up: a chance to get a free meal followed by a gymnastic workout to the counts of her list of "No's!" After all, a girl has to have some exercise to keep in shape. But he and a few Ward Eights had interfered with this program. Even then he did not impress her as the best man she had ever known. In fact, she was disappointed in him when he left so soon.

He came right back, though, and not only once but five times! This surprise had made her Peter the grandest man of them all. She even thought he was good-looking now. She had come to think of a *real man* as a myth. Then a real live myth had come into her life!

She had feared that Peter's first-night performance would not be duplicated. Perhaps on their next date he would turn out to be like the rest of the men. Just when *her* interest was becoming really aroused, he would be saying, "Well, when will I see you again?" But Peter's first-night behavior had been a genuine demonstration of his normal behavior. "Some man!" still described him.

Bertha was amused by Peter's eccentricities. Such a wonderful man was entitled to all the peculiarities he happened to have, and she could accept any of them as the ideal form of conduct. She had come to like the way he went outdoors "to cool off." These brief intervals of solitude proved to be an additional pleasure he had to offer. It was a nice sensation to stretch out on the couch alone, a waning afterglow telling her that this man was like all the others, and her thoughts assuring her that Peter would be at her side again in just a moment. The feeling of suspense, that possibly he might not come back, made his return all the more welcome. And the afterglow became more intense than before when he suddenly announced, "Here I am again."

It was strange that Peter's hands always got so cold just from hurrying outdoors and back to her room. But they became warmed in short order. It was strange, too, how he was so refreshed by these short trips. Sometimes his hair would be a bit mussed or his tie out of place when he left. He would be back in less than a minute in immaculate condition again.

And his greetings and conduct on each reappearance were as enthusiastic and ardent as though he were seeing her for the first time that evening. Even on his fifth and sixth trips up the stairs, he usually ran. He certainly was a man! "When God made him, He must have used the stuff that was left out of half a dozen elves and fairies," she laughed to herself.

Bertha wondered just why Peter took his short time-out periods. Was this one of his jokes? Or did he like to go out and comb his hair and straighten himself out before renewing his love-making? Evidently he brushed off his clothes, too. Several times there had been powder on his coat when he left. There was no sign of it when he got back.

Perhaps he had some medicine he took that he did not want her to know about. It would be embarrassing for him to turn his back and say, "Just a minute while I take my tonic." If this was the case, she hoped his supply was not limited.

But probably he got some strange additional pleasure out of leaving her for a moment, just as she did in being alone during that brief interval.

Peter had a peculiarity of conversation that was decidedly different. He generally talked about taking her out, but, instead of sticking to the topic of where they were going that night, he usually spoke of plans for entertainment two, four, six, eight, and even ten nights after that. Once during the evening he would be enthused about to-night's program, then he seemed to forget all about it until she started getting ready to go out with him.

Bertha liked to have Peter take her so many places, but it was hard to keep track of his plans. He would start by talking about the fun they were going to have some night drinking Ward Eights. First it had been eight nights from now, then six nights, then four. Apparently Ward Eights were the only concoction fit to drink, and this imbibition would constitute a very special occasion. Well, why not drink them to-night? Why wait so long?

"No," Peter would say, "we've got to go to that theater (or that cabaret) to-night." (The Peters compared notes as to intended destinations, so that Bertha's Peter did not appear to suffer from complete lapses of memory.) His tone of voice would suggest that the performance would be the worst ever produced and that they would have a very miserable evening.

Then in a few minutes he would have forgotten about the Ward Eight panacea. He would be equally as enthusiastic now about champagne, or some other intended means of diversion. Six nights from now they would drink champagne again. Of course, champagne was expensive. Probably he couldn't afford to buy it until the night in question. And Ward Eights perhaps were offensive to him when he was thinking of champagne. But why, if she happened to mention it, did he show no enthusiasm for champagne when he was talking about Ward Eights?

Peter certainly had a one track mind. When he was discussing a date for a certain night, she could not arouse his interest in their plans for any other night. Then—after he had told her about as many as five prospective evenings that were each to be much better diversion than to-night's theater date— his original enthusiasm for the show would return, and he became as happy about attending it as though this were the best of the five better nights he had been describing.

"Maybe each swig of his tonic makes a new man of him mentally as well as physically," Bertha laughed to herself.

She let Peter keep track of the complexities of his schedule of dates. She knew he would call every other night, so she could see to it that no dates were broken. And she knew he would take her somewhere each time he called. She did not worry about the details beyond this point. She could not be sure whether this was to be the Ward Eight night or the movie night until they were seated at their destination. At any moment up until then, she expected he might change his mind again as to the best way of spending an evening.

Bertha Render looked forward to the dates she had with Peter that were eight and ten days or more away, but the next meeting was always her chief anticipation. Peter's generosity was unusual, but she did not appreciate this as fully as his myth-man qualifications. She could go to a show or get drunk with any man. The arrangements for the latter part of these evenings, whether champagne or fresh air, were comparatively unimportant—when she knew what the opening program was to be.

CHAPTER XIII

BUSINESS BEFORE BREAKFAST

When Teresa Beetle reached a certain stage of drunkenness, the religious inspiration that had started her career as a Vestal Vertical was reawakened, and she insisted upon going to church. She would not be standing up by the time such an urge became active. Upon rising, or trying to, she would find the path to God unpaved and filled with pitfalls. Each step onward sent her headlong into a deep hole. In her struggle to regain an upright position, the sides of the hole would disappear, and she would have little to cling to for support.

Clad in a silk kimono without buttons, she had once reached the hallway outside her room on one of these pilgrimages. Then the depths of Hell had loomed up, and she fell into space. The landlady and her son had carried Teresa upstairs to her bed.

Teresa did not recall these attempted journeys upon sobering up. They would have been embarrassing to her if she had known of them. Religion had been her girlhood racket, as she referred to it, and she claimed to have suffered no ill effects from its teachings.

"Religion was all right as long as it was supporting me," she explained, "but I'm not going to turn around now and start supporting it."

Teresa felt that she had won in a sort of contest with religion. She had been given food and quarters as a Vestal Vertical. Religion thought he had her as his captive. Then she had escaped and joined a profession whose name alone should have caused a religious lady to shudder. After being fed and housed those years by the chuckling jailor who assumed she was in his power, she had shown that religion was something she could take or leave alone. She hadn't been fooled herself but had only been fooling the captor.

That contest was finished and called for no more consideration. The contest with Dorothy Dolly remained the issue of the moment. Dorothy's slanderous remarks about her, both to others and directly to her, had continued without fitting retaliation. Teresa thought that she had held her own in the face to face skirmishes but was not sure that the gossip she had conceived about Dorothy had been equivalent to the sharp-tongued comments Dorothy had made about her.

And even if they were back on equal terms, as measured in terms of demonstrated malice, Teresa wanted to be ahead in the contest. There was no flush of victory to be had in letting it continue as a tie. Fitting compensation would come only when she was proved master.

Revenge had been duly obtained for the scandal story spread by Dorothy that Teresa's professional record had been without pay. Teresa had hired twenty-five newsboys to wait outside Dorothy's apartment. When Dorothy came out for a walk, she and Tinker Avenue were informed by twenty-five loud voices, "Here we are, Dorothy! You hired us to make a new record! You hired us for a new record! . . ."

Dorothy Dolly's replies had been unheard in the uproar. Her walk was delayed, for the boys started to follow her down the street with their shouts, and she had to return to her room to escape them.

Teresa Beetle did not feel very well this afternoon. Early in the morning she had insisted upon going to church. She had waked up a few hours later beside an overturned table. She lay in bed now with two sore elbows and a throbbing head, thinking of unpleasant things she would like to do, or have done, to Dorothy Dolly.

The worst infliction she could conceive in her present mood was to have her rival be forced to eat a large meal. Picturing this scene of torture made Teresa feel still more uncomfortable. She had to change the view to one of Dorothy nailed on a cross in the manner of a Christian martyr.

There was a knock on her door. Teresa hoped it was a customer. Doubtless her money was all gone. It usually was when she awoke in this condition. She did not feel like working now, but a two-dollar bill would enable her to buy a few eye-openers that would take away this deathbed sensation—if she could keep them down.

A man and a woman entered. Miss Mabel Shoe, wearing her own clothes, had resumed her search for a prostitute. With many blushes, she had brazenly explained the nature of the Society for the Resurrection of the Fallen Woman to a man who had applied for charity and asked him if he could help her locate a worthy case. In return for five dollars, he had led her to Teresa Beetle's room.

"You can assure me that this woman is a prostitute?" Miss Shoe said timidly to the man.

"Yes'm," he replied, "and a good one, too."

"What did you think I was, a sailor?" added Teresa.

"Madam," Miss Shoe began.

"Hey, I ain't no Madam," interrupted Teresa. "I'm still doing business on my own."

"I have come to help you."

"I ain't got time to listen to any sales talk," said Miss Beetle.

"But I am not a saleslady. I am really here to help you."

"All right, then—scram, and let me talk business with your boy friend."

"Yes," said the man, "if you'll wait outside just a minute or two, I think I can make her listen to reason."

CHAPTER XIV

TWENTY-TWO DOLLARS CAN BUY A LOT OF EYE-OPENERS

Mabel Shoe stepped back into the hall. The man closed the door after her. No doubt it was hard for one of the fallen women to believe that a society had actually been formed to redeem the souls of their lost bodies. Such a woman probably considered herself a hopeless case. This man who knew her could explain the benevolent enterprise better than a stranger. As soon as the woman could be made to realize the blessings that awaited her, she would come flying out the door with open arms, tears, and thanks.

Miss Shoe was very happy at having finally located a real prostitute. Her society was to be a success after all. This poor girl would rejoice over the chance that was offered her to become an honest woman and would hasten to tell others of her kind about the society. In a few days, unfortunate women from all over the city, and perhaps from other cities, would be swarming to her. She would have to hire an office in this section—and a large one—to accommodate them all. She would put up a big sign, "Streetwalkers' Shrine."

Her feeling of reckless stimulation had returned when she started to explain the nature of the Society for the Resurrection of the Fallen Woman to the guide who had brought her here. She had felt wicked in walking to a brothel with a man. Standing here alone in the hall of this house of ill fame made her feel more abandoned than ever. The fascination that accompanied missionary work among harlots was making this society the most diverting of them all. The sensation was undoubtedly one of inspiration for her cause. She had found the reform movement for which she was best adapted.

But suppose a man should appear now? He would naturally assume that a woman in a house of ill fame was a prostitute. What would she do if he seized her rudely and started to lead her into one of the other rooms? Miss Shoe still believed that any woman, whether fourteen or ninety, who was willing to become a member of the demimonde would be instantly accepted. The Devil didn't care anything about the age or beauty of his converts. He wanted their souls. If a woman should mentally say, "I am willing to be a harlot," no doubt Satan would supply a customer instantaneously.

The combination happy-wicked feeling still remained predominately pleasurable, much to Miss Shoe's attempted disgust. Proximity to carnal sin should not make her feel this way—why, criminal congress might be going on in one of these rooms at this very minute! She should feel sad and sympathetic.

Then her mind explained that the strange thrill was due to the dawning success of her society. Being inspired in her cause, how could she help becoming thrilled, excited, and pleased by such a prospect? She was going to be the means of putting an end to this illegal intercourse. Eventually, she could perhaps erect a large monument in the form of a gravestone and inscribed:

HERE LIES THE UNPARDONABLE SIN
DEATH DUE TO
THE SOCIETY FOR THE RESURRECTION
OF THE FALLEN WOMAN
MISS MABEL SHOE, PRESIDENT

Or, it might be better to have MISS MABEL SHOE, PRESIDENT, come first, followed by the name of the organization.

This pleasing thought was interrupted by footsteps. Miss Shoe saw a man coming up the stairs. She was lost! Helpless! What could she do? Her terror did not lessen its intensity when she caught a glimpse of Alfred Wopple, of Uncle Ben Wopple domination. She knew Alfred Wopple, the Bible Authority. What if he should see her? There were more flights of stairs. Miss Shoe frantically ran up to the next floor. Would he come up here? Had he seen her? She would have been hysterical but for the great effort of will which held back the cries that would have made her presence known.

Footsteps in the hall below ceased, and Miss Shoe began to calm down. What was Alfred Wopple doing here? Surely he was not a patron of brothels. This was inconceivable. Probably he had started a society similar to hers—and was beginning his campaign with the same girl who was to have brought success to the Society for the Resurrection of the Fallen Woman.

This was unbearable. After all the trouble she had had in locating a prostitute, to have a rival organization steal her away. She ought to go back to the woman's room and put in a claim of priority. But this would not be safe. Alfred Wopple might not have heard of her society. In that case he could draw only one conclusion if he should see her in a brothel.

He would doubtless say he was greatly disappointed in having found what lay behind the hypocritical veil of her pretended social service career but that it was fortunate he had discovered her secret degradation in time. Then he would start trying to reform her as well as the other woman. Miss Shoe knew that she would be too upset to speak coherently about her society under such circumstances.

And, of course, it would become common knowledge that Miss Mabel Shoe had been caught in a disorderly house. Those who knew of her society could rectify her reputation, but they might assume that the organization had been merely a name, an excuse to account for her presence if she ever were caught. She would be unable to cite any cases to prove the society had been legitimate.

There was one hope, though. The man who had brought her here knew what her real motives were. He could prove that her intentions were honest—and he could bear witness to the fact that she had first claim and was entitled to reform this prostitute which a rival organization was trying to take away from her. She was redeemed! She might reverse the situation on Mr. Wopple by entering the room and accusing him of being a libertine, attempting to degrade still further this girl whom she had been about to reform.

She knew the charge would be ridiculous, but its utterance would make it necessary for him to account for his presence, instead of her. Then she could apologize and appear very sorry for having allowed herself to be deceived by appearances. This procedure seemed to be the only possible escape. Alfred Wopple might go from room to room and come upstairs. If he found her trying to hide from him, the situation would be doubly compromising. She could keep one floor ahead of him only until they reached the roof.

· · · · · · · ·

Uncle Ben Wopple had talked to his nephew about holy subjects all that morning. Having escaped after lunch, Alfred Wopple had decided to make this call on Teresa Beetle and her Vestal Vertical costume, despite the facts that it was not Sunday and that he would have to forego the pleasure of letting his wife wait outside. Another man was paying Miss Beetle two dollars when he arrived.

"Remember, now, we're gonna split whatever she gives you," he was saying.

"She?" asked Wopple.

"Yes, there's some rich woman that wants to do business with me," explained Teresa. "And remember," she added to the other man, "you're going to split whatever you get out of her for keeping quiet."

· · · · · · ·

With the aggressive attitude attributed to a tiger trapped in a corner, Miss Shoe came down the flight of stairs. She was ready to utter indignant sentences to the representative of the rival reform society. The man who had brought her here had just come out of Teresa's room and was looking about the hall for her.

"It's all fixed up," he said. "Go ahead in. I'll wait here."

"You come in with me," she told him.

Miss Shoe entered Miss Beetle's room with the witness who could verify her account of the society and its aims. But Alfred Wopple was not in sight. Evidently he had called at some other room. Her fears that he had been stealing her first case had all been groundless. She could proceed with her original mission without the annoying interference of others.

"Are you ready to accept the assistance of my organization?" she asked.

"Sure, twenty bucks," replied Teresa.

"All right, I will give you twenty dollars if you will do what I say."

"I'll do anything for twenty bucks."

"Very well, you must promise never to ply your immoral trade again."

"Get to the point," insisted Teresa. "What do you want me to do?"

"Simply this: promise me you will not commit adultery any more," said Miss Shoe.

"Cut out the stalling," replied Teresa. "Let's get down to business."

"But all I want you to do is to make that promise."

"And you'll give me twenty bucks for that?"

"Yes."

"Lady, give me the money."

Miss Mabel Shoe proudly walked down Tinker Avenue. Prostitute number one had been rescued from the pit of iniquity. Now she could begin to make definite plans for establishing the Streetwalkers' Shrine.

Teresa Beetle opened her closet door. "I don't know whether that woman is crazy, or whether she suspected there was somebody in here," she said.

"Both," laughed Alfred Wopple.

CHAPTER XV

AMONG OTHER DUTIES

With a white rose that was really a carnation over one ear, Dorothy Dolly was walking along Fleet Street. She had had four clients this evening. After three more she decided she would stay in bed until morning. This total of seven would not better her six-man record, for they would not have visited her in a group. Customers obtained singly or in pairs were only retail trade. The wholesale record, comprising the highest total of men who all called at the same time, was the recognized achievement in Tinker Avenue trade circles.

Dorothy took out a cigarette. "Got a match, big feller?" she asked a passing man. He gave her a match. "Got two bucks?"

"Oh, so you're one a them kind! No, thanks."

"Lavender boy, huh?"

"Lay off the sales talk. I tell you what I will do, though: I'll give you four bits if you'll walk up to the next corner with me and wait until my girl shows up. We got a date, and she'll get all excited if she sees me with another dame."

"O.K."

"She gets jealous over nothing—"

"So I fill the bill, huh?"

"No, I mean she'll be so jealous when she *sees* me with another woman I don't know what she'll do. Say, there she is now. Here, lemme grab your arm."

The other girl sighted them and turned around abruptly to walk away from the corner where she had been waiting.

"I guess that sort of breaks up your evening," said Dorothy.

The man laughed. "No, that fixes everything up fine," he replied. "The only times me and my girl get anywhere is when she gets mad. Now I'll go over and call on her in a few minutes, and she'll throw everything at me in the place and call me every kind of a name that ever was. Then after a while she'll sober up and be sorry. She'll start bawling and offer to do anything I say if I'll forgive her. I have to keep thinking up ways to get her mad. I can't even mug her up until after she gets in a tantrum. So you've saved me a buck and a half. So long."

Dorothy Dolly spoke to another man.

"You're just the girl I'm looking for!" he answered. "Come on over to Three Hundredth Street with me, and I'll give you two bucks. A friend of mine is throwing a big party, and everybody has to bring somebody else's wife with him in order to get in. You can be my admission ticket. We'll say you're Mrs. Tiffery. You can sneak out after we get inside if you want to."

The man stopped a taxi and took Dorothy to the address of the revelry. A face appeared through a hole in a thick door which, to its owner, was a cherished relic of the prohibition era. He had purchased it from a speak-easy proprietor after repeal and now used it in place of his own front door. Mrs. Tiffery and her escort were admitted after explaining she did not wear a wedding ring because it had been a common law marriage.

The entire floor was one large room. All along both sides was a series of booths in each of which was a bed. Couples were sitting and reclining on some of the beds. Shades in front of three of the booths were drawn. There was considerable noise and laughter. Two girls were doing a strip dance to the combined tunes of a phonograph and a radio.

Dorothy had a few drinks at a bar in the rear. Parties of this sort did not appeal to her. The drinking was all right, but getting all excited about naked bodies was too much like going back to kindergarten. "You'd think none of these girls ever saw a man before and none of the men ever saw a girl," she said to herself. "And the girls ain't getting paid for it neither—except the dancers." Getting drunk on liquor was a legitimate diversion, but getting drunk on sex stimulation was comparable to a business man being thrilled by the excitement of his office routine.

Each man had at least one girl. There was little prospect of drumming up trade here. Dorothy decided that this childish atmosphere was not even conducive to drinking free liquor. She discovered a back door and departed to take a bus to her section of the city. While waiting for transportation, a youth of about eighteen spoke to her. Some kid looking for a handout, she decided.

"Two bucks and it's a bargain," she told him. The boy appeared frightened and hurried away.

Dorothy got off the bus at One-Tenth Street. Somebody seemed to be speaking to her, and she stopped to investigate. A white-haired man seated in front of a store was making her a business proposal, but it had to do with the purchase of celery. She invariably replied when a man spoke, but the proposition now in question did not appeal to her. She did not make her customary response.

Back on Fleet Street again, she greeted a man wearing a derby. "Doing anything?" she asked.

"Maybe I will be if you'll help me out," he replied.

"Anything you say."

"Well, I know a swell girl, but the trouble is she's married. We both want to see each other tonight, but her husband might break in on us if I call on her, and she's afraid to come out for a date. She lives over a store where her husband works. Now if you could go in and talk to him and keep him interested, I could run up and see his wife. You know, smile at him and tell him what a nice guy he is, and all that."

"Two bucks and she's yours," said Dorothy.

The man pointed to the cuckold clerk through the window of the store. "Promise now you won't let him out of your sight," he said. "I won't be long. Just keep talking to him."

When the man returned from his visit, he looked in the store window to signal the girl that the husband needed no more of her attention. Neither the clerk nor the girl was there. Dorothy Dolly had found another customer for her services.

CHAPTER XVI

HOME BREW FROM HEAVEN

Uncle Ben Wopple was indulging in one of his week day religious excesses, kneeling in silent prayer in a corner. He kept both his forehead and knees tightly pressed against the walls at their point of junction. Although he was explicit in explaining that he was bowing to God alone, he took care to make it as difficult as possible for the Devil to hold any invisible idols in front of him. Nephew Alfred Wopple and his wife were guests to-night. But Uncle Ben always prayed when he felt in the mood (which was quite often) whether others were present or not.

He seemed to be communing with God in a very temperate manner. There were no indications of inner intoxication. Cocktails were, of course, forbidden, but Uncle Ben was having the equivalent of several of them in carrying on this silent conversation with God. For it was not just a monologue. God was replying.

He was listening to Ben's thoughts and saying, "Stay with it, Brother," in the joy-language of Heaven. Uncle Ben accounted for the stimulation which surged through him as being the result of a direct contact with God, a sip of Heaven itself. A psychic communication had been established between God and him. His messages to God brought direct recognition and reward. Such a pious man, God thought, was entitled to a few advance nips of the ecstasy that awaited him after death.

The glow from Heaven and the views of Heaven which God was providing constituted a non-alcoholic form of drunkenness. God and His luxuries were awaiting Uncle Ben. All buildings in Paradise were castles and palaces. Lambs with golden fleece were the emblem of this Holy Empire.

He was thanking God for His assurance that this land of bliss and glee was to be his eternal home. He would have not only everything he wanted but everything that could give pleasure. The angel-body, no doubt, had countless capacities for enjoyment which had not been provided in the human body. The whole earth with its riches would appear like a marble in comparison to the extravagances of Heaven.

Mr. and Mrs. Alfred Wopple remained with heads bowed during Uncle Ben's silent prayers, but they sat in chairs, presumably offering prayers of their own. When Ben Wopple reached his amen, he was at the stage of mental effervescence that in drinking people leads to the suggestion, "Let's have just one more." He remained in meditation, dancing thoughts of Paradise sparkling through his mind. Another sip of Heaven would be quite welcome, in fact seemed quite in order. God was inviting him to have another nip.

Then dinner was announced. The words of his butler could not have been more emphatic if they had come from God Himself—they had really come from God Himself: Having dinner meant saying grace. Saying grace meant speaking with God again. God had put the dinner announcement into his butler's mouth as a means of *insisting* that Ben have "just one more."

Uncle Ben hurried into the dining room and told his guests to hurry, too. The heads of Alfred and his wife quickly fell forward once more as their host proceeded to thank God for this which they were about to receive.

There was a long pause before the amen. Additional stimulation came to Uncle Ben. New powers of Heaven were conceived, more glories that were to be his. He would have a new palace there every day. He would be so sensitive to pleasure as an angel that the most intense joys of his earthly body would seem like pain in comparison.

Uncle Ben wished these guests were not here to-night. He wanted to have "just one more" nip of Heaven. But he had said grace and offered a prayer. If he performed either of these functions again, Alfred and his wife would wonder why he hadn't included the postscripts the first time.

He shouldn't have stopped thanking God so soon. He might say, "We thank you a *second* time," though, with emphasis to show that he was aware of the repetition and was not becoming absent-minded. The heads of Mr. and Mrs. Alfred Wopple bobbed forward again.

Three tastes of Heaven in succession left Uncle Wopple in the stage of inebriation at which one's motions are governed more by instinct than conscious effort. If his body had been affected as well as his mind, he would have been in danger of slipping from his chair. His inspired thoughts concerning celestial wonders were interrupted by the discovery that he had finished eating a fruit-cup.

At least the cup was empty, and he had a spoon in his hand. Yes, and he could taste the residue of the last swallow. It would not do to interrupt the meal to speak with God again. He would have to wait until dessert was finished and then give thanks for what they had eaten.

Uncle Ben managed to get enough control over his thoughts to remark, "God is a jealous God, but He forgives us, for we know not what we do." No, no. He was quoting Jesus. "I mean, God is jealous because most people are so ignorant as to listen to Satan instead of to Him. God is too happy in Heaven to bother coming down to drive away the Devil. But Hell is such a miserable place that Satan spends most of his time on earth— sending souls into Hell in the hope that they will quench the flames so he can be more comfortable there."

"Just so," said Alfred.

"Yes," said Mrs. Wopple. Religion to her meant agreeing with Uncle Ben.

Talking about God was a stimulant for Uncle Wopple but not of the same intensity as direct communication. The topic would prolong the effect of the three direct contacts—in the manner of a light table wine—until the meal was over, when a goblet of Heaven's liqueur could be enjoyed.

"God is so omnipotent—why, the earth may be nothing but God's junk-pile," he continued. "He is certainly benevolent to offer its occupants a chance to return to Heaven."

"I think I shall make that the topic for tomorrow noon's Bible talk," said Alfred.

"Yes, do," remarked his wife.

"Always serve God," said Uncle Ben.

"Of course," replied Alfred, adding mentally, "I'd like to serve Him on a platter."

CHAPTER XVII

CAN YOU HEAR ME NOW?

"You're Peter Pike."

"No, I am."

"Well, then *you're* Peter Lyman."

"Nope. That's me."

A neighbor of the six Peters was indulging in the conundrum of trying to establish their identities. Such a procedure solved the problem of thinking up a topic of conversation and evaded the alternative of saying, "Nice day," and its synonyms.

"If you'd tie yourself together in pairs, you fellows could make a lot of money in a circus. You could be the Siamese-twin triplets. Ha, ha. Imagine a woman getting three sets of them."

This remark indicated that the neighbor considered his conversational duties fulfilled. It was his parting comment whenever he stopped the six Peters to guess who they were.

"Well, Romeo, now that he's gone, how about taking up the collection," said Peter Jones.

The Peter who was to be Bicycle Bertha's escort following their next visit was referred to as Romeo. The one in this rôle was also appointed to be the polite bandit in their hold-ups. Peter Sadler was Romeo at present.

The new Romeo was given the name after its preceding holder had returned from his date with Bertha. The predecessor would say, with much evidence of disgust, "Well, that's over," or some equivalent. The next Romeo would be surrounded by five Peters and given the revolver with various comments about the need for doing something to prevent his complete degeneration. As a gunman, he would at least be keeping up appearances as a normal individual even though his social inclinations had become depraved.

Romeo was subject to two days of derision by the other five. He was in love, a disgraceful affliction. He had been sucked in by a girl. Bertha had hypnotized him. She had trained him and tamed him. He had gone out of his head. He was wasting money on a girl who didn't charge. Instead of being a hold-up man, he was being held up by a girl. Being a gunman again would perhaps help him see his many errors.

Apparently this poor, misguided Peter was the only one of the six who ever entertained Bertha after their visits. If Romeo attempted to point out that the others were equally guilty, five loud voices would cooperate in ridiculing the charge with additional raillery. Romeo was a hopeless case, a pervert, a damn fool, and a disgrace to the other five.

Hooked by a woman. If he *had* to take her out, it would be excusable. But she had not even asked for compensation for her services. Why didn't he buy a window dummy and take it to a restaurant? That would be equally sensible, more so in fact because a dummy wouldn't be able to talk or run up his liquor bill. A girl's place was in her room, or in his room. Taking her anywhere else voluntarily was a shameful form of insanity.

An insane man might be expected to do anything. Perhaps he would go to the zoo next and try to date up an alligator. Romeo, meanwhile, could only memorize any new remarks that were made to save for use when another Romeo took over this rôle of dishonor and disgrace.

Romeo served two purposes. Each of the other five was enabled to show his resentment at the nonsensical custom of taking Bertha out. Romeo, of course, was to blame for establishing this precedent. And, even though the five non-Romeos did not mention having their turns at playing the part, there was no way of denying their guilt. Their consciences, or their attempts to convince themselves that they did not want to be alone with Bertha for social purposes, attended to this stigma. And Romeo also served as a butt for their jealousy at having to share Bicycle Bertha with five others.

The dread and discomfort of being Romeo was compensated for by the anticipation of the date with Bertha. Each Romeo in turn abandoned his arguments with himself that Bertha offered no more inducements than any other girl. When he was Romeo, each Peter let himself accept the fact that he did want to be alone with Bertha and take her to a theater or restaurant. The sanity of this desire was emphasized by the obvious jealousy of the other five. They were only saying the things he usually said to himself, and these deterrents were no longer convincing.

Despite this attitude, Romeo could not allow himself to show that he looked forward to the date. He had to give the impression that he was being forced to do something very distasteful. He was still paying the forfeit for having been one of the losers when they drew lots.

Six plans for secret dates were still under way, but five Peters were also alert to excuses offered when a sixth decided to do an errand.

Hold-ups were conducted now on the alternate nights that the Peters did not see Bertha. This was more often than formerly, when sometimes one or two "collections" a week would provide enough income. Each Peter wanted to be sure his supply of cash would be sufficient when his turn as Romeo came around again. But the spoken reason for the additional robberies was that they had been getting too lazy to take this extra money which had been waiting for them all along.

To-night's collection, or the first collection—depending on its amount, was to be taken on One Hundredth Street. An alley provided a convenient waiting place. A man with a cane appeared, and Romeo Sadler put on the mask.

"Hands up, please," he requested.

The man kept right on walking. Romeo spoke to him again, flourishing the revolver.

"What?" said the man, who was evidently deaf.

Peter repeated his request in a louder tone.

"No, I don't know how to fix a gun," replied the man.

"Hands up!!" shouted Peter, becoming exasperated by the man's attitude.

The loud command made no impression on the intended victim, but there were other people in the neighborhood. Six Peters found themselves running, as planned, but, instead of helping a man with a cane to catch a thief, they were being chased as thieves themselves.

CHAPTER XVIII

MADAM, HOW DARE YOU!

Alfred Wopple, pious Bible man for impious purposes, was not well. He had received a letter containing sickening information. Facts were known by another which, if told to Uncle Ben, would cause immediate removal of Nephew Alfred's name from his will. The message was not an attempt at blackmail, since it was from a wealthy woman. And it could not be merely a facetious inspiration, for the text was not appropriate to her sense of humor.

The letterhead had amused him:

*THE SOCIETY FOR THE RESURRECTION OF THE
FALLEN WOMAN
Redeem the Souls of Lost Bodies*

MISS MABEL SHOE, *President*

Until he had seen her through a crack in Teresa Beetle's closet door, Alfred Wopple had always suspected that Mabel Shoe did not know what a harlot was.

The chuckles caused by these printed lines, and the indelicate motto at the bottom of the stationery: MAKE THE PROSTITUTE A RESPECTABLE WOMAN, had been quickly squelched by the body of the letter:

"I see that we are both engaged in the same sort of social reform work. On a recent visit to 217 Tinker Avenue I observed you making a call there, too. I do not find your name on our lists, so I assume that you were present in the interests of an organization of similar nature to this society which I have formed. You disappeared before I had a chance to speak.

"May I offer the suggestion that these two welfare groups of obviously identical purposes be united into one. As a united body, we could plan a joint campaign which might prove more effective than the efforts of two individual and rival societies. I suggest that we continue with the name the SOCIETY FOR THE RESURRECTION OF THE FALLEN WOMAN (An erasure at this point gave evidence of a habitual tendency to write "Mabel Shoe, President"), as this has already become known in the underworld, and another name might cause confusion.

"I trust that your organization has been meeting with as pleasing success as ours. To cite just one case, we can offer an instance of an erring sister who, under our guidance, became a resident member of a strict religious cult. Yes, this is an actual fact, as our records will show. I called on this girl myself on the occasion when I saw you at 217 Tinker Avenue. She was rather reluctant to change her ways at first, but I finally managed to show her the light. She promised to reform.

"I called again a few days later to see if I could be of any further assistance in guiding her along her new path of life. What was my astonishment and amazement to see this woman wearing white robes which, she explained, identified her as a member of a sacred society known as The Vegetarian Vestals—a group which abhors the most trivial sins of the flesh! She explained that she had taken religious vows but had returned to her former haunts to help carry on the work of our society herself.

"Although I had never heard of these Vegetarian Vestals and was unfamiliar with their teachings, I offered no criticism and congratulated her upon having chosen the right God.

"Results like this show the tremendous possibilities our field of endeavor has to offer. I am already arranging for an office on Tinker Avenue where fallen girls may come and be rescued of their own free will without waiting to be sought out. I have pledge-cards printed for each convert to sign."

Alfred Wopple felt hot, cold, faint, and sweaty all at the same time upon reading this. His life's work as a man of God would have been in vain if Uncle Wopple heard of his having been seen in a brothel. Uncle Ben would not be able to follow Miss Shoe's reasoning. People did not go to brothels to reform the women. Furthermore, Uncle Ben knew that he did not represent any society which had professed this intention.

Miss Shoe probably had told others that she had seen him in a bawdyhouse. The news might be on its way to Uncle Ben. If not, it soon would be, for she would show no discrimination in circulating the information. Everybody she told would suspect his real mission at 217 Tinker Avenue despite his reputation as a sinless lover of God. When Uncle Ben heard the account, it would be frankly stated with evidence to show that his nephew was a whoremaster.

"I guess the only hope is that Uncle Ben will be so shocked he'll have a stroke and die before he can get his hands on the will," Alfred commented mentally. "But I'm afraid he's too healthy an ox."

If there were only some way to make Mabel Shoe shut up. She would think it strange, and incriminating, if he told her he wanted his benevolent enterprise kept secret. . . . What organization could he tell her he had been working for? . . . Why didn't his group wish to merge with hers? . . . His might be a secret society—but why the secrecy? she would ask. . . . If he hadn't been representing any society, how could he account for his being in the disorderly house for devout purposes?

But had it really been him that she saw at 217 Tinker Avenue? He might telephone her and make an indignant denial of her insulting charge. No, she must have had a good look at him, judging from the confident tone of her letter. She hadn't said the man looked like him, or that she thought it might have been him; she had said it *was* him.

And what would his wife have to say if she heard the address and learned that she had waited for him so many Sundays while he visited a woman instead of a sick friend? But his wife's reactions in this crisis were not of much importance. Alfred Wopple felt that he had earned the bequest that his uncle's will would give him several times over by so many years of outward holiness. He could overlook the loss of his wife, but it was pitiful to lose the inheritance and his job like this—his uncle would surely discharge him. He should at least offer some defense. He *would* call up Mabel Shoe. He took a pencil and started to write out an alibi he could read off to her:

"Miss Shoe, I am deeply offended and insulted by the allegation against me in your letter. And I am shocked by the nature of your new society and the depraved associations which you are making—but that is your affair. My complaint is that you charge me with being a party to a similar vice—yes, vice. To associate with fallen women for any purpose whatsoever is a vice—and a vice which I can proudly say I am innocent of.

"The prostitute must go, I grant you. But there is only one place fit for her: jail! Modern society has no room for the prostitute—reformed or otherwise. But that is your affair. Don't interrupt, Miss Shoe. You said a great many things in your letter which I wish to contradict.

"Do you realize, my good woman, that it was not until I received your communication this morning that I knew the Tinker Avenue address was a brothel? I was actually stunned by the news. I stumbled into that den of iniquity—I will take your word as to its nature—quite by accident while making a sick call on one of our church members. The address I was in search of was on Pinker Avenue, not Tinker, and I soon discovered my grievous error.

"The surroundings had seemed rather unattractive, but I would never have suspected that I had crossed the threshold of a bawdyhouse if you had not informed me. I almost feel that I have sinned in having entered such a sty of filth.

"I trust that you have not informed anybody that I have been guilty of this unintentional sin. To spread the report that I was seen seeking the company of degenerate women would be most unfair, malicious, and slanderous. If you have spread any such story, I call upon you to make the necessary corrections at once. Consider my name, my reputation, my wife!

"This has been a most unfortunate misunderstanding, Miss Shoe, and I am sure that you must regret it fully as much as I do. My presence at that house of ill fame was incriminating, I admit, and there was no other conclusion to be drawn except the one you did—unless you were to suppose—I can hardly say these words—that I had come there as a—let's not even say it."

Alfred Wopple began to feel better. He consulted a city directory. Yes, there was a Pinker Avenue, and it was in a respectable neighborhood. He read over what he had written, mentally stressing certain words. It would be best to take the aggressive and not show any signs of anxiety which might give him away. There was no danger of his laughing. This was too serious a predicament. And his histrionic abilities in the rôle of a representative of God were too well trained. He telephoned Miss Shoe and reread the message to her with fitting expression.

He was soon smiling happily—picturing his name safely back in its place in Uncle Ben's will—while adding, "There, there, Miss Shoe, of course I accept your apologies. I realize you wouldn't do anything to slander me or anybody. . . . My indignation got the better of me for the moment. It is my turn to apologize to you. Your cause is a worthy one. Any prostitute who can be reformed should *not go* to jail.

"You are much braver as a woman than I am as a man. I should be prevented from cooperating in such a noble undertaking by the feeling of repugnance and loathing which the very word 'prostitute' arouses in me. You have gone ahead with your work in the face of these inner tortures. . . ."

CHAPTER XIX

THE LORD IS MY SHADOW

Having said a long prayer for an eye-opener and grace before breakfast for a bracer, Uncle Ben Wopple felt his usual morning enthusiasm for eggs and tea. When he awoke in the unpleasant state of partial sobriety, he never had to fear that last night's bottle would be empty. Nor was there any doubt as to whether or not a swallow from it would remain inside him. A few words to God brought the glow of Heaven's luxuries. The palace reserved for him was still waiting.

The stimulation of the day's first revelation of some of the grandeur God had ready for him provided energy that brought Uncle Ben out of bed happily singing a hymn—but the tone was funereal. The hymn was an additional stimulant, telling of the glories of God and the joy that awaited him, but it lacked the full invigorating effect of direct communication with the deity. It was a substitute for a glass or two of beer while preparing himself to say grace and have the second dose of Heaven's improvement on whisky.

Breakfast tasted good, but Uncle Ben knew it would not seem good enough for a pig if he were in his angel-body. The earth had no dish that was fit for God and His angels. Heaven's food would make earthly offerings seem nauseating—if such a reaction was possible in Heaven. Probably earthly food would merely appear to be something which did not arouse the appetite. But no such garbage would be there anyway. Everything in Heaven would arouse a pleasurable response.

God's greetings this morning had reminded Uncle Ben of other facts about Heaven, his future home: There would be no need to sleep. Angel's bodies were not subject to fatigue, and there would be no possibility of boredom. There would be no whiskers to shave. It would not even be necessary to wash. Everything in Heaven was clean and pure.

There would be lakes of Heaven's champagne—something non-intoxicating, of course. All men of God were strict teetotalers. His mere presence would serve as money for whatever he wanted. The wish alone would produce the desired article. Probably it would appear before the wish was able to make itself known in his mind.

The anticipation of these prospects, as pictured in inspirations direct from Heaven, would have prolonged Uncle

Ben's ecstasy for some time, but he wanted to get into communication with God again. The eye-opener and bracer alone would be tantalizing if no more could be had. He stuffed the rest of the egg into his mouth and poured some tea in after it. It was not necessary to give spoken thanks for this repast. God could read his thoughts. He rose, his mouth still full, to bow his head in a silent message to God.

In recent months Uncle Ben had over-indulged in religion to greater excess than ever. Through his years of piety, messages from Heaven had gradually lessened in potency. Like the toper who needs three drinks to get the effect that one used to provide, Uncle Ben had found it necessary to take more frequent sips of Heaven.

Business associates were frequently told, "Mister Wopple is busy just now," as a result of morning or afternoon prayers in his private office and their afterglow. Before seeking these extra potions of God's advance hospitality, he would notify his secretary that he wished to be alone. Sometimes word would come that Mr. Wopple was no longer busy. Sometimes no more was heard of him until he appeared at Nephew Alfred's Bible talk for employees at noon or until the close of the business day.

Not even a W.C.T.U. reformer could have condemned Uncle Ben as a habitual drunkard. And as a habitual religionist, he was above reproach, except that the wives of his neighbors could not understand why he never said, "How do you do," to them. When criticisms were being made by other ladies for this failing, Miss Shoe always managed to get in the delicate remark, "He always speaks to me." Since she was not another man's wife or maidservant, Ben Wopple could nod to her without arousing God's suspicions that he was coveting forbidden acquaintances.

Having swallowed the mouthful of egg while giving mental thanks to God for breakfast and for a nip of Heaven, Wopple repeated the words aloud. These two additional tastes of God's delights left him in no mood for earthly business. He would devote this whole day to God. Why bother going to the office at all?

He telephoned his secretary. "Miss Alley, I have some very important matters to attend to and will not be with you to-day."

At this point a drinking man would have poured out a nice long, high one and perhaps spilled a little in the process. Uncle Ben reached for a Bible. There was one within reach of every chair in his home.

This was the Lord's book. He owned it in common with God. He held the Bible to the light. The shadow was not all his, any more than was all of the Bible. Part of the shadow must be God's. God was not visible anywhere in the room. The shadow might be part of God himself.

CHAPTER XX

LEWD LADIES

The Society for the Resurrection of the Fallen Woman had established a duration record for a Mabel Shoe organization. It had been in active existence for over two months. A new social service society's letterhead was long overdue, and Miss Shoe had no other one in prospect. She had found the field of work in which she could do the most good. She had the interest of the whore at heart and was determined to have the signature of every such woman on a pledge-card beneath the promise, "I shall forever refrain from fornication."

Just what the future means of income would be was a problem that Miss Shoe had not considered.

Establishing headquarters on Tinker Avenue had not proved to be merely a matter of hiring office space. Real estate agents had been quite pleased to offer her a choice of many desirable locations until she explained her intention to have a large sign "Streetwalkers' Shrine."

"But, lady, you can't advertise like that," one man had told her. "You'd be pinched the first day. You'll have to sort of keep things looking respectable on the outside."

"Oh dear, so many people think my work is wicked," Miss Shoe had replied.

"It may not be wicked, but it's illegal," the agent told her. "They've got some funny laws in this country."

"Illegal?" asked Miss Shoe. "Surely it's not illegal to reform fallen women."

"Oh, so you want to *reform* them. I'm afraid we can't take care of you. Some of the other tenants might not like—well, having the neighborhood cheapened like that."

Miss Shoe could understand this explanation. It would be a reflection upon an honest girl to have a large sign announcing that she lived near the red-light district. But why the man had been surprised at her intentions of reforming other kinds of girls was not quite clear. His first impression must have been that she was merely planning to inform on them and arrange for their arrest. Even so, she had not realized such a procedure was illegal.

Other real estate men had offered similar excuses for refusing her a lease. Playing this rôle of an undesirable tenant had been humiliating to Miss Shoe, but she was still willing to be a martyr to her cause. To have carried on after Alfred Wopple's denunciation of her mission was the best instance of her determination. He had apologized, but, just the same, he had said her work was a depraved vice which he would be ashamed to be a party to.

Miss Shoe was pleased by the hearty cooperation being given by her first convert. Teresa Beetle—Vestal Beetle now— apparently had become so enthused by life's new appearance as seen on the path of virtue that she was devoting more time to the reform work than to her new religious duties. She had been at her former room whenever Miss Shoe called and had already secured twenty signed pledge-cards. Miss Shoe had paid fifteen dollars for each—"a surprise gift for each girl as a sample of the good fortune now in store for her."

So much money had at least enabled Teresa to start toward the path of virtue, for she had taken a vacation—except from the work for regular customers.

Vestal Beetle had been so successful that Miss Shoe felt rather ashamed of her own record: she had only one reformation to show for Vestal Beetle's twenty. There was a little consolation in the fact that her one was Vestal Beetle, who had negotiated all the others. Vestal Beetle seemed proud of her own accomplishments and reluctant to tell her the names of fallen girls on whom she could call with pledge-cards. This attitude was rather selfish, Miss Shoe thought, but the new thrill of life which this reformed woman now found in reforming others doubtless made it excusable.

Miss Shoe would not have dared go from room to room at 217 Tinker Avenue, for probably not all of them were occupied by fallen women. Yesterday, after much persuasion, and an additional twenty-dollar bill, she had managed to obtain from Vestal Beetle the number of an apartment that was definitely a brothel. "Ask for Madam Funnybone," Vestal Beetle explained. "You won't have to talk much. Just ask to see the girls—there's five of them. Give them the cards and the money. They'll sign."

Teresa had arranged with Madam Funnybone—her real name was Mrs. Blythe Dyle—to divide the profits.

Miss Shoe had hurried to this suite on the first floor but had seen a man at the door. She had run past him and into a taxicab at the curb. She was returning now to reform the five girls—and the madam, too. She hoped Vestal Beetle had not called on them in the meantime. She wanted the credit for their rescue.

To reform six fallen women all at once would be a remarkable record. This did not compare with Vestal Beetle's total, but she probably hadn't obtained as many as six at one time. Despite over two months of perseverance, this was to be Miss Shoe's first visit to a brothel containing more than the one girl, Teresa Beetle. She was excited by the thoughts of seeing six lewd women. What would they look like, and how would they act?

Her fears that a man might be there or might come while she was inside were being replaced by other thoughts. Six lewd girls would soon be honest women. There would be six less women selling themselves to men. Six men—no, perhaps a hundred or more men would have to look for other women. Vestal Beetle and her converts made a grand total of twenty-seven less women available for men. Hundreds of men were being affected. Hundreds of men without women. Men who did not want to be without women.

Mable Shoe felt a pleasurable vibration, a strange sensation of joy. She told herself not to think about the men involved. They would have to reform, too, when there were no more prostitutes to be had. These wicked men—she had escaped them for over forty years.

Miss Shoe knocked on the door of the bottomless pit.

"Glad to see you," said Madam Funnybone. "We've been expecting you. Come on, girls! Here she is."

Her enthusiastic welcome was very gratifying. This was the sort of reception she had expected from the demimonde, offering redemption and salvation to women who thought themselves too deep in sin ever to be rescued. Vestal Beetle, who had repulsed her at first, had been a problem case, but she had finally been won over.

Five girls wearing slippers ran into the room, one with a thin pink ribbon tied around her stomach, and all equally as enthusiastic as Madam Funnybone. These were certainly bawdy women. Miss Shoe knew that she *should* be shocked, but, instead, the strange pleasant feeling became more intense. She could not think of anything to say, an unusual predicament. She hastened to pass out pledge cards.

"Oh, can I have one, too?" said Madam Funnybone. "Thank you."

Miss Shoe had six pairs of ten- and five-dollar bills folded together all ready to provide a happy surprise. She passed these out as she collected the cards. Still she couldn't think of anything to say. These were all honest women now, but this fact did not seem to make the proper impression on her. She felt a sort of elation, but it was not the kind of elation this victory over sin should have produced.

There was no need for her to stay here any longer. Her work was done. Why didn't she go? This was not a den of iniquity now, but the fact was not yet known to its frequenters. A man might appear and think she was a seventh girl of joy—no, sin, sin! A man might appear. A man with only one purpose—to hire a woman's body. She had a woman's body. And she was the only woman present who had not signed the pledge.

These other six completed a total of twenty-seven former prostitutes who would have to say, "No." Twenty-seven—that was just a beginning! Every harlot would sign a pledge card before she finished. Every man would have to come to *her!* Mabel Shoe felt a sudden conscious desire to be with a man— with men—as a prostitute.

Her whole body tingled with anticipation. She wanted a man, a wicked man. She wanted to be a girl of joy—yes *joy!* She wanted carnal sin, criminal conversation, physical expression— every synonym there was.

Madam Funnybone and the girls noticed that Miss Shoe was trembling. She began to squeeze one of her drooping breasts with a ferocity that must have been painful. She walked up to Madam Funnybone.

"Let me have the next man," she pleaded in a low tone. "Please! I'll go into one of the rooms and put out the light. It will be dark. He won't be able to see me."

Madam Funnybone stopped smiling. "So that's it," she replied, glancing up and down at Miss Shoe's face and body. "I'll see what I can do—and you needn't worry about the light. I'll be sure that's out."

CHAPTER XXI

*WE DON'T LOOK THE SAME
IN THE DARK*

A man, namely Uncle Ben Wopple, stepped out of a taxicab which had stopped in front of 217 Tinker Avenue.

"Just ask for Madam Funnybone," the driver told him.

"Buy yourself a couple of drinks with the change," said Uncle Ben. He started toward the door of the brothel.

Ben Wopple had arrived at a stage analogous to *delirium tremens* in his long religious drunk. His hallucinations would have been merely the usual outlook on life for another, but Uncle Ben's usual outlook on life in the past would have constituted hallucinations for another. And, if not shaking in proper D.T. manner, Uncle Ben was at least trembling slightly with excitement and expectation. The long neglected side of his make-up had asserted itself, overcoming the formerly dominant part which had finally been weakened by religious dissipation until it was powerless to resist further.

Uncle Ben, like all of us, was only partial master of his body. Through the years he had succeeded in checking unholy actions and even desires, but the nerves and cells arousing such calls of Nature had not atrophied entirely. The barrier of resistance he had built up against them had been a strong one. Nerves and cells of opposite variety had been able to dominate the unwanted urges. They had been strengthened by constant usage, somewhat like the muscles of an athlete, until they were able to prevent ungodly suggestions of the body from appearing in the arena of consciousness.

When the opposition became reenforced by stored up energy, the athletic brain-cells had packed the arena of consciousness full of substitute-stimuli of a holy nature. Most forms of bodily pleasure were sinful, and the desire for pleasure was a powerful one. Holy pleasure had to be conceived as a substitute.

The duplicate of drunkenness had been provided in Uncle Ben's anticipation of his future joys in Heaven through communication with God. When in this happy state, mere desires for other forms of indulgence could not be effective even if noticed. It is hard to lure a drunken man away from a full bottle, and the holy cells were able to keep the invisible bottle filled.

Having been able to cool his natural instinct by means not specifically opposed by either God or Satan, the two most vigorous rivals for mental authority were squelched: sex-hunger and the desire for pleasure of intenser form than sobriety permits.

The cerebral barrier thus established around the arena of consciousness might have remained impenetrable if Uncle Ben had not gone in for excessive libertinism of a religious nature. His pleasures being legitimate forms of godly expression, there was no need to set any limit on them. Having gradually increased his number of daily communications with God, it would have lessened the cumulative pleasure from Heaven to which he became habituated if he said fewer prayers.

The joys of Heaven's drunkenness became his favorite dissipation, for they could be spread over the whole day. Providing this form of intoxication constantly was a strain on the athletic cells. They became weakened and could not give the usual full effect of one prayer until after two or three had been said. The suppressed energies were striving for entrance, battering the wall from the outside. Uncle Wopple's demands were crumbling the wall on the inside.

Death did not intervene, and so the wall had finally crashed. Uncle Ben Wopple was suddenly informed that his forty-nine years of piety had been enough. A new sort of message from Heaven was telling him of divine pleasures right here on earth which he was now entitled to. He had served his term as an ascetic and proved himself a man of God. Now he was entitled to have the things he had been going without.

His broken resistance did not bring visions of alligator-snakes and other monsters. Instead, he received visions of earthly life that replaced the former visions of Heaven's grandeur.

He became aware of many possibilities in his liberated state, but the first definite impulse was to find a woman. The quickest means seemed to be to locate a brothel. His chauffeur might not understand this freedom which came after so many years of reverence, and he probably didn't know where there was a whore-house anyway. Uncle Ben had consulted a taxi driver, that great fount of universal knowledge.

Madam Funnybone looked at her new customer suspiciously. He seemed more like a snooping reformer in search of data for police warrants than an honest patron.

"Let's hear you swear," she said to him.

Uncle Ben let loose a volley.

"I guess you're all right," said Madam Funnybone. "Come on in."

The five reformed girls stepped forth for him to select from. Uncle Ben felt like saying a new form of grace, but another instinct prevented this delay. These smiling bodies gave him little choice. Each one was the best. He pointed straight ahead to what happened to be the girl with the thin pink ribbon. Madam Funnybone had delayed the financial arrangements.

"I'll be in this room," said the girl, making her departure.

Uncle Ben stayed behind to pay five dollars to Madam Funnybone, who explained, "Daisy has to stay in a dark room. Her eyes are weak. You don't mind, do you?"

Uncle Ben did not mind. In fact, he preferred that the room be dark. He would probably be somewhat confused on this initiation into what had once been a sin, and the darkness would make his condition less noticeable to Daisy.

He had a glimpse of a bed before the door of the room was closed behind him. Instinct serves for virgin animals who have no apparent means of communicating information. The universal language of instinct, which needs no oral synonyms, served in this case.

The afterglow of Ben Wopple's pleasure came in the plural. The light in the room suddenly glared forth. One of the girls had succeeded in drawing Madam Funnybone's attention away from the electric light button which she was carefully guarding, and another girl had pressed it.

Mr. Ben Wopple found himself looking into the face of Miss Mabel Shoe, and in a bawdyhouse, an impossible situation. Wopple knew that Miss Shoe, pious religious reformer, was not a prostitute and would never be found in a brothel. Miss Shoe knew that Mr. Wopple, saintly churchman, would never knowingly enter a brothel. Even if he did by mistake, as his nephew had, he would never enter into the spirit of the practices there. But this impossibility was true. They could not doubt their eyes.

"I . . . I . . . I must have gone out of my mind . . . why this is . . . this is . . . outrageous . . ." stammered Mr. Wopple, with the natural impulse of a drunken man, hardly able to stand, who unconsciously reels around into an opposite course at the sight of a policeman ahead.

"Oh dear! a white-slaver has kidnapped me," Miss Shoe moaned.

The light was switched off again. In the darkness came low voices:

"That was wonderful, Daisy."

"Wasn't it, Mister."

CHAPTER XXII

AN OVERDRESSED FINGER

Bertha Render was happily powdering her body. This was the alternate night on which her Peter called, the one and only Peter Hatch, myth-man, super-man, love-athlete.

Most girls were enthusiastic about the athletes of rugged sports, but Peter did not waste his energies in exhibition contests and races. Love was his game, and he was a champion.

Bertha patted the powder puff against various parts of herself, saying, "A dab for Peter here, and a dab for Peter there. . . ." "Peter uses up too much of my powder," she laughed. "Naughty boy."

The bell rang. Peter The Great had arrived. Bertha pressed the button that released the lock, then threw a fancy silk kimono around herself.

"How's my nice Bicycle Bertha?" asked Peter Hatch (the real one and only Peter Hatch).

"Fine—now that my nice Peter is here."

They sat down on the couch, but Peter paused a moment before putting his arms around her. He took a very small box out of his pocket.

"We're going to be married," he announced and displayed a shiny diamond ring.

Bertha kissed him, and they proceeded with other acts of love.

As Peter Hatch made ready to leave, she rebuked him playfully: "Got to go take your tonic, huh?" This had become her stock joke whenever Peter went out for his customary breaths of fresh air.

"This is our Ward Eight night, you know," he reminded her. "We'll have a big celebration." Bertha knew that he would not mention Ward Eights again until they were about to depart. When he came back, he would refer to the fun they would have drinking champagne the night after next or going to a theater eight nights from then. She didn't care how they celebrated this happy occasion. The champion's engagement ring was her ticket to all the pleasure she could conceive of.

Romeo Hatch returned to enjoy the ridicule of his companions. Their mockery of his disgraceful rôle to-night would provide the necessary damper to keep his exhilaration from causing some sort of an internal explosion. Bicycle Bertha was to be his wife—his wife alone. This was insanity, but insanity had proved to be a far happier state than sanity.

Peter Sadler hurried up to Bertha's room. "I'm back already, Bicycle," he informed her. He sat down on the couch, and Bertha placed a hand against his cheek.

"You certainly cool off fast," she said.

Peter Sadler did not embrace her immediately. He took a very small box from his pocket and remarked, "We're going to get married."

"Yes, won't it be wonderful!" said Bertha.

Peter Sadler noticed the ring she was wearing.

"I've got another ring," he told her. "It's better than that first one I gave you." He removed Peter Hatch's offering from her finger and replaced it with a similar ring. "You can probably get a few dollars for the other one."

Peter had been refreshed just as much as ever by his hasty trip outdoors and back. Before leaving he spoke of the cocktail party he was planning for four nights from then.

"We won't really celebrate to-night; we'll wait a few days and have a big time," he told her.

Bertha smiled at him. She knew he would celebrate to-night. His enthusiasm for this evening's diversions would return by the time they were ready to start.

Peter's invigorated return was made by Peter Pike.

"Has my little Bicycle been a nice girl while I was gone?" he asked and then kissed her.

"No," she replied a few moments later, "while you were going downstairs and back, eight men came in to see me."

"I've got a surprise," he told her and brought forth a very small box containing a diamond ring.

"*Another* one."

Peter Pike saw two rings around her finger. She had put the first one back on.

"This is a still better one," he explained. "Take off those other two I gave you."

Peter's next appearances were made by those of surnames Dean, Lyman, and Jones. It was time for Peter Hatch (the real one) to separate from the other five and fulfill his degrading duties as Romeo. His abuse, while waiting, had been even more caustic than Romeo was usually subjected to. Each returning visitor made very indignant accusations concerning this companion's helplessness at the hands of a woman. But customary taunts that Romeo was about to propose marriage were omitted. Engagement rings had suddenly become an unmentioned subject.

Romeo ran upstairs to take out *his* Bicycle Bertha for the Ward Eight celebration of their engagement. He should have asked her to hide the ring. But evidently none of the others had noticed it.

Bertha Render, still reclining on the couch, was trying to adjust six diamond rings to one finger. Peter's choice in rings changed as often as his choice in entertainment. He must have been unable to select any one he liked best at the jewelry store and so had bought his six favorites. She wouldn't sell any of them as he had suggested, for the one he preferred would doubtless continue to vary from moment to moment. She could wear the one he wanted at a particular time and carry the other five in her hand-bag. Then she could change rings as his choice changed.

Six rings from Peter somehow seemed quite appropriate and symbolic. Other girls would get only one ring. But her man, who was six times better than theirs, had, with proper consistency, given her six rings.

The door opened, and Peter Hatch's excited voice asked, "All ready to start the celebration?"

"No, hubby—can I call you that now?—but I will be as soon as I dress."

"You mean undress," replied a startled voice. Peter had seen six glittering rings where there should have been one. Details of a secret wedding were due for cautious revision. The problem of a secret date had become a vital one.

CHAPTER XXIII

THE GEISHA GIRL PERIL

Dorothy Dolly had decided that her neighbor Teresa Beetle was not an honest woman. Dorothy had devoted much conversation to accusing her of many crimes in the past, but now there was definite proof. No honest professional woman could earn the amount of money Teresa had been spending lately. And Teresa had not even tried to pretend she was earning her wealth at her usual trade. All she did was spend money, making no effort to earn any. Dorothy had actually seen a man try to stop her on the street and heard Teresa's reply, "Don't get fresh." Such conduct was disgraceful.

Teresa's financial success had set an undisputed high as income for a Tinker Avenue girl. Her figures were unquestionably exaggerated, but her display of bills made her the acknowledged money-record holder. This was a new sort of record for Tinker Avenue. Occasionally a rich and drunken patron could be charged a high price or rolled. There had been rumors of fifty and hundred dollar customers but no official proof. And never had the results enabled the girl to retire, as Teresa seemed to have done.

Teresa and her money were the main topics of the avenue. Dorothy's wholesale record had become ancient history anyway, but, even if it had just been accomplished, it would not have been worth more than casual mention in comparison. Dorothy's rival had risen to new fame, and Dorothy was jealous.

"First the skunk goes in for free love to make a name for herself," Dorothy's thoughts were saying, "now she steals a bale of money and tells everybody she's hooked a rich sucker. Where is he? He must be invisible. Nobody has seen him."

Dorothy had only one clew to the real source of income—although she had many detailed explanations. She had seen the disgusting old maid who had practically called her a fallen woman enter the building in which Teresa lived. There was no proof that this obvious outcast from the profession endowed by Nature had visited Teresa, but Dorothy took this for granted. The woman would be out for no good, and Teresa was entirely unprincipled. It was obvious that they were being drawn together by some criminal interest they had in common.

Possible wealth on the part of the outcast was overlooked, for such thoughts would have been disturbing. Dorothy had refused to talk with the woman on the occasion of the insult. Surely she had not thrown aside the fortune that was now Teresa's. If the old maid had had any honest intentions, she would have been more polite when they met. Dorothy was convinced that Teresa had received tainted money—not an endowment.

An outcast woman who insulted Nature's girls on the streets, and a girl of Nature who had become unworthy of her calling, provided a pair of criminals that performed a variety of interesting felonies in Dorothy Dolly's mind. They might have stolen and subsequently sold a large supply of dope. Perhaps they had created a lot of new addicts in the process and made sales to little children, too.

The subject of drugs brought to mind the Orient and geisha girls. Perhaps Teresa and her partner had gone in for yellow slavery and started a vogue for Japanese and Chinese girls. Such a project would lessen the income of native white girls by just that much and thus would be decidedly criminal.

"That would be a trick almost low enough for Teresa," Dorothy told herself as she considered this possibility now. "Every dollar she gets is stolen right out of the hands of the rest of us. They probably charge half rates.

"Damn it, if they get enough of those yellow joints started, it will drive the rest of us out of business. There's been a slump already. Teresa the Rat-Eater—she probably helps the Chink girls eat rats. We'd ought to lynch her. She's probably got a laundry out in front and a sign, 'Have Your Suit Pressed While You Wait.' The girls that ain't working are pressing clothes in the window and trying to wink in more trade. If any place with white girls tried to advertise like that, everybody would be pinched."

There had been no rumors of competition by Oriental brothels, but this did not detract from the convincing conclusions of Dorothy's reasoning. Teresa Beetle had unquestionably been obtaining money from some such source, and immediate action should be taken to eliminate the yellow peril. Otherwise, Nature's chosen white girls would find themselves forced to meet sweatshop rates or to try to find work other than that for which Nature intended them. The only way to eliminate the geisha girl menace was to eliminate Teresa Beetle.

Tinker Avenue should be aroused to its danger, and Dorothy decided to start the offense that would make the best defense. The other girls were being fooled by Teresa's money. Teresa had bought them a few drinks to give the impression she was still their friend. They would remain unaware of the monster that was among them until the yellow peril was brought right to Tinker Avenue.

Dorothy went out to spread the real facts, confident that a crowd of enraged ladies would soon be storming Teresa's quarters with clubs and knives. Dorothy could watch the arrival of the police from a safe distance. She would have done her part in informing the girls of the crisis. She saw Madam Funnybone and ran across the street to tell her of the yellow menace that Teresa Beetle had created. She could enlist her five girls for this emergency. Madam Funnybone laughed.

"Teresa won that money playing cards," she said.

CHAPTER XXIV

"DON'T BREAK THE BOTTLE,"
CRIED THE SEXTON

Ben Wopple had been missing for two days. His nephew was worried. The death of Uncle Ben would be the long awaited climax of Alfred Wopple's strenuous career as a docile man of God. He hoped there would be no such anticlimax as an unfound or unidentifiable body to further delay his financial independence.

Uncle Ben had not mentioned any contemplated out of town trip. Nobody at his home or office knew where he was. The prospects for Nephew Alfred seemed to be good, but where was the body? There had been an omen that Alfred feared might be a bad one. The stained-glass church window—the one he had planned to make the target for a bottle after his bequest was definitely in his own name—was broken.

Alfred had discovered this fact on his way home to-night. When walking past the church, he usually stopped to gaze at this window in outward admiration and devotion—wondering how it would look after the bottle had passed through it and wishing this were the happy day of the bottle throwing.

To-night he had seen how the broken window looked. Just when it had appeared that his chance to fulfill this ambition was at hand, the window had been smashed by another. There were many other windows in the church. Why had this particular one been broken? It might be a sign that the inheritance from Uncle Ben was to be snatched away from him as had the pleasure of watching the broken angels' wings flutter gently to the ground.

There was a moment of hope when the telephone rang, and he was asked if Ben Wopple was missing.

"Have you found the body?" he asked excitedly.

"I guess so, but it's still a lively one. There's a drunk here at Station Five who seems to be Ben Wopple. You better come down and look him over to make sure."

Uncle Ben drunk and under arrest? This couldn't be true. He must have been in an accident that had stunned him in some way—perhaps left him out of his mind. Well, if Uncle Ben could be proved insane, Alfred's financial independence doubtless could soon be arranged. The broken angels may have been a good omen. Alfred was amused by the thought of his holy uncle being in jail for drunkenness. This situation was almost as pleasing as the satisfaction of breaking the stained-glass window would have been.

• • • • • • •

Uncle Ben was loudly shouting through the bars of his cell. "Give me back my liquor! Give me my liquor! God damn bastards! Kidnapers! I want a drink! . . ."

Usual methods for quieting a prisoner were not used. The identification of this man as the rich Ben Wopple might be correct. The arresting officer regretted having been so rough in bringing the prisoner to the station—he hadn't known who this drunk was. He regretted now that he had made the arrest. But what else could he have done upon seeing a man throw a bottle through a church window?

For this had been Uncle Ben's final act as an unrestrained citizen. His investigation of earthly life the day before had turned from women to alcoholics, and from cocktails to bottled goods. A hotel had provided an intermission, and several bottles had been standing on the floor by his bed to remind him that morning prayers were no longer necessary.

Four quart bottles were protruding from his coat and pants pockets when he was arrested. A knapsack hanging over one shoulder contained ten more quarts and pints of various brands.

The eleventh bottle of this reserve supply had been thrown to the angels. Other church windows were scheduled for similar donations, but a policeman had intervened.

Uncle Ben's battle arena of consciousness had become reorganized. The influx of unholy impulses through the broken barrier of holy cells had led to the building of a new wall. The long excluded mental reflexes cooperated in erecting an equally strong barrier of their own. Holy thoughts found themselves outside the wall. At the end of this process Uncle Ben had decided that church windows should be broken.

. . . .

Alfred Wopple could hear an indignant voice that sounded like Uncle Ben's as he entered the door at Station Five. What was that he was shouting? He must have misunderstood. Alfred listened and started to laugh. Yes, Uncle Ben was crazy. There could be no doubt of that. Alfred was delighted by the strange symptoms of this variety of insanity. Blasphemy from the mouth of his uncle was as gratifying as it would have been to have the stained-glass angels come to life during a church service and fly overhead shouting a chorus of profanity.

And he was yelling for liquor, too. This was too good to believe. Saint Wopple cursing God and demanding whisky. If he should ever regain his sanity, the shock of recalling such heinous heretical crimes would be fatal. Uncle Ben being in this state, anything seemed possible now. Probably the window had been broken by the angels coming to life and flying out of it amid merry curses, bawdy songs, and an inharmonious refrain of, "Who's got a drink?"

Alfred tried to keep a straight face as he was escorted to the cell by the lieutenant. Strange sounds of explosive laughter that refused to remain silent were covered up by Uncle Ben's shouts.

"Is that Ben Wopple?" he was asked.

He had to look several moments to be sure. He hoped this was his uncle, but it hardly seemed believable, even with cursing angels flying about the city.

"Yes," he replied.

"He's had a little too much to drink," the lieutenant explained. "You better put up a bond and take him home."

"Surely he isn't actually drunk," said Alfred, becoming aware that an alcoholic odor was coming from Uncle Ben's cell.

"I'm afraid he is—but he'll be all right when he sobers up."

Uncle Ben . . . sober up . . . these two terms didn't fit into the same sentence. Surely he couldn't sober up from this insanity and be "all right" again. The officer must be trying to break the supposedly bad news gently.

Ben stopped shouting, but only for a moment. He had recognized Alfred. His words took up a new subject:

"So there's that God damn son of a . . ." (Ben Wopple's vocabulary had become enriched by a choice selection of terms which might involve unesthetic combinations of type) "nephew of mine. I been looking for you . . . you and your damn Bible talks . . . trying to turn my office into a bunch of pansies. And you go to church as though you thought God was—God. Not a brain in your head. God is the guy who invented swearing . . . but you pray instead of cuss. No damn fool religious nut is going to get any more favors out of me. You're fired! . . . and you'll get exactly one dollar when I die . . ."

Alfred's teeth were making chattering noises. "I'll get in touch with the insane asylum," he said.

"No, no, don't be alarmed," the lieutenant reassured him. "He's only drunk."

CHAPTER XXV

HERE'S THE MAN;
WHERE'S THE MOON?

"Why, I had no idea such conditions existed."

A group of "I prefer tea" guests from the Loyal Ladies' League was being given a drawing-room account of the activities of the Society for the Resurrection of the Fallen Woman.

"Yes, it is sad but true," said Miss Mabel Shoe. "Such persons know no shame. It is hard to believe one's own eyes—and still harder to believe that these lewdsters could have been born pure and innocent babes. Their sale of their bodies to man and the Devil has become an organized business, a veritable industry. They have made our female sex a mere trade name in their localities.

"Why, I actually discovered a woman flaunting this business card!" Miss Shoe showed the guests a card on which had been printed by hand in red ink:

AGNES MOON,
STREETWALKER

"It is unfortunate that our bodies permit such abuse . . ."

"Please!" said a prim old lady who did not approve of the pronoun "our."

"These beasts have desecrated the female body," Miss Shoe continued. "It is our duty to remove this disgrace of our sex and to rescue the fallen. . . ."

"I had no idea there were such women," observed another member of the sex in question.

"Have you never read the Bible?" replied Miss Shoe. "Christ Himself forgave a prostitute."

"Don't talk like that," said the woman. "Christ had no dealings with such degenerates."

"But He really did," another woman whispered to her.

No new members for the society were obtained as a result of this gathering. Miss Shoe remained the only worker for her cause—except Vestal Beetle. Miss Shoe had continued to entrust her with fifteen dollar presents for each new convert and now had over sixty signed pledge cards.

Madam Funnybone and her girls were not workers for the society. Vestal Beetle had warned her in advance that to give them a supply of blank cards and send them out among their former friends seeking converts would place temptation in their path. They might find themselves unable to resist the evil influences they would have to face. It was best to leave them to find new and uncontaminated friends who could help keep them on their new path of virtue.

Miss Shoe was sure that they were still living up to the pledge. Each time she had gone to see them since they had signed the cards, the formerly immodest girls all had on the kimonos she had bought them. She was doing her best to keep temptation from them. As soon as a man came to call, he was turned over to her.

Miss Shoe set out for 217 Tinker Avenue after her guests had left. Her discovery of the fact that her body was an animal had revealed for her a cruel deception underlying society and its teachings. She realized that she had not escaped men for over forty years, but that men had escaped her. She had been led to believe that men, and only men, were human animals—vicious and wicked—respectable women were exempt from this animality. Relations with men were a painful marital duty only pleasurable to the man. Every man was a potential means of torture.

She had been shown that this was not true. Women were animals, too. She had been deceived and denied the pleasures that should have been her animal-body's through the years. The body's greatest joy had been disguised for her with the label "Poison." The really dishonest women were the so-called honest ones who had lied to her.

She had discovered a secret that many women did not seem to know. She was glad now that they didn't. And she was not going to say anything to enlighten them. They were so many less women from whom she would need to obtain signatures. They represented so many more available men.

In reforming the active animal-bodies of other women by convincing them that they were doing something wrong, she was only using the form of deception she had been taught herself. A week ago she would have believed she was telling the truth. To-day she was an animal, and she had been without mates all her life.

She had explained to Madam Funnybone that her frequent calls were made in order to take over the former duties of the girls and prevent their falling again in the event that an insistent man should arrive who did not know of their reform. Madam Funnybone thanked her for this kind consideration each time and tucked several bank notes into a stocking. A dark room, following a customer's choosing from a row of more eligible maidens, enabled Miss Shoe to "cleanse the man's mind of its evil intentions," she explained.

During the week since the revelation of the real purpose of her society, Miss Shoe had started to make a name for herself— or rather for Betty Biller. A return customer who had gone into the dark room before pointed to Betty on the next visit and said, "I picked you last time, and you were pretty nice." Betty had thanked him for the compliment.

Miss Shoe hoped her example would not serve an opposite purpose and tempt the members of this household to break their pledges. But, even if it did, Madam Funnybone and her girls only made six. Nearly sixty *other* girls were telling men to look elsewhere, and Vestal Beetle was constantly obtaining new names. To reform all but six, besides herself, would be practically as good as reforming them all when the millions of unreformed men were considered.

Millions of men. Millions of momentary husbands all for herself. This would be the situation if her conspiracy worked. She could take her pick of men. She would have so many at her disposal that she would need a few assistants to help her. But she did not want too many assistants. Men had thought they could get along without her. They would soon realize that she was a necessity.

Nevertheless, she felt that men were not yet sufficiently aware of her, Mabel Shoe, in coming to her in the dark after selecting another girl in the light. She wanted men to choose her in the light.

She did not think it would be advisable to stand in the line-up with the other girls for a man to select from, for she realized they were much younger than she. It would be nice if she could bring her own man to Madam Funnybone's instead of waiting to be supplied with one. She had considered calling up Ben Wopple, but she still found it hard to believe that he would be interested.

Then she had had another plan which she intended to try to-day. She had been watching the men she passed on the way to Tinker Avenue. They would all be more observant of her soon. But for the present it would be necessary for her to take the aggressive. It was hard to get up courage to speak to one of them.

"I'll take the next one—whoever he is," she informed herself with determination.

Mabel Shoe had realized she would have difficulty finding the proper words on such an encounter and had carefully prepared a card which she handed to a man—white, although the need of a shave gave a black tinge—who stepped out of a doorway in front of her just as she made this resolution. The card read:

AGNES MOON,
STREETWALKER

"Where is she?" asked the man.
Miss Shoe hurried away toward number 217.

CHAPTER XXVI

"Imagine a guy bein' sap enough to want to marry a girl."

"Yeah, and to buy her a diamond ring and tell her they're engaged."

"You should have handed her a rope tied to a ring through your nose."

Romeo (Peter Sadler at present) was taking the blame for Bertha Render's engagement rings. But only one ring, Romeo's, was ever mentioned in the derision by the others of the member of their sextet who had degenerated to the point of becoming engaged to a girl.

Marriage, to the Peters, was still officially a disgrace to the man involved. A man who reached the stage where he was willing to settle down with one girl was as bad as an ascetic who was willing to eat nothing but milk toast at every meal for the rest of his life. The word "girl" or "date" should bring a variety of types and possible selections to mind, not just one particular female.

This attitude might have prevented Bertha's receiving a ring if there had been only one Peter. But the guilty rôle of Romeo being filled by one of them enabled the other five to work off enough of their taunting consciences to allow room for disgraceful thoughts of marriage to continue. The objections to monogamy that constantly accompanied the desire to be Bicycle Bertha's only husband could be shouted forth at Romeo.

When such words came to mind as, "I want Bertha all for myself. You poor damn fool, she's got you hypnotized," the second sentence was repeated aloud to Romeo.

Being able to express such arguments with a disgusted tone and in the form of an accusation against somebody else removed much of their sting. For the moment, each Peter could tell himself that Romeo was the guilty party in question. Romeo was the God damn fool who had been hypnotized by a girl. Then each Peter could resume the contemplation of his own marriage with Bertha until reminded by new annoying thoughts that he himself was the God damn fool—and Romeo would receive another outburst.

There were other trends of disgraceful unspoken thoughts that brought accompanying spoken charges against Romeo: The wish of each Peter that it was his turn to be Romeo and be alone with Bertha after their next visit. The wish that these five other Peters did not exist. And vague plans for escaping their vigilance and going with Bertha to some far away and hidden locality where these rivals could never find them.

Each Romeo, in turn, became the happiest Peter of the six. Not only was he to be alone with Bertha again, but he could celebrate or re-celebrate their engagement. The details of eluding the others to get married were still to be worked out, but at least they were engaged. Bertha's five other engagement rings were of no consequence now. She would wear his ring on this date. It was his turn to be her fiancé.

Bertha's engagement had been duly celebrated six times. A second series of celebrations was in progress. It seemed fitting to Bertha that they should say they were celebrating their betrothal each time they went out. It did not seem fitting to each Peter that he should be allowed to celebrate his engagement only once in twelve days.

Peter Hatch had devised a scheme for escaping the other five for a personal visit to Bertha. Rehearsing such a feat in advance might suggest better ways and means for accomplishing the permanent secret date which would start on their elopement day. He had had to keep his intention just as secret from her as from the others for fear she might mention it to the wrong Peter Hatch. The problem of how to say to her after his private date, "Don't ever remind me that I called tonight," was an irritating one.

But, if the discovery of this personal date by the others was not made until after he had spent a whole extra evening alone with Bertha, the consequences, whatever they were, would not be too great a price. Peter Hatch's repeated decision on this point was followed now by the remarks to Romeo Sadler, "Crazy ain't a good enough word for it—any fool who is willing to throw himself to a woman is too far gone to be anything. Why don't you get wrapped up and mail yourself to her?"

Peter Hatch's plan was already under way. He had stayed in bed all day and taken frequent peppermint pills from a black and grewsome bottle. A headache, a back ache, an ear ache, and a stomach ache were his professed ailments. Other Peters had brought him sandwiches and coffee during the afternoon. Romeo being the center of attraction, Peter Hatch had not been given much further attention.

They had called on Bertha last night, and this was the alternate day of the polite bandit's activities. If the other Peters continued to believe that he was sick; if they left him alone without a guard to make sure; and if Bertha was home, Peter Hatch's scheme would have succeeded.

He tried to get up strength enough to join them when it came time to leave but succeeded in demonstrating that his depleted energies would make this impossible. He also requested that one of them stay behind to keep him company. But Romeo, the gunman, was accompanied by all of the other four. Without having Romeo at hand to release annoying thoughts upon, it would be an uncomfortable evening.

Bertha proved to be in her room and nicely powdered and painted as well. Peter Hatch picked out his ring for her to wear.

"I suppose I can hock the other five now," she said, with one of her winks that made Peter Sadler like her so well. "That's what you always tell me—then, before I hardly get it on my finger, you pick out another one you like better. You'll wear out my finger."

"I won't change my mind once to-night," Peter told her. "You wait and see."

They sat down on the couch but did not remain seated long.

When it came time for the rejuvenation process, Peter did not seem interested in running down to the front door and back. Instead, he remarked, "Well, Bicycle, let's go out and have a nice Ward Eight celebration."

"Don't you feel well, Peter?" she asked.

This remark was disturbing for the moment. How did she know he had been playing sick all day? Had one of the other Peters worked out a secret scheme for seeing her alone? No, none of them would have mentioned him even if they had seen her. It wouldn't make sense to come to visit Bertha and say, "I'm home in bed sick." Probably staying in bed so long had made him look exceedingly wan and pale.

"I feel fine," he assured her. "Come on, let's get ready."

"I know what's wrong: you forgot your tonic," she replied, with another wink which Peter Sadler would have enjoyed even more than Peter Hatch.

"Ward Eights will be a good tonic—we won't stay out all night."

"I thought you were all better yesterday—now you have to go and get sick again," said Bertha, pouting in the way that

Peter Jones liked. "Night before last you weren't feeling good either."

Night before last—Romeo Dean had been in action as gunman then. Peter Hatch recalled that Peter Lyman had become separated from the others while helping a victim chase a bandit.

"I guess I been eating too much," he explained. "But I'll be O.K. to-morrow night."

"To-morrow night" had an unpleasant sound. This recovery would depend upon the cooperation of five other individuals. How was he going to account for the lack of cooperation after they were married?

CHAPTER XXVII

HERE'S LOOKING AT YOU, GOD

After sobering up, Ben Wopple no longer believed that church windows should be broken—by him, at any rate—but should simply be ignored along with the rest of the building. Even so, the flying stained glass of the angels' window was a happy recollection. Ben Wopple being the church's best customer, a settlement for damages had been made very quietly out of court. News was spread about that the window had been broken by a passing communist and that Ben Wopple had immediately donated money for a new and better one.

"I broke two windows and only paid for one," was Wopple's consolation for his final contribution to godly purposes. At the time of the bottle throwing, he had distinctly seen—or at least seen—two shattered windows.

Ben Wopple, holy man, having become Ben Wopple, unholy man, his pew was empty the following Sunday. The absence of Mr. and Mrs. Alfred Wopple was noted and regretted, too, but the uncle was the present holder of the Wopple wealth and thus the more beloved and sadly missed figure.

Rev. Nehemiah Dick thought there would be mention of a new parish house and perhaps a personal present in Ben Wopple's will. Of course, he hoped the window breaking had not been an indication of a serious illness and that this man who had done so much for the church was not in discomfort—but evidently that was the explanation. For Ben Wopple's attendance could always be counted on with as much certainty as that of the stained-glass angels. Having neither these favorite angels nor his favorite mortal, Ben Wopple, to address his sermon to, Rev. Dick had felt as though he were still rehearsing these remarks at home, not delivering them to his parish.

Sunday worship did not seem complete to Rev. Nehemiah Dick without the Wopple idol out in front of him. When lowering his head to God in the pulpit, Ben Wopple had always been directly in line with his bow. The start of the services had been delayed for ten minutes, but the rich man did not appear.

The minister had hastened to Ben Wopple's home as soon as devotions to God were concluded. It was his duty to help this devout member of the fold in his hour of need. The Sunday School classes soon to follow could be carried on by their leaders on this one occasion without his interruptions.

Ben Wopple, who had already enjoyed several liquid eye-openers and was reading a book of bartenders' secrets in the art of mixing, was glad to see Rev. Dick.

"Well, well, if it isn't Oyster Eyes himself," he greeted him. "You never got very far with this God stuff, did you? Here you've been preaching all these years and haven't learned to do any of his tricks yet. Well, you've made a good racket out of it. Sit down. I want to talk to you."

"Why, my dear Mister Wopple—" The prized parishioner was delirious. This was indeed Mr. Wopple's hour of need.

"You certainly had me fooled for a while. Imagine falling for those fairy stories. Well, meet the atheist. You've got your last dime out of me. I'll give you a drink though. Here, get that into you."

It would be best to humor this madman. He might become violent if his wishes were opposed. Rev. Dick picked up a tumbler filled with Benedictine. Ben Wopple continued drinking his attempt at making a silver fizz.

"You'd ought to be in jail, you and the rest of your ghost-faced gang and your mourning clothes," he added. "Selling people wings to wear after they die—and when they're dead it's too late for them to get their money back. I think I'll sue you and your church for all the money you hooked me for."

"Mister Wopple, has the doctor been here recently?" This was indeed a serious illness, doubtless a fatal one. Rev. Dick hoped that Wopple would be allowed to recover his mind before passing on. Surely he would want to make further compensations to God in his will if his sober senses should receive a hint of the nature of these ravings. This drink tasted sweet and harmless. It did not contain the flames of alcohol.

"Doctor? I don't need one any more. I had some kind of stupid-sickness for forty-nine years, but I've recovered now, thank God—or somebody. We need another Emancipation Proclamation. Slave-trading isn't over yet. You ministers and priests have made more slaves with your ghost-trading than Uncle Tom and his tribe could ever count up to including the bloodhounds and the entire underground railroad."

Having nothing better to do, Rev. Dick was finishing this sweet drink. There was no point in reasoning with a maniac. Perhaps the pious man's soul was on its way to Heaven already. This was only his earthly body that was talking. The soul had been spared the sufferings of the flesh in its final sickness. In this case, there would be no change in the will, but no doubt the soul had arranged for adequate bequests.

"Even if there was such a thing as a soul," Ben Wopple continued, "how would our supporting you guys do it any good? Why build fancy churches and waste a lot of money? The soul won't be here long. There's plenty of fancy stuff for it in Heaven, you claim. It don't cost money to pray, but you fellows have made it a pretty expensive racket."

Rev. Dick was beginning to feel a strange sensation. He felt exhilarated and youthful. He wanted to talk—but it would not be wise to irritate this madman. A few words from a vulgar popular song he had heard on the radio danced through his mind. He changed them to a stanza from a hymn, but the jazz tune continued to accompany them. He wanted to laugh. He had never felt so happy before.

This must be the way people felt in Heaven. He could imagine no better sensation. He must be in communication with Heaven now. Was the hand of God being extended to him? Was he being called to the eternal joy of Paradise? But he was not dying—Ben Wopple was the sick man.

Then it occurred to him: God was sending relief to Ben Wopple's body in its final sufferings. But evidently the angel in charge of the divine duty had made an error and delivered this happiness to him instead. The angel had been deceived by this blasphemy and thought that such a heretic could not be a favored man of God. The angel had probably been delayed so that Wopple's pious soul had left the body before succor from Heaven had arrived.

Having had this accidental gift from Heaven, would he be returned to his mortal existence again, or would he join the soul of Ben Wopple in its journey to God? One did not return from Heaven, and he had been allowed to enter part way at least. It would be depressing to become a mere mortal again after this introduction to Paradise. Why, his soul was already becoming separated from his body. He could see two doors where there should have been only one. The eyes of his rising soul and of his earthly body were causing this double impression.

A full tumbler of Benedictine can cause many strange results. Ben Wopple was surprised to see Rev. Nehemiah Dick jump from his chair and cry, "Whoopee! I'm an angel!"

CHAPTER XXVIII

DID YOU BREAK ANY STONES?

Efforts of a discharged employee to prove his uncle, the employer, insane were not successful. Alfred Wopple was despondent. His career had come to an abrupt end. His life work as an actor in the rôle of a devout man of God had been so effective that prosperous results had seemed certain. Then the taste of his audience had suddenly changed to burlesque shows and the cheers to boos, leaving him in an empty theater with nothing but his holy man make-up.

Alfred's talents as an actor had been too convincing. It was inconceivable to Ben Wopple that Nephew Alfred could ever be anything but an ardent church-goer and Bible authority. Alfred's similar opinion of his uncle had been horrified by unbelievable demonstrations to the contrary. Uncle Ben's transformation would still be very amusing if it could be shown to be insanity. But when he found himself unable to have Uncle Ben declared mentally incompetent, the comedy became too ruthless a personal tragedy to permit further laughter.

With no job and no further pleasant anticipations of the climax of his career that had been due upon Uncle Ben's death, Alfred Wopple was faced with the necessity of starting life all over again. His attitude was what that of a prospector might have been who had mined a ton of gold and then been informed that this metal had lost all value.

His only hope seemed to be that Uncle Ben would recover from his delirium and resume his former beliefs. It was inhuman, Alfred thought, to be disinherited for being too pious. And doubly so in his case because the piety had not been genuine. If he had lived his normal life openly and been cast out by Uncle Ben years ago, they might be having a happy reunion now.

Alfred had considered the possibility of trying to show Uncle Ben that his religious beliefs had changed, too, and that whatever Uncle Ben's opinions were at present had been adopted simultaneously by him. This course might be unwise, for, if Uncle Ben should recover, he would then become an outcast all over again.

Efforts at reconciliation had been useless. He was always told that Mr. Wopple was not at home when he called to see him. If he telephoned, Uncle Ben would say something to the effect of, "Just keep on praying, Alfred. The divine solace of prayer, you know, is far more priceless than that job you had with me. I've done you a favor in letting you have all your time to pray in."

Once a girl's voice had added, "And he tells me to tell you you're a God damn fool."

The employees who had formerly attended Alfred's noonday Bible talks and whom Alfred had intended to discharge when he took over the business had had the unexpected pleasure of ejecting him. Alfred had gone to the office the morning after his own discharge expecting Uncle Ben to make profuse apologies for his disgraceful conduct and probably to offer a raise in pay as partial recompense for his remarks. But Ben Wopple arrived just as the Bible talk had started and did not have to speak more than once to obtain assistants to lead Alfred out to the elevator.

Alfred had seen his uncle twice since then: Once he had been assuring a young and pretty blonde companion that he did not need her help in getting into the taxicab they were boarding. The second time he had been protesting a taxi driver's offer to brush off his coat, which had sopped up part of a mud puddle.

According to his secretary, Ben Wopple was devoting a little more attention to business than before despite these indulgences. He did not spend as much time in the office now, but, while he was there, he was not isolated in solitary prayers and "busy" when any one wanted to see him. When at the office, and in sufficient control of his faculties, he was attending to company business.

Rev. Nehemiah Dick, whose soul had been forced to return from Heaven to complete its allotted span with his mortal body, had not heard of Alfred Wopple's disinheritance and thought it advisable to investigate the cause of this faithful's absence from church. A visit to Alfred might also furnish information as to the nature of the uncle's illness and what the consequences were expected to be. Rev. Dick had decided that Ben Wopple's soul probably had not been called to Heaven yet but was still suffering in the blasphemous flesh of which it had lost control in this sickness.

Mrs. Alfred Wopple welcomed Rev. Dick courteously, for this minister had been Ben Wopple's best friend. Alfred did not know whether to continue his holy rôle or to tell this man what he really thought of him and his teachings. His habits as an actor were working automatically before he reached a decision.

"We have missed both of you as well as Mister Ben Wopple at Sunday services," said Rev. Dick.

"We have been so busy taking care of him, we haven't been able to get away for church," Alfred explained.

"It is very sad. And how is the poor man getting along?"

"There has been no sign of improvement."

"It is very sad. If there is anything I can do, I should be only too glad to help."

Alfred Wopple subdued his actor impulses. It was not going to replace his name in his uncle's will to continue to coddle the minister. He went to a window and opened it.

"Yes, there is something you can do," he replied. "I think it would help Uncle Ben a great deal if you would jump out this window. This may sound unusual, but you know Uncle Ben's condition is a strange one. The correct cure is doubtless equally strange."

"But, my dear man—"

"Come, let me help you out. Surely you are willing to jump ten feet to the ground for my uncle's sake."

"Your uncle's illness has been a great strain on you. Don't you think you had better get a little rest?"

Alfred Wopple took Rev. Dick's hand and attempted to lead him to the open window. Mrs. Wopple watched with little concern. This procedure seemed no more fantastic than many other phases of religion which she had always accepted without question.

"I must be going," said Rev. Dick.

"Yes, right out the window. I should hate to have to tell Uncle Ben that you, the very pastor of his church, had failed him in his hour of need."

Would it be best to humor this strange fancy? It would be better to jump than to be thrown out and perhaps land on his head. Evidently Ben Wopple's disease was catching. Rev. Dick sat down on the sill. The driveway below looked very far away.

"We will all be very grateful to you for this," said Alfred. "I was just reading a book on witchcraft which explained many sure cures for otherwise incurable ailments. Dropping a minister out of a window was recommended for insanity."

Rev. Dick felt the ground strike him. He must have been pushed.

"Oh, I forgot," Alfred Wopple yelled down at him. "That's a cure to use when the minister is crazy. Did it work?"

CHAPTER XXIX

THEN HE PULLED DOWN THE CURTAIN

Romeo Jones was being censured for secret visits to Bicycle Bertha Render. Each of the six Peters had finally succeeded in making one of these private visits, but, of course, whoever happened to be Romeo received the blame for all of them.

The pleasure of these one-man calls had been dimmed for each clandestine visitor by the unpleasant realization that Bertha did not love him as an individual but only as one of six individuals. It required all six Peters to provide the fiancé that Bertha wanted. Any one of them taken alone was tolerated as a replica but by no means the equal of the man she was engaged to. One Peter on a solitary visit could not convince Bertha that he really felt well.

This situation had been given considerable thought by each Peter. Bertha would not want a "sick" husband, but each of them wanted Bertha just for himself with no other Peters to assist. Peter Hatch's reasoning was typical of the others':

It would be different after they were married. Bertha was probably being kittenish now, acting like a girl will who is engaged but not married to a man. Some girls wouldn't even sit in a man's lap, he had heard, until the marriage had taken place. Bertha had no scruples about sitting in her fiancé's lap, but she was going to the opposite extreme and accusing him of giving her too little affection when he was "sick."

A girl who wouldn't sit in her sweetheart's lap soon became adjusted to this and other functions, he hoped, after marriage. And so would Bertha become accustomed to the one-man husband who replaced her six-man suitor. The marriage in itself would prove to her that he loved her even more than ever, and she would have no grounds for chiding him with, "Don't you love me as much as you used to?"

But—there was always a "but" to interfere after the problem had been so nicely solved—suppose she was not being kittenish? In creating Bicycle Bertha Render, the world's finest girl, Nature—realizing that she would be sought by many men— might have provided her with a corresponding desire to have more than one man. Nature may not have approved of letting one man have this whole lovely girl just for himself. One husband might not be enough for this masterpiece of Nature's art.

But—a "but" for the other side this time—evidently Bertha did not want more than one man. She thought the successive Peters were all the same person. If Nature had told her to let several men share her, she would permit more suitors than this "one." And she would not have agreed to marry her Peter and repulse all other men.

But her Peter was really six men. And she really had six suitors. She was following Nature's orders even though she did not realize it. Nature knew there were six Peters and six intended husbands.

But Nature wouldn't want to deprive this masterly maiden of a home of her own and let her have just an endless series of new husbands. Perhaps Nature wanted Bertha to be shared only up to the time of marriage. Then, having displayed sufficient of Nature's genius to other men, she could settle down with one.

Such mental processes became so involved that Romeo would sometimes be without reproach for several minutes at a time. Then one of the other Peters would become conscious of the marriage-disgrace he was deliberately bringing upon himself, and Romeo would be told:

"If she was a magnet and you were a tack, there might be some excuse for it. But she's just another dame. They're all the same in the dark. You damn fool, she's got you kidnaped. You'll be paying out your hard-earned money for ransom the rest of your life."

Romeo would be happily conscious of the fact that it was not always dark.

Secret meetings with Bertha were not approved by the others. There were uneasy feelings that similar visits might be arranged after the marriage. It would be necessary to find a very secluded home in which to live with Bertha, and a permanent escape from the other Peters would have to be carefully planned.

"She's a menace, this Bicycle Bertha," said Peter Dean.

"Yeah, she's got Romeo eating skunk-cabbage out of her hand," said Peter Sadler.

This was an alternate night when Bertha's fiancé would be in the best of health. Romeo Jones, being in the light-hearted mood which his rôle induced, thought of a scheme for providing her with an extra bit of entertainment. Other Peters agreed to cooperate.

Bicycle Bertha, nicely powdered, was greeted as usual by her lover. When it came time for his first hasty trip to the front door and back, he told her, "I've been studying magic, Bicycle, and I'm going to show you a trick. Now watch closely. Here I go out the door. Watch now."

As soon as the door had closed, there were rappings on a window. She raised the curtain and found Peter standing on the fire escape looking through the glass at her.

"The hand is faster than the eye, you know," he said. "Watch again now."

Peter stepped to one side, and the door opened.

"Here I am back again," Peter announced.

Bertha looked at him, then back at the window, and screamed. "You've left your foot out on the fire escape!" she cried.

Peter could see part of another Peter's foot still showing in the window. "That must be an old shoe," he said. "I did the trick with mirrors."

CHAPTER XXX

GOD'S BOOT WITH THE HOLY SOLE

Mabel Shoe had been as surprised as everybody else by the continued absence of the Wopples from church. Her impression had been that these devout believers would attend Sunday religious services even if they had to be carried there from their death-beds on stretchers. Probably they were making an out of town visit and had gone to some other church.

She would not have been particularly interested in this absence of the Wopple church fixtures but for a happy recollection of a man who had looked like Ben Wopple. It couldn't really have been he, of course, but there had been a decided resemblance. This man who had provided her initiation at Madam Funnybone's was the only one she had been given a chance to see in the dark room. A more careful guard had been maintained over the light switch after that.

Ben Wopple's double had left a lasting impression. And he had seemed to enjoy the experience almost as much as she—he could not have enjoyed it fully as much. Other men had been rather impersonal and blunt. The first man had said nice things to her before leaving.

She had no way of finding out who the man had been. He had given no name, and Madam Funnybone did not know him. Unless he should return to 217 Tinker Avenue when she was there, Miss Shoe's only hope of meeting him again was to imagine Ben Wopple to be the man in question. She only saw Wopple at church. Miss Shoe had looked forward to watching him from her pew during the services and telling herself he was the man who had introduced her to her body.

Merely looking at someone who resembled the man who had said nice things to her in the dark would not be as satisfactory as duplicating that experience, but there would be something pleasing about it. It would enable her to picture that first adventure more vividly and to imagine for the moment that they would soon be together again. Then she could make another visit to Madam Funnybone.

It would also be very amusing to make this intended use of pious Ben Wopple in church to recall an erotic inspiration. If he could read her mind, the shock would so horrify him that he might be forced to leave the scene of such psychic sin—even though he was in church. At any rate, he would turn red all over and probably glare back at her with an offended expression intended to show his resentment of such insults.

Miss Shoe could readily reconcile her especial interest in this one man with her scheme to have so many men at her disposal.

Probably there would be others she would like equally as well as the stranger who looked like Ben Wopple.

Others had been very nice, but none of them had provided the additional thrill of pleasing remarks about her before departing. If they spoke at all, the comments were either of a general or a coarse nature. The first man had shown himself to be more aware of her—

After attending church to-day, Miss Shoe started for Tinker Avenue despite the fact that Ben Wopple's stimulus had not been available.

"I just thought of an errand I must do," she told a woman who had invited her to dinner, "but I will be at your house in ample time."

Miss Shoe had been giving more attention to lip-stick, rouge, and powder of late. She applied additional cosmetics when making Tinker Avenue visits. She stepped into a doorway to adjust her make-up after all her church acquaintances were out of sight. She might meet a man who would be willing to accompany her to number 217. But Miss Shoe did not take the aggressive. She had decided it would be best to let the man speak first.

She saw six men—all dressed alike—approaching in a body. They were looking at her—all six of them. This was delightful. She began to walk slower. Her importance to men was being realized already. Men were seeking her out in groups. What an achievement it would be to arrive at Madam Funnybone's and say, "Meet six of my boy friends."

It was time for these men to speak. They were still looking at her and seemed very much interested. Probably they were bashful. She understood men now. These men's eyes gave them away. She knew what they wanted. They were perhaps dazed by the thought of accosting a woman who had—or would have— millions of other men to choose from. She would show them that such success had not turned her head. All they needed was a word of encouragement from her to overcome their feelings of inferiority. She could still be democratic.

"Hello, boys," said Miss Shoe in a sociable but at the same time a slightly superior tone. A woman of her dawning fame must retain the proper dignity.

"Howdy," replied Peter Lyman. The six Peters did not stop.

"Oh dear, why are some men so bashful?" Miss Shoe said to herself.

The six Peters had considered consulting this prosperous looking woman but were glad that they had not done so.

"She must have known us," said Peter Jones.

"Yeah, it's a good thing Romeo didn't walk up to her with a gun like he wanted to."

Madam Funnybone had only recently finished her night's sleep but was as genial and cordial as ever when Miss Shoe arrived. She liked to stuff bank notes into her stocking.

The first man who arrived accepted the customary explanation that the girl he had chosen preferred a dark room because of her weak eyes.

When he was ready to leave, he remarked, "If the woman I work for knew I had come here—and on Sunday of all days—she'd have hysterics. We all call her 'God's Boot' and 'The Holy Sole.'"

This voice sounded natural, but Miss Shoe could not identify it for the moment.

"Who is she?" she asked.

"Mabel Shoe—I'm her butler."

"Oh, yes," she said, trying to disguise her voice. "I've heard she's quite strait-laced."

CHAPTER XXXI

GIN DAISY PETALS

Romeo Peter Hatch and Bertha Render were celebrating their engagement again with Ward Eights which blended nicely with the color of her lips. Five other young men named Peter were patronizing another bar, celebrating the fact that they had escaped the fate of Romeo and his disgraceful entanglement with a girl. Secretly, each of the five was alternately consoling himself with the information that it would be only so many more days before he had another turn as Romeo and cursing himself for his flabby personality which could be so completely corrupted by this girl.

"He's a fool and a damn one," said Peter Jones with reference to Romeo.

"He's so weak he can't even resist a dame," commented Peter Pike. "No principles. He acts as though she had him covered with a gun."

Gin Daisies had appealed to Peter Sadler this evening. For these drinks recalled daisy petals, and daisy petals were a means of determining a girl's affection. Thus it had seemed feasible that Gin Daisies might be used as a substitute for daisy petals.

He was making a private investigation by means of his drinks. The one he was downing now was accompanied by the mental comment, "She loves me." On the one before he had said to himself, "She loves me not," and on the one before that, "She loves me." His theory was that the verdict on the last drink he was able to down this evening would be the correct one.

In case he did not remember to-morrow what this finding had been, he would not consider that the investigation had been in vain. For he was the sole judge in this test, and the verdict, "She loves me," would be the only reasonable one. A girl did not become engaged to a man unless she loved him, and Bertha was engaged to him. She was engaged to five others, too, but—well, a few more drinks would help him overlook this fact. Gin Daisies had a decided advantage over flower-daisies.

"Two more," said Peter Sadler.

He drank the first—"She loves me not"—in one hasty draught, then took up the second one for a more careful consideration of its message, "She loves me."

"Beware of the wiles of women," had always seemed like senseless advice from a misinformed reformer. Women had their pleasures to offer, and there was no more reason for avoiding them than for signing a temperance pledge and bewaring the delights of demon rum.

Then came Bicycle Bertha with her invisible snares which did not allow a victim to suspect he was even in danger until he found himself a helpless prisoner. The wiles of women could not be realized in advance. The reason for the advice to beware could not be seen until one was trapped, and then it was too late, just as it was too late for the chronic alcoholic in an insane ward to escape from demon rum.

"She's got me," Peter Sadler said to himself. "She's put the curse of love on me. Imagine it! Me being in love. But, damn it, how was I to know she would play such a dirty trick on me? No other girl was ever mean enough to do it."

Another swallow of the Gin Daisy changed the trend of his thoughts to, "This drink proves she loves me. Ain't that great? I'm glad the others aren't drinking Daisies. Bicycle and me will get away from them somehow and settle down by ourselves.

Won't it be wonderful? Just Bertha and me. Nobody else to step in each time after I leave."

He poured the rest of the drink into his mouth and was given the mental message, "They talk about women being the weaker sex—God, it's the male sex that's the weak one. A woman just makes a man fall in love with her, and he's her slave from then on. A man can knock a woman down, but he can't do anything to break the strangle-hold of the love curse once she gets it on him."

"Two more," he said aloud.

He gulped the first one, despite its words, "She loves me not," which might have been interpreted as breaking the love curse for the moment. He took a hasty sip from the second drink to be assured once more. "She loves me."

"She'll probably have a kid after we get married," he told himself. "And it will be my kid. We'll see to it that none of the other Peters have anything to do with it. And we can hock those other five rings I gave her if we happen to run low on cash."

Another sip brought another thought, "What chance has a man got with women having this power to put love curses on him? A man can't lay off of girls altogether. And there's no way of telling which one is going to grab him. It's dangerous being a man and not knowing when you're going to find yourself helpless. The best way would probably be to stick to a girl who didn't put on the curse. But that would be worse than the love curse: having only that one all the time and not being in love with her."

Peter Sadler ordered two more Gin Daisies. The other Peters were keeping pace with drinks of other kinds. There had been several minutes of silence. Peter Sadler's thoughts might have been those of any of the others. But continued silence and continued drinks are not an agreeable combination. Peter Sadler felt the urge to say something out loud. The Gin Daisy chain within him removed the caution he would otherwise have shown in selecting his words. The one predominant thought of the moment was given to his larynx for translation into sound:

"She loves."

Peter Sadler and each of four other Peters were equally astonished to hear this identical sentence being spoken by four voices simultaneously with his own.

A moment of embarrassed silence followed, but the internal liquids had become intolerant of moods that allowed discomfort.

"We're all getting to be mind-readers: we can read Romeo Hatch's thoughts like a book," said Peter Lyman. "'She loves me,' that's just what he's thinking now."

"Yeah, what a damn fool he is," said Peter Dean.

CHAPTER XXXII

YOUTH COMES AT LAST

Ben Wopple did not remain an atheist long. His body had many neglected stages which demanded expression in the attempt to neutralize forty-nine years of piety and provide a total result that approached the human norm. The body's normal period as a pretentious atheist while a young man was condensed into a few weeks of intense atheism as a middle-aged man.

Then came the stage known now as paganism and representing an age of antiquity when the human race accepted openly and glorified the pleasures of life for which the body is specialized. To-day we can look upon the centuries as but a step from the animal-man who knew no wine or god to Nature's man who discovered wines and gods. Ben Wopple in the animal-man atheist period had by no means been a perfect duplicate of this ancestor, for he had had not only wines but liquors and liqueurs.

Thus, as a pagan, his change came chiefly in the recognition of a benevolent donor of sex distinction and alcoholic intoxication to the human race. There must be at least one god or goddess or both, he concluded. Such pleasures could not have originated of themselves. Some kind deity had endowed the body with these capacities for enjoyment. It followed that this deity—or some deity—must have created life and the universe. The pleasure-endowments had called this latter fact to Ben Wopple's attention.

His conception of the chief deities would have coincided with Bacchus and Aphrodite. In this present state, he would have been a faithful believer had he been living in the days when those divinities were recognized, before the human race began its long hang-over of asceticism.

Had his body followed a more conventional course of development, this stage of paganism would have succeeded the period of atheism many years ago. But Ben Wopple's mental reactions had been abnormally retarded by intense religious beliefs of a modern variety. Instead of settling down in this modern stage in later years, he had found himself just emerging from it at the age of forty-nine. Wild oats which are normally sown as a young man were still available to provide a late crop.

The final result would be the same if he lived long enough to offset these forty-nine years of holiness. For the standard process had merely been reversed. Instead of enjoying Nature as a young man and becoming holy later in life, he had been holy as a young man and was starting his investigation of Nature in his fiftieth year.

With its span of piety behind it, rather than as a vaguely recognized possibility of the future, his body could enjoy itself now without need of restraint. Its penance was fully paid for whatever it might do that modern society regarded as sinful.

Ben Wopple's basic program as a pagan of forty-nine was patterned after his previous life as a man of God. His morning prayers which had provided intoxicating versions of Heaven were abandoned for one or two eye-openers from a bottle—the amount depending on the severity of the day's hang-over. Cocktails were substituted for grace before meals, liqueurs for grace after meals. Drinks with happy companions between meals provided the former stimulation of prolonged and private prayers.

He no longer regarded smoking as a vice—in fact, he smoked cigarettes himself. And he had bought, and enjoyed, several books which had been recommended by his new companions as smutty. Visits to Tinker Avenue were made frequently: once a week as a customer, three or four times as a patron. In this latter rôle, he came in search of a pretty girl to escort to a night club or other social function.

It was said by some that, "He's always got a slut on at least one arm."

Ben Wopple's attitude toward Nephew Alfred was not altered by the change from atheism to paganism. He remained as intolerant of his nephew's apparent piety as a pagan son might be of a pious father. Ben Wopple had the advantage in his delayed state of paganism: being in a position to disown the moral blight provided by the holy relative on his family tree.

He was often amused by a recollection of the illusion he had had on his first visit to Madam Funnybone's when Miss Shoe's face had seemed to appear as a mask on Daisy Blue. The effect had been so real that he had actually been embarrassed. Who wouldn't be, finding himself looking into that saint's face under such circumstances? "Imagine Mabel Shoe, the reformer, working as a prostitute!" This thought could produce a laugh from Ben Wopple whenever it came to mind.

On each subsequent visit to Madam Funnybone's quarters as a customer, he had selected Daisy Blue. Her eye trouble had suddenly cured so that she did not have to entertain him in a dark room again. But she had seemed ever nicer to him in the dark. Whenever he thought in terms of Aphrodite and personal experiences, he recalled the first evening with Daisy. He chose her again each time hoping that first experience—either with or without the Mabel Shoe mask comedy-effect—might be duplicated.

She had been more affectionate and less matter-of-fact the first time. On no other occasion had she shown any amount of enthusiasm.

Ben Wopple had visited other Tinker Avenue Aphrodisions. Girls had been nice but never quite up to the standard of Daisy Blue in the dark. He had not told Daisy this for the information might offend her, and he wanted to continue on friendly terms.

Ben Wopple had discovered a boyish delight for dirty stories among the other suppressed faculties which had been made available to him. The anecdotes told by his new acquaintances were all welcomed as masterpieces of entertainment. For not only had he never heard any of them before, but he had never heard any like them before. Ben Wopple had years of erotica to catch up on, and had yet to undergo the experience of listening to a story for the third, fourth, or even a second time.

He liked to stop former churchly associates and recount to them stories that he recalled. Such encounters were especially satisfying if he was noticeably enjoying the effects of alcoholic beverages at the time. He was amused by the horrified attempts to escape upon seeing this former man of God "reeking with whisky" and "raving filthy talk."

They had reeked with whisky and raved their filthy talk many years ago when holy Ben would have run from them. They could have added to his store of erotica now, just as he could have added to their Bible lore. But neither party was ever interested in making this incriminating exchange of information.

On one occasion Ben Wopple had met Rev. Nehemiah Dick on the street. The clergyman had been unable to get away before being seen and loudly greeted with, "Hey, there, Oyster Eyes." He felt that he must humor this formerly upright man who had been possessed by the Devil.

"Stop me if you've heard this one," Ben said facetiously before launching into the most graphic bit of pornographic humor he could think of.

Rev. Dick's face turned red, for Ben Wopple continued to talk in a loud tone, and many people were passing by. But it would not do to tear himself away from Ben's grasp on his coat collar. This rich man might eventually recover, in which event he did not want him to have any unfriendly recollections.

It occurred to Rev. Dick that perhaps the deranged man no longer held the antipathy toward him that had been manifest on their last meeting. This story-telling was a friendly gesture. There was no more talk of suing the church. It might be wise to encourage this friendship—with the view of reconverting him, of course. And, if that was not possible, a bequest from a man of the Devil would build just as good a parish house as the same gift from a man of God.

". . ." Ben concluded the story in a raucous climax of ribaldry.

Rev. Dick bent his head to Wopple's ear and whispered, "Next time have his wife hide under the bed with the salesman."

CHAPTER XXXIII

A QUEEN BEE COMPLEX

Madam Funnybone had thought it advisable not to let her two best customers meet again. Whenever Miss Shoe inquired about the man who looked like Ben Wopple, she shrugged her shoulders and replied, "He ain't been here since." His repeated selections of Daisy Blue after the dark-room experience awakened Madam Funnybone's intuition to the suspicion that he might not be indifferent to a reunion with Miss Shoe—despite the fact that he had had a glimpse of her in the light.

Strange phenomena of peculiar attractions were not merely printed pages of case histories listed in sexology text-books for Madam Funnybone. She had never read Ellis or Stekel, but she could have given more colorful, though less scientific, descriptions of many equally curious aberrations. In comparison to peculiarities of some customers she had accommodated, it would not seem unusual to have a man prefer an unattractive woman of forty-four to a choice of five young and pretty girls.

Miss Shoe was quickly hidden in her dark room as soon as she called. Madam Funnybone was thus enabled to use her own discretion in sending her a man. Many years of dealings with men, and women, had developed her natural intuition for sizing up people into an almost telepathic power. Some men would catch on to the trick being played upon them at once if she were to try to send them into the dark. Others preferred the dark and would experience a feeling of relief as soon as she mentioned a dark room. Some would know that Miss Shoe was not the girl they had chosen in the light. Others wouldn't. Madam Funnybone had received no complaints from those she had considered eligible for the trickery.

Miss Shoe often referred to the fact that the dark room was only to conceal her identity. She liked to have Madam Funnybone agree that it would be most unwise for her to expose herself in the light and take a chance that the man might know her or might recognize her at some future time and place. Madam Funnybone's tone of voice would have the implication that Miss Shoe possessed every requirement of beauty which could be expected in the light.

Miss Shoe liked to believe this was so, but she found it hard to reconcile the fact of her beauty with the fact that men on the street did not seem interested in her. "Probably I look too respectable," she told herself. "They're afraid of getting a slap in the face if they speak to me. Or else they're too bashful—like those six men who almost ran when I said, 'Hello.'" This explanation was too satisfying for Miss Shoe to spoil the delusion by offering an Agnes Moon card to any more men.

Besides, her scheme which would bring men to her in swarms was working out fine. It would appear undignified later if it could be said that this woman who had become such an idol had but recently been accosting men. Miss Shoe had over three hundred signed pledge cards. Figuring fifteen regular customers for each girl, these represented over forty-five hundred men who were looking for other women. She had appointed Vestal Beetle her campaign manager, and more signed cards were being obtained in constantly increasing numbers.

Vestal Beetle had offered to enlist other reformed girls in the work of the Society for the Resurrection of the Fallen Woman. She explained that she had better attend to the selection of these workers, for, being a former fallen girl herself, she was more fitted to determine which converts could be trusted to brave the temptations to break the pledge involved in mingling with lewd associates while obtaining other signatures.

None of these volunteers were ever at Vestal Beetle's room when Miss Shoe called. But they had always left ample evidence of their continued integrity and faithful and efficient service to the society in the form of cards with new signatures. These pledges had become so numerous that Miss Shoe had reduced the reward given each convert to five dollars.

Miss Shoe was pleased by the gullible manner in which the girls of joy were being deluded by her plan. When enough of them had been reformed, they would suddenly discover that she had really been buying an option on the man market. These girls, and their predecessors, had been having the men she might have enjoyed in past years. Now they would find themselves pledged to the sad rôles of honest women, while *she* had all *their* men at her disposal.

The final detail of how to make the announcement to men that Mabel Shoe was one female who had not signed the pledge was still to be planned. But this would doubtless work itself out at the proper time. The news of her desirability would spread quickly. Those six bashful men had obviously been aware of her importance even though they had hardly dared to speak.

Miss Shoe had previously had her eyebrows and other facial hair plucked by a beauty expert. She had been having a permanent wave and a facial massage to-day. A cosmetician had applied an artistic mask of beauty paint and powder, and the final effect—with all gray hairs dyed and fancy painted wigs on her eyebrows—made her look much different and many years younger.

Rev. Nehemiah Dick was able to recognize her, however.

"Miss Shoe," he said, "I understand you have been doing some very commendable work among the—ah, degenerate women of our city. It has occurred to me that I might cooperate by spreading the Gospel among some of those you have succeeded in reforming. If you could give me a few of their addresses, I would be glad to visit them and help glue them still more securely to their new honest ways by telling them the word of God."

Miss Shoe felt obliged to comply with this suggestion, although the only address she knew was 217 Tinker Avenue. She told him the number of Madam Funnybone's apartment rather than Vestal Beetle's. She was beginning to suspect that some of the girls there might have violated their pledge.

Later in the day Miss Shoe visited Madam Funnybone. When the door of the dark room opened to admit a man, she saw a familiar face that immediately disappeared in the darkness. Rev. Dick had come to spread the Gospel! Why in the world had Madam Funnybone let him into her room? Had she become so completely converted herself that she thought her original rescuer needed conversion? Probably Madam Funnybone would put on the light. She couldn't explain this present compromising position as part of her reform work. Rev. Dick would doubtless spread the news of the real mission of her society, and her plans would all be thwarted. She would be disgraced among her friends, a social outcast—

What was this? Why, Rev. Dick was not here to spread the Gospel!

CHAPTER XXXIV

THEY TOPPLE FOR WOPPLE

Dorothy Dolly and Teresa Beetle were prominent figures in the Tinker Avenue contest which ensued several times a week upon the arrival of a wealthy forty-nine year old man. The capture of Ben Wopple was the main event of the days on which this notable put in his appearance. To be escorted by—or to escort—this Tinker Avenue celebrity into an automobile in full view of all the other jealous girls was an ambition realized. In fact, it would have been even if there had been no other girls to witness the accomplishment.

Ben's style of entertainment was of the most elaborate ever described by Tinker Avenue girls. Being with him was a ticket to exclusive night clubs and other resorts to which a Tinker Avenue lass could not otherwise obtain admission. And being with him was almost like having temporary access to the mint. One girl had casually mentioned the fact that she liked Ben Wopple's car. She had come driving home in it alone early the next morning, wearing the chauffeur's cap and holding a transfer of ownership certificate in one hand.

Ben's visits as a customer, rather than just a patron, were still more welcome to the fortunate maiden chosen. For she won the additional distinction of having entertained the great man in her room and having obtained still more of his dollars. She would invariably be on his arm as the companion of the evening when he got into his car. A girl who obtained access to the Wopple arm maintained a tight grip while she was on Tinker Avenue.

Daisy Blue's frequent selection at Madam Funnybone's made her something of a distinguished figure herself. Teresa Beetle could not resist the opportunities of the Ben Wopple contest, despite her many surplus dollars obtained from Miss Shoe. Dorothy Dolly wanted to have a higher score of parties with Ben than this girl she did not like. One date with the rich man was the answer to most girls' highest hopes. Dorothy wanted several. And Teresa, being a lady of money herself, concluded that she was the one who should be eligible for all dates with this man of money.

Teresa could devote most of the day to watching for Ben Wopple. Dorothy still had to support herself and could not keep as constant a vigil. Teresa was generally among the first to arrive in the bevy of excited girls that was on hand to open the door of the Wopple car. Dorothy was there, too, as often as possible.

Teresa had won the contest one afternoon and been invited to dinner and a night club. Another time Dorothy had tied the score. She became the victor upon running to the Wopple car, which had stopped nearby, after saying, "Just a second," to a man who was walking home with her.

Except when he insisted that he was going to visit Madam Funnybone, Ben Wopple's choice of a girl depended chiefly upon the one who got hold of his arm first. In the event that both arms were seized simultaneously, he would generally use the process of elimination which begins, "Eeny, meeny, miney, mo." On more than one occasion he had found black and blue marks which he could not account for on his arms.

Dorothy Dolly's resentment of Teresa Beetle's mysterious supply of cash had not abated. She needed many, many victories in the Wopple contest to even this score. Miss Shoe's activities on Tinker Avenue had been kept in strict secrecy, for there were numerous others who would have liked to share her payments. Madam Funnybone and her girls claimed she was a friend of Daisy Blue's and always came to borrow money. Teresa maintained that she was a real estate agent who had heard of her new income and came to see her repeatedly in an attempt to sell her a house. There were various other rumors.

Teresa's financial success had made her so triumphant in her feud with Dorothy that she no longer recognized their former rivalry—in spite of Dorothy's uncomplimentary remarks whenever they met. Dorothy was just a no-good whose comments did not even warrant a reply. The only time Teresa had noticed this lowly former enemy since her dealings with Miss Shoe was on an occasion when Dorothy had come up behind her in a bar and spilled part of a glass of beer down her neck. Then Teresa had spoken, but she managed to retain enough dignity not to take physical measures of retaliation. Dorothy had walked away with composure that could not be ruffled by unseemly words from such a low person.

Both of these girls happened to be watching when Ben Wopple's car stopped on Tinker Avenue to-day. To win Ben Wopple a second time would be a feat for Dorothy that Teresa had not equaled, in addition to the lavish entertainment it would provide. Dorothy ran to the curb, the machine having stopped on her side of the street. Teresa and several others came hurrying across from the other side.

Dorothy reached the door at the curb ahead of those who were racing there from her side. She did not wait for Ben Wopple to get out. She opened the door, stepped in, and curled her arm under his as she sat down. The car was now surrounded by disappointed girls who had arrived just too late.

"Do you live near here?" Ben asked. This was his usual question when his visit was as a customer.

Dorothy was delighted. "Yes, just two doors down," she replied. "Come on."

She looked for Teresa's envious face in the group around her. All of Teresa's money could not buy the distinction she had won in obtaining the honor of this dignitary's selection. But Dorothy had not seen Teresa hand a bill to one of the other girls.

Dorothy had to let go of Ben's arm for a moment in getting out of the car. At this strategic instant the face of Teresa appeared, also her arms. Dorothy felt herself being given a sudden push, and she found herself falling backwards over a girl who had crouched down on all fours directly behind her.

When Dorothy got back onto her feet, she saw Ben Wopple walking across the street arm in arm with Teresa Beetle. Teresa could not resist the temptation to recognize the existence of her former enemy just once more: Still trying to maintain all of her superior dignity, she turned her head and thumbed her nose behind Ben Wopple's back at the lowly streetwalker who had tried to take away her boy friend.

Dorothy's vocabulary started to explode: "You . . ."

Let us paraphrase the remarks and say, "You're an unesthetic combination of type."

CHAPTER XXXV

HITCH HIKING ON THE SIDEWALK

There were two possible solutions for the Bicycle Bertha problem, Peter Lyman decided. Either the five other Peters would have to be done away with, or Bertha herself would have to be done away with. If he had approved of this latter alternative, the situation would not have been a problem. Thus, his only hope was to get rid of these five Peters in a more permanent way than by merely arranging a secret date.

It would be a dirty trick to do anything that would hurt them physically. They were his pals and his half brothers as well. But discords had been introduced into the harmony of their friendship. They had all been infected and deranged by a contagious love epidemic. Probably the only reason they were still on friendly terms was that their co-operation enabled them to convince Bertha that there was only one Peter. And this system enabled each of them to keep closer tabs on the five rivals.

Peter Lyman was going to let his friends off easily. He would not use poison or bullets. His scheme was just as bad ethically, but it would enable the other five to go on living. He was playing the part of Romeo to-day and would be called upon to be the polite bandit. Instead of saying, "Hands up," he planned to take off his mask and whisper to the victim, "I just heard five fellows planning to stick you up. They're hiding in that alley."

He would offer the loan of his gun, and the man he had befriended would hold the other Peters by means of it until he found a policeman. Peter Lyman would insist upon wearing different clothes than the rest, and he would not shave when the others did. It would not do to have any confusion at the station house as to which of the six was the hero. With these five Peters in jail, he and Bertha could make open and deliberate arrangements to wed and elope to remote parts.

Having decided upon this procedure, he was able to reconcile the scheme both with the sincerity of his friendship for the others and with his official opinion that marriage was a synonym for insanity. Peter Lyman stepped into the rôle of a martyr. He was even willing to undergo the disgraceful sacrifice of marriage to save his five best friends and fellow sufferers from the love-disease to which they had succumbed.

Instead of trying to become cured, they had all continued to flock back to the source of the love curse for further contagion. This repeated reinfection would go on indefinitely unless forceful quarantine measures were taken. He would provide an effective quarantine despite the fact that it meant sacrificing his life for the others. The punishment of a possible jail sentence for these five would be nothing compared to the lifelong infliction he was taking upon himself for their sake.

They would think at first that he was a squealer, a double-crosser, and a rat when he gave his gun to the man he had started out to rob. They would curse him and consider him a species of lower caliber than any previously recorded. But, as the days passed in the quarantine provided by the jail cells, the love-disease would begin to lose its hold. When they were released, the source of contagion would no longer be available.

Finally they would find themselves cured. Then, instead of wanting to get hold of him for purposes of revenge, they would want to seek him out to give thanks and reward. They would realize that he had been the truest friend of the six. He had rescued them from the shameful pit of love by taking a life of martyrdom upon himself. And Peter Lyman was determined to live out this span of sacrifice by remaining in hiding and keeping the original source of infection forever hidden from the five fortunate Peters whom he had saved.

Peter Lyman loaded the revolver in full view of the other Peters and remarked, "These slugs would be nasty things to have bite you. Hope no customer ever makes me pull the trigger."

• • • • • • •

This was evidently a day of active minds. Miss Mabel Shoe had devised a scheme, too. The impression made upon her memory by a white-haired man with his remark, "Twenty cent," had been indelible, but there were possibilities for retaliation and an evened score. It would not be fitting for a woman of her growing importance to overlook the incident. Having lost her abhorrence of strange men, she could humiliate and insult him in return.

She had seen this white-haired man sitting in his usual place several times while walking along the other side of One-Tenth Street. This evening she intended to walk on the Dew side of the street. She would stop in front of him long enough to remark, "Why don't you get a job in the waxworks? Nobody would know you were alive. You degraded lout." Then she could walk away with befitting dignity.

When the Peters came downstairs, John Dew was laughing. "Lady go quick," he said. "She call me degrade—I call her old maid. . . ."

Peter Lyman had a blind alley in mind for tonight's hiding place. The others saw no reason for doubting his hunch that this would be a good location. They waited there until a somewhat unsteady individual—Ben Wopple, in fact—came into sight. Peter Lyman put on his mask. A man who was a little drunk would have sufficient courage to hold a gun to five desperadoes.

"So long," he said in a low tone. This would be his last friendly remark to these five pals. But he was doing them a big favor. They would be grateful in the end.

On the sidewalk he brushed the mask back under his cap. Ben Wopple was moving very slowly. He stopped to rest against a pole as the martyr came up to him.

"Say, mister," Peter whispered. "I just heard five guys in that alley say they were going to hold you up."

"That's fine," replied Ben. "I need someone to hold me up."

CHAPTER XXXVI

WHO SAYS THERE AIN'T A GOD?

A man stopped on a bridge over a river. Jumping from this height into the water far below would probably be painful. But what of it? Life, with no income, had become a hopeless routine. Even if he had had any unusual business ability, no employer could have been convinced of the fact. As soon as he gave the name Alfred Wopple, it was concluded that, if this man had even imbecile intelligence, his rich uncle could have found a place for him in his company.

Alfred had no thoughts of Heaven or Hell, for he did not believe there were any such places. He was wondering how long it would take to lose consciousness in an attempt to drown and just how uncomfortable it would be.

He had heard that one's whole life was re-lived during the process of drowning and that seconds became years. This fact annoyed him. Would his life be worth living over again? Would his years give a balance of pain or pleasure? Theoretically, he would be getting the best of Nature by living two lives in the course of one life span. But, if his life's balance was pain, Nature would still get the best of him if he re-lived it.

He tried to recall past events. His chief recollections were based around his uncle's sudden change which had disrupted his own life plans. The climax of his life's repetition would be most unhappy. His uncle still had a dominant place as his thoughts went into past years. It had not been a happy predicament to have to follow Uncle Ben's version of the Bible in public and make an apparent fool of himself as a man of God. Still, there had been secret sins: unholy delights whose pleasure had been intensified by the fact that they would have horrified Uncle Ben. Alfred put his hand on the rail.

But his chief pleasures had been based around thoughts of what he would do with Uncle Ben's bequest. He had lived a restricted life in a scheme for storing up pleasure for the future. Living through all this restraint again would be like serving a jail sentence. Death was the solution, but not death that involved working out another long and unpaid term of painful service. This rail was cold. The water would be equally cold. A live rail would be better.

Alfred put his hand in a pants pocket to warm it. He felt a slip of paper and remembered that this was a two-dollar bill, his last piece of currency. He should at least spend this before he died. Two dollars immediately recalled Teresa Beetle, her white robes, and other details—he could explain that he would owe her the usual extra dollar. He had not visited her since his estrangement from his uncle. He had been spending his savings sparingly, hoping Uncle Ben would recover.

Teresa Beetle was wearing her robes when Alfred arrived, just as she used to for their former standing appointment on Sunday mornings. She said, "come in," in response to his knock, for she was not expecting Alfred Wopple. She had lost all interest in customers who had only one extra dollar to offer.

"I've gone out of business," she told him. "Try the next door. There's a girl in there. I don't think she's doing anything now."

Alfred was already inside Teresa's room. There was a sound of footsteps coming up the stairs.

"Get out, quick," said Teresa.

Alfred started but did not get out quickly enough. He collided with a man in the doorway. "Sorry," he said. Then he noticed that the man was Uncle Ben. Teresa's religious robes had appealed to this member of the family, too.

Ben Wopple laughed loudly. "Well, if it isn't Little Lord Fauntleroy," he greeted his nephew. "You'll have to do an awful lot of praying to make up for this. You sure got the wrong address. God probably never will forgive you for stepping into a place where they specialize in breaking one of his commandments. What was he trying to do?" he asked Teresa, "sell you a prayer book?"

Alfred decided to make the most of this last meeting with his uncle. Here was a chance to show him that he hadn't been such a fool in the past as he had appeared.

"Listen here," he replied. "I was coming here all along back in the days when you were wearing callouses on your knees. You're the family saint. You'll never live long enough to make up for all the praying you've done. I just talked about the Bible to keep on the right side of you."

"Dear, dear, such heresy from Pious Alfred," said Ben. "Don't let yourself be tempted to send your soul to eternal damnation now just to get on the right side of me. You can't fool me. Now run along home and pray. You've said naughty things. God's face is blushing."

"Just ask Teresa. She'll tell you how long I've been coming here."

"I've never seen him before," she insisted. She thought it best to side with Ben Wopple in this argument.

Ben laughed again. "You'll have to pray for weeks to make up for this," he said. "You better do some fasting, too."

"Well, I'll prove *I've* seen *her,* the damn liar," Alfred retorted. "She's got a tattoo mark high up on her right thigh, a strawberry birthmark on her stomach, and a white patch on her right breast."

Ben was not aware of these characteristics. "If your Sunday School class could only see you now," he replied.

"Come to think of it, I made you wait outside one time with the wife while I came up here," Alfred continued. "Remember? We were coming home from church and going to my house for dinner. I told you I wanted to stop in and see a sick friend."

Two disconnected threads in Ben Wopple's mind suddenly came into contact. This location on Tinker Avenue had seemed familiar on his first visit, but he had not been able to place it. Now he remembered having waited in a parked car at the curb on that occasion to which his nephew referred. At the same time he became aware of Alfred's having used Teresa's name in speaking about her a moment ago.

"Say, let me see if there's a tattoo mark on your right thigh," he said to Teresa. There was.

"So, you see, I've had a few laughs on you in past years," Alfred remarked. "So long."

"Say, wait a minute," Ben insisted. "You may not be such a bad egg at that. Here, let's see you take a drink."

Alfred swallowed twice from the bottle of whisky his uncle handed him.

"Holy jumping! and you didn't even cough," said Uncle Ben. "I can take it straight, too, but I have to have a chaser." He produced a second bottle and demonstrated this point. "I've had you sized up all wrong. You certainly had me fooled. I want to apologize. How would you like a job, a good job?"

Alfred Wopple tried to recall whether he had jumped off the bridge or not. Perhaps there was a Heaven, after all, and he had arrived there.

"Here, take this note over to the cashier," Uncle Ben added after writing a few words on the back of an envelope. "And here, here's a few dollars to liquor up with on the way so he'll know the note is on the level. I'll meet you there after a while, and we'll throw a big reunion party. It's great to find a good fellow in the family."

"One of the best fellows I've ever known," Teresa remarked.

CHAPTER XXXVII

WE HAD BODIES BEFORE WE HAD MINDS

Teresa Beetle's iconoclastic willingness to wear a religious garb while fulfilling a function of quite different nature appealed to Ben Wopple. Having a Vestal Vertical costume on a harlot provided an even more pleasurable novelty than breaking the church window with a whisky bottle. Although no longer an atheist, Ben still enjoyed ridiculing accepted religions of modern times.

The added enjoyment of the iconoclasm involved in dealings with Teresa had substituted her for Daisy Blue as his favorite. Evidently on his introduction to Daisy in the dark, she had shown him the special consideration only given a new customer. If he went to Madam Funnybone's in disguise, perhaps she would be like that again. But this destroyed his original illusion. Whispering nice things and making unpaid-for gestures of affection to a new customer was not the same as showing this consideration to Ben Wopple.

Now Ben was determined that this would be his last visit to Teresa. She had shown herself to be very untruthful in claiming that she had never seen his nephew before. She might have prevented their happy reunion and the big party they would have to-night—perhaps it could be prolonged for two or three days. Anyway, a party for a definite reason was much more satisfactory than just a party.

He had realized Teresa's stereotyped remarks of affection had always lacked sincerity. But they were merely the harmless line of an honest saleslady, similar to Alfred's former religious comments in his presence. This other type of lie was different. There were plenty more girls. Probably most of them would be willing to wear any kind of religious garments that he was willing to buy.

It was a sad disappointment to Teresa to have Ben tell her that he had decided to make to-night's party a stag affair. (He hoped the blonde with the nicely rounded hips who had been among those to greet him at the curb would reappear when he returned to the street. There had been a shapely brunette, too, with a white carnation over one ear, whom he might take along as a surprise for Alfred.)

"And I was looking forward *so* much to tonight," Teresa whined.

Ben was not concerned with the footsteps outside as he walked to the door. He opened it and found another barrier in his path. Saint Ben Wopple and Saint Mabel Shoe were looking into each other's faces once more. Teresa Beetle was terrified. How could she account for having a man in her room?

Ben started to laugh at this second vision of the devout reformer in a brothel—but she did look different than she used to in church. Her lips and eyebrows and hair. Her eyelashes were even curled. Was he seeing things, or could it be that this was really Mabel Shoe?

Miss Shoe smiled at seeing the bigoted man of God at 217 Tinker Avenue again. Probably this was the real Ben Wopple. Vestal Beetle must have enlisted him in the work of her society. But, no, this man couldn't be Ben Wopple. He smelt of whisky. Ben would die rather than permit such contamination of his body.

The amusement was momentary and was immediately replaced by other feelings. This was not a meeting of Ben Wopple and Mabel Shoe. It was a reunion of two bodies who had once hired each other's services and obtained more than they had paid for. Ben Wopple knew Miss Shoe was a prim and religious old maid. Mabel Shoe knew Mr. Wopple was a would-be saint. Their bodies knew differently and refused to obey the minds' orders to nod and pass on.

"I saw a lady once who looked like you," said Ben.

"And I saw a man once who looked like you," replied Miss Shoe.

"It was my life's happiest experience," said Ben.

"And it was my life's happiest experience," replied Miss Shoe.

Ben whispered his next sentence: "Will you marry me?" (Marriage was a custom that originated in pagan days.)

"Do you need to ask me?" answered Miss Shoe.

She said in a louder tone to Vestal Beetle, "You can tear up any more pledge cards you've got." She didn't want millions of men now. One man had picked Mabel Shoe as his permanent mate.

"Just for the fun of it, will you wear a Vestal Vertical's robe at our wedding?" Ben asked as they started down the stairs. "White would symbolize light—an electric light bulb."

"Sure, if I can take it off when the ceremony is over—I wouldn't want to dress like that all the time."

"You can take it off just as soon as we get through saying, 'I do.'"

CHAPTER XXXVIII

PETER CHEATER, PUMPKIN-EATER,
HAD A WIFE AND COULDN'T KEEP HER

One of the Peters was standing beside Bertha Render in the church which had a new stained-glass window of sad-faced angels. On each side of them was a stranger who had been obtained from the sidewalk outside after Rev. Nehemiah Dick had mentioned the need of witnesses.

This elopement had been arranged with such haste that there had been no thought of the details of a best man or bridesmaid. The Peter who had negotiated a permanent escape from the other five had been unable to confide his plans to Bertha until he arrived at her room as she was about to start for work this morning.

"Hurry up—we'll just have time to get another ring onto your finger before we catch a train," he had said.

"Look out, I haven't got any time now; I'll be late at the store," Bertha had replied, somewhat hazy from several Ward Eights the night before.

"We're eloping," Peter explained. "I wanted to surprise you."

"Really? I wish you'd told me last night. We could have made it for this afternoon, and I could have slept longer."

But the realization that she was about to marry her super-man quickly aroused all of Bertha's unawakened faculties. The couple had arrived for the appointment with Rev. Dick with one suitcase. Peter had had to tiptoe out of his apartment with only shoes in his hands.

He had been determined that the wedding should take place before they boarded the train. As soon as this ritual was over, he could relax. The escape from the others and the abduction of Bicycle Bertha from them would have been practically successful. Society's laws would then help him keep his wife out of the hands of the other five. He would be able to enjoy the trip to a secluded hiding place with less premonition that some of the other Peters would suddenly appear and interfere. They would be arrested if they tried to steal his wife. They might be able to show justifiable cause for stealing his fiancée, since she was their fiancée, too.

Rev. Dick, who had not had a stimulus such as had been provided Bertha and Peter, was unsuccessfully trying to suppress his second yawn. He opened a large book of holy nature preparatory to proceeding with the ceremony. The type looked a little strange. Then he noticed that the book was upside down. The scrub-woman had evidently been dusting the pulpit. It seemed like a laborious task to turn this big book around.

The minister cleared his throat. He wanted to spit, but this would not be in keeping with the present occasion.

"What am I supposed to do?" the witness beside Peter whispered.

"I dunno," replied Peter. "Just buy a drink and a cigar after it's all over, I guess. Here's a couple of bucks. Get the other fellow something, too."

Rev. Dick had to make his opening sentence louder at the end to be heard above footsteps that began to echo about the empty pews. Five sets of feet were thumping down the aisle. Peter felt as though he had suddenly been locked in a refrigerator. He did not look around. He had heard these steps before. Rev. Dick looked up from his book and rubbed a hand across his eyes. Bertha turned her head and immediately seized her groom's arm. "Look, Peter—they look just like you," she whispered.

"I know it," said Peter.

"What are you gentlemen doing here?" asked Rev. Dick.

"We're the rest of the groom," one of them answered.

"Save your pranks until after the ceremony has been performed," said Rev. Dick.

Bertha Render had an uncomfortable reaction that informed her these men were not merely made up to look like her fiancé as a joke. This was the way they really looked. This was why her boy friend had been six times better than any other. This was why he went out for breaths of fresh air when he visited her, and changed his opinions so often, and had such a poor memory. There were six of him.

"So you thought you could fool me, did you?" she burst forth angrily. "You bunch of freaks. Go marry the Siamese twins. I wish I had a gun. I will have, though, if I ever see any of you again." Bertha had been fumbling in her hand-bag. "Here, take back your damn rings!" Six engagement rings were thrown to the floor, and Bertha walked to the entry where her suitcase had been left.

"I need a lot of drinks," said one of the Peters. Six of them walked slowly to the door.

"That will be all," said Rev. Dick to the two witnesses. He stepped from his pulpit into the empty church and started to pick up six diamond rings.

THE END

Franklin Perry Collier Jr. was born on June 16, 1905, in Boston, Massachusetts. His father, Franklin Sr., was a newspaper cartoonist known for the character Otto Grow. After graduating from Dartmouth in 1927, Franklin Jr. worked as a newspaper reporter and editor, and later as a writer for the WPA. By 1950, he was the manager of the Communist Party's bookstore in Boston, and he would become a national news story for having issued a party membership card to an undercover FBI agent. Collier committed suicide in 1958.